IT WAS THEIR HONEYMOON.
ALICE WAS INTOXICATED
BY THE PARISIAN NIGHT.
"I LOVE YOU SO MUCH,"
SHE WHISPERED.

If there ever was a night for making love, this was it. Her whole body yearned for it. She longed to feel his warm, firm flesh pressing against her, holding her down, dominating her. And she would yield to him blissfully in total surrender. And she would know then, for sure and forever, that their marriage was the most wonderful in all the world.

"Don't spoil a pleasant evening," Arthur said. "There will be plenty of time for making love when we return to New York."

"A happy find . . . touching, ruefully funny, affectionate."
—Publishers Weekly

The Lady Who Loved New York

R. L. GORDON

A DELL BOOK

Published by
DELL PUBLISHING CO., INC.
1 Dag Hammarskjold Plaza
New York, N.Y. 10017

Dell ® TM 681510, Dell Publishing Co., Inc.

ISBN: 0-440-14958-4

Reprinted by arrangement with
Thomas Y. Crowell Company, Inc.

Printed in Canada

First Dell printing—September 1978

To
My Mother
and
Tom and
Ruth Bredin

Chapter 1

It was the first week in April and the sunlight, filtering through the light gray haze, gave everything the pale, washed-out, unreal look of a sentimental watercolor painting. There was no sharpness or hardness about the world.

It was a raw day but Alice was not concerned about that. She had on her heavy tweed coat, her woolen scarf, a sensible felt hat, and sturdy shoes. There was a rug for her knees, too, which the driver would help her spread over them once she was seated on the bench. No, she wasn't in the least worried about the damp or the chill; she had spent hours in the Park in weather far worse than this.

She wished that Mr. Wilkins, who had driven her to and fro so often during the past years, could have driven her again today—this final day—but he had retired from the Limousine Service last November. This new young man seemed pleasant enough and courteous but she would have preferred Mr. Wilkins—today of all days.

Though it was Sunday, the Park, to her disappointment, seemed almost deserted. Perhaps children would come along to play later on but, if she didn't have them to watch, she could still spend a pleasant hour and a half looking at the trees and the grass and perhaps some squirrels. There might be some young lovers, too. She always enjoyed watching young lovers.

She peered anxiously out the window. "Stop here!" she commanded suddenly. "That's my bench over there under the elm."

The driver pulled gently over to the side of the road, turned off the ignition and, getting out, came around to open her door.

"You have got my rug?"

"Yes, Mrs. Melville. Can I carry your handbag for you?"

"No, thank you," she replied crisply. "I can manage perfectly well. Just keep your hand on my elbow in case I stumble."

They reached the bench safely and she instructed him on

how to tuck the rug around her. Her handbag rested on her knees, clutched firmly in her gloved hands.

"What is the time?" she demanded.

"It's five minutes before two."

"Then I'll expect you back at three thirty sharp. Is that clear?"

"Perfectly clear, Mrs. Melville."

"I want to be back at the Waldorf for tea at four and I shall have to get myself tidied up first."

"Yes, Mrs. Melville."

"You won't forget which bench you've left me on?" She smiled up at him. He really was quite a nice young man.

"No, Mrs. Melville, I won't forget." He smiled back at her. "Have you lived in New York all your life, Mrs. Melville?"

"Yes, it has always been my home. I can't imagine why anyone would ever want to live anywhere else. It is the most wonderful city in all the world though, I must admit, Paris has its points. They say New York is going bankrupt. I never heard such nonsense! What about you? Are you a New Yorker?"

"No, I'm from Minnesota, from a little place called Thief River Falls."

"Never heard of it."

"Not many people have."

"What brought you here?"

"I wanted to see New York. I'm driving a limousine during the day and studying commercial art at night. In another three months I'll be finished and I can go back west."

"You mean you want to?" asked Alice incredulously.

"Oh yes. I've got a job lined up in Minneapolis."

"You *want* to leave New York? How strange."

"But, Mrs. Melville, you told me that you yourself are flying west tomorrow morning."

"Indeed I am. I didn't, however, say I *wanted* to do so. Three thirty on the dot."

"Yes, Mrs. Melville."

Oh dear. This really was the end now. It was almost too sad to bear thinking on, though she couldn't somehow bring herself to think of anything else.

Her life—her meaningful life—had really come to an end that frightful night a few days after the play opened. It had had a sort of resuscitation during the years of her and

Jenny's Help-The-Children work together. Now Jenny was gone and the apartment building she had come to regard almost as home was to be torn down and rebuilt. There was no longer any real excuse for not going to Vancouver to be near her daughter for the few years that remained.

Thank goodness she had at least won the battle about not actually going to live with Patricia and Michael. She would retain some independence at any rate. Patricia had assured her that there was "a fine view of the Pacific" from the living-room window of her apartment. "On a clear day," Patricia had written, "you'll almost be able to see Japan." It was an apartment hotel so there would be no worry about furniture. She was taking very little with her in the way of furnishings. What was the point?

A few framed photographs—her mother and father; one of herself as a child of nine, in the garden wearing a frilly dress; a rather formal one of Arthur standing with his right hand on an immense urn containing a potted palm; another of the wedding party in the garden. That was all except for a few odds and ends—a lamp or two, a small amount of china, a crystal sherry decanter which had been a favorite of her mother's . . .

The four trunks and three suitcases had gone off to Vancouver the day she moved from her apartment to the Waldorf. The furniture and other things had been disposed of through Mr. Durant's office. She didn't know where they had gone but at least they would remain in New York, which was where they belonged. It was where she belonged, too, but there was nothing more to keep her here now and Patricia would be deeply hurt if she refused to come. It might not be too bad.

So this, her first visit to Central Park that season, was almost certainly also her last—ever. That thought was not merely strange; it was well nigh incomprehensible. Even though, in the past few years, weeks and months had gone without a visit to the Park, she had always known it was there waiting for her only a short drive away. But by tomorrow afternoon it would be as remote as the hanging gardens of Babylon or wherever. The papers said it was no longer safe at night. There were muggings and suchlike. She didn't believe that. That was just another of those sensational rumors the papers went in for these days. It all looked much the same to her.

A young woman wheeling a baby carriage walked slowly along the path. She seemed to be looking in a vague sort of way for somewhere to sit down. Alice caught her eye and tried to look welcoming and presently the young woman wheeled the carriage over and sat down on the bench beside her.

"It's a chilly afternoon," Alice said. "There aren't many people out."

"How did you get here?" the woman asked. "Did you walk?"

"No, I was driven and in a little while I'm going to be picked up."

"In a car you mean?"

"In a car."

The woman thought about this for a time. She was a thin, sallow-cheeked young person with big eyes, high cheekbones, and very light brown hair. She had, Alice thought, a sensitive mouth. She was plainly but respectably dressed.

"You live near here?" Alice asked.

The young woman smiled a sad half smile. "My real home is in Ohio," she said. "Right now I'm living over there on Fifth Avenue with some people called Nevinson. I look after their little boy." She peered into the baby carriage. "I'll be going back home in a few weeks though. I can hardly wait. The Nevinsons are going to Europe for the summer. I could have gone with them but I said I'd sooner go back to Ohio."

"Don't you like New York?"

"It's O.K. I'm glad I saw it. It's not like Sandusky though."

"Is Sandusky a very special place?"

"Oh yes." The thin face became animated. The gray eyes lit up. "It's friendly and . . . and it's fun. People talk to each other. Sandusky's the kind of place you can really think of as your home town. You can love it. No one could think of New York as their home town and love it."

"Of course they can," Alice replied indignantly. "I do. It certainly is my home town." She spoke the words boldly but there was, somewhere behind them, a faltering feeling that they weren't quite true. Not as true as she made them sound. The New York she claimed as her home town was the New York she remembered as a child. Well, all things changed. All things changed . . .

"I guess it's what you're used to," the young woman said. "Of course Sandusky's changed a lot since I was a kid."

"I suppose it has," said Alice. The changes which had taken place in Sandusky, Ohio, were of no interest to her. She was taking her last long look at Central Park.

After a while the young woman got up and wheeled the baby carriage away and, not long after, the young man turned up to drive her back to the Waldorf.

Chapter 2

Alice Sanford Elizabeth Melville (nee Barrington) had been born at seven o'clock on the morning of November seventeenth, 1881. Two sisters had preceded her and it had been decided that she should be a boy. Alice, however, had a mind of her own even then and, confounding her parents' plans, elected to be another girl instead.

Ward Barrington Jr., her father, was a kindly man and didn't want his wife to feel unduly guilty. "Don't fret yourself, Amy," he said, bending over her bed a short while after Alice's arrival. "It can't be helped. I'm sure you did your best."

He was a clothing merchant, both wholesale and retail, who with the talented help of an aggressive young partner, promoted from the ranks, had built his father's fashionable but comparatively small business into a large and prosperous concern. His father's establishment had advertised itself as "Gentleman Clothiers for All Occasions"; Ward Jr. had democratized and greatly expanded the operation and now proclaimed Barrington's to be "New York's Finest Outfitters for Men, Women and Children." There were, however, two departments which retained the traditional gentility of his father's day and it was made subtly clear by the decor, the superior manner of the sales attendants, and the prices that these departments were not designed to cater to just anybody. A Brooklyn mechanic and his family, say, who might blunder in, would quickly be made aware that this was not their part of the store. The male department was called "Pour Monsieur" and the female one, "Pour Madame." Ward had thought of the names himself and was very pleased with the arrangement. The Barringtons had a substantial stone residence on Fifty-Second Street which, though of course in no way comparable to the Fifth Avenue mansions of the Astors, the Vanderbilts, and others, was not—at least in the eyes of little Alice—without a certain grandeur. They had a carriage, a coachman, a matched pair of bays, and five full-time servants.

One of her very early memories was walking along Fifty-Second as far as Fifth Avenue with her father and gazing with awe at the vast château which stood there.

"I knew Mr. William Kissam Vanderbilt personally," her father told her, "and in March of the very year you were born your mother and I went to a costume ball there to celebrate the official opening. It was on that night too that your mother was presented to Mrs. William Astor."

"Did they ever ask you back again?" she had asked.

"No," her father answered reluctantly.

"Did you ever ask them to our house?"

"Don't ask silly questions, Alice, or I won't tell you interesting things. I didn't know Mr. Vanderbilt intimately."

"What did you dress up as?"

"I went as Julius Caesar and your mother as Marie Antoinette. There were five Marie Antoinettes but only one other Julius Caesar."

Sometimes her father took her to the store with him. The sidewalks were very crowded with tall men in dark gray suits and derby hats. They were always in a hurry. There were hucksters along the way peddling all manner of amazing things which Alice, dragging along behind her father like a little skiff being towed behind a yacht, would love to have bought. There were raggedy boys with shoeshine boxes or newspapers under their arms. They all had black hair and some of them would grin at her and sometimes she would grin back, though that was forbidden. And beggars, too. Some of them sat with their backs against buildings with an old cap or a tin cup beside them into which people could put pennies or even nickels. Her father never did.

"Why do they beg?" she asked him once.

"Because they are shiftless and lazy. Any money you give them merely makes them more depraved. They spend it on cheap wine and gambling."

"But are they poor to start with or do they get poor because they are wicked?"

"God helps them that help themselves, but he doesn't help the idle wastrels and neither do I."

"Some of them are blind."

"Nonsense! They just make themselves look that way to fool people into feeling sorry for them."

"How do you know?"

"They wink at each other when no one is looking."

"But if no one is looking how . . ."

"Alice, I have warned you before about this annoying habit of yours of asking silly questions."

"Yes, father."

After that Alice had a proper contempt for beggars, especially the ones who pretended to be blind. She kept trying to catch them in the act of winking at each other. Some of them didn't seem to have any eyes in their heads at all and she wondered how they managed it.

At the store she realized what a great and important man her father was. She liked the way the young men and women said, "Yes, Mr. Barrington, sir" and hurried to do anything he asked them. Once, when she was eight and her father had left her briefly and gone into his inner office, she decided to test whether any of her father's prestige and authority had rubbed off on her. She seated herself on one of the chairs conveniently placed for weary shoppers and snapped her fingers at a young male clerk standing nearby. When he turned she said, "I wonder if you could bring me a glass of water."

"Yes, of course, Miss Barrington." He hurried away and presently returned with a small glass of tepid water. "There we are," he said, handing it to her. She didn't want the water, though she forced herself to drink it. She was delighted, however, to discover that she too was born to be obeyed.

Much as she admired her father's power and wisdom she always thought of her mother as being "the superior person." The phrase came from an inscription in a book her mother had received when she was a girl from a parishioner of her father's. The book was called *The Way to Virtue* and the inscription on the flyleaf read: "The truly superior person is one who, by her noble bearing, her shunning of all vulgarity and her devotion to what is good and true in the preservation of our society, commands admiration, respect and obedience from those around her." For as long as Alice could remember back—a long, long way— she had always thought of her mother as one who lived up fully to this definition of superiority.

While Alice enjoyed the ventures with her father into the hustle and bustle of the world of commerce, she found the long walks with her mother in Central Park to be, on the whole, more satisfying, though she sometimes wished they were not so much dedicated to her improvement. She thought the Park must be the most beautiful place in the whole world with its grass and trees and ponds and outcroppings of mossy rock and birds and squirrels and flowers. They would walk along the path side by side, sometimes in silence, sometimes chatting, and then they would sit down on a bench or a little hummock or on the grass itself and Alice would know that her mother was going to talk about what sort of a lady she should be when she grew up.

On fine days Alice was dressed in a dress somewhat shorter but similar in style to her mother's long one and they both carried parasols. On cold and rainy days they dressed up warmly and Mrs. Barrington carried an umbrella under which they both huddled as they hurried purposefully along. There was little talking on these rainy walks. They were taken ostensibly for exercise but actually, Alice presently realized, because Mr. Barrington disapproved of them. "This is *not* weather for ladies," he would say at breakfast. "You'll get pneumonia or, worse still, pulmonary consumption. Even I don't go out more than I have to." His wife would merely laugh and, when he saw that he had lost, he would say, "Well, if you are determined to jeopardize your health then breathe very shallowly. Don't for heaven's sake draw this dank air down into your lungs." They would go out the front door and the first thing Alice's mother would do would be to inhale as deeply as she could two or three times. Alice would do the same. Then they would laugh.

It was the fine weather walks of course that Alice remembered most clearly. There were a lot of other children about but, for the most part, they were with nursemaids or nannies. She was with her mother and her mother was a very superior lady. The nursemaids and nannies and other, lesser females gazed at her with admiration and then modestly lowered their eyes as she went by. Her mother, chin high, erect and fearless, swept along apparently quite oblivious to the mute admiration of those who drew aside to make way for her. Alice quickly learned to follow her mother's example. She too held her head tilted slightly back and looked straight ahead, though she would have liked to stop and play.

They never paused to sit down until they found a secluded spot, free from the curious eyes of the vulgar. "I am not opposed to the use of Central Park by the general public," her mother used to say, "but I do think there should be certain days of the week or certain hours of each day when admission is restricted."

Mrs. Barrington was tall, fair-haired, and blue-eyed. She dressed beautifully, avoiding anything approaching vulgar ostentation while still conveying unmistakably that a display of such superlatively good taste could only be achieved at considerable expense. She was a woman of moderate intelligence and great ambition. Growing up motherless as the only child of an impoverished minister in New Hampshire, she had come to New York at the age of eighteen and found a position as assistant governess in the household of a large, suddenly rich family by the name of Nesbit who had recently moved to New York from Oregon. Then, one day, as a particular treat, the Nesbits allowed her to attend a large ball they were giving. Mrs. Nesbit even bought her a dress for the occasion. That evening she met young Ward Barrington and decided to marry him.

She was forty-seven now and well satisfied with what she had achieved. Her two older daughters were married very satisfactorily, one to a banker and one to an architect, both still living in New York. Now she could give her undivided attention to this last one.

"You're eight years old," she told her on one occasion, "so it's time you began thinking like a young lady. The first and most important thing to remember is that you are better than other people."

"Why am I better than other people?"

"Because you are my daughter."

"I'm Daddy's daughter, too."

"Yes. Well, we'll come to that in due course. For the moment just think of yourself as my daughter and do exactly as I tell you. Is that clear?"

"Yes, Mama."

"The first thing you must understand, Alice, is that our whole society—in fact our whole civilization—is based on showing proper respect for each other. Do you understand?"

"No, I don't think so."

"I can explain it this way. I don't go down to the kitchen when I know the servants are at lunch or supper and I try not to ring for them at those times unless it is necessary. I don't go into their bedrooms and poke through their personal belongings. I always treat them politely. Why do I do these things?"

Alice thought for a moment and then said, "Because you're afraid they'd pack up and leave if you didn't?"

"Don't be absurd. I'm certainly not intimidated by a mere servant. If any of them want to leave they may certainly do so. A servant can be replaced as easily as a worn-out shoe."

"But I heard you telling Mrs. Crampton that good servants were so hard to get."

"That may be"—there was a distinct edge to her voice—"but that is *not* why I don't ring for them while they are eating. Alice, for heaven's sake put your mind to the question and don't give me silly, flippant answers."

"I was trying to think. I didn't mean to make a silly answer. If you aren't afraid they'll leave, I don't know. Anyway you do ring for them when they're eating. You ring the bell and say, 'I hate to disturb Elsie at her lunch' and then when she comes and you ask her to bring in sherry you say, 'I'm so sorry to have disturbed you at your lunch, Elsie,' and she says, 'That's quite all right, ma'am, I'd all but finished.' You do that all the time."

Mrs. Barrington smiled a tight little smile. "Why do I bother to show such consideration?"

Alice was becoming increasingly bored by the whole discussion. She was watching some boys flying kites a few hundred yards away. She would like to have joined them. Kites were wonderful things. She wished she could have one.

"Well?" her mother demanded.

"Well what? I'm sorry, I was watching those boys with their kites."

"I asked you why I showed such consideration for the servants."

Alice creased her forehead, closed her eyes, pulled down the corners of her mouth, and clenched her fists in order to demonstrate to her mother that she was giving the question her most powerful concentration. Suddenly she relaxed. She opened her eyes and unclenched her fingers. "So you won't have to pay them higher wages," she said confidently.

"Because I respect them as individuals," said Mrs. Barrington, who was unwilling to become involved in any more guessing games. "I can't expect them to have respect for me if I show no respect for them. Do you understand?"

"A little."

"You will. Until now the servants have called you Alice."

"That's my name."

"Of course that's your name, just as my name is Amy. The servants, however, do *not* call me Amy."

"Well, they can't call me Mrs. Barrington."

"Of course not. Don't be silly. From now on they will call you *Miss* Alice. I have so instructed them. You must begin to learn to accept respect. If any of them should forget and call you Alice you will not answer."

"Should I start to call them Miss Jean and Mr. John and . . .?"

"Of course not. Don't be absurd."

"What about Mrs. Grimble? When I go into the kitchen to help her cook does *she* have to call me Miss Alice?"

"You won't be going into the kitchen much anymore."

"Why not?"

"Because I say so. Also because, starting tomorrow, you are going to have a tutor. Now that the room is all ready I've found a very suitable young woman. Miss Laura Cosgrove is coming for tea. We'd better be getting home if we're to arrive before she does."

Alice drained the last of her gin and tonic. She had made it last an hour. She would have liked another but the doctor had said only one a day and, on the whole, she obeyed him. She had to admit that sometimes two glasses did bring on those annoying fits of dizziness. Anyway, it was almost time for supper and then she would watch "Wednesday Night at the Movies." This evening it was *The Scarlet Pimpernel* with Leslie Howard. Despite the blurb about it in the program guide it hadn't been *that* long ago since she had seen the original. With Arthur? No, that seemed unlikely. With Geoffrey? That seemed unlikely, too. Perhaps she had taken Patricia or just gone alone.

Outside the window the rolling yellow fog had completely obscured the ocean.

Chapter 3

Though Alice saw no necessity to confess the fact to her daughter, she admitted privately to herself that the Chalfont Apartment Hotel was a good deal better than she had imagined it was going to be.

Mrs. Owens, her housekeeper, cook, and occasional companion, was pleasantly efficient and tactful. Now, after six weeks, Alice was beginning to feel reasonably settled. Canada was not the United States and Vancouver was, very definitely, not New York. She couldn't comprehend the politics at all and the theatre page of the paper seemed drab indeed. However, she wouldn't complain. The country wasn't anything as primitive as she had feared it might be. A routine was beginning to establish itself. There had been a time when Alice resented routine but now it comforted her. It was something one could rely on.

Patricia came on Wednesday afternoons. If the day was fine she arrived at two thirty and they went for a drive through Stanley Park before coming back for tea. It was pleasant enough, Alice thought, but it was no match for Central Park. No park in the world could compare to *it*! If the day was rainy Patricia came an hour later and they just had tea and talk. On Sundays either Patricia or Michael called for her and she went to their house for tea, sometimes staying on for an early supper.

Alice liked her daughter and son-in-law well enough and appreciated their kindness but she found them boring. That wasn't, she realized, entirely their fault. It was just the way they were. Patricia never had shared her own sense of excitement at the mere fact of being alive. She was her father's daughter.

The time of day Alice enjoyed most was five thirty, when she could tell Mrs. Owens to bring in her gin and tonic and could sit at her window, looking out over the Pacific Ocean towards Japan, sipping her drink and remembering the old days. That was the best hour.

Today was another Wednesday. Patricia had departed. Alice sat with her cold glass in her arthritic hands and looked at the rain-streaked window. "Poor Laura Cosgrove," she thought to herself. "I suppose I really was rather horrid to her but what happened to her wasn't my fault. If only she had confided in Mother."

Alice, being a child of her parents' middle age, seldom had any children to play with during her first nine years. The children of her parents' friends were much too old—the age of Alice's older sisters, Dorothea and Prudence, or at least in their teens. The only other possible companions were the boys and girls she saw flying kites and playing tag in Central Park but, when she suggested joining them, her mother always said, "I have no idea who they are and I suspect many of them are very common children."

Though Alice envied other children she saw playing games and having fun together, it never occurred to her, at that stage, to doubt that she was more fortunate than they were. Her mother had frequently told her so and of course what her mother said was right.

For a time there had been a nanny, a seemingly pleasant English girl, Hilda Moorhead, who, despite her cockney accent, had come with impeccable references. However, she was presently discovered to be with child. Mrs. Barrington, who had been keeping an increasingly suspicious eye on Hilda's waistline for some time, at length summoned the wretched girl to the small, sparsely furnished room which she called her "office" and which was used mainly for interviews of servants. She demanded the truth. To her astonishment, the brazen hussy, instead of bursting into tears and pleading for mercy, had had the audacity to say: "Oh, didn't Mr. Barrington tell you? He said he would. It was that weekend you went to Bridgeport to see your aunt or something."

Alice, crouching outside the door to hear and relish the drama she only partially understood, heard her mother draw in her breath sharply.

"You slut! Do you dare to insinuate to me that Mr. Barrington . . ." She hesitated, uncertain of how to finish the question.

"I wasn't insinuating anything. One night while you were away I'd just put Alice to bed and Mr. Barrington came up for a good-night kiss. From little Alice, I mean. So afterwards I stepped out into the hall with him for a moment and I said, 'Mr. Barrington, you do like children, don't you?' and he said, 'Yes, I do,' and I said, 'I'm going to have one myself one day and I hope it turns out to be as nice a little girl as Alice is.' 'Good for you,' he said, 'I'll tell Mrs. Barrington what you said.' So I thought you knew."

"Get out!" commanded Mrs. Barrington. Alice was poised to flee but she lingered just long enough to hear Hilda Moorhead answer, "You didn't think your husband was the father, did you? I'm shocked, I am."

She went out, slamming the door behind her, and Alice, who had sought refuge on the stairs leading down to a side entrance, watched her walk proudly and smilingly by.

It had never occurred to Alice that anyone could possibly speak to her mother in that way without being struck dead by a bolt of lightning.

After that there were no more nannies.

So, without a nanny or companions of her own age, Alice was allowed far more time with her mother and father than was normally considered appropriate for most little girls her age in "nice" families. She was not encouraged, however, to speak unless she was spoken to, and so she got used to sitting silently with a picture book open on her knees and listening to what the grown-ups were saying. So silent and motionless was she that her parents seemed to forget that she was there at all or to assume that, because her clear blue eyes were riveted on the colored pages, her mind was concentrated on the adventures of the delightful animals or charming elves and fairies who lived on them.

"Tell me more about this tutor you've engaged for Alice," her father said.

Her parents were having their nightly glass of sherry before dinner and, since there were no guests that evening, Alice was to be allowed to dine with them. Going slightly squinty-eyed, in a way she had taught herself, Alice was able to watch her mother while apparently never glancing up from her book.

Her mother smiled vaguely and then said, "I assure you that, when you see her, you'll understand why she isn't in the marriage market."

"I was interested in the young woman's cultural background and training."

"She is the youngest daughter of a retired Harvard professor of philosophy. He had, apparently, five children and was able to launch four of them on successful careers or marriages. Then he retired and his wife died. He decided very sensibly that he had done quite well by his children and now it was time that at least one of them repaid the debt. So he told Laura that that would be her responsibility. She would not rush off and get married—a quite superfluous decree, I should have thought, unless she had an immense fortune to go with her. She would, he informed her, stay at home and keep house for him. In return he would teach her some English, History, Mathematics, and Philosophy so that, when he died, she might possibly open an old maids' school or, failing that, find a job as a tutor. She agreed, which, since she had no choice in the matter, was very sensible of her."

They both laughed and he picked up the decanter and refilled their sherry glasses.

"Her father died a couple of months ago and she found to her horror, poor dear, that the house they had been living in was mortgaged to the hilt. She had hoped and expected that her father would leave her enough money to get a little school started, instead of which she finds herself obliged to pay off some of his debts. The other members of the family have apparently lost interest in the whole affair and so she is quite on her own. She has picked up a little money tutoring and I've given her two weeks pay in advance. Apart from that she has nothing."

"Sounds like a good find. I like the Harvard background."

"Yes, she'll do very well, I think, for a year or two until Alice is ready for Ashcroft. She's coming to tea on Tuesday so that Alice and she can meet and I can gauge their reaction to each other."

So, even as they were hurrying back from Central Park on that Tuesday afternoon in September, Alice already knew at least a little bit about Laura Cosgrove. She did not, however, know the whole story.

The full-length mirror in Alice's room gave her great pleasure. She looked at herself in it every day. Unlike Snow White's wicked stepmother, she did not consult it for reassurance that she was indeed beautiful but rather for the very considerable satisfaction which her beauty gave her.

She admired her long, shiny, light golden hair which her

mother enjoyed brushing and which Alice enjoyed having brushed; she admired her clear blue, sparkling eyes, her delicately upturned nose, the creamy pinkness of her cheeks; she admired her red lips which smiled so fetchingly and the firm shapeliness of her chin. She was, without a doubt, the prettiest little girl she had ever seen.

Looking at herself before going to bed on the day before she was to meet Miss Laura Cosgrove she thought how taken her tutor would be by her appearance. There was no doubt in her mind that Laura Cosgrove herself would be thin and bony with a pale complexion, dull, mouse-colored hair pulled back and fastened in a bun behind her narrow head. Her neck would be too long and she would wear thick glasses which would magnify her rabbity little eyes. Her drab dress would hang from her narrow shoulders as if from a wire coat hanger. Poor Miss Cosgrove.

It came therefore as something of a shock to Alice when she had washed her face and hands, put on her yellow frock with the pink roses on it, and come downstairs for tea to find that Laura Cosgrove was big-boned, tall, and almost formidable in appearance with heavy eyebrows, dark eyes, a large nose, and very thick lips with the hint of a moustache. She had black hair done up in a great swirl above her ample shoulders. She had big breasts. Her complexion, however, had an unhealthy sallowness about it. Her voice, when she greeted Alice, was deep—almost like a man's.

"So this is the little girl," she said.

"Yes, this is Alice," Mrs. Barrington replied proudly. "I think the two of you will get along very well."

"I am sure we shall," Miss Cosgrove agreed in her masculine voice. "She looks like an intelligent and obedient child. 'A disciplined mind in a disciplined body,' my father used to say to me. 'Those are the essentials of sound scholarship.' "

"I'm sure you are right," Mrs. Barrington replied. "How do you take your tea?"

"In the same way that my father took his: cream and a healthy portion of sugar."

Alice had long ago learned not to let her outward behavior interfere with the inner workings of her mind and so, though her manner was demure to the point of coyness, her mind was intent on evaluating the strengths and weaknesses of the enemy. Even as she dropped her little half curtsy and extended her slim hand to Miss Cosgrove on introduction, she had decided that she was certainly not going to be intimidated by this large and fearsome woman who was to be set in charge over her.

"School" began at nine the following morning. Alice went up to the room ten minutes before the hour and found Miss Cosgrove already there.

"Bright and early and eager to learn, I see," said Miss Cosgrove.

Alice treated her to one of her dazzling smiles and said, "Good morning, Miss Cosgrove."

"Your mother tells me you read well and have a good command of simple number work."

"Yes, I think I am quite good in those things. My mother has taught me most mornings."

"Well, let's see where we stand. This book is a McGuffey Reader and it is full of beautiful things." She advanced towards Alice like a man-of-war. "I've opened it at a poem called 'Lochinvar' by Sir Walter Scott. It is a fine poem. I want you to read it through to yourself first and then I want you to read it aloud to me. I think you'll find it very exciting." By this time she was bending low over Alice, indicating with a thick index finger where the poem started on the page.

Alice looked up innocently into Miss Cosgrove's large, ugly face and asked, "Is that smell from your breath or from under your arms?"

Laura Cosgrove straightened up as though someone had pinched her ample behind. "What a perfectly dreadful thing to say!" she exclaimed. "What would your mother say if I told her you asked such a frightful question? My standards of personal cleanliness and hygiene are of the highest. Whatever you smelt, it was not me."

"I'm awfully sorry," Alice said contritely. "I didn't mean to hurt your feelings. Perhaps it was a smell coming in the window."

"The window isn't even open."

"Oh no. How foolish of me."

Miss Cosgrove went back to her desk before the blackboard without further comment and Alice bent her head over her book.

After a little while she said, "I think I'm ready, Miss Cosgrove, but there are two words I don't understand."

"When we don't understand words we look them up in a dictionary. Do you understand how to use a dictionary?"

"Yes."

"Well, here's a small Oxford dictionary. My father always preferred Oxford to Webster. He said it was purer." She put the book on Alice's desk and asked her what the words were.

" 'Galliard' and 'scour.' "

"Let's see you find them," Laura Cosgrove said; but she didn't bend down to help.

Mrs. Barrington came in at about eleven thirty, just after they had embarked on their first Geography lesson, which was concerned with the roundness of the Earth. "Well," she asked, "how are you two getting along?"

Alice wondered if Miss Cosgrove would now get her revenge by reporting her. But, no, all she said was, "Very well, thank you, Mrs. Barrington."

"Oh yes," echoed Alice. "We're getting along very well. Miss Cosgrove is a marvelous teacher."

Chapter 4

"I wasn't a cruel child," Alice thought to herself, looking back. "Not really. Children sometimes seem to be cruel but almost always it's a curious form of experimentation. I'll say or do this and see what will happen. That's all. I wasn't malicious. I didn't really think of Miss Cosgrove as my enemy. Of course, in my girlhood, growing up in the sort of household I did, servants were fair game. They would seldom risk dismissal by complaining about their employer's children. And we knew it. I knew it anyway."

Alice had wondered in retrospect why she hadn't realized what a terribly lonely time that must have been for Laura Cosgrove; but the imagination of a small child, so fertile in many, many ways, is rarely capable of perceiving the misery of a grown-up who tries bravely to conceal it. Her parents, she had sometimes thought, might have been more discerning, but they apparently never thought of it either.

Miss Cosgrove occupied a small and sketchily furnished room on the third floor and shared a bathroom with Mrs. Grimble, the cook, to the latter's intense and unconcealed annoyance. It had been one of Mrs. Grimble's proudest achievements that over the years she had fought for and won a small bathroom all to herself. "All I can say," she told Laura when they first encountered each other, "is that you'd better pop in and pop out again pretty quick when you use it, because if I ever catch you in there when I want to go you'll not forget in a hurry."

Though Mrs. Grimble was certainly no match for Laura physically, being almost a foot shorter and a hundred or more pounds lighter, there was a tigerlike quality about her when aroused that was capable of intimidating beefy tradesmen and was more than adequate in dealing with Laura Cosgrove. Laura was made sufficiently nervous by the threat that, though she tried to confine her bathroom visits to times when she was reasonably sure Mrs. Grimble would be otherwise occupied, she frequently thought she heard her approaching and would "pop out" with her mission unaccomplished.

Oh, it was easy enough later to realize their unkindness and everyone, even Mrs. Grimble, felt badly about it, but how was anyone to know at the time how miserable she was?

"She kept herself so much to herself," Mrs. Grimble sighed, as if to imply that all her overtures of friendship had been rebuffed.

Though the servants made it abundantly clear that she was not a welcome addition to their dining table, they were resentful when she took to carrying her meals on a tray up the back stairs to her own little room. Of course, when Alice was not with her parents, the two of them dined together in the nursery and they frequently had lunch together when Mrs. Barrington was out. She was never invited to dine with the family.

She got seven dollars a week plus room and board, which was twice what the maids got.

On an occasional fine afternoon, instead of staying in the classroom, they went, with Mrs. Barrington's permission, for a walk in Central Park and Miss Cosgrove sometimes told Alice little stories about her life with her father.

"I was very fortunate," she said more than once, "because I was able to serve my father right up to the end, and he repaid me by teaching me what a disciplined mind in a disciplined body really meant. We weren't rich, you know, and I remember once I was cooking a roast of beef while reading a book and forgot it. It was almost burnt to a cinder. There was barely enough to give him one decent helping.

"Very well, my girl," he said, "you'll live on bread and water for the next two days. That will remind you that the world of literature must not take precedence over the practical world of everyday. It isn't a choice of books or bread. We need both."

"I think that was unkind. Were you just a little girl like me?"

"No. I was twenty-six. It was a very good lesson. My father was a wise man. 'Never too old to learn,' he said."

But Alice didn't really like her much and she tried periodically to make that clear, just in case Miss Cosgrove ever began to think that she could take her obedience for granted. She put honey in the ink bottle, which clogged up the fountain pen Miss Cosgrove had inherited from her father; she sometimes played stupid, especially in arithmetic, or "number work," as Miss Cosgrove called it, until poor Laura was herself completely confused and the problem had to be abandoned.

Once—only once—she got her so angry that tears came to her eyes. They had just started to read *Black Beauty* and had come to the part where Beauty's mother calls him aside to advise him about his conduct. Miss Cosgrove was reading aloud. " 'I wish you to pay attention to what I am going to say to you. The colts who live here are very good colts, but they are carthorse colts, and of course have not learned manners. You have been well-bred and well-born; your father was . . .' "

Alice interrupted. "She's really talking about people, isn't she?"

"The author is drawing an analogy between well-bred people and well-bred animals. We'll proceed."

"Well-bred people are rich, aren't they?"

"Not necessarily at all. I am extremely well bred but I am not rich."

Alice giggled. "I don't see there's any advantage in being well bred if you're still treated like one of the servants."

It was then that the tears came to Laura Cosgrove's eyes.

Except for such occasional gibes Alice was, on the whole, a well-behaved if reluctant student. She found her confinement in that one poorly lit room alone with Miss Cosgrove tedious in the extreme, and longed to be in a bright classroom surrounded by other girls. Autumn turned into winter and winter slowly and reluctantly yielded to spring.

More and more frequently, as winter was drawing to an end, Miss Cosgrove did not come down to the kitchen to collect her supper and, much as Mrs. Grimble despised the woman, she began to be concerned. One day she expressed her concern to Mrs. Barrington.

"Always was uppity and never would sit down to table with us but she'd come for her plate regular enough. Now all she does is swig a cup of coffee in the morning and then of course she eats lunch with Miss Alice in the classroom at noon. She hardly ever comes down to collect her supper. I leave it in the oven until I'm finished in the kitchen and then I throw it away. It's all dried and wizened up by that time anyway. If you ask me it's a waste of good food."

Mrs. Barrington thought of calling on her daughter's peculiar tutor that evening to see if anything was wrong but, in the end, she decided to wait until the next day. There was no point in making a big fuss. She respected Miss Cosgrove's right to privacy. Besides, they had guests coming for dinner.

It was after nine fifteen the following morning that Alice came to her mother's bedroom. "There's something wrong with Miss Cosgrove," she said. "When she didn't come to the classroom I waited for a while and then I went up and knocked on her bedroom door. She just said, 'Go away.' I could hear her moaning but I couldn't get in because the door's locked."

Mrs. Barrington rose promptly and, taking the master key from the small drawer in her writing desk, she proceeded up the stairs with Alice following excitedly behind.

Laura Cosgrove was lying on her bed attired in a voluminous nightgown. Her knees were drawn up almost to her chin and she clasped them with both hands. Her bed clothes were in complete disarray and she had vomited on them.

"Go to your room at once," Mrs. Barrington commanded Alice, "and stay there until I send for you." Alice, however, lingered long enough to see her mother go to the bed and, putting her hand on the forehead of the groaning woman, say, "You poor thing. I'll get the doctor at once."

From her window Alice watched the doctor arrive and then, a little later, saw Miss Cosgrove carried out, swathed in blankets, to be taken to the hospital.

She died that night. Alice was never quite sure what she died of but there was some talk of internal bleeding and she overheard her mother tell her father that "Dr. Winston said it had probably been going on for some time. I do wish the poor dear had said something earlier."

Alice was mildly saddened by the event but her main feeling was one of bewilderment. The fact of death was as far beyond her comprehension as Darwin's *Origin of Species,* which was still being much discussed although it was over thirty years old.

There would come a time when death would be of more significance to her.

Chapter 5

There was a postscript to the affair.

Going through Laura Cosgrove's belongings Mrs. Barrington found no record of next of kin. There were brothers and sisters, but apparently Laura did not correspond with them. The only name and address she discovered was that of a Mrs. Reginald Bender who lived in Brooklyn. She couldn't be a relative, because at their first interview Laura had said she had no relatives in New York.

Mrs. Barrington didn't know what to do. She asked Alice if Miss Cosgrove had ever mentioned a Mrs. Bender to her.

"Yes," Alice said, "she did. I remember now. She lives in Brooklyn, I think. She was a friend of Miss Cosgrove's mother. She's very old. Miss Cosgrove used sometimes to visit her on Sundays."

"I expect I'd better write to her."

"Why don't we go to see her?"

"All the way to Brooklyn? Don't be absurd."

But in the end Alice had her way. She had been so moody and so frequently tearful since Miss Cosgrove's death that Mrs. Barrington was quite concerned about her. She kept saying, "If only we could take her things to Mrs. Bender and I could tell her how sorry we are I'd feel better." She also said, "Miss Cosgrove would have wanted us to take her things to Mrs. Bender, and if Mrs. Bender dies before we deliver them I'll never forgive myself." It never occurred to Mrs. Barrington that Alice might be playing a rôle.

So Mrs. Barrington gave way. She wrote to Mrs. Bender saying she could expect them on a certain day and, despite Mr. Barrington's grave doubts, they set off one morning with Laura Cosgrove's belongings in a suitcase and a large paper bag.

It was a Saturday in late June and it was hot. The street, when they eventually found it, was dotted with semiclad children who stopped in their play to gaze with curiosity at the unaccustomed sight of a carriage in that neighborhood.

Men in undershirts and women in cotton dresses sitting on steps also turned to stare. They seemed neither hostile nor friendly—just curious.

When they found Number 17, Roger, the coachman, stopped the horses and Mrs. Barrington and Alice got out.

"Wait here, Roger," Mrs. Barrington commanded in an unnecessarily loud voice. "I don't expect we'll be very long." The street seemed very silent to Alice. There were half a dozen people on the steps of Number 17 completely blocking the entrance and Alice wondered if they were going to have to scramble over them in order to get in; but they shifted to either side and made a narrow space as Mrs. Barrington approached.

"Does Mrs. Bender live here?"

The fat-armed woman to whom the question had been addressed looked at Mrs. Barrington as if she were a visitor from another planet and then, after a long silence, asked, "What do you want of her? She never did nobody any harm."

"I have some things for her."

"Third up, turn left and first on the right," a man said, and they went in.

It was very dark and there was a smell which was different from any Alice had encountered before. "What is that smell?" Alice asked in a loud whisper, as if she were in church. Her mother didn't answer and, as they began to mount the first flight of wooden steps, Alice repeated the question. Her mother stopped and, turning her head to face her daughter, she said, "It's the smell of the poor." Alice said nothing. It was the first time she had realized that the poor had a smell all their own. She wondered if the rich had a smell of their own which she had never detected.

By the time they reached the third floor they were both out of breath. Mrs. Barrington was carrying the suitcase and Alice the paper bag. They rested for a moment or two and then went along and knocked at the door.

It was opened so instantaneously by a small, hunched old lady in a black dress that it seemed she must have been poised and waiting with her hand on the knob. "Come in! Come in!" she said brightly, "I've been expecting you."

"I'm Mrs. Barrington and this is . . ."

"I know, I know. Your daughter Alice. I've heard so much about you. You were both so wonderful to poor dear

Laura. She spoke of you often and said such nice things about you. Please sit down. The kettle's boiling and I got some cookies to go with the tea."

"We really can't stay," said Mrs. Barrington. "It's such a long journey to Brooklyn and . . ."

"But you'll stay for a cup of tea, won't you? I'm pouring the water in the pot now. I've been waiting for your visit. I was so excited I couldn't sleep last night."

"Well, perhaps just for a moment."

"That's better," she said with pleasure. "Sit at the table. I got my tablecloth out last night and my best cups. I still have a few nice things left. When my husband was alive we had a house in Hartford but things happened. I suppose things always happen. Then I came to New York to be near my son and he died, too. Oh well, I'm quite cosy here, but it gets hot in summer. I would have made my little buns but I was afraid the stove would heat up the room and make it uncomfortable for you. So I went out yesterday afternoon and bought cookies from the bake shop at the corner."

Alice was fascinated. Mrs. Bender chirped on about this and that, kept passing the cookies, offered to refill their cups after they had only had two or three sips and was indeed quite beside herself with enjoyment. Alice hoped her mother would say, "You must come and have tea with us one day," but she didn't.

Mrs. Barrington was, however, sufficiently impressed by the hospitality; they stayed on for nearly three quarters of an hour and, when they finally stood up to leave, she said, "This has been most kind of you, Mrs. Bender. I'm glad we came. I felt Laura would have wanted us to come. We were all so fond of her."

"Yes, she was a nice girl. Her mother was my closest friend once upon a time. A sweet person. I wish you didn't have to go but I know it's a long journey back to where you live. You never told me how Laura died."

"It was an internal trouble that had been going on for some time. She never mentioned it."

She pursed her little wrinkled lips and thought for a moment. "Well, it's God's will I expect. Thank you for bringing her things. They won't fit me but I'll find someone."

When they reached the door she and Mrs. Barrington shook hands and then, impulsively, she stooped and kissed

Alice on the cheek. "I looked like you once," she said.

They went down the stairs and out the door into the sunshine. Once again the step sitters shifted to give them passage.

"Isn't she a wonderful person!" Alice said as they set off.

"She was very hospitable. She didn't kiss you on the lips, did she?"

"No, on the cheek. Why?"

"I didn't want you to catch a germ. When you get home I want you to gargle well and have a good bath."

In later years Alice couldn't remember for sure whether it was the evening of that same day or some days later that her father and mother announced that they and their friends the Dysons had rented a private car on the railway and were going to the Chicago World's Fair.

Whenever the announcement did come it swept away all morbid memories of Laura Cosgrove.

"And next autumn," her mother told her, "you are to enter Ashcroft School for Girls."

Alice's cup was full to overflowing.

She remembered the train ride to Chicago, sitting at a window and watching the forests and lakes and fields and streams whirl by and listening to the clickety-clackety of steel on steel, eating splendid meals with the grown-ups while the train rocketed on and the waiter, balancing a laden tray on one hand, swayed with the motion, spilling not so much as a drop of soup. She remembered lying in her berth at night feeling the surging power as the great monster rushed through the darkness. At one stop she and her father walked along the platform right to the front and the engine driver himself looked down from on high and asked her her name.

She remembered too the importance of having her very own hotel room with her very own key and the huge lobby of the hotel with its immense chandeliers and overstuffed furniture and potted palms, so crowded with people.

They were all there to see what was billed as "The World's Greatest Extravaganza." Some New Yorkers, including her parents and the Dysons, kept saying they wouldn't have believed Chicago was capable of staging such a show if they hadn't seen it with their own eyes, and others said that of course most of the truly imaginative planning had in fact been done by New Yorkers.

She remembered these things but of the big Fair itself, strangely enough, little remained in her mind. It was a blur of white buildings, of noise, and of more people than she had ever before seen in one place at one time. The only incident she recalled really vividly was somehow getting separated from her parents and finding herself wandering along behind a row of tents. She came to a clown, all made-up and his crazy costume, sitting on an up-ended box. She went up to him and said, "I'm Alice Barrington from New York City and I've lost my parents."

He looked at her thoughtfully for a few moments and then said, "We're looking for a pretty girl like you to hang from a trapeze by her teeth. How would you like to join up with us?"

Alice *thought* he was joking but she wasn't absolutely sure. However, she answered, "I think I ought to at least try to find my parents first."

He sighed. "Oh well, I expect you're right." He got up and she took his hand. "Do you remember where they were when you saw them last?"

"They were going to look at some things from France."

They walked along together hand in hand and she wasn't frightened any more. People turned to stare at them and she was so proud to be walking with a real clown. When she saw her parents, almost too soon it seemed, she pointed them out and he took her up to them and said to her mother, "I offered your daughter a career as a trapeze artist but she preferred to come back to you."

Alice was afraid her mother might be cross with the clown, who spoke to her as if he were her equal, but she laughed and thanked him and Mr. Barrington offered him some money which he refused. He asked them if they were enjoying themselves and they said they were. Then he looked down at Alice and said, "If you change your mind, Alice, come and see me. Ask for Gombo." Then he walked away and was lost in the crowd.

"That," said Mr. Barrington, awed in spite of himself and gazing after the disappearing figure, "was The Great Gombo, the most famous clown in the world." Alice had the feeling her father would almost have liked to ask him for his autograph if he had realized in time.

"He's very well spoken," her mother said. Alice had the feeling that her mother was going to add "for a clown" but checked herself in time.

Then, before they knew it, summer was almost over and Alice and her mother were involved in having school uniforms fitted, having teeth looked at, a medical examination, and checking off various purchases on a printed list headed "Required Equipment for Girls of Ashcroft School."

She had collected an enormous number of pamphlets, leaflets, and other bits of propaganda from the various national pavilions at the Fair. She was always going to study them but somehow they remained, tied in neat bundles, in her bottom drawer. Eventually they were thrown out.

They belonged to The Past. She was now entering The Future.

Chapter 6

On one of their late summer shopping expeditions they went into a bookstore and Alice saw and persuaded her mother to buy for her a slim volume called *The Boy Prince of Rajasthan*. It had nice pictures.

She read it the last weekend before school started and it made a deeper impression on her than any other book had made up to that time. It told of a boy growing up in northern India who, at the age of fourteen, inherits his father's title and vows to avenge his father's murder by a wicked, antiBritish, lawless tribe of hill people. Though most of them worship him, the boy's own subjects doubt that he is capable of realizing his ambition. He thwarts a plot to overthrow him, goes on to slay the tyrant who murdered his father, converts the tyrant's erstwhile followers to the true cause and, in the end, seeks out and wins the girl of his dreams to be his Princess.

Near the end a loyal follower asks him how he has managed to achieve so much and he replies, "Fate would have it so. It was Fate which ordained that I should become a Prince at such a young age. It was Fate which enabled me to seek out and destroy the evil Singar Ramin. It was Fate which enabled me to find the beauteous Princess Kahmin who is to become my wife. I am a child of Fate."

It was, Alice thought, a most marvelous speech. The fact that the dust jacket blurb said of the author, "It is one of Mrs. Agatha Finch's great ambitions to visit the land of which she writes so vividly," did nothing whatever to diminish Alice's conviction that this was a truly great and authentic book. She, too, she was convinced, was a child of Fate and, though she could not marry the Boy Prince of Rajasthan, because he was now too old for her and married already to the Princess of his choice, she would marry someone like him. Fate would guide her.

She said nothing to her parents about this and, when her mother asked her if she liked the book, she answered with what she was masterful restraint, "Yes, I enjoyed it very much. I think, when I have time, I shall read it again."

The front picture was in color and showed the Boy Prince sitting proudly on a large and extremely handsome white horse. He was in a splendid jeweled uniform and the harness of his horse had jewels on it, too. He wore a fine jeweled turban and held his sword high in the air. Most evenings, after she had knelt by her bed, been tucked in, and kissed good night, she waited to make sure that she was safe and then climbed out of bed, turned on the light, opened the book at the picture, and took a last longing look at it. Sometimes she kissed it.

It had always been Mr. Barrington's custom to be driven only part way to work. To walk the last few blocks "set him up," he used to say, and besides it was a good example for the juniors. Roger, the Barringtons' coachman and general handyman around the place, now began each day by taking Mr. Barrington part way to work and then taking Alice on to her school. Roger was a sad man in his middle thirties. Life had not been kind to him and he cherished no expectation of better times ahead.

"Sometimes," he confided in Alice one day, "I almost wishes I was one of them there horses. They gets their meals regular; they gets cared for and they've no cause to think."

Alice resisted the temptation to say that he looked rather like one of "them there horses" with his large brown eyes, long nose, and long, lank hair. Instead she asked, "Do you do a lot of thinking, Roger?"

"All the time," he answered sadly. "My mind never stops working. You have no idea the thoughts I think, Miss Alice. Sometimes I amaze even myself."

"What do you think about?"

"Everything. Mostly about life."

"About life?"

"The meaning of it."

"Have you figured it out yet?"

"Oh yes. I can't tell anyone, though."

"Why not?"

"It's too depressing. I've got to keep the secret all bottled up inside me and that's what makes me sad."

"You could tell me if you like. I wouldn't tell anyone else and it might make things easier for you."

Roger seemed to consider this proposition for some time

but eventually he said sadly, "Wouldn't work. Then I'd be worried that maybe I'd ruined *your* life. I wouldn't want to do that."

"It wouldn't ruin my life. I'm going to be very happy and successful. I'm going to find an Indian prince."

"Go on thinking you're going to be happy," Roger said. "Go on thinking that as long as you can. I used to think that myself once."

"But are you unhappy all the time, Roger? I heard you whistling when I came out after breakfast."

"Me?"

"Yes, you."

"Strange. Trying to keep my courage up, I expect."

"You're from England, aren't you?"

"That's right. I was born an orphan in Brighton."

"Why did you come to America?"

"Why not? I had to go someplace. I couldn't just stand around. People kept saying this was the land of opportunity, like. I believed them. Worse luck me. Of course no land would be the land of opportunity for the likes of me. I wasn't meant to succeed."

"You're a very good coachman," Alice told him hopefully. She didn't like to see anyone so unhappy.

"Me and the horses," Roger said, "birds of a feather."

Alice couldn't think of any comment on that remark that might be suitable and not insulting so she remained silent until they pulled up in front of the school.

The Ashcroft School for Girls was a day school which, according to the prospectus, "cares for the moral, physical and intellectual needs of young ladies from the age of nine to eighteen and is 'progressive' in the sense that it emphasizes academic disciplines to a greater degree than most girls' schools without sacrificing training in deportment and in the social graces." It had just short of two hundred students. It was situated in the lower Forties near Fifth Avenue when Alice first attended the school; the location had shifted several times already since its founding, moving with the ever-changing City.

From the very first day Alice loved school. For the first time she was with girls her own age with whom she could romp and play and argue and fight and, of course, she had Miss Conner. Miss Conner was wonderful—the most wonderful person, in fact, in all the world.

"I sometimes wonder," Alice told her mother, "what the world would be like without Miss Conner. I simply can't imagine it."

Miss Conner was tall, redheaded, green-eyed, and knew everything.

"I wish you were like Miss Conner," Alice told her mother. "She's so wise."

"That's nice," said Mrs. Barrington.

"Miss Conner's very old."

"I don't think she's *that* old. I *did* meet her when we first went to the school."

"I asked her how old she was and she said she'd lived almost a quarter of a century. That's pretty old."

"Yes," Mrs. Barrington agreed, "that's pretty old. But Alice, my dear, you must not go round asking people their age. It isn't nice."

"Why not?"

"It just isn't. A person's age, especially a lady's, is a personal matter."

"People ask me my age."

"That's quite different. You're a child."

"But if someone wanted to write down my age now they'd know when I was thirty or forty."

"No one would do such a thing. Besides, people grow older at different rates."

"I don't understand."

"You will, dear, in time."

"Oh," said Alice. It all seemed very puzzling. "But a year is the same length for everyone."

"I don't want to get impatient. It all has to do with birthdays. Now do run along. I'm busy." So there the matter was left—another bafflement that would only be understood when she was grown up.

Miss Conner was more than a teacher. She was a friend and moral guide. To Alice's amazement and delight it turned out that she too had read *The Boy Prince of Rajasthan* and admired it greatly. "I think it must be one of the best books in the world," Alice said. "I think it must," Miss Conner agreed.

Alice's affection and admiration for Miss Conner was reciprocated. For almost a month Alice, who was supposedly recuperating from the flu, was "E.P.E."—excused physical exercise—which meant she could stay in her classroom and read instead of putting on bloomers and running around the small, stuffy gymnasium. It was during this "E.P.E." period that she really got to know Miss Conner. Miss Conner presided over the "E.P.E." students. There weren't many and, for a week, Alice was the only one except for a girl called Gladys Strong who had very weak eyes, thick glasses, and bow legs. Gladys Strong was a permanent member of "E.P.E." No one had any use for Gladys Strong. Her father, so the story went, was a librarian. That seemed a very strange way of earning a living. None of the other girls could even imagine what it would be like to have a father who was a librarian.

"Well," Miss Conner said brightly to Alice one day, "and what kind of a life are you planning for yourself?"

Alice was better prepared for the question than most children her age might be, having given the matter considerable thought. "I'm going to marry the right man. I shall know he's the right man when he comes along because I believe in Fate. Then, when we're married, I'm going to have ten children, five boys and five girls, and we'll all travel together and see the world."

"That sounds like a very good plan," said Miss Conner.

"Yes," said Alice complacently, "I think so."

Apart from Miss Conner, who was in a special category, Alice's main friend at the school was a girl called Jenny Robertson. Jenny and her family had moved from Scotland a little over a year before and Alice liked the way she talked. Her father was an architect. "My father," Jenny confided in Alice, "is very fashionable at the moment, but he says it may not last."

Jenny Robertson, straw-colored hair, shiny eyes, snub nose, wide mouth, pointed chin, had a wonderful, wonderful laugh which began as a sort of a shout and then trilled and ended in a gurgle. Years and years later, whenever Alice felt depressed, if she thought back on Jenny's laugh and heard it over again in her memory, it never failed to cheer her up.

It was Jenny Robertson who introduced Alice to the sinful delights of talking about sex.

"Have you ever seen a naked boy?" she asked one day. It was early spring and they were outside for art class and were supposed to be drawing a tree.

This caught Alice off guard but she didn't show it. She gave her full attention to the tree for some seconds and then, when a decent interval had been observed, she said, "I've seen statues."

"They always cover the important part up with a leaf."

"That's what Adam and Eve did."

"Have you ever seen the important part without a leaf over it?"

Alice toyed briefly with the idea of saying that she had once come unexpectedly upon a lake where a whole lot of naked boys were bathing but she rejected this notion because of the problem of when? and where? and other awkward questions which would be bound to follow. So she was forced to answer lamely, "No, I haven't."

"I have."

Alice felt that Jenny was being insufferably smug and would have liked to ignore her statement entirely, but her curiosity was greater than her will power. So she said, "Who?"

"My fifteen-year-old brother and a friend of his who was staying with us. They'd come in from running and were undressing in Donald's bedroom and the door was a little bit open and I looked through the crack and saw it as plain as plain can be."

"What was it like?" Alice asked.

"And how are you girls getting on?" demanded Miss Laurence, the Art Mistress. "You haven't made much progress, Jennifer, and Alice, your tree looks like a vertical boa constrictor which has swallowed a number of footballs. I think we'd do better if we didn't sit close enough to talk. You come over here, Jennifer, and draw the tree from a new angle; and remember, the branches get thinner as they go out from the trunk, not thicker like yours."

Alice believed in Fate. Things that were going to happen happened. But they were more likely to happen if one willed them to with all one's heart and soul. Take the case of Mrs. Barnstable, for example.

Mrs. Barnstable was the wife of the Reverend Austin Barnstable, one of New York's most popular preachers. They were a formidable couple but she was the more imposing of the two. She was very tall and immensely fat. Alice had thought to herself that if the Rev. Barnstable ever lost his job or if collections didn't measure up, his wife could always get a job as a fat lady in a traveling circus.

Mrs. Barnstable was a close acquaintance, if not exactly an intimate friend, of Alice's mother. She came often to tea and frequently requested that Alice should be allowed to join the party. This was not, Alice realized, because Mrs. Barnstable was particularly fond of her, but because she was useful as a conversation piece. Dorothy Barnstable held strong views on every conceivable subject but what she referred to as "the decent modesty of the female" was the subject on which she waxed most eloquent. "I do hope," she was fond of saying to Alice's mother, "I do hope, Amy, that little Alice here is being brought up with a strong sense of the decent modesty of the female. It is through this modesty and decency that we ladies set an example for the world."

"I'm sure you're right, Dorothy," Alice's mother would reply. "I think it is wonderful that Alice can be exposed to your influence."

"So do I," Dorothy Barnstable agreed. "Yes, I do think it good for the child. I've been speaking to Austin about African women. I have seen pictures and you know, they walk around with their breasts quite uncovered. What kind of an influence is that on the children? What would happen in New York if you and I walked up and down Fifth Avenue naked to the waist?"

Alice had to bite the inside of her cheek almost hard enough to make it bleed in order to check her laughter.

"I've asked Austin to look into the matter. I thought perhaps the Women's Auxiliaries of St. Aiden's, St. Luke's, and St. Swithins' might all combine to make a number of simple little cotton blouses in assorted sizes which we could send to the missionaries for distribution. For that matter think what an effect these seminaked African women might have on some of our younger male missionaries. They would, I am sure, welcome the blouses with open arms."

"But Eve was naked all over," Alice said suddenly.

Dorothy Barnstable looked at her with scorn—the way, Alice thought later, that Mrs. Grimble looked at a piece of cod which she suspected was slightly "off."

"When I was a little girl," she said, "we were seen but not heard. Besides, there is no documentary proof that Eve

was naked. Austin believes, and I strongly endorse his belief in this, that the language in that part of Genesis is fig-
urative, allegorical, poetic, symbolic, and full of imagery.
Whatever else Eve was she was definitely not *naked*."

The Barnstables had a small place in the country. "It's
nothing much more than a shack—only five rooms," she
told Mrs. Barrington, "but Austin and I do feel the need to
escape from all the fripperies and artificialities of the City
and get close to good old Mother Earth from time to time.
We live much as the early settlers did. We take Lucy with
us to get the meals, wash up, clean our little place, and do
the laundry but otherwise we do everything ourselves and
quite often I go and help Lucy in the kitchen—making a
sauce or something like that. It's great fun. I grow petunias,
lovely petunias. I mean I do it all myself, with Austin's
help. We are great believers in the dignity of manual labor
and getting back to the soil."

Mrs. Barnstable was indeed a believer in dignity of all
sorts and so it was right and just, Alice thought, that when
Fate eventually did catch up with her it was to expose her
in an exceedingly undignified situation.

The Barringtons were giving a late summer garden party
for about fifty people. The huge dahlia bed was at its gorgeous best, all the annuals were in full bloom and the lawn,
dotted with tables and brightly colored garden furniture,
was like green velvet. Alice, Jennifer, and two or three
other girls had been allowed to attend, partly for their dec-
orative value and partly because it was good for them to
learn to be useful passing plates of sandwiches and cups of
tea.

Mrs. Barnstable, a cup of tea in one hand, was just
reaching for a piece of fudge almond cake on a plate Alice
was offering her when it happened. The seat of the cane
chair she was sitting on gave way under her and slowly,
inexorably, her ample bottom sank to the ground while her
pillarlike legs rose higher and higher in the air. "Austin!
Help me!" she cried and everyone turned to look. Her tea-
cup toppled over onto her dress.

So firmly was she wedged in that it took four men to
extricate her. Two held the legs of the chair, one her arms
and another—her husband—grasped her ankles. All four
tugged and jerked until she eventually popped out like a

cork from a bottle. Alice laughed so hard her tummy ached.

It was an example of Fate at its very best, she thought as she went to bed that night.

Chapter 7

So far as Alice knew her parents had never actually been invited to Newport, Rhode Island when it was in its heyday in the early 1890s. They had talked about it a good deal, however, and Alice, as a child of ten or eleven, was quite convinced that the only reason they didn't go was because of their disapproval of what her father referred to as the "animal grossness of the Newport mentality" and what her mother termed "boorish ostentation."

She was proud of her parents for spurning such vulgarity. There were fancy dress balls that cost $200,000; there was a stable where the horses had monogrammed linen sheets to sleep between (before learning of this Alice had always thought that horses slept standing up); there was a children's party at which the young guests, watched by their doting parents and grandparents, chased balloons with hundred-dollar bills in them across the lawn. The Vanderbilt "cottage" cost $2,000,000 to build and another $9,000,000 to furnish which, Mrs. Barrington declared, was "perfectly scandalous." Her daughter nodded her pretty head in complete agreement.

Looking back, Alice had sometimes speculated on whether or not her parents would have managed to stifle their admirable distaste for such affairs if a handsomely engraved invitation to a gathering at one of these robber barons' summer retreats had actually been received. She could never quite decide. She herself would have been delighted to attend the hundred-dollar-balloon party.

She remembered her childhood summers as happy, lazy, sunny times, but their chronology was hazy in her mind. They had gone to Maine for one or two summers and she remembered scrambling about on the rocks and plucking tenacious little snail-like creatures from them. When the tide was out there were pools to explore; once she found a lobster in one and eagerly called her mother, thinking she had discovered a strange new creature of the deep.

They had gone to Saratoga another time and stayed at a fashionable hotel where Alice was bored and suspected her parents were, too. All she remembered were the flamingoes who turned their heads round and round and a fat, freckled boy called "Hicky" she went swimming with and who would crouch down and imitate a frog. Another time they went to Atlantic City where it was very hot. All Alice remembered clearly of that summer was promenading endlessly up and down the Boardwalk in the sun and eating salt water toffee until she felt sick.

One summer, however, they didn't go away at all and Alice recalled her adventures then very clearly indeed.

`She had a friend at that time called Carla Sandhurst who was a radiantly beautiful, dark girl with obvious Spanish blood in her, though her parents had come from England. She had big eyes and very red lips and wore her black hair in pigtails. Her father was a surgeon and her mother, from whom Carla got her looks, was supposed to have been an opera star who gave up her career for marriage to the young London doctor who had saved her from dying of some mysterious disease. Alice couldn't remember the details, if she had ever known them.

At any rate the Barringtons and the Sandhursts were friends and, after some consultation between the mothers, it was agreed that Alice and Carla were now old enough to go and spend afternoons together in Central Park without adult supervision. This decision was announced at tea one day at the Barringtons'.

"You're getting to be big girls now and we have decided to trust you," Mrs. Barrington said. "We know you won't let us down."

Both children indicated by the pained expression on their faces how abhorrent the mere idea of betraying their mothers' trust was to them.

"And no romping around with other children," Mrs. Sandhurst added.

"Of course not," said Carla.

They had agreed in advance that their first expedition would be to Madison Square Garden. They were both very keen to see Diana's toes.

Carla had done the initial research on this one and knew where they had to go to catch the cable-car which would take them there. They had stolen enough money from their mothers' purses to finance the project.

On the Twenty-sixth Street side of the magnificent building the tower rose three hundred and thirty-two feet high, and there on top was the nude statue of Diana with bow and arrow raised. An elevator took them up to the solid part of the tower and from there a winding staircase led up to the toes they had both read about. Now, a little breathless but with eyes shining with pleasure, they were experiencing them for themselves.

"You don't suppose," Carla said suddenly, with a little twinge of apprehension, "that our mothers would go looking for us in the Park?"

"My mother wouldn't anyway."

"How do you know?"

"Because, when she trusts me, she always says, 'Now I won't check up on you, dear, because I know I can trust you.'"

"Well, we'd better be getting back anyway."

"What would your mother do if she did find out?"

"She'd spank me with her slipper and I wouldn't be allowed out alone again for the rest of the summer. What would yours do?"

"She'd say, 'The next time anything like this happens I'm going to spank you.' Then she'd give me a long talking to about how important it is to trust people. Then I'd make tears come to my eyes and she'd say, 'I'm glad to see you're sorry.'"

"It sounds very complicated," Carla said. "I think I'd sooner have a spanking."

They ran a good deal of the way after they got off the car and then, having paused briefly to compose themselves a little, they went in. Their mothers were in the upstairs living room.

"Here you are at last!" Mrs. Barrington said. "We were beginning to be worried. Did you have a lovely time?"

"Yes, thank you," Carla answered coolly. "We walked and we sat under a tree and watched the birds."

"We were wondering if the next time we could take our lunch with us and stay for the day. We'd have a little picnic."

"What do you think?" Mrs. Barrington said, consulting Mrs. Sandhurst.

"I think they've shown us we can trust them. I could have Carla dropped off here at nine thirty or ten."

"We thought Saturday would be a good day," Alice said.

"Very well then," said Mrs. Barrington, "we'll say Saturday. Now you children may go down to the kitchen and ask Mrs. Grimble to give you a glass of lemonade and then look at the *London Illustrated News* in the sun-room until it's time for Carla to go home."

On their way downstairs Carla asked, "What is this thing about Saturday? You never said anything to me."

"I only suddenly thought of it," Alice said. "On Saturday we'll go to Coney Island!"

"But it's . . . it's a place where all sorts of people go, like ditch diggers and people like that. My father says it's very vulgar."

"I know," Alice said.

The two girls stopped, looked each other in the eye, grinned widely and shook hands. Then they clattered down to get their lemonade.

Luna Park, Coney Island!

It was sheer enchantment—the crowds, the smells, the noise, the gaiety, the sun, the dust, the frankfurters (which neither of them had ever tasted before), and above all, the exhilaration of being on their own, free and independent from fussy parents and tiresome restrictions. They had each managed to steal three dollars, which they realized must be a once-in-a-lifetime crime; repeated thefts of this magnitude were bound to be discovered.

They had some difficulty in justifying their criminal activities morally but Alice eventually worked out a two-pronged formula which more or less satisfied their consciences. "If our mothers don't notice it's gone it proves they didn't need it and every cent we spend helps a poor person feed his family. Besides, if God didn't want it to happen, He wouldn't let it happen." The more they thought about it, the more convinced they became that they were benefiting society by their thefts.

Early in the afternoon they found themselves standing in front of a show which called itself "Congress of the World's Greatest Living Curiosities" and starred Jolly Trixy, who weighed six hundred and eighty-five pounds. They read the words painted on the front above the illustration of Trixy and her friends. "Holy Smoke, She's Fat! She's Awful Fat! She's So Fat That It Takes Seven Men To Hug Her!"

"Should we?" Alice asked. "We could look at Trixy and then go home."

"I think maybe we should go home now," Carla answered doubtfully. "We're already late."

Then a man's voice behind them asked, "How would you girls like an ice cream?"

They turned. He was a tall, nice looking man about the age of their fathers. But, nice looking or not, it had been firmly impressed on both Alice and Carla that they were never on any account to talk to strange men, so Alice answered promptly and primly, "No, thank you. We are just about to go home."

The man laughed. "You've been told not to talk to strange men," he said.

The girls answered "Yes" in unison.

"Where are your parents?"

"Our parents aren't here," Carla said. "That's why we have to go home right away."

"Perhaps I can take you home. I've got my carriage here. Where do you live?"

"I live on Fifty-second Street not far from Fifth Avenue," Alice said.

"And I live on Fifty-seventh," said Carla.

"And I live on Fifty-ninth so it would be quite convenient. I probably know your parents so I'm not really a strange man. What's your name?" he said, looking at Carla.

"Carla Sandhurst. I'm the daughter of Dr. and Mrs. Sandhurst."

"Of course, of course. Your father was speaking of you to me just the other day. I almost feel I know you, Carla. I'm Mr. Carberry." He extended his hand and Carla took it shyly. Then he turned to Alice. "And you?" he asked gently.

"I'm Alice Barrington."

"Of Barrington's Clothes?"

"Yes."

"Isn't that nice. I know your father, too. Do your parents know you are here on your own?"

The two girls looked at each other and Carla indicated by a slight raising of her eyebrows that Alice could answer that question.

"I'm not sure whether they do or not," Alice replied

calmly. "They trust us but I think it would be better if you didn't mention it to them."

"Not a word," said Mr. Carberry. His hair was gray around the edges, his eyes were smoky blue, his face was tanned, and he had a nice smile and shiny white teeth. "Well, young ladies, if you are ready to depart, my carriage awaits."

He led the way and they followed, though it didn't seem to Alice they were going the right way. The gaiety of the show ground faded in the distance and presently they approached a scruffy clump of trees and bushes. "This isn't the way out," Alice said in a high voice.

"I want to show you something," said Mr. Carberry. "Take my hands."

The little girls, suddenly fearful, stopped and held their arms rigidly at their sides like soldiers. They were about to turn and run when Mr. Carberry pounced and, grabbing them by the hair, dragged them in behind the bushes. They both screamed.

"Now," he commanded, "take off your clothes and keep your mouths shut or I'll kill you." He let Carla's braids go and relinquished his grasp on Alice's fair hair. "I mean it," he said, and he no longer sounded like a benevolent uncle.

"No!" exclaimed Alice decisively. "I don't even let my own father see me naked anymore. My mother says it isn't nice."

"Isn't nice?" Mr. Carberry looked at them both. "Isn't nice? I think it's nice. If you girls aren't out of your dresses before I count ten I'm going to strangle you both and then your parents will never see you again, naked or dressed. If you behave yourselves and don't make a fuss I'll buy you each an ice cream when we're finished."

Carla began to cry, silently. The tears oozed from her large, dark eyes and trickled slowly down her cheeks. Alice, her heart beating like a trip hammer, was made of sterner stuff. "I like your ring," she said. "Show me your ring and then we'll undress."

He extended his large, fleshy hand to her and allowed her to lift it to her lips. Then, like a tiger she took it into her mouth and bit down as hard as she could. At the same time she kicked him in the crotch with all the force of her strong right leg. She didn't know much about male anatomy, but enough to know that that was a vulnerable spot.

"Come on!" she shouted at Carla. "Run!"

They ran.

They were, of course, much too late in arriving home. They knew they would be and had their story ready. Alice was, as usual, the spokesman. The Sandhursts had been invited for a sort of family dinner that night and the parents were having predinner sherry when the girls arrived back.

"We fell asleep under a tree," Alice said, "and then I must admit, we did leave the Park and went for a long, long walk up Fifth Avenue and then we suddenly realized how late it was and we hurried home."

"But you promised you wouldn't leave the Park," Mrs. Sandhurst said.

"We won't do so again," Carla answered contritely.

"Let's forgive them this time," Dr. Sandhurst said. "I'm sure they've learned their lesson."

Glancing at her mother, Alice realized that she didn't believe the story.

The Sandhursts left early and, when Alice was in bed, her mother came in and sat down beside her. "What were the two of you up to today?"

Alice had toyed with various alternate versions—a blind man they had escorted home, a crippled child, an elderly lady whose companion had deserted her. In the end she decided to stay with the agreed version.

"We weren't up to anything. Don't you trust us? Don't you believe us? We walked along Fifth Avenue."

"If you say so, dear, I must believe you. That is the meaning of trust."

"Do you know a man called Mr. Carberry?"

"No, I don't think so. Why?"

"We stopped him to ask what time it was. He seemed very nice."

"There are all sorts of nice people in New York, but you must not talk to strange men. I've told you that."

"We just asked the time."

"Good night, dear," said Mrs. Barrington, and she switched off the light.

Alice lay awake for a time, wide-eyed in the dark. She wondered whether or not to get up and have a look at the Boy Prince of Rajasthan. She wondered what would have happened if she and Carla had in fact taken off their dresses and stood naked before Mr. Carberry. It had been a momentous day.

Would Carla crack under pressure? She doubted it.

Then she fell asleep.

Chapter 8

The school included ballroom dancing as part of its regular curriculum, and it was said of Ashcroft girls—at least by their parents and the staff of the school—that the waltz and the minuet achieved a new grace and beauty when danced by them. Fortunately for both schools Ashcroft was able to work out an arrangement with Westside Academy, a nearby boys' school of comparable gentility, to share the weekly lessons and, towards the end of May, the two schools combined forces to put on the annual Tulip Dance. However, it was really Ashcroft's dance, held at Ashcroft and paid for by Ashcroft; all Westside did was provide a sufficient number of boys to match the number of girls. It was at this affair that Alice met Randolph Maybank and almost immediately concluded that life would never be the same again.

She was fifteen and Randy was nearly sixteen—almost a man. He was strong, dark-skinned, exceedingly handsome, and treated her with exactly the right blend of gallantry and contempt. He paid her what she regarded as the ultimate compliment of her life when, near the end of the evening and after three dances together and a long talk during supper, he said, "You're not bad for a girl."

"Why did we never meet at the dancing lessons?" Alice asked.

"I never took them. I learned at home. If you already know all about dancing you don't have to come and you can play football instead. That's what I do."

"I'd like to come and watch you play."

"It's pretty rough."

"Do many boys get hurt playing it?"

"Some do. But if you are in top physical condition and are never afraid, then you don't get hurt too often. Even when you are hurt the thing is not to show it. That way your opponents get discouraged."

"Are you a very rough player?"

"I give as good as I take. I play fair but I play very hard. When I tackle someone he stays tackled."

Alice gave a little pretended shudder and said, "You're very strong, aren't you?"

"I'm quite strong, I suppose. I don't go around talking about it."

"And brave."

"Football isn't for cowards."

The Maybanks had a tennis court and, during that long, lovely summer of 1897, the Maybanks' tennis court became a favorite gathering place for the Ashcroft-Westside crowd. A maid would bring out large jugs of lemonade and they would sit, the boys in their crisp white ducks and the girls in their pretty pastel dresses of green and yellow and pink, watching whoever was on the court at the time, sipping lemonade, waiting their turn, laughing, chattering.

As the summer meandered along in this inconsequential way, it became increasingly obvious to Alice that Randy Maybank preferred her to the other girls and that this was a very satisfactory arrangement, because she preferred him to the other boys. She had always been tall for her age and, now that her young body was rounding out so very satisfactorily, she realized that she and Randy, side by side, made a very handsome sight.

Sometimes they wandered a little way away from the others and sat on the lawn under a tree and talked. They talked about what they wanted to do when they left school. Alice told him about *The Boy Prince of Rajasthan* and he didn't laugh.

"How do you know I'm not the one?" he asked her.

And Alice smiled because life was so perfect and said, "I'm not old enough to be married yet, but I don't think it's an accident we met and maybe you *are* him. You're just as handsome." Then she looked into his eyes and asked, "You don't think I'm being silly and childish, Randy?"

"A little bit," he answered. "But I like it."

Alice's mother was delighted with the tennis gatherings in general and with her daughter's growing friendship with young Randolph Maybank in particular. Alice was associating with all the right people.

"Of course I know the Maybanks," she said when Alice had duly reported her first encounter with Randy at the dance. "Your father can tell you more about Mr. Maybank. For many years he was an associate of Mr. Andrew Carnegie and now I think he just sits and looks at paintings. Your friend Randolph must be a son of their old age. Mrs. Maybank was a Mowat. There was some vague connection with the Astors. She wildly exaggerated it, I think. At any rate she has no real business having a child the age of your friend, but I'm pleased she has."

"So am I. I've never met her but Randy always speaks so nicely of his mother."

"Of course. But Alice, I do wish you would stop using that dreadful contraction. The young man's name is Randolph."

"But everyone calls him Randy."

"His parents as well?"

"I—I don't know. I've never met either of them."

"Then please don't make sweeping statements about 'everyone' when all you really mean is other children your age."

Then one day, towards the end of August, Alice was invited to a family dinner at the Maybanks'. "It will be awful," Randy warned her. "All my aunts and uncles will be there and afterwards we'll dance. My mother said I ought to invite a partner my own age. If you agree she'll write your mother a letter to make it . . . you know, to make it sort of legal. Would you like to come? You'll hate it, but it will make it much better for me."

"I'd love to come," Alice assured him.

Alice's mother was very pleased to get the note from Mrs. Maybank and replied immediately that her daughter would be delighted to attend the party and would also, as Mrs. Maybank had so kindly suggested, be pleased to spend the night as the Maybanks' guest, because it would be late for a girl her age to be out without a chaperone.

Alice looked forward to the day immensely.

She was late in arriving because her mother, who normally insisted on punctuality, spent so long over the dress she would wear for the party and also over the dress she would wear for breakfast the following morning. Then, of course, she had to listen, as she always did before she went anywhere, to her mother's lecture on manners, becoming modesty, and ladylike behavior in general. As a result, by the time the gloomy Roger deposited her at the front door of the Maybank mansion all the other guests had already assembled. This, plus the fact that they of course all knew each other and she knew only Randy, got the evening off to a bad start as far as she was concerned. It was to get worse as it progressed.

A maid answered the door and took her at once to her bedroom, which was considerably larger and a great deal more opulent than her own at home.

"Mrs. Maybank said I was to tell you when you arrived that the other guests have been here for some time, and would you please be as quick as you can." She spoke in a tone Alice instantly recognized as one of hauteur. It was a tone which she had read about in books and one she had heard her mother use to a servant she was displeased with. Alice didn't think a maid had any right to use it.

"I shall explain my delay to Mrs. Maybank," she said with what she hoped was a more impressive hauteur than the maid's. "You may show me down now." She tossed her head. She knew she did that well because she practiced it in front of the mirror. She liked the way it made her long, fair hair swirl about her face. Normally she smiled when she did it but not this time. This time she tried to look haughty.

Alice was met by Randy at the entrance to the blue and gold drawing room where everyone had assembled for sherry. He had obviously been on the lookout for her. Alice thought he looked even more handsome than usual in his dark suit, and he said to her, "You look beautiful."

"I'm sorry I'm late."

"You aren't really. It doesn't matter anyway. Come and meet my mother and father and then you have to make the rounds of everyone, I'm afraid. Mother said so. I warned you you'd hate it."

"I'm going to love it," Alice said with somewhat diminished conviction.

Mr. and Mrs. Maybank stood at the far end of the large room in front of the gothic windows with leaded panes which looked out on the garden. They stood, sherry glasses in hand, as if, Alice thought during the approach, they were posing for a formal portrait and had been doing so for a very considerable time. Their faces were completely devoid of any real or meaningful expression, though each wore a smile. They were both a good deal older than even her mother's reference to their ages had led her to expect, and they looked very regal. Alice felt she should drop a

low curtsy before them, but she wasn't very good at low
curtsies and so she just did a sort of bob and took the extended hands in turn.

"So very nice to meet you," Mrs. Maybank said. "We've
heard about you. You're Amy Barrington's child?"

"Yes," said Alice rather breathlessly.

"How is your dear mother? Lovely person. Haven't seen
her in years."

"She's very well, thank you, and she sent her regards."

"Did she? How sweet. Take mine back to her."

"And mine to your father," Mr. Maybank said.

The preliminary audience was over, but there were still
the relatives.

Glancing quickly, and furtively, around the room, Alice
realized in an almost panic-stricken way that all the old-
sters were watching them while pretending to carry on their
own conversations. She and Randy were thirty, forty, fifty
years younger than anyone else there, and they were being
watched and judged against the memories each of the
watchers had of his or her youth. She was used to this in a
small way because her mother and father were both fond of
sentences which began "When I was your age . . ." but
she had never faced up to a jury as large as this before nor,
she felt, as critical.

"Aunt Elsie, I'd like to introduce a friend of mine, Miss
Alice Barrington. Aunt Elsie is my mother's sister, Miss
Mowat."

"How do you do, Miss Mowat."

"How do you do, Alice. I'm delighted to make your acquaintance. I like young people—on the whole—and I'm
glad that Randolph is old enough to have a female companion."

In her dark green dress with her short legs, short arms,
short neck, Alice thought Aunt Elsie looked rather like a
mobile cucumber but, trying to look "becomingly modest,"
she said, "It's so kind of Mrs. Maybank to invite me to
meet Randolph's relatives."

"Yes," Aunt Elsie agreed, "I think it is."

Then there was Aunt "Iffy"—Alice never did discover
what "Iffy" was short or long for—and her husband, Uncle
Carlyle. Aunt "Iffy" was another of Mrs. Maybank's sisters,
but whether younger or older Alice couldn't guess. Her
name was Mrs. Swain-Smith.

She was more animated than Mrs. Maybank and more frightening. A large, florid woman with blue hair, immense earrings, a big nose and a large voice, she said, "So *this* is the little girl! Tell me, my dear, when you and my nephew Randolph are alone together, is he as much the perfect little gentleman as he is when in the company of his elderly relatives? Is he? Does he ever make naughty suggestions or do you just talk about the weather? You and I must get together after dinner. Shall we? Ah, she's blushing. There's more here than meets the eyes, even old and experienced eyes like mine." She laughed.

Alice shook hands with Mr. Swain-Smith, a weedy little man who would certainly be no match for his awesome wife. Alice hated her instantly and wondered what strange arrangement of mysterious circumstances could conceivably have made them man and wife.

Everyone had been looking covertly at them before, but Aunt "Iffy" had changed all that. Now the assemblage had fallen silent and everyone was openly watching their progress around the room.

There was Uncle Paul, a brother of Mr. Maybank and his wife, Aunt Olive; there was Uncle Timothy, another brother, and his wife, Aunt Margaret; there were two much older brothers of Randy's and their wives and an older sister, called Charlotte, and her husband. Finally there was Great Aunt Katie, who lived with the Maybanks, an aunt of Mrs. Maybank, seated in the corner. Of all the people she had been introduced to in that dreadful ordeal only Great Aunt Katie appealed to Alice, and she did so strongly and immediately.

She was a short, stout woman with dark, wrinkled skin and snowy white hair pulled tightly over her head and tied up in a bun behind. She wore a net over it. Her face, which was small anyway, was made smaller still by age so that in a sense it had regained, almost ninety years later, some of the characteristics it had possessed when Katie was a small girl. There was in it a curious blend of wisdom and innocence.

"I'm so glad you came," she said to Alice. "You look delightful. Stand back a little so I can see." Alice did so, and the old lady smiled with quite genuine pleasure and then motioned Alice forward again. "Randolph has cousins or second cousins or tenth cousins twice removed and that sort of nonsense but they're afraid to show up. Randolph's mother makes him come and I think it very brave of you to keep him company."

Alice laughed. Then she said, "So do I." Then all three laughed.

It was a dreadful evening—every bit as bad and, in fact, worse than Randy had forecast. At dinner she was seated next to Mr. Swain-Smith, Aunt "Iffy's" weedy little husband. He looked so miserable, and as if he felt even more out of place than she did, that she decided to try to cheer him up. It was a bad decision.

"Do you think Mr. McKinley is doing a good job as President?" she asked brightly.

All men, she thought, were interested in politics, and her father, who thought all parties other than the Republican to be subversive and their leaders complete charlatans, believed that William McKinley was "the right man at the right time."

Mr. Swain-Smith pondered the question for some time, his slightly protruding front teeth seeming to bare themselves even more fully as he thought. He even stopped chewing, apparently because it was better to concentrate on one thing at a time. Then, just as Alice was about to say, "Please don't let it spoil your dinner. I was only making conversation," he said, "I was a Bryan man myself," and looked so sad that Alice wondered if he had ever been on the winning side in anything or if he always picked a loser.

After that she devoted most of her attention to the food except for replying to very occasion bland questions from James Maybank, one of Randy's older brothers, second on her right, such as, "I hope we have a nice, long, warm autumn" to which it fleetingly occurred to her to answer, "I was hoping for a nasty, short, cold one."

Toward the end of the seemingly interminable meal, when a horrid looking pink parfait had just been placed in front of them, Mr. Swain-Smith, apparently feeling that he had failed again—this time as a dinner companion—suddenly asked, "Have you ever ridden an ostrich?"

It seemed such an incredibly unlikely question that Alice couldn't really believe she had heard correctly. "I'm sorry," she said, "I don't think I quite . . ."

She took a small spoonful of her parfait and found it tasted inexplicably of pineapple, which she loathed. He repeated the question and it *was* what she thought it had been.

"No," she said, "have you?"

"When I was three my parents took me on a visit to an ostrich farm and they told me I rode on one. They're both dead now and I don't remember."

Alice didn't know what to say, so she said nothing, and presently Mrs. Maybank announced that the ladies would now retire to the drawing room; the gentlemen must join them there in not more than twenty minutes, because the pianist and fiddler had arrived and dancing could commence any time.

On the way out of the dining room Alice found herself next to Aunt "Iffy," who said to her, "I watched you flirting with my husband during dinner, you shameless thing!"

Alice felt the blood hot in her cheeks and was quite sure she looked as though she had been detected in a sordid attempt to lure Mr. Swain-Smith into her clutches. Aunt "Iffy," seeing the dismay on the young face, laughed in her vulgar way.

Alice *hated* Aunt "Iffy."

Chapter 9

Wednesday. She appreciated Patricia's visits, and felt guilty at her sense of relief when the time came for Patricia to look at her watch and say, "My goodness! I hadn't realized how late it was. I must fly."

She *did* appreciate the visits but she couldn't help wishing that Patricia wasn't quite such a bore. It was common enough, she knew, for children to find their parents' addiction to the mores of the past somewhat tedious, but surely it wasn't natural for a mother to find her daughter overly staid and old-fashioned. Of course Patricia had always been like that—even as quite a young girl. Alice had never had any qualms about Patricia behaving in a wild, irresponsible way and tarnishing the family reputation but Patricia, she well knew, did not have the same confidence in her.

Though Alice thought frequently and with affection of the past, she knew perfectly well that she was living in the present and she didn't fight against it. Patricia behaved as if nothing had changed or ever would. There was a serenity about her but, unfortunately, there was also a dullness.

How different, Alice reflected, her relationship with her own mother had been. Patricia had departed and she sat with her gin and tonic looking out the window. It was her special time of day. Her mind went back again to the family party at the Maybanks'.

It wasn't dancing at all as Alice understood the term. The piano made sounds and so did the violin—though Alice was never sure that they were even attempted to play the same tune at the same time—and people wandered about with their arms vaguely intertwined and sad expressions on their faces. All the men had to dance with all the ladies before the dancing part of the evening could be declared over so Alice had only one dance with Randy, during which he said, "When this is over we'll go and sit in the library. They'll play whist. I warned you. It's awful, isn't it?"

The violinist would announce the nature of the dance

but it didn't matter whether he said minuet, waltz, polka, or whatever; there was no discernible difference in the music or in the solemn shuffling movement of the dance.

When it came Alice's turn to dance with Randy's father he approached like a portly and solemn police constable about to make an arrest and to Alice's confusion said, "May I ask you to trip the light fantastic with me?" Alice decided later it was his little joke for the evening. He had probably made it up in his bath.

Old Great Aunt Katie went to bed early but she insisted, before she was taken up by her maid, that Alice come to say good night. Alice was pleased to do so, particularly as it meant she could miss the rest of her dance with Uncle Paul, who seemed to have been drinking more than was good for him and had said, "I'm not as old as you think I am" as he squeezed her to him.

"You don't know how old I think you are," Alice had replied, disengaging herself.

"I hoped, my dear," Aunt Katie said, "that we would have a chance for a little talk, but we can't do that tonight. Promise me you'll come again when all this . . . this nonsense is just a bad memory. You and Randolph and I could have a nice talk." She blinked her eyes. "I so seldom have a chance to talk to the young these days and I feel I have so much more in common with them than I do with their mothers and fathers and uncles and aunts."

"I'll come," Alice promised. "I'd like to."

The old lady smiled with unmistakable delight and said, "Bless you." Then she allowed herself to be helped into her wheelchair and was wheeled away.

They sat alone together at last in the dimly lighted library.

"I'm sorry," Randy said. "I should never have asked you to come. I never realized how really bad it was until I sort of saw it all through your eyes tonight."

"I didn't mind. You said you would tell me about some of your camping trips. I've never been camping."

"I hope one day we might . . ."

"So do I," she said.

Alice knew perfectly well, in her mind if not her heart, that *The Boy Prince of Rajasthan* was nothing more than a romantic legend of childhood. It remained on the bookshelf in her bedroom, however, and she would no more have thought of throwing it out because she never read it anymore than of cutting off her long glossy hair because it was of no practical use. She believed in the *idea* of "The Boy Prince." He was brave and handsome and led a life of adventure (always with honor) and grew up and, in the end, met the Princess of his dreams who turned out to be a girl he had played with when he was ten, before his father's death made him the Prince.

And that was the idea which Alice cherished, and Randy hadn't laughed at it. He hadn't disagreed with the notion that there was a destiny, a Fate, a whatever you wanted to call it, which perhaps didn't exactly control our lives but could make or break them just the same. When the "right moment" came you had to recognize it as the "right moment." Alice studied *Julius Caesar* and fell so in love with the "There is a tide in the affairs of men" speech that she seemed to almost absorb it into herself as she read.

She and Randy had their talk with old Aunt Katie and it was, as Alice told her mother later, "absolutely perfect."

"What did you talk about?" her mother asked.

"The Irish famine of 1846."

"How extraordinary!" said Mrs. Barrington.

Old Aunt Katie had been known as Aunt Katie for so many years now, even by those who could claim not even a trace of kinship, that few realized she still thought of herself as Mrs. Donald O'Brien, wife of the late Dr. Donald O'Brien who had come to New York in the emigrant vessel, *India*, Liverpool to Staten Island. Aunt Katie's mother, who had been a Harrison of Dublin, had been to school with Donald O'Brien's mother and they had kept in touch ever since. "That's interesting, isn't it?" she said and she was smiling with her old-young eyes, looking backward and forward at the same time.

She told them about her first meeting with Donald O'Brien. "My mother had heard he was coming, of course, and somehow knew when he had arrived, so she sent him a letter inviting him to come and take tea with us. They'd almost given up hope of getting me married off but I expect they thought they'd have one last try. Donald wasn't that young either, come to that. My father, who had some Irish blood in him himself, said that tea was an insult and went out and bought a big bottle of Irish whiskey 'so the poor

man can at least go away with a decent taste in his mouth.'
Dear old father. He liked that 'decent taste' so much that in
the end it killed him. But he went to heaven, I'm sure of
that. He always insisted on the best accommodations.

"So Donald came to have tea and somehow he managed
to spill a full cup of it on our British India rug. He was like
you, Randolph, with his black hair and laughing eyes. I got
to know him a little and he told me about Staten Island
and the terrible condition of the fevered emigrants. He
wanted me to help raise money for clothing and things and
I said I would if he would take me with him to the Island
to see the conditions for myself. We had to plan it secretly,
of course, because my parents would never have agreed.
Even though I was over thirty they still thought of me as a
girl. Nor would the authorities, if it had been 'official,'
though many New Yorkers were visiting relatives. It was
terrible. I'd been very protected of course. I'd never been
allowed to see people who were within an inch of starving
to death, though there were lots of very poor people in
New York. Of course there still are. The smell . . . I can
almost *feel* it now. A lot of them had almost no clothes on.
That was the first place I ever saw a man naked.

"I helped raise a bit of money around and about. And I
went back again with Donald several times. Terrible it was!
But do you know what I thought?" She looked from one to
the other. Randy and Alice shook their heads.

She smiled again—sadness and humor mixed. "I thought
how noble I was."

"But you did marry Dr. O'Brien?" Alice asked.

"Of course I did and a fine wedding it was, I can tell
you." Her eyes fairly sparkled. "We never had any children
because . . . oh, I don't know . . . we thought we had
lots of time. And then of course it was suddenly too late to
think of such things. It was only just over two years after
our marriage that Donald got typhus himself. We had two
years though—two magic years." She didn't cry. No one
had ever seen Aunt Katie cry, but her eyes shone brighter
than usual.

"So plan for happiness, children. Whatever else you plan
for, be sure to plan for happiness."

Although Alice was a year younger than Randy, the fall of
1897 was to start the final year of schooling for both. Al-

ice's parents were not in fact at all sure that perhaps she wasn't getting too much education, but she pleaded with them to allow her one more year and, thanks in part to Miss Conner's support, she won her point. Though Alice had long ago 'outgrown' Miss Conner, they remained friends. "But," said Mrs. Barrington firmly, "if we let you have another year at Ashcroft you're going to have to work all the harder next year at your music, painting, and needlework. You're going to have to put first things first and forget about English and History and Mathematics and so on. As you know, I am all for Ashcroft's policy of treating girls as if they had minds but I think your mind has been quiet sufficiently developed and now we must work on your talents, both social and artistic. No self-respecting man ever married a girl because he admired her *mind*."

She saw Randy at two or three Saturday tea dances for young people that autumn and early winter but, apart from these occasions, neither made any effort to get together. When Alice thought about that fact, as she did occasionally, she concluded that they were both being very sensible and getting on with their main responsibilities. But Alice hated talk about being "sensible." As long as she could remember, whenever she had proposed a scheme which had no "educational" value nor any "edifying" potential but which she thought would be great fun—like getting up a kite-flying party in Central Park or chartering a paddle-wheeler for a trip around Manhattan Island, inviting as many as possible, playing games on deck and having ice cream—her mother would say, "Oh Alice, for heaven's sake be sensible. You have quite enough entertainment as it is. You don't want to dull your appetite for worthwhile things by too much frivolity." Even at the Chicago World's Fair her mother kept saying, "It's the architecture and the paintings I want you to retain in your memory, dear."

So, Alice told herself without conviction, she and Randy were just being sensible by not seeing too much of each other. They were being sensible and, of course, they were both now living under a winter discipline which restricted life much more than a summer one. When they did meet at the tea dances things were as they had always been.

"It's wonderful to see you," Randy would say. "I wish we could see more of each other. Of course I'm studying pretty hard and, when I'm not studying, I'm training or playing badminton. The time certainly gets filled up."

"It certainly does," Alice agreed. "I'm so busy myself."

The big annual dance at Westside was the Snow Ball, which was held just before the Christmas holidays, and Alice was looking forward to it immensely. Those of her friends or acquaintances who had attended it said it made the Ashcroft Tulip Dance seem like a children's party by comparison. One big difference was that instead of inviting guests of the opposite sex en masse, individual boys asked individual girls, and whereas at the Tulip Dance all the girls came from Ashcroft, for the Snow Ball the boys were not obliged to confine themselves to Ashcroft girls. However, because of the close relationship between the schools, many Ashcroft girls were invited and as the date of the dance approached there was a good deal of nervous tension.

Alice was invited early on by a boy called James McGrath, one of the tennis players of the previous summer. She was flattered, of course, but not unhappy to be able to tell him she was going with someone else. It was strange, she thought, for James McGrath to ask her. Surely he would know she was going with Randy. In a way, she thought to herself, it would have served Randy right if she had accepted James McGrath's invitation. He obviously took her so much for granted that he didn't feel obliged to ask her until the last moment.

Then one morning a girl called Joanne Dowler, another of the summer tennis crowd, and, Alice had thought until then, a nice girl, asked her, "Who are you going to the Snow Ball with, Alice?"

Alice saw the jaws of the trap just in time and answered in what she hoped was a calm and slightly disdainful tone, "I told Randy I decided not to go and suggested he ask you because I knew no one else had. I hope he did?"

"Yes," Joanne answered in a slightly strangulated voice, "he did."

Alice was inwardly shocked at Randy's faithlessness, but that did not detract from her pleasure at seeing Joanne's hoped for triumph turned to dust and ashes. Now, even if Joanne asked Randy if he had invited her first, she wouldn't believe his answer. Serve her right!

Alice was nonetheless somewhat out of sorts on the Friday evening in mid-December when the Snow Ball was finally held, without her in attendance. What, for instance, would James McGrath think of her when he saw that she wasn't there after all? She really *should* have accepted his invitation. These and other similarly morbid thoughts filled her mind as the melancholy Roger drove her back through the rain and sleet of a dirty New York winter afternoon.

But as she let herself in the front door all thoughts of Randy Maybank, James McGrath, Joanne Dowler, and the Snow Ball vanished. Her older sister, Prudence, was standing in the hall, her face streaked with tears. "Thank goodness you're home," she said. "I've been standing here waiting for you. The most terrible thing has happened."

Alice's two older sisters, both living in New York, so seldom appeared that, when they did, it signified an event of some considerable importance. Once Dorothea, the one married to the architect, had dropped in casually for tea one afternoon. When her arrival was announced Mrs. Barrington had gone out into the hall to greet her daughter and asked, "Who's dead, or did you come to tell me of your divorce?"

Prudence, the banker's wife, had no sooner finished her tearful greeting of Alice than she was joined by Dorothea, looking wan but determinedly brave. Something must *really* be wrong if both sisters were here.

Alice didn't know her sisters at all well and didn't much care for the little she did know of them so, in the face of this emotionalism, she decided to remain cool and detached.

Dorothea kissed her and said, "You poor dear. Take off your coat and come into the living room. Prepare yourself to be brave."

Alice disliked intensely being kissed by Dorothea, and to be told to be brave, as if she were a little girl about to have iodine applied to a scratch, was the final insult. She said nothing until they were seated in a corner of the living room and then she asked, "Well, what dreadful thing has happened?"

"It's Mother," Dorothea answered in a tone of voice which made Alice think to herself how proud Dorothea was of her ability to control her emotions.

"What's wrong with her?" Alice asked the question in

what she hoped was a casual manner, but her heart was thumping.

"Cancer," Prudence blurted out. Prudence felt Dorothea had been upstaging her. She thought the mention of that dreadful word, which was almost never spoken aloud, would shock Alice into a proper state of mind.

"But . . . but there was no sign. I mean I never thought . . ." She recovered herself. "When did all this happen?"

"It happened this afternoon," Dorothea answered quickly, determined to recapture the initiative from Prudence. "Mother called us on the telephone. Well, as soon as I heard her I knew something terrible had happened. I knew by her voice. It was so strained and unnatural. She said she wanted to see us."

"She was already in bed. It had been a shock for her," Prudence said. "She told us she hadn't been feeling well the last few weeks and she'd been to Dr. Winston and he had called in others and then this morning he came to tell her she had cancer of . . . cancer of something inside her and she couldn't expect to live for more than another two years at the most."

Dorothea's eyes suddenly overflowed with tears. She stood up and embraced Alice again, saying, "Be brave, my dear. You can always lean on me."

"At the moment," said Alice, who had remained seated, "you are leaning on me and you're hurting my neck."

Whenever Alice heard a lady described as "striking," she immediately thought of her older sisters. Prudence and Dorothea were the most "striking" women she could possibly imagine. If they had lived in ancient Greece, she always thought, their memory would have been preserved as great tragic heroines, like Jocasta, the mother of Oedipus. (When she told her mother they were studying a translation of the play at school, Mrs. Barrington had said, "A strange choice, it seems to me, for impressionable young girls.")

The thing that annoyed Prudence and Dorothea most about their younger sister Alice was that she was unimpressed by them. In this case, even their tears had no visible effect on her. As they left the house Dorothea said to Prudence, "I'm afraid Alice is an insensitive child."

"Yes," Prudence agreed, "very insensitive."

Alice was frightened.

She had always thought of her mother as indestructible, and now she would be gone within two years at the most. Alice had heard of and read about mothers and daughters who were described as being "very close." She wasn't sure that she fully understood what was involved in being "very close" and she was not sure she wanted to. She had always respected her mother and, more than that, admired her. She had recognized her authority and had, on the whole, shown herself an obedient daughter. She thought her mother unduly strict and terribly old-fashioned but she was perceptive enough to realize that *her* daughters would almost certainly think the same of her. That was what mothers should be.

She had been determined not to display her feelings before Prudence and Dorothea, but now that she was alone she was hard put to force the tears back. She remembered the early walks in Central Park and, although she would have liked to have been allowed to play with the other children, she had taken a certain pride in striding along the path with her mother, aloof and unapproachable, parasol or umbrella in hand when indicated, head up, the object of all eyes. She wasn't as sure now as she had been then that she and her mother were better than other people, but she still remembered with pleasure the warm feeling such a conviction had once given her.

What would her father do? He had always pretended to be the head of the household, and Amy, his wife, had let him huff and puff and growl his way around the place. She even at times pretended to consult him about something or other.

A week or so ago at dinner her mother had said, "Ward, I need your advice."

"Of course, my dear, what is it?"

"The evergreen shrubs along the driveway. I'm sure you'll agree they're a perfect disgrace. They're all tattered and torn and brown. I think they must be dying of some dreadful blight. I'm ashamed of them. Should I, do you think, ask Mr. Ambrose, of that excellent Gardens Incorporated firm we dealt with before, to come up with a new plan for the front of the house, replacing shrubs where necessary and perhaps enlarging the front border? Do you think that's a good idea?"

Her father had gone on eating for a time in silence. He

was pretending, Alice well knew, to be considering the proposition. Then, at length, he said, "I was going to suggest it myself. It is high time we did something about the front of the place. It's a perfect disgrace."

Alice had been vaguely amused and perhaps a little annoyed by that conversation a week ago. Now it seemed sad. What indeed would her father do all by himself when her mother died? Recently she had wondered on occasion how he could have been so successful in business and the unworthy suspicion had crossed her mind that Mr. Crombie, the partner, was more important than her father ever admitted.

What would he do? Even had she thought she might be able to take her mother's place, Alice had no intention of trying to do so. She wanted to leave home as soon as she could after she finished school. There was a great big world out there waiting to be explored, and she wanted to explore it.

It was with a mixture of feelings more complicated and conflicting than she herself cared even to try to comprehend that she eventually made her way upstairs to talk to her parents. As she took the carpeted stairs one at a time she thought fleetingly to herself that Joanne Dowler would be beginning to get ready to go to the Snow Ball with Randy. She smiled at the thought.

Chapter 10

It was still raining. It had been raining steadily for two days.

Alice sipped her morning coffee and looked at the spattered window. In a little while she could have the prelunch glass of sherry she allowed herself and watch the Americans and Russians meet in outer space. Surely no one had lived through so much as the few surviving members of her generation—the first motorcars, the first airplanes, the first telephones, radio, wars in Europe and in Asia with millions of people killed after which old friends became enemies and old enemies friends and the ones who had won discovered that they'd really lost. And now there was television and men on the moon and frozen food and topless waitresses and strikes and violence, hideous crimes and . . . so much, much more that she didn't understand and didn't really want to understand.

She had lived too long. She knew that. No one had any business living as long as she had. She didn't particularly want to die but she wasn't afraid of death and, in a way, when it did come as it must do soon, it would be a relief. It would, she hoped, be like going to bed after a long, tiring day.

It was strange, now that she was so much older than her parents had been when they died, that she still missed them.

The doctors had underestimated Mrs. Barrington's defiance. She would allow Death to take her when she was quite ready and not before. 1899 had turned into 1900 and a brand new century had begun. Alice found that fact exciting. The newspapers were full of the most wonderful prophecies concerning the twentieth century and, though she didn't say so to anyone, even to her mother, Alice felt strongly that this was *her* century. The nineteenth had belonged to her parents and people like Randy's dear old Great Aunt Katie, but the twentieth belonged to her.

Mrs. Barrington had lost a good deal of weight over the

past year and was in almost constant pain, but her courage and tenacity were equal to the challenge and she remained firmly in control of the household, seeming to know with an uncanny instinct if a servant was being slack, if the butcher's beef was not up to scratch or if the grocer's lettuce was a little tired and limp. She herself was existing mainly on gruel, creamed chicken, toast, and dry white wine.

"We must plan your coming-out party," she had told Alice one day.

"I don't want a coming-out party," Alice said. "It always seems to me like a way of saying, 'Our daughter is now available for marriage. Come and look her over.' Like a sort of highly civilized social slave market."

"Don't be absurd," Mrs. Barrington replied. "Prudence and Dorothea both had coming-out parties and you must have one, too."

But the days and weeks drifted by and the subject was not mentioned again. Alice knew very well that if she had really wanted the party her mother would have somehow summoned the strength to put it on, but she didn't want it and she suspected that deep down her mother was relieved, yet still critical of her for not submitting herself to the ordeal.

Though Alice was no longer at school, her days were fully occupied. Her mother had made sure of that. She was enrolled in a ballet class, took French lessons three half-days a week, was studying the violin with Madame Kobrinsky and, at her own particular request, was enrolled, for a time, in Professor Francini's philosophy classes at the New York Public Library.

There were parties, too, and, though the Barringtons no longer gave them, Alice had not been dropped from the invitation lists of those who did. It was at one of these parties, one given by Mr. and Mrs. Courtney Alexander to celebrate the redecoration of their Fifth Avenue mansion, that Alice met Arthur Melville. At the very moment of their introduction she thought to herself, "This is it. This is indeed the Boy Prince of Rajasthan."

He was four years older than she was and had the most charming manners of any young man Alice had ever encountered. He had graduated from Harvard the previous spring, danced divinely, and talked with wit and apparent understanding about art, literature, music, the theatre, and international affairs. Alice had never met anyone so enthralling before. How could she possibly have ever imagined that she was in love with Randy Maybank?

Tall and thin, he had a face which, though not handsome in any conventional sense, was not one which escaped notice even in a crowded room. With its deep-set eyes, high cheekbones and firm but sensitive mouth, it was perhaps the face of an intellectual but an intellectual who, far from living in a dream world, is a keen and perceptive observer of all about him. He had thick, black hair which he wore quite long. Alice liked black hair on a man. It contrasted so well with hers, which, now that she was no longer a school girl, was put up in a fine, fashionable style.

1900. Mr. McKinley was again elected President. This demonstrated, her father explained to her, that although America was embarking on a new century, it was not forsaking the tried and true values of the past. "I must admit," he conceded, however, "I have grave doubts about Roosevelt as Vice-President. I didn't like him as Assistant Secretary of the Navy, I didn't like him as Governor and I don't like him as Vice-President. He is not my idea of a Republican." He consoled himself with the thought that McKinley, gentle as he was, wouldn't tolerate any nonsense from Roosevelt. "Of one thing you may be quite certain," Ward Barrington told his daughter, "this is the end of the road for Theodore Roosevelt politically and he knows it."

She asked Arthur what he thought and was glad to find that he agreed with her father completely. "He's a bellicose fool," Arthur told her with the impressive wisdom of his twenty-two years. "But fortunately the Old Guard have trapped him. There's no chance of Roosevelt making a mark for himself in national politics now. Vice-Presidents are never remembered."

"You know so much," Alice said admiringly.

Life, of course, went on as usual. It always does. Even with the best will in the world the mood of crisis can only be maintained for a short time, unless it is bolstered up with additional bad news. Once everyone concerned knew that Amy Barrington was dying of cancer, though the actual name of the dread disease was mentioned, if at all, in whispers, and had come to take a sympathetic and curious look at her, there was not much to interest anyone in the situation until the actual dying was about to take place. When Amy Barrington's name cropped up in conversation people said, "Isn't it sad?" and others added, "Isn't she brave?" Most of those who lauded her courage thought secretly to themselves that she couldn't really be suffering that much pain or she wouldn't be able to smile so easily. Besides, she was up and about and even attended "At Homes" and tea parties on occasion.

But Alice knew.

She saw her mother off guard when she didn't have to pretend for the benefit of guests or hosts. She saw her mother doubled up with agonizing pain and unable to suppress the fierce gasps or to hold back the anguished tears. Alice watched her mother grow old day by day and she came to love her as she never had before. Never before had she been able to embrace her mother, put her young cheek against her mother's old one, and sit together on the side of the bed for whole minutes at a time without either of them speaking, without either of them feeling awkward or in any way self-conscious. They never put it into words.

And she grew closer to her father, too. She saw how much, now that her mother was ill, he wanted to assert himself and be a father in more than just name. She let him lay down the law and was suitably submissive because it pleased him and because she had no particular escapade in mind and because she knew he would never attempt to thwart her if she had really made up her mind on a course of action of which he disapproved. So she said, "Yes, Father" and "Of course, Father" and "Whatever you say, Father" and was happy to see how pleased he was by her attitude.

"I'm glad you don't set yourself up against parental authority as I read so many modern girls do these days," he said to her one evening at dinner.

"The girls who do that haven't got fathers like you."

"Perhaps not," he said complacently.

After the initial excitement had worn off neither Prudence nor Dorothea showed much interest in the situation. They didn't come even at Christmas, because as Dorothea explained to Alice on the telephone, "In view of the situation Prudence and I have decided that a quiet Christmas is the best scheme. We want Mother to rest so we're having a little party of our own and would love you to come along, but you probably feel you ought to stay with Mother."

Early in the new year, however, Prudence and Dorothea together with husbands and children descended on them one evening. "We didn't let you know we were coming because we wanted it to be a wonderful surprise. We've just had dinner so we don't need any refreshment. We won't stay long."

In the hall, as they were leaving, Prudence said, in a husky whisper, to Alice, "We thought we ought to bring the children so they could see their granny before she alters any more. We want them to remember her as she was."

"How sweet," Alice said.

She had stopped ballet, though she still did the exercises from time to time, and she had given up the violin and formal French lessons. A good deal of her time was spent tending to her mother's needs, reading aloud to her or simply sitting by her bedside. What time she had to spare was shared between household duties, her father, and Arthur.

The more she saw of Arthur the more she thought that almost certainly the two of them were made for each other. If he did ask her to marry him she would probably say yes and yet there was something about him . . . something she couldn't quite define which made her just a little bit uneasy. Was he perhaps a little too sure of his erudition? Was he a little, tiny bit condescending or was that just a manner he had picked up at Harvard?

Alice still looked at herself in the mirror and what she saw now was every bit as satisfactory as what she had seen half a dozen years ago. When she stood naked before the glass she saw the fulfillment of the earlier promise. Her legs were long and shapely, her stomach was flat, her waist narrow, her breasts firm with youth and eagerness, and her long, fair hair as lustrous as ever. When the time came to give herself to some man he must be worthy of such a gift. She wasn't now *absolutely certain* that Arthur was. She no longer thought of him as the Boy Prince of Rajasthan.

One afternoon, at her mother's request, she brought Arthur for tea. He didn't want to come but Alice insisted.

"My mother does not have much longer to live," she told him, "and I am determined that she shall have everything she wants during the time she has left. She wants to meet you and so you must come."

With Alice's help, Mrs. Barrington left her bed, put on her pale rose dress, and presided at tea as a hostess of a fine house should.

And Arthur, despite his initial reluctance, was charming, considerate, and amusing. He told her how he and three of his Harvard friends had one evening written a letter on parchment in very bad German, signed it Arthur Schopenhauer, dipped it in tea, dried it and taken it along to old Professor Pillsbury's house, claiming to have found it in a secondhand book store and antique shop.

Professor Pillsbury, who was then at the pinnacle of his fame as *the* Harvard philosopher, next, of course, to George Santayana, invited them in and offered them beer. They sat around talking for a time before a welcome coal fire in the grate. It was a bleak January evening. He glanced at their forged document but made no comment. Then, as they were finishing their beer, he stood up with the supposed letter in his hand.

"Have you any further use for this, gentlemen," he asked, "or shall we put it where it belongs?" None of them answered and, moving the screen aside, he placed it on the fire. They all laughed.

And Mrs. Barrington laughed too and then asked, "Who was Arthur Schopenhauer? I've never heard of him."

"Arthur Schopenhauer," Arthur answered, "was a German philosopher who was born, oddly enough, in Danzig, near the end of the eighteenth century."

There it was again. That patronizing note. His tone said, "Never heard of Schopenhauer? Good heavens!" Why on earth should her mother have heard of an eighteenth-century German philosopher? If Alice hadn't gone to Professor Francini's philosophy classes she would never have heard Schopenhauer's name. She wondered if Arthur had ever read him or just read about him. Did he know for instance that he had said, "Character lies in the will and not in the intellect. Popular language is correct when it prefers the 'heart' to the 'head' "? Alice remembered those sentences because they had appealed to her so much when she first read them. She didn't think intellect was her strong suit, but she never doubted the dictates of her heart nor her will to follow them. Did Arthur, she wondered, know that Schopenhauer's mother had once pushed him down a flight of stairs? What would he make of that?

But perhaps she was wrong about Arthur. Perhaps it was just his manner. Certainly her mother didn't seem to notice any condescension and when, a short time later, Arthur got up to take his leave he behaved so very charmingly that Alice was ashamed of her mean thoughts.

"This has been delightful, Mrs. Barrington," he said, taking her hand and bending low over it. "I wondered where Alice had acquired her beauty, wit, and charm, and now I know."

When he had gone and Alice was helping her mother to undress and crawl back into bed her mother said, "He will ask you and I think he's worthy of you, my dear. You could do a lot worse."

"Maybe I won't get married at all," Alice replied.

Her mother pulled her pink nightgown quickly over her head. "Of course you'll get married," she said emphatically. "I should consider my life a failure if you didn't marry. I want no more talk of that sort."

"I was just teasing."

"In very bad taste," her mother said.

Chapter 11

The time with Help-The-Children for all those later years before her friend from childhood, Jenny Robertson, died and she herself became too old for anything much had been fun but they seemed, curiously, much farther away and more faded in her memory than the years which preceded them. If she had been allowed to play a more active role in the actual operation of the hostels and play centers she might recall it all more vividly now. All that they had really wanted, she thought now, was her money, and they accepted her desire to meet the children and talk to them as a necessary but regrettable part of the arrangement.

She didn't let that worry her. There were whites, yellows, browns, and blacks and she *had* gone among them and talked to them. They were all New Yorkers!

A few had written to her later and she had appreciated that. There were no letters now. They were all grown up and doing whatever they were destined to do. Some of them perhaps had a kindly thought for her now and again. If so, they didn't put it down on paper.

Fat Mrs. Bimbaum, the widow of Bimbaum Pickles, who had occupied the apartment down the hall near the elevator, had said, when Alice announced that she was departing, "I'm going, too, you know. You and I are the last of the somebodies. When they build the whole thing up again it will be filled with nobodies. I wouldn't come back if they paid me. I'm going into that home on Riverside Drive. It's not ideal but at least quality is respected there."

"Tell me about your husband," Mrs. Bimbaum had once demanded during a morning coffee session.

"There isn't much to tell," Alice replied.

"How odd. I could tell you plenty about Herman if I'd a mind to. He was a man, he was. Would have spent all day in bed if I hadn't shoved him out. Then he turned queer. Did your husband turn queer?"

She didn't wait for an answer. "It's fine at the beginning but it turns queer later on. I knew my marriage was starting to turn queer when Herman insisted on wearing his winter coat in the house."

"Why did he do that?"

"He said it was nonsense to pay so much to heat the place when we could be perfectly warm if we just wore our coats and gloves inside. There was no talking him out of it. I had to take to wearing my coat, too. We did it all the last year before Herman died. He loved having parties but he wouldn't turn the heat up even for them and I'd have to tell the guests when they arrived not to take their coats off. We'd all sit around the table eating dinner with coats and gloves and scarves and all. After a bit Herman wondered why people turned down our invitations. I could never make him understand. Near the end he went off hot water as well. He stopped having baths then. He said they made him faint. Did your husband turn queer?"

"Not exactly," Alice answered. "Not in the same way."

Mrs. Bimbaum sent her weekly postcards and, though Alice considered the woman somewhat common, she appreciated the spirit behind these meager communications. One had arrived that morning. "Is Canada cold? Am doing my best to keep the flag flying here. Most are nobodies but Astor cousin, recently moved in, is tolerable. Best wishes."

It was near the end of February before Arthur eventually got around to mentioning marriage, and when he did so it was obvious that he had never entertained the slightest doubt as to her enthusiasm for the idea. They were having afternoon tea in the cosy little room which Arthur called "my work room." A fire was flickering in the grate.

"I wonder if you could find out when it would be convenient for your father to see me about our marriage."

"Is that meant to be a proposal?" Alice asked.

"I didn't think a formal proposal was necessary. I assumed you realized I intended to marry you."

"Did it occur to you that I might want to have a say in the matter?"

He looked genuinely puzzled. "I took it for granted. It never entered my mind you wouldn't want to marry me. You do, don't you?"

"I'm not sure." Then, because he looked so hurt and puzzled, she said, "Of course I do," and got up and kissed him lightly on the forehead. "But not just yet, I have responsibilities at home."

"You mean your mother?"

"Mainly. My father, too. I can't just walk out on them at this moment."

"I realize that. How much longer do the doctors give your mother?"

Alice was shocked not so much by the question itself as by the completely insensitive tone in which it was asked. He might have been inquiring what time the train for Chicago left instead of asking about her mother's life.

"How can you ask such a question in such a way? I'm sorry if my mother's continuing to live is inconveniencing you. I shall tell her and I'm sure she'll agree to die at once."

"Aren't you being somewhat overly emotional? Your mother is dying, after all. There's nothing I can do about that."

Alice didn't get angry often, but now she felt a wave of anger surge within her and she turned on the man she had agreed to marry only a few moments before and said, "I've seen you for the first time as you really are, Arthur Melville, and I don't like what I see. I wouldn't marry you now if you were the last male creature left alive. How can you speak of my mother that way? What if it were your mother who was dying?" She stood up.

"We're all dying. From the moment of birth we are all journeying towards death." Mrs. Melville stood in the doorway—tall, serene, dark, imposing. She had on a long purple dress and wore a white shawl over her shoulders. "Arthur, have you been unkind to your bride-to-be? Have you been tactless and uncouth? I'm sorry, my dear," she said, advancing on Alice. "You must be patient with him. He can be very difficult at times. I think he gets it from his father. I shall turn over his management to you after you marry and move in here with us."

"But I'm not at all sure that I shall marry your son."

"Of course you will, my dear. You are by far the best possibility so far. How is your dear mother? I wish to come to see her. Is she well enough for that? Shall we say Wednesday at four?"

Her eyes, tawny and unblinking, were like twin drills.

Arthur had stood up when his mother appeared. He had been taught to do so as soon as he was capable of balancing himself on two feet. She turned those eyes on him now and Alice, seeing the color fade from his cheek, realized with something of a shock how afraid he was of his mother.

"We'll have no more of this sort of nonsense," Mrs. Melville said.

"No, Mother."

He was like a frightened schoolboy.

"My father was a surgeon," Mrs. Melville told Alice later. "He believed strongly in discipline and he taught us discipline. I remember him saying 'There is nothing a man or woman can't do if they set their minds to it and, if they refuse to do it of their own free will, then they must be made to do so.' I was the only girl with three older brothers but I was not pampered. He only beat us when there was no other way. Usually his voice and his eyes were enough. He was a great man. He taught me firmness. I adored him. He didn't spare himself and he didn't spare us."

Mrs. Barrington rose from her bed to take tea with Mrs. Melville on Wednesday. When Alice, backed up by Mrs. Barrington's nurse, had suggested that tea could be served in the bedroom, her mother had replied, "I don't entertain in my bedroom. I'm not going to have Agnes Melville think I'm some sort of an invalid."

So they had tea in the drawing room on Wednesday.

"I am delighted, Amy," Mrs. Melville said, her Minton cup poised between her knee and her lips, "that our two young people will be perpetuating the Melville tradition."

"I rather think, Agnes," her hostess replied evenly, "that Alice will bring up her children as young Barringtons in all but name."

"Perhaps the best of both worlds—the Melville polish and the Barrington business acumen."

Mrs. Barrington smiled faintly and pursed her faded lips. Various replies occurred to her but she was really too tired for this sort of thing now and the effect of the pain killers she had taken earlier were beginning to wear off; and anyway, she knew that Alice would be able to stand up to Mrs. Melville without her help. "I hope they'll be happy together."

On Friday Amy Barrington died at five in the afternoon.

Both Alice and her father were in the room with the doctor and the nurse when, after listening for a heartbeat and putting an ear to her gaping mouth, he put a thumb and forefinger to her staring, vacant eyes and closed them firmly forever. Then he raised the sheet over her face and said, "It's all over."

Alice had often thought back on that moment. She had not cried. She had lowered the sheet, kissed her mother's cheek and felt, with a small shock, how cold it was to her lips. Then she replaced the sheet and, taking her father by the arm, led him gently from the room.

She took him to the living room, poured him a drink, and then went out to telephone to Prudence and Dorothea. The doctor had been very insistent that he should call the undertaker and Alice had wondered, in a numbed, uncaring way, if he got a commission.

As she knew they would, Prudence and Dorothea "took charge" and, within an hour of their arrival, had everything and everybody in a state of confusion. They began by taking Mr. Barrington's whiskey away from him because, Dorothea said, "When people come to call you don't want them to think you have to seek solace in a bottle, do you?"

"I don't want to see any callers."

"You can't refuse to see people when they call to pay their last respects," said Prudence firmly.

Then the undertaker's men came to make Mrs. Barrington respectable to receive these same callers. After considerable debate and much rummaging through closets it was decided that the dark blue satin dress would be most suitable, though of course all her dresses were much too big for that shrunken, wasted body. Then there were flowers to order, people to telephone to, people to write to, suitable light refreshments to be ordered for impending visitors and of course funeral arrangements to be made. Though she refrained from saying so, Alice could not help thinking that her older sisters, during that dreadful weekend, were enjoying themselves thoroughly. She left them to it, spending a good part of her time with her father or alone in her room. Prudence and Dorothea did most of the muted entertaining of callers, conducting somber little groups up the wide stairs to view their mother in her satin dress with her almost transparent hands folded across her breast. They forced their poor father to make an occasional appearance at first but, after a bit, he refused and they left him alone to endure his solitary misery.

On Sunday afternoon Arthur called with his mother and Alice came down to take a glass of dry sherry with them. After a time Prudence and Dorothea took Mrs. Melville up to the bedroom and she and Arthur were left briefly alone.

"I'm terribly sorry about the other afternoon," he said at once. "I behaved very badly. I hope you'll forgive me. I realize that I can't see your father now but I hope you will marry me as you said."

Alice thought of her mother's words. "He will ask you and I think he's worthy of you, my dear. You could do a lot worse." It had been her mother's wish and yet . . . she wasn't quite certain.

"I . . . I can't make up my mind for sure at this moment," she said. "Somehow funerals and weddings don't go very well together."

"I know. I don't want to hurry you. I'll wait for your answer."

He didn't have to wait long.

After the funeral on Monday various friends of the family, including the Reverend and Mrs. Barnstable, came back to the house for a time and, after they had gone, Dorothea said, "Now I think it's time for a family conference." Prudence agreed and so did their husbands, who always agreed with their wives.

"First of all there's you, Father. We must organize you."

"I think if you don't mind," Mr. Barrington replied quietly, "I'll just organize myself."

"But you won't eat properly," Prudence said.

"And if you're not careful," Dorothea added, "you'll start drinking too much."

Mr. Barrington stood up. He was not an impressive man, but, at that particular moment, Alice saw a strength and a dignity in him which she had not perceived before. "I am your father," he said, "and you will not impose your will on me. I shall live the rest of my life in the way I choose without interference from you." As he left the room he passed the chair where Alice was sitting and, pausing momentarily, touched her gently on the top of her head. Alice looked up into his face. He was crying, but his back was to the others and they didn't see.

"Poor Father," Prudence said complacently. "It's been a hard day for him. We'll have to work gradually."

"Now the problem of Alice's future," Dorothea said. "She's too young and it wouldn't be fair anyway for us to desert her and leave her to look after Father and the house. She mustn't be cheated of life. I propose we get a very capable and superior housekeeper who can really take charge. Prudence and I can take turns looking in to make sure things are as they should be."

"I quite agree," Prudence said. "As for Alice, what about a year at that nice school in Boston—I forget its name—where she could continue with her music and French? It would be good for her to get away from it all."

For a moment Alice didn't trust herself to speak. She had only been annoyed before but now she was outraged. What right had they to try to organize her life? But she would keep her voice down.

"No one need worry about me. I'm engaged to Arthur Melville and, as soon as Father is settled, we are going to be married. And now I think I'll go to bed. It's been a long day."

She was out of the room before any of them could think of anything to say.

She called Arthur on the telephone which had been installed in her mother's bedroom. Years later she was to think that if the instrument had been out of order, as it quite often was, and she had gone to bed, she might have reconsidered in the morning. How different things might have been.

But the telephone was in order, and Arthur sounded pleased by her decision but not particularly surprised.

Chapter 12

Alice herself had comparatively little to do with the arrangements for her wedding. Her father was eager to spend a lot of money; Mrs. Melville was eager to prove herself Alice's second mother; Prudence and Dorothea were eager to demonstrate their sisterly devotion. Carla Sandhurst, with whom she had remained good friends, was determined to leave nothing undone that a prospective maid of honor should do and this meant coming to talk to Alice while she was trying to write thank-you notes for wedding presents and making helpful suggestions such as, "Why don't you let me look after your packing for you?" or "I've been wondering about that going-away hat. Let's go upstairs and have one more look at it."

There were parties too, including a mammoth one given by the Melvilles, at which she and Arthur had to appear as eager love birds about to fly off together so that people could say, "Aren't they an adorable couple?" and, "They're perfectly matched" and other such things. It was at the Melvilles' party that Alice, overhearing such a remark, turned and said, "The marriage was arranged by our parents when we were both infants. We can't stand each other, really." The laughter was nervous and uncertain.

Mr. Melville, a tall, quiet, austere looking man who had inherited a fortune in railway stock from his father, did his duty at the various affairs but appeared to have little enthusiasm for them. His chief interest in life was collecting paintings and, in one of the very few conversations Alice had with him before the wedding, he said, "I have asked Arthur to attend to a few things for me in Europe when you are on your honeymoon. I hope you won't object."

"Of course not," Alice assured him.

An excellent, motherly Irish widow like a character out of a warm, sentimental play had been engaged as housekeeper for Mr. Barrington and he had settled into a placid routine of rising late, lunching at the club, visiting the store once or twice a week for the pleasure of being deferred to (he no longer even pretended to be active in its management), going for walks on fine days, reading back copies of the *Illustrated London News* and just sitting, contentedly sipping a drink. Alice didn't mind leaving him too much.

The wedding itself, when it happened, was a splendid affair and, though Alice knew how much, on that day of all days, her father must have longed to have her mother at his side, there was no doubt that he thoroughly enjoyed playing host at the reception in the garden. It was a perfect June day.

Two or three weeks earlier Alice had asked her father if people would think it was too soon after her mother's death. "We could put it off to the fall," she told him.

He had looked at her and smiled. "No, my dear. Your mother always thought you should take happiness where and when you found it. I don't care what other people think. Can you imagine your mother saying, 'You must avoid being happy for at least six months after my death'? I can't."

"Nor can I," Alice answered.

"I'm not a very religious man but I like to think your mother will be looking down from heaven on the day and giving you her blessing."

"I love you so much," Alice said, "and I agree—she will be."

The plan was for the newlyweds to spend that first night at the Waldorf and board the *Olympia* for Southampton the next morning. Mrs. Melville had suggested that they take "at least one servant" with them, but Alice had firmly vetoed that idea. Eight weeks or so in Britain and then France and Switzerland, returning to New York at the end of August. The day before the wedding Alice, to her horror, was told by Mrs. Melville, "By that time the apartment we're going to have made ready for you will be finished and you can move into your very own place."

"But I thought our stay with you when we got back was to be just until we could find a place of our own."

"Perhaps eventually you may want a house of your own," said Mrs. Melville, "though it would seem quite unnecessary extravagance when we have so much room here and Arthur is our only child. However, we won't worry about such things now—not just before the most important day of your life."

Alice didn't pursue the matter. There would be ample

time while they were in Europe to make Arthur realize the importance of making a home which was really and truly their own and in which they could raise their children. Alice still looked forward to a large family through whom she could enjoy, even if secondhand, the companionship among each other and with other children of which she, until the untimely death of Laura Cosgrove, had been deprived.

Arthur was seasick on the way across and was annoyed with Alice because she wasn't. "I don't see why you keep rushing away to walk around the deck," he told her. "I should have thought that, as a bride of only a few days, you would want to spend more time with me."

She made the mistake of thinking he was joking and laughed. "I'm glad you find my discomfort so amusing. If I were really seriously ill I expect you would find the situation positively hilarious."

"But Arthur, my darling, you're not seriously ill. I'm sorry I laughed. I only did so because I thought you yourself were making light of the situation. I will spend more time in the cabin if you wish but, when I am here, you seem to spend most of the time groaning and trying to go to sleep. I really thought you scarcely noticed whether I was here or not."

"Suit yourself. I don't want you to stay with me out of a sense of obligation. I expect the strangers you walk with find the situation as comic as you do—the wife hale and hearty with a voracious appetite, the husband lying helpless on his bunk. You must have some good laughs about it with your new companions."

"Oh please, Arthur, don't be like that. I have no new companions and I certainly wouldn't discuss your seasickness with them if I had. I am truly sorry that you feel so miserable."

"I'm not at all sure it *is* seasickness. I think it may be something more serious."

"There is a ship's doctor," she said.

"I don't want to be prodded and poked by some ignoramus just out of medical school."

When they landed at Southampton Arthur recovered his health and good spirits almost instantly. While they were in England they were to visit a number of distinguished patrons of the arts, all of whom were friends or acquaintances of Mr. Melville. Alice had been too excited about the

whole idea of getting married and going abroad and so involved with wardrobe planning, packing, and other preparations for these events that she had paid little attention to
the details of the European venture. She had a vague general idea that they would be dropping in for afternoon tea
or dinner with various friends of the Melvilles; it had not
occurred to her that they would be spending any apprecia-
ble time with them.

Now, however, she heard Arthur saying, "We're to meet
Lord Ackerly at the White Hart. He came down especially
from his home in the New Forest to welcome us and take
us back to Ackerley Hall. He wants us to spend our first
five days with him and Lady Ackerley and then we go to
London to stay with the Merrihews."

Alice didn't quite know how to phrase the question to
make it sound casual and innocuous and, deep down, she
knew it would be better not to ask it at all. But she had to.
She suddenly felt she had to know.

"I'm looking forward so much to meeting Lord and
Lady Ackerley, darling."

"Yes, you'll like them. They're a good deal older than
us, of course. I mean they're friends of my father's but I've
met them. When I was just a boy they came to New York.
I don't remember them very well."

"I'm looking forward even more to the two of us just
being alone together. How much time do you suppose we'll
have by ourselves?"

Arthur gave her a puzzled, slightly annoyed look. "We
can be alone together any time we like back home," he
said. "I looked on this European trip as a great opportunity
to meet important people—people who might later help me
with my literary career. I expect we'll manage a few days
of just the two of us in Switzerland but, apart from that,
you don't want to spend time simply mooning about in an
idiotic, lovesick way, do you?"

"I want to do whatever you want to do," she told him.

Arthur nodded as if that was such an obvious desire on
her part that it scarcely required putting into words.

So they met Lord Ackerley, a short, dull man who
looked like a turtle on its hind legs at the White Hart as
had been arranged; they spent their five days at imposing
and uncomfortable Ackerley Hall, where Arthur passed
most of his time with Lord A. in his study and Alice di-

vided hers between admiring the big oaks and watching Lady A. at her loom.

Then they moved on to the Merrihews, who had a luxurious flat in Mayfair. The Merrihews, a shy, elderly couple, told them all about the death of Queen Victoria in January—an event from which, Mrs. Merrihew assured them, the Country would take years to recover. In London Alice enjoyed the plays and evening concerts which the Merrihews took them to, but the endless hours in art galleries and at dealers' showrooms bored her exceedingly. She had no idea as to whether Arthur was genuinely knowledgeable about painting and music and so on; she suspected that most of it was bluff. But she could have forgiven him that if he had shown any desire to make her a real part of their activities and a participant in discussions, instead of treating her as a sort of camp follower who trailed along after him and sat in humble admiration as he expounded at some length on why America would never develop an artistic tradition of its own or whether the influence of the French Impressionists was altogether healthy.

She did say to him one nice sunny day that she thought it would be fun to go for a walk in the park.

"Why?" he asked.

"As a little girl I used to go to Central Park with my mother. I like parks. We could feed the ducks."

"My darling," he said, and the condescension in his tone quite overwhelmed the affection in the words, "we surely didn't come all the way to London to feed ducks, did we?"

They spent a week with the Merrihews and then, in accordance with an arrangement which had been made before they left New York, but about which no one had bothered to tell Alice, they moved in with an American family, friends of the Melvilles, who had come to London on a semipermanent basis so that they could "really be a *part* of British culture and *feel* it from the *inside*."

These people, Mr. and Mrs. Tom Travers and their unmarriageable daughter, Jodie, in spite of their efforts to become far more British than the British, had found themselves to be easily resistible by London society. However, pride would not allow them to return to New York too soon and they were delighted to welcome the newlyweds to their palatial flat not far from Marble Arch.

"We've gained a tremendous amount both culturally and

spiritually from our time here," Mrs. Travers assured them. "I wish that there were more young people for Jodie, but she's never been one for a hectic social life any more than we have and she *has* got a tremendous amount out of the British Museum, haven't you, Jodie?"

Jodie, who had been staring vacantly out the window, pulled herself together, closed her mouth, which had a habit of sagging open in moments of deep reflection, and then opened it again to ask, "Were you talking to me?"

"I said that you had got a tremendous amount out of the British Museum."

"Those Egyptian mummies, you mean. I could sit and look at them for hours. Never saw anything like that before." She smiled hopefully.

"Alice isn't quite as keen on art galleries and dealers as I am," Arthur said, "so perhaps, while I'm looking about and making some inquiries on my father's behalf, Jodie would take Alice to the British Museum."

"Sure would," Jodie said. "Ever seen an Egyptian mummy?"

"Yes," Alice replied calmly, "we had one in the corner of our drawing room at home with a hollow head and a light inside which shone out through the eyes."

"Oh," said Jodie and her jaw sagged open again.

"I think Mrs. Melville is just joking, dear," Mrs. Travers said coldly.

"Oh," said Jodie again.

That night, when she had him in their bedroom, alone at last, she decided that the time had come to make her feelings clear. "I do not intend," she told him firmly, "to spend the next week or ten days or however long you have in mind, gazing at Egyptian mummies with that slack-jawed, cross-eyed, half-witted creature called Jodie. You seem to have forgotten that this is our honeymoon. It is normal on honeymoons, I believe, for the bride and groom to spend a good deal of time in each other's company."

Arthur, who was in the process of taking off his trousers, came to a sudden halt with one leg in and one leg out. He looked like a frightened contortionist. "You astound me," he said.

"If we don't start having a proper honeymoon soon I shall astound you even more. I want Paris; I want it soon; I want it on our own."

Arthur, after doing a little hop, skip, and jump with his trousers, managed to collapse into a chair. "Is this one of your silly jokes," he asked, "like that unfortunate remark about the Egyptian mummy?"

"Try me and see," Alice answered.

Chapter 13

Sunday. Patricia had telephoned that they couldn't have her over because she and Michael were involved in a medical convention reception or some such thing. "Arthur and Polly said they'd be glad to have you for tea if you'd like to go and Arthur said to tell you that he'd call for you and take you home again but their little Jennifer has come out in a rash and I told him I thought you'd probably prefer a quiet afternoon to yourself. Am I right?"

"Quite right, of course, dear. I've got that book you brought me, *New York in Pictures*, and I'll look at that."

"Good for you. I'll see you on Wednesday."

"Yes, dear. Have fun at your party."

"We'll try. It's more a duty than a fun thing. Michael feels we have to go."

"You'll enjoy feeling noble then."

Patricia laughed a little uncertainly. She didn't appreciate such a remark, which was why Alice had made it.

Mrs. Owens was out visiting her cousin, so Alice had got her own gin and tonic and made it a little stronger than usual. There was an evening haze which blurred her view of the ocean and the houses and buildings in between. She didn't mind it. The pictures of old New York had made her feel a bit hazy herself.

What a strange thing time was. So fast and yet so slow. So short and yet so long. Those honeymoon days were an age ago and yet they were merely yesterday. She had been nineteen going on twenty then and she thought she was immortal. There was lots and lots of time to work out her real or imagined problems with Arthur. Lots of time . . . lots of time . . . and yet time was almost gone now—*her* time, that was. Time would go on for other people and no one would really notice that she had disappeared, because almost everyone who might have noticed had already preceded her.

The occasions in Alice's life when she had seriously considered the possibility that she might be wrong had not been frequent, but at one point in those early days of married life she had tried hard to convince herself that she and not Arthur was being too critical.

"Of course Arthur has things he wants to accomplish," she told herself. "He is after all gaining knowledge and experience for his career as a gentleman writer about and critic of Art. He also has commissions to perform for his father. I was told about that by Mr. Melville and said I didn't mind. One doesn't come to Europe two or three times a year. He has to make the most of his visit even though it does happen to be our honeymoon."

But, lying awake beside him at night and listening to his rhythmical breathing, she couldn't help asking herself what had happened to the charming, witty, suave, polished, erudite man she thought she had married. Had it all been in her imagination? Had he changed so soon? Had it all been an act before? Was he disappointed in her? They should be making love, not lying here side by side with him sound asleep and her staring wide-awake. It was too early—much too early—in the marriage for this kind of worry. Tomorrow they would be in Paris. She would tease him out of it. Perhaps she had been too solemn about his parents' friends. Tomorrow they would be together in Paris! If that didn't work nothing would. Paris would be magic. Paris would do it.

The Channel had been rough and Arthur had been sick again. The boat train from Dunkirk had been late in leaving and there had been a mix-up about their seats. Arthur had been in a foul mood and Alice had been as submissive and solicitous as it was possible for her to be. She didn't even show annoyance when Arthur, from the depths of his misery, sitting in the stuffy first-class compartment on the train, had said, "You've been so protected all your life. I don't think you know what it is to suffer."

Now, however, they were at last in Paris. They had spent the previous night in Dover and departed early in the morning. Despite all the delays and confusions, here they were. Alice decided that now was the time to begin her campaign to cheer Arthur up and reawaken in him those traits which had won her heart.

They were in their large, ornate, dome-ceilinged bedroom at the Hotel du Louvre and they were changing for dinner—their first dinner in Paris! Alice was not the least bit tired. In her bodice and petticoats she stretched herself out luxuriously on the immense bed and gave a sigh of contentment which she hoped would draw Arthur's attention and make him realize how irresistible she was. He was busy pulling on his trousers and didn't seem to notice. At important moments Arthur *always* seemed to be pulling on or taking off his trousers.

"I don't suppose you'll approve of me exploring Paris alone," Alice said, "so you'd better come with me."

"I am as keen as you are to enjoy some of the diversions, my love, but there are commitments. I am, after all, collecting a wealth of information which will enable me to write with some authority about the arts on our return. I also have certain commissions for my father."

He had somehow got his right leg in the left leg of his trousers and was extricating it with difficulty. "I could take you more seriously," Alice said, "if your legs were not so spindly. You look so much better with trousers on."

"I'm sure I do," he said. "I expect we all look better decently clad. Why don't you get dressed?"

"What about the Rubens pictures you're so keen about?"

"I don't follow you at all. Rubens died two hundred and fifty years ago. Besides, he was Flemish."

"You mean those fat, naked Flemish ladies don't seem vulgar and I, in my petticoat, do? How do you decide?"

Arthur looked at her with some apprehension and eventually managed to say, "Art and Life are two quite different concepts. I shall have to explain."

"Yes, you will," Alice answered. She waited while he sorted his trousers out but, when he was no longer preoccupied with them and still hadn't said anything further about Art and Life, she asked, "Are you going to go and see the dancing girls?"

He looked at her with surprised disappointment. "What *are* you talking about, Alice?"

"You know perfectly well what I'm talking about. I'm talking about the attraction that lures more tourists here— more *men* tourists anyway—than all the museums and art galleries combined. Girls without clothes on. That's what I'm talking about. You may find excitement in looking at paintings of buxom, big-bottomed ladies lounging naked in

Italian vineyards or beside Grecian fountains, but most men prefer the real thing. Perhaps you feel safer with the nudes on canvas than you do with me." In spite of herself there was an edge to her voice. She had meant to be gay and bantering but she was afraid she sounded sarcastic and even strident.

Arthur didn't look at her. He was, by this time, arranging his tie in front of the mirror. Alice waited for him to speak and at last he said, "This is a most idiotic conversation and I don't wish to continue it. I am thankful my mother can't hear you."

"What on earth has your mother to do with it?"

"A great deal, if you must know. I happen to admire my mother very much indeed."

"Arthur, please come and sit down on the bed beside me. I don't want to quarrel on our honeymoon. I admire your mother, too, but you didn't marry your mother, you married me." She stretched out her hand towards him and, after a momentary hesitation, he came and sat down beside her. "I don't mean to make you cross," she said softly, "but . . . but . . . oh, I don't know . . . you aren't acting at all the way I thought you would before we got married."

He took her hand in his but it was an almost mechanical gesture, as though he were a somewhat nervous actor obeying the director in an amateur production. "I don't know what you mean. I gather I have already disappointed you as a husband, I'm not sure what you expected."

"When I first met you at the dance at the Alexanders' I thought you were so handsome and so wise. I still think so. You were witty and your manners were so graceful . . . I don't know. You seemed so perfect. When we got married I thought our honeymoon would be the most wonderful experience of my life."

He got up impatiently. "Isn't it time you finished dressing?"

She didn't answer and, turning back toward her, he thought he saw tears in her eyes. Or did they just glitter that way when she was angry?

"I don't mean to sound cold," he said. "It's just that . . . Oh, it doesn't matter."

"It *does* matter. It matters very much. Can't you understand, Arthur, that if . . . if you and I have made a mistake in each other, if I'm not the woman you thought I was and you're not the man I thought you were, then the years ahead are going to seem very long?" She dried her eyes, sat up, put her bare feet on the rug and tossed her head in the way she had practiced before the mirror so often as a child so that her hair swirled and fell back softly over her shoulders. "It's a long time since I cried," she said. "I didn't cry even when my mother died."

Arthur heard her out, his dark eyes intent and his swarthy face immobile. He didn't look annoyed and he didn't look apologetic. He just looked faintly puzzled. It was some moments before he answered. Then he said, "I think you're being overly dramatic. We aren't very experienced in marriage yet. We'll learn. I expect it's always more difficult for the wife."

"Why?"

"Because she must learn to accommodate herself to her husband and, even though she belongs to the weaker sex, I expect there is some natural tendency to fight against such subjection."

Alice looked to make sure he was joking. But no, there was not a trace of a smile nor a sparkle in his eye. He couldn't mean it! This was the twentieth century! She gave a little uncertain laugh, intended to show him that she quite understood he was just having some fun, but his only response was to say, "Come get your dress on and we'll have an apéritif on the sidewalk." Then, at last, he smiled.

It was all right after all. More fool she for taking him seriously. She took no more than five minutes to get into her dress, toss up and pin her hair in place, put on her stockings and shoes, inspect herself in the mirror and extend her hand to him as he stood waiting for her by the door. "I'm sorry," she said, "I think I was being foolish."

He gave her hand a little squeeze and then, holding her at arm's length, his strong, long-fingered hands on her shoulders, he smiled again in his grave, handsome way. He gripped her so hard that it hurt, but she smiled back; she didn't show that he was hurting her.

"We'll learn," he said quietly.

"Yes," Alice answered, "we'll learn."

Then they were out the door and walking down the broad, carpeted corridor side by side.

"Everything is going to be fine," Alice told herself insistently. "Everything is going to be just fine."

Alice had read of air that was like wine but, even when she had inhaled the air of Central Park right down to the bottom of her lungs, it had never seemed like wine to her; but now, walking along the Champs Elysées with the Arc de Triomphe in the distance and the burnished horses lifting their legs proudly and the elegantly attired Parisian ladies and the beautifully turned out boys and girls and the colorful umbrellas shading the tables of the sidewalk cafés and, above all, the pale blue sky with its little puffs of purest white cotton clouds, she breathed the air of that blissful summer morning and it was indeed like wine. This was what she had been waiting for all her life.

Arthur had an all-day appointment with a Monsieur Parent, a gentleman of impeccable reputation who made a specialty of guiding wealthy American collectors around the galleries and helping them discover bargains they might not have been able to find on their own. Alice had declined an invitation to accompany them and Arthur had not insisted but he had asked, "What will you do then? I don't like the idea of you wandering around Paris by yourself."

Alice had laughed. "Paris is full of people wandering around by themselves. I shall just be one more tourist out for a morning stroll. I'll come back here for lunch, have an afternoon snooze, and then wait for your return."

The conversation had taken place while they were having dinner and, to Arthur's horror, while Alice was trying snails for the first time.

"I wish you would have done with those revolting things and get the waiter to take your plate away. You've almost spoiled my appetite for duck."

"Just one more to go," said Alice, pulling the final little rubbery morsel from its shell. "They're delicious." The waiter hovered solicitously behind her. "You wouldn't worry about me going around by myself in New York."

"This isn't New York."

"Don't worry, darling, I can take care of myself." She signalled the waiter to remove her plate.

So now here she was. Life was perfect. A little whisper of a breeze kept the day from being too hot. Everyone was on holiday; everyone was happy. There was a special quality to the sunshine; it was never as golden as this in New York.

"Américaine?"

Alice turned to the voice on her left. It belonged to a young woman about her own age and height with short, dark brown hair, hazel eyes under exaggeratedly arched eyebrows, high cheekbones emphasized by too much rouge, and scarlet lips.

"Oui."

"Welcome to Paris. A beautiful day, n'est-ce pas?"

"Yes, beautiful."

"You speak French?"

"Oui, un petit peu." It was, Alice thought to herself, an overly modest answer but perhaps it was better to be cautious. She spoke excellent American French, but she wasn't certain that Parisians spoke the language the same way.

She was on the whole relieved when her newfound friend said, "Do you mind if we speak in English? I want to improve mine."

"Not at all. Your English is very good."

She shrugged her shoulders and pouted. "It is passable." She pronounced the word in the French rather than the English way. "You are alone in Paris?"

"No, I'm here with my husband."

"Your husband? You are very young to be married. It is your . . . your lune de miel?"

Alice laughed delightedly. "Our honeymoon. Yes, it is. My husband had some important business to conduct today. He is an expert on painting."

"A connoisseur?"

"I think you could call him that."

"So for today you are seeing Paris on your own?"

"A little bit of it."

"Your first visit?"

"Yes."

Alice had at first been pleased and even a little bit excited at being accosted by a real live native of Paris but now, suddenly, she wasn't so sure. There was something about the woman she didn't like—an overeagerness, too much perfume. Turning to look at her again, Alice saw that her companion's neck was dirty and that the red and yellow cotton dress had stains on it. She was definitely not a lady.

"If you would like to pay for a carriage," the woman said, "I will be pleased to show you the real Paris. There is much more than the Champs Elysées, the Eiffel Tower, and the tomb of Napoleon."

"Perhaps some other time," Alice said. "I think I'd better be getting back to my hotel now." She stopped walking.

"Why? It is not time for lunch yet."

"I . . . I have some letters I want to write."

"But we must walk as far as the Arc de Triomphe. We are almost there." She seemed very insistent.

"Yes, I suppose we should do that." It would, she thought to herself, be a more natural place to stop and go back. She only hoped the woman would not try to accompany her on her return.

In the cool shadow of the mighty archway the woman plucked Alice's sleeve. "Venez ici," she said and drew her to one side away from the other people. Alice thought she was going to show her something special. Almost at the same moment Alice became aware that a man had joined them.

"Mrs. Melville?" he asked. For a fleeting moment Alice thought he must be a friend from home.

"Yes," she answered brightly. "Have we . . .?"

"No, we have not met before. If you wish to see your husband again you will please do as I say. You feel that prick in your back? It is the point of a knife. If you make any fuss I shall be forced to push it the rest of the way in."

"This is absurd!" Alice exclaimed. "I am an American citizen."

"I know," the man replied quietly. "So am I."

They got into a waiting carriage.

Chapter 14

It wasn't until they were in the carriage that she had a chance to get a good look at her captor. He had the face of a worried and not particularly intelligent squirrel, with two protruding, yellowish front teeth, little tufts of hair on his cheekbones and bushy red eyebrows. His eyes were strangely colorless and sad. He was almost completely bald. He was thin and tall. Alice found herself wondering if he had played basketball in high school and decided that he was probably the type who had tried out for the team, worked very earnestly and then, just before the season started, been told by the coach that he hadn't made it.

She wasn't very afraid. A strong sense of unreality overcame any deep fear she might have felt. The whole business was so absurd. He kept the point of the knife touching her side and he looked straight ahead. Occasionally his cheek twitched and then he looked even more like a squirrel. "He hasn't done this before," Alice thought to herself. "He's more nervous than I am." The woman sat and contemplated her hands. Alice noticed that her fingernails had been chewed.

"How did you know my name?" she asked.

"I know more than you might suppose," the man answered mysteriously.

The horse clip-clopped on its way. "I should be nervous," she thought. But she wasn't; she was, in fact, beginning to feel a not unpleasurable excitement. It was an adventure. She looked at the man; she looked at the woman. Neither of them appeared at all happy about the situation. "How very strange," she thought, "for an American to be kidnapped by an American in Paris."

"Isn't it a lovely day?" she said.

No answer.

"Well, I think it's a lovely day. The only thing I'm sorry about is what's going to happen to the two of you. I shall do my best, of course, but I'm afraid it will be out of my hands."

No comment.

"I shall say that, apart from the knife in my ribs, you didn't mistreat me. I shall say that and I'll ask for mercy for you. I expect it will just be a long time in prison. I'm quite sure the French wouldn't guillotine an American who had kidnapped an American. I think the Secretary of State would have something to say about that."

Not a word.

"On the other hand, of course, I'm sure the French will think that kidnapping is bad for the tourist trade and must be discouraged. Perhaps they'll send you to Devil's Island and you can write a book about it when they let you go in fifteen or twenty years. It should be a best-seller. Perhaps you'll dedicate it to me—'Alice Melville, the lady who made it possible.' I'd appreciate that."

Silence.

"I wonder where they're waiting."

"Who?"

"The police, of course."

"What makes you think they are waiting any place?"

She laughed. "I feel sorry for you."

"Sorry for me? What do you mean?"

"You can't possibly sleep at night."

"Why not?"

"Your conscience. You weren't really cut out for this kind of life and you must wonder what your mother would think if she only knew. Do you ever think of going back to America?"

"I don't want to talk to you."

"Very well, I won't warn you then." She closed her lips tight and looked straight ahead. For a time there was silence.

"Warn me?" he asked at last, unable to contain himself any longer.

"It doesn't matter," Alice said. "Let's just wait for it to happen. It will be more exciting that way."

"For what to happen?"

"You said you didn't want to talk to me. I think you're right. You are a desperate, ruthless killer and I am a young bride on her honeymoon. What could we possibly have in common? You have a knife at my side and may plunge it in at any moment. This is no time for lighthearted conversation."

"I have taken the knife away. I didn't hurt you." He

sounded sad and defensive. "You said you were going to warn me."

"So I did. Do you want me to?"

"If you care to. I have no fear."

"Good for you. So you don't need my warning. You are a man who can cope with any emergency. I shall be absolutely fascinated to see how you deal with the one you are about to face up to."

"I don't know what you're talking about."

"You will."

Another silence. Alice was enjoying herself now. She would be late for lunch but she would be back at the hotel in plenty of time to greet Arthur. The woman, who took no part in the conversation, seemed increasingly apprehensive. Her mouth puckered occasionally and she kept looking across Alice at the man. The smell of her sickly sweet perfume filled the carriage.

"Well," said the man at last, "what is it you want to tell me?"

"Don't you mean, what is it you want to hear?"

"Have it your own way."

"Your friend in the hotel made a bad mistake. He was much too obvious."

"What friend? Who said I had a friend in the hotel?"

"Oh, don't treat me like a child. You think I don't know what the game is?"

"What is it, then?"

"Your friend gave you my name as a likely kidnapping possibility—young, newly married to a wealthy man. He heard my husband and me speaking of our plans at dinner last night. It's all so silly and obvious. You station this woman in the lobby and, when I leave, she follows me and lures me on to the Arc de Triomphe where you're waiting to take over. Please give me credit for some intelligence."

"Aren't you afraid?" His voice was nasal. He tried to pitch it lower than was natural and succeeded only in sounding like a man with a very bad cold in his head.

"Afraid?" Alice asked. "Afraid of you? Why should I be? At any minute now the gendarmes will catch up with us and you and the woman will be taken away. You surely don't think a man as protective as my husband would let me leave the hotel on my own without taking suitable precautions? At the trial I shall have to say that you threatened my life but, as I have said, I'll do the best I can for you. You are, after all, a fellow American."

They had crossed the Seine and were clip-clopping their way down a narrow, cobbled street with tall, forbiddingly dark structures on either side. Presently the man leaned out the window and gave an order to the driver, and they came to a stop.

The man turned to Alice. He really was like a squirrel. His eyes bulged and he looked as though he had acorns in his cheeks.

"You may go," he said.

"Go? Go where? I have no intention of going. You brought me here and if you want to get rid of me, you can take me back where I belong."

"I don't believe the police are on our trail at all. I think you're bluffing."

"Then why let me go?"

He looked at her sadly and didn't answer.

After a time the woman said to him contemptuously, "Vous êtes un imbécile." The man did not dispute this judgment. In fact the expression on his face seemed almost to indicate agreement. Then the woman thrust her hand across at him. "Mon paiement, s'il vous plaît. La dame est votre responsibileté maintenant."

"Cochon!" the man said petulantly. He thrust his hand into his pocket, however, and placed some money in her outstretched palm. The woman thereupon opened the carriage door and departed without another word.

"She is not a nice woman," the man said gloomily.

"No," Alice answered, "I didn't care for her much."

"Are the police really looking for us?"

"Take me back to the Champs Elysées and, if they stop us on the way, I'll say we're just going for a little ride together."

"All right," said the man abjectly. He gave the necessary instructions to the driver.

As they went along Alice said, "I really don't think you should try any more kidnappings. Another victim might not be as kind to you as I have been and besides, you're not very good at it."

"I only did it to see if I could get enough money to pay my way back to Wilmington."

"How do you happen to be in Paris?"

"I met that man who's a waiter at the hotel. He has a married sister in Wilmington he was visiting. He talked me into coming to Paris on a holiday. I've spent all my money. I spent most of it on that woman you saw."

"That's too bad," Alice said. "Why don't you get a job?"

"I had a good job in Wilmington. I worked in a drug store. They don't have drug stores like that in Paris. Besides, my French isn't very good."

"How were you going to collect the ransom if you hadn't changed your mind about kidnapping me?"

"I was going to telephone your husband and get him to mail it to me. I was just going to ask for five hundred francs. It wasn't much. But I'm glad it didn't work. I probably would have been caught anyway and then things would have been even worse."

He looked so inutterably miserable that if Alice had had five hundred francs, she would most gladly have given it to him.

They reached the Champs Elysées and Alice prepared to dismount. "Were the police really after us?" he asked.

"Not so far as I know."

"I didn't think so," he said gloomily. She hesitated and then, groping in her bag, she produced ten francs. "I hope this will help cover your out-of-pocket expenses," she said. "I wouldn't want you to be poorer just because you kidnapped me." He thanked her profusely and she was glad she had helped him.

"Good-bye," Alice said. "I hope you get back to Wilmington."

"Good-bye," said the man. "Thanks for being so nice."

She stood for a few minutes watching the carriage disappear, and then she set off for the hotel. She decided not to tell Arthur she had been kidnapped. He might not understand and would make difficulties about exploring Paris on her own.

He was late in getting back to the hotel—nearly six—but he was in excellent spirits and, as they sat on the sidewalk sipping their vermouth, he told Alice what a delightful gentleman Monsieur Parent was and how he was negotiating for a Degas and two Renoirs "at very special prices."

"Good," said Alice. "Your father will be pleased."

"Yes, if we bring it off it will be something of a triumph.

Monsieur Parent congratulated me on my grasp of the whole Art situation in Paris at the moment."

"What is the situation at the moment?" Alice asked, trying her best to sound at least moderately interested.

"Confused. The days of the wildly inflated prices caused by American purchasers who just wanted to show off and knew nothing about paintings as such are over. Many of the Paris dealers either don't realize this or . . ." Arthur talked on and Alice let her mind wander.

Surely, she thought to herself, Arthur hadn't been as pedantic as this before they were married. No, that was unfair. She was thinking of him as he was at parties, as he was when he was courting her, as he was when he was charming her mother. He was the same as he had always been. To study and write about this kind of thing was going to be his life's work. Just because she was ignorant didn't mean Arthur was pedantic.

"So then I said to Monsieur Albert, 'Just because I am an American doesn't mean I am eager to buy at any cost.' He knew then that he was dealing with someone who knew a thing or two."

"Who's Monsieur Albert?"

"The man I've just been telling you about, the proprietor of the gallery. Weren't you paying attention?"

"Of course I was, darling. I just didn't quite catch the name at first."

He looked at her quickly to make sure she wasn't laughing at him and, reassured, he took a sip of his vermouth and continued. "I'm afraid many Americans have only themselves to blame when they get robbed by the European dealer. I make it clear right from the start that I know what I'm talking about. Monsieur Parent, who has taken a lot of Americans around the Paris dealers, was delighted with my acumen. I really think, my dear, you might learn a great deal if you came with me on some of my excursions."

"If you'd like me to I'll be happy to come."

"Good. It will give you a better understanding of what I'm trying to do. I'm meeting Monsieur Parent here at ten o'clock tomorrow. It should only be a couple of hours. Then we'll have lunch and in the afternoon we might do some sightseeing together. I wouldn't mind seeing Notre Dame and Napoleon's Tomb."

She fought against the thought and did her best to banish

it from her mind when it intruded but surely, now that she was his wife, Arthur's attitude towards her *was* different. He spoke to her just now as though she were a child. She wasn't a child! She was Mrs. Arthur Melville! No, that too was unfair. He did, after all, want to include her in his activities. She should be pleased. She was pleased. At least it now looked as though they might have some time alone together.

After a while they went in for dinner.

"The trouble with French cooking," Arthur said, "is that they cover up everything with sauce so you can't really see what you're getting. The chicken is quite nice but I would prefer it if it wasn't smothered in all this creamy buttery nonsense with mushrooms. What's that you're having? I thought you were joking when you told me what you had ordered."

"No, they're frogs' legs."

"Real frogs' legs! My God! I've heard of them but I've never met anyone who really actually *ate* them. I was quite sure you were joking. You mean the legs of live frogs?"

"They're very nice. They chop the legs off fat bullfrogs. I expect they kill the frogs first."

"Alice, how can you talk that way?" There was no mistaking the distaste in his voice.

"Oh, Arthur, for heaven's sakes! We're in Paris. We're on our honeymoon. Can't we have some fun?"

He looked at her. "Do you consider frogs' legs *fun*? Perhaps your idea of fun and mine are different."

"Perhaps they are," Alice said casually. "In that case, we each have fun our own way." She was determined not to get sentimental as she had in the hotel room the night before.

Arthur said nothing for a time and they ate on in silence. Alice ate slowly and with, she hoped, obvious enjoyment. Finally she said, "You haven't asked me what I did today."

"Well, what did you do?"

She had changed her mind. Perhaps it would do Arthur good to know after all.

"I met a charming young man from Wilmington who tried to kidnap me."

It worked! Arthur, his wine glass halfway to his lips, twitched violently and spilt some on the table. Alice calmly went on eating her frogs' legs.

Chapter 15

He didn't ask for further details.

After a long silence, during which Arthur twice opened his mouth as if to speak and then closed it again, he apparently concluded that she was trying to make a fool of him in the same way she had tried to make a fool of Jodie Travers about the Egyptian mummy. She would leave it at that. There was no point in going on about it, and yet she would have loved to have told him the whole story about the pitiful little man, his prostitute friend, his first abortive venture into big-time crime, and his pathetic longing to return to Wilmington.

Why couldn't she? Why couldn't they laugh about it together over their liqueurs and coffee? Arthur *did* have a sense of humor. Of course he did. He had made her mother laugh at the fake Schopenhauer letter and that, she supposed, showed a sort of sense of humor; but it was too precious and intellectual. It was all right in its place but it needed a sense of fun, a sense of joy in the absurdities of the world to go with it. She would develop that in Arthur, but she wouldn't begin this evening by going on about the kidnapping.

"I'm looking forward to meeting Monsieur Parent," she said as they spooned delicately into their Gâteau aux Fraises.

"Yes, I think you'll find it interesting."

"What are you thinking about?" Alice asked. "You look as if you have something very profound on your mind."

"I'm sorry to disappoint you. Nothing profound. I was wondering if, when we finish this, it might be amusing to go for a stroll and take our coffee and liqueurs at a side-walk café. Does that appeal to you?"

"It appeals to me very much," Alice answered with enthusiasm.

"Good. That's what we'll do then. After all, this is our honeymoon." He smiled in the old way, in the way she remembered him smiling when they first met, with the corners of his mouth turned up and his deep-set dark eyes gentle and friendly. Oh, what a fool she was to think, even for a moment, that there was anything wrong with their marriage.

They walked for a half a mile and found a delightful place called Café de L'Etoile and had two little glasses of Benedictine each and two cups of café filtre.

"In America," Alice said, "this would be called the Star Café."

Arthur laughed. "Indeed it would. It would be hot and smell of fried onions and too many people in too small a space and the proprietor would be wearing a sweaty shirt open to his waist."

"You've been in such places?"

"Of course. When I was in Boston we used to go slumming. I've even been to such places in New York. My mother would be shocked if she knew it."

She had never told Arthur about the venture with Carla to Coney Island. She thought of doing so now but decided against it.

Why? Why couldn't she tell him? It had all happened so long ago. She would have to admit that she had lied and that she had stolen and, even though it was when she was a little girl, Arthur might still take it seriously. She doubted that, even as a small boy, he had lied or stolen. Perhaps she would tell him one day, but not just now. Why risk spoiling the evening?

"A penny for your thoughts," he said.

"Must I tell?"

"Of course."

"I was just thinking how lucky I was to be your wife."

"If I hadn't asked you it wouldn't have been long before someone else did. I'm glad I was the first." He paused. "I was the first, wasn't I?"

"Not quite. When I was fifteen I was practically engaged to Randy Maybank but he deserted me for another."

They both laughed.

When they got back to their hotel room, Alice threw her arms around his neck and kissed him. "Thank you for a lovely evening." She pressed close against him so that he would feel her firm round breasts. She rested her head on his shoulder. "I love you so much," she whispered. If ever there was a night for making love, this was it. Her whole body yearned for it. She longed to feel his warm, firm flesh pressing against her, holding her down, dominating her. And she would yield to him blissfully, giving him her body in total surrender. And she would know then, for sure and forever, that their marriage was the most wonderful in all the world.

Arthur submitted to her embrace for a moment or two and then, very gently but with unmistakable firmness, he removed her arms from around his neck.

"I don't know about you," he said, "but I'm weary."

"Oh, Arthur,"—she wanted him so much she was willing to humble herself, to humiliate herself even—"Oh, Arthur I . . . I want to make love. It's not late. Please, Arthur. It would be so perfect. Couldn't we . . .?"

"Don't spoil a pleasant evening," Arthur said. "We have a busy day tomorrow with Monsieur Parent in the morning and sightseeing in the afternoon. There will be plenty of time for love making when we return to New York."

The anger welled up within her and it was only with a superb effort of will that she thrust back the words which came tumbling up, clamoring to be let out. So she said nothing at first, pressing her lips together with dramatic firmness so that Arthur would observe her restraint and realize that he had wounded her. It was only when Arthur persisted in not noticing and continued to undress in his irritating, methodical way—removing everything from his pockets, placing the contents on the dressing table, folding his trousers neatly over a clothes hanger, putting his jacket over it and hanging it in the closet, then removing his undershirt and draping it over the back of the chair by the desk, then putting on his pajama top, then . . . It was only after some moments of this that Alice could restrain herself no longer.

"I'm sorry," she said acidly, "that you think that making love on our honeymoon would spoil an otherwise pleasant evening. I should have thought it might possibly enhance it."

Arthur said nothing in reply. He removed his overly large blue underwear pants, struggled into his pajama trousers, sat down again to pull off his socks, which he placed with his underwear over the back of the chair. Then he put on his slippers and dressing gown and disappeared into the bathroom.

Alice stood for a few seconds biting her lips and tense

with fury. Then she made up her mind. From the bathroom came sounds of splashing water, then silence, then the tumultuous sound of the ornate toilet being flushed. It was even less efficient than the English contraptions and she guessed he would have to flush it again once the tank filled. Then there was the sound of Arthur gargling. He gargled every night with salt and water. His mother had insisted he take a jar of special salt along with him. She had offered Alice a jar, too.

"It guards against all sorts of infections one might pick up in foreign countries," she told her. Alice had accepted the jar out of politeness but had left it at home.

So she had plenty of time to undress and, when Arthur emerged after the second flushing of the toilet, she was in her dressing gown and ready to go into the bathroom herself. She wasn't nearly as long in there as Arthur and she came out just as he was in the act of climbing in between the sheets. She was stark naked. She flung her dressing gown carelessly on the chair in the corner and turned towards him.

"You're not coming to bed like *that*!" he said in horror.

"You can wear what you like in your half of the bed and I'll wear what I like in mine."

"But you're not wearing *anything*! I think it's indecent."

Alice laughed but there was a sharp edge to her laughter. "Do you think sex is indecent, Arthur?"

"Don't be absurd. Do you think I'm a prude?" He was sitting bolt upright in bed. "I think sex has its place, of course."

"But if poor Venus had arms and was able to do so, would you just as soon she draped something over her upper self instead of standing around half-naked gazing into space?" Putting her hands behind her back and thrusting out her elbows, Alice assumed a Venus de Milo pose.

"I think the wine and the liqueurs have gone to your head," Arthur said tensely.

"I wish they had gone to yours too. Arthur, it's not the wines and liqueurs. It's Paris! It's the air! It's love! Why can't you feel it too?" She flung back her arms, stretching as far back as she could so that her back arched and her breasts were thrust out. She took a deep breath and exhaled it joyously.

"Oh for heaven's sake stop that!" Arthur was suddenly shouting.

"They'll hear you in the next room," Alice said coolly. "They'll think you're angry."

"I *am* angry. What are you trying to do?"

"I'm not trying to do anything. I'm trying to get *you* to do something. I'm trying to give you a chance to prove you're a man." She hadn't meant it to come out the way it did—suddenly, she sounded loud and strident.

He gazed at her appalled. His cheeks flushed. For a moment he had trouble finding words. Then he asked, "What do you mean by that? Are you serious?" His voice was husky and intense.

There was no backing down now. "Of course I'm serious. Did I sound as if I were joking?"

"I hoped you were. You wonder if I'm a man. Perhaps not by your standards. I'm not a sex-starved coal heaver if that's what you mean by a man."

"And I'm not a Bowery prostitute or even a Montparnasse one but I am a woman. I'm your wife and I want to be treated as your wife, and not just as a woman who happens to be traveling around with you." She went across and sat down on the bed. She tossed her head back so her hair swirled and came to rest over her bare shoulders. "Can't you understand that? Can't you see how I feel, Arthur?"

"If you want to be treated like my wife it's time you started to behave like my wife and not like an infatuated schoolgirl. Moral values and good taste go together and you are showing no evidence of possessing either at the moment."

He had got over his momentary shock and his voice was hard and cutting. Yet there was in it, Alice thought, a hint of fear, a note of defensiveness. His words were intended to hurt her but his eyes seemed to plead with her not to continue the battle.

"All right," she said quietly, "I'll put on my nightgown and come to bed."

In the darkness Alice lay awake hoping that Arthur would kiss her or at least say something. His breathing was regular, but she didn't know whether that meant he was on the edge of sleep or merely pretending.

She herself was staring wide-awake. The evening had seemed as if it might turn out to be their best as man and wife so far. Had it been her fault? Was it her pride that was hurt? Alice posed the questions dutifully to herself in order that she might dismiss them as being unworthy of serious consideration. They had perhaps fifty or sixty years of married life ahead of them. Oh my God! Neither of them could possibly endure it that long if it was all going to be like this. Perhaps she should have waited. But there had been no one else and, if she had delayed, Dorothea and Prudence would have moved into her life and tried to "organize" her and . . . Oh dear, wasn't life complicated!

If Arthur was asleep she didn't want to wake him, but she couldn't get comfortable. She tried her right side with her arm underneath her head and thought if she lay perfectly still and made her mind a blank sleep would come; but her arm began to ache and her mind refused to become a blank. Very gently she rolled over onto her front with her hands under the pillow and her head turned to the right, but after a time that wasn't satisfactory either. Ever so carefully she manipulated herself onto her left side and brought her knees up. In this position she couldn't quite decide what to do with her arms. Arms were a nuisance in bed. Yet how could one turn over without them? She settled for her right arm at her side and her left forearm under the pillow. Almost at once she realized that that wasn't going to work. Her right side was the answer. If she hadn't abandoned that position she would probably be asleep by now. Slowly and with utmost caution she maneuvered herself back again.

Her mind was the real problem. It simply refused to stop working—like some idiotic carousel at Coney Island that keeps going round and round because no one knows how to stop it. She went round and round with it all night until she saw the first light of day coming in under the heavy curtains and creeping across the rug.

Switzerland was the best.

There were no pictures to buy there, no agents to confer with, no vast art galleries to tour and suddenly Arthur was again the man Alice thought she had married. Neither of them had made mention of that night, but the remaining days in Paris had not been easy and relaxed. Alice had dutifully accompanied Arthur on his rounds with Monsieur Parent, a pompous little man with slicked-down black hair, bulging eyes, and a jerky manner who flattered Arthur so outrageously that at times Alice had to bite her cheek to keep from laughing. "You are not only a superb critic," he told him, "but also a genius of finance. Your understanding of values, both artistic and commercial, makes me amazed. And you are still a young man. In a few years it is you who should be conducting me through the maze." It seemed to Alice that he smirked after delivering himself of such an oration, but Arthur didn't appear to notice.

They had gone to Napoleon's Tomb and to the eleven-year-old Eiffel Tower of which, of course, they had read descriptions. "I should have thought," Arthur said, "that when the exhibition was over they would have torn it down."

"Why should they?" Alice asked.

"It was just a sort of trick to lure tourists. It's badly constructed. It's ugly."

"I think it's very impressive."

"In a vulgar way. It won't last. In a year or two it will fall down and be forgotten."

But in Switzerland everything was different. They stayed in a small hotel—originally called Keller's and now rechristened the Henri Dunant after the Nobel Peace Prize winner who founded the International Red Cross—in Interlaken and made excursions from there, generally on foot. They wandered the alpine meadows, carpeted with wild flowers such as neither of them had ever seen. They seemed to be able to walk and walk and walk forever without tiring and they took lunch with them—a crusty loaf, a wedge of cheese, a bottle of wine. They would leave the wine to cool in a convenient mountain brook, climb for an hour or so and then return, retrieve their bottle and sit in the shade of the trees sipping the cool, nutty wine and munching on cheese and bread. Then they would continue on down, watching the peasants cutting hay on the sunlit slopes, puzzling at the rocks on the roofs of the cabins and outbuildings, waving at the little shepherds driving flocks of white and black sheep ahead of them. It was like something out of a fairy tale.

Alice thought she had never been happier and Arthur too seemed carefree and eager. They slept together now and made love without any constraint. Every night was a perfect end to a perfect day. Their earlier problems were blown away like a puff of smoke. They had been no more substantial than that, Alice told herself, and then they drifted out of her mind entirely.

If they could only live like this forever and ever. She didn't know exactly when Arthur had decided they had to return home and she didn't ask him, because perhaps he had forgotten about it and perhaps they could stay on here for a longer time.

Then one late afternoon they got back to the hotel and, when they came into the entrance hall, which was too small to be called a lobby in the American sense, the boy behind the desk said, "There's a cablegram for you, Mrs. Melville."

Alice took the envelope from him and tore it open. "Father died this morning. Funeral Monday. Love Prudence."

She handed it to Arthur who read it and handed it back. "I'm very sorry," he said, and he bent and kissed her there as they stood in that little lobby that wasn't really a lobby.

As they went slowly up the stairs to their room Alice thought to herself, "Now, except for Arthur, I'm all alone. Pray God it will all work out."

When they got to their clean, wooden-walled bedroom with its red curtains, green bedspread, and vase of little flowers on the small table, he took her in his arms and kissed her as he had never kissed her before.

"We're leaving for home tomorrow," he told her.

She hadn't cried when her mother died and she didn't cry now, not at first, not until she got into the bathroom. And then it was only a few tears quickly stifled. She dashed her face with cold water and came out.

"Let's go and get something to eat," she said, "and then I'd better do some packing of suitcases."

He looked at her. "I love you," he said.

"I can't think why."

"Everything will be all right."

"Of course it will."

They went down to dinner hand in hand.

Chapter 16

"Did you see in the paper that the leader of a sect called 'The Chosen Ones' says that the world is going to come to an end next February?" Patricia asked.

"It was supposed to come to an end the year I was born," Alice answered, "but despite everything it still seems to go rolling on."

"It's ending because of sin this time," Patricia laughed.

"Is that why it was to end when you were born?"

"Oh no! There was a much better reason then. You see, 1881 was a year that could be written upside-down or back-to-front and come out the same. There won't be another such year until 8008. People didn't think the world could last another six or seven thousand years so it was almost certain to end then."

"I'm glad it didn't, Patricia said. She paused thoughtfully for a moment or two. "I wish I'd known your mother," she said at length. "Was she like Grandmother Melville?"

"Not much, I think. My mother had a better sense of humor." Even as she said it she realized that Patricia would resent the remark. Anything that could conceivably be construed as a slight on Arthur was instantly resented by Patricia.

"Where do you suppose Father got his wonderful sense of humor from?" Patricia asked tartly.

It occurred fleetingly to Alice to reply, "I didn't know he had one," but that would have provoked an angry and emotional scene because Patricia herself had inherited her father's inability to enjoy the absurd. So she replied, "I expect you are right, dear. I hadn't thought of that." Patricia gave a smug little smile.

The Melvilles Senior met them at the dock. They had engaged a separate carriage for the four trunks and eight suitcases which had accompanied the newlyweds on their travels, so they went home as a little procession. The footman was on the front steps waiting for them when they drew up and he and the coachman carried the luggage upstairs to the new apartment.

As soon as she saw it Alice realized that her mother-in-law did not contemplate the possibility of them setting up an establishment of their own in the near future.

It was magnificent. The house was U-shaped and the entire second floor of the west wing, which had consisted mainly of seldom-used guest rooms all these years, had been redesigned and decorated in elegant style.

Mrs. Melville had employed for the job Donald Robertson, architect father of the Jenny Robertson with whom Alice had gone to school, and she had given him full scope artistically and financially. From the rich creamy entrance hall to the spacious drawing room with its dark greens and reds and beyond into the panelled dining room with its glittering chandelier, the emphasis was on color rather than period. "It's all what he calls 'traditional contemporary,'" Mrs. Melville told them. There was a study for Arthur, a large master bedroom, three guest rooms, each with its own bathroom, a splendid large kitchen and pantry and, of course, plain but adequate servants' accommodations at the far end. "I was determined to have it all ready for you when you got back," Mrs. Melville told them, "and Mr. Robertson entered into the spirit of the thing and was most helpful with furniture, curtains, and rugs. Your father, Arthur, of course selected the paintings and supervised their hanging. So there's really nothing for you to worry about, Alice my dear. You'll want to choose your own servants, of course, but I'll help you with that."

The date was September fifth. The following day the President of the United States, William McKinley, was shot by an anarchist.

"He will not die," Arthur assured Alice with confidence. "It is quite unthinkable that that bombastic fool Roosevelt should become President." He spoke with the assurance of one who is in close consultation with the Fates and privy to their decisions. Eight days later, however, McKinley did die. Arthur regarded the event as an almost personal betrayal. "I was quite sure he wouldn't die," he told Alice. "It's wrong."

"Benton can serve as butler for all of us," Mrs. Melville told Alice. "He certainly isn't overworked. So you should be able to make do for the time being with a cook and two other servants. Your maid and Arthur's valet won't be so busy that they can't look after the cleaning and tidying. Of course I hope you'll have many of your meals with us, but when you want to be by yourselves I think the maid and valet can wait on table as well. Read *Mrs. Seely* and then we'll go down to the agency and see what we can find. In the meantime, of course, you'll be our guests."

"I thought perhaps, until we had servants of our own, I would cope," Alice said.

"Oh no, dear. I don't think so. I wouldn't want you living in our house and doing your own housekeeping. What would people say? I appreciate your desire to be independent and I respect it but you can't possibly manage without servants. We'll go and find some next week. In the meanwhile we'll all be one big happy family." Arthur appeared to accept this arrangement without hesitation and Alice, who strongly suspected that the time to take a stand would come shortly, decided it was a little early to have a row with her mother-in-law. The issue wasn't a big enough one—yet.

Mrs. Melville was a person who never, even fleetingly, entertained either the possibility that she might conceivably be mistaken in her judgments or that anyone might contest them. She was exceptionally tall and held herself with queenly erectness. Her dark brown almost black hair was swirled and pinned about her head and down the back of her neck almost like a turban. Her eyes were catlike and commanding. She always wore dark dresses. Even for their spring wedding she had worn purple. When she moved she seemed to glide rather than take steps. She was going to be a formidable opponent, Alice decided, in those first early days. Mr. Melville spent most of his time in his study or the gallery. He was a shadowy figure about the house.

It had been plain to Alice some time before the marriage that Arthur would never care to offend his mother. Now it became obvious that he would do everything in his power to win her approval, to placate her when she showed the slightest hint of annoyance.

To make him into her husband rather than his mother's son was going to prove an even greater challenge than she had originally supposed.

MRS. SEELY'S COOK BOOK WITH CHAPTERS ON DO-
MESTIC SERVANTS, THEIR RIGHTS AND DUTIES

A servant has a right to ask questions about the
place in a respectful manner, and he should gain all
the information he legitimately can about the character and demands of the household to which he thinks
of going.

A servant obtaining employment by any false or
forged letter or certificate of recommendation is
guilty of a misdemeanor. A misdemeanor is punish-
able by imprisonment in a penitentiary or county jail
for not more than one year, or by a fine of not more
than $500.00, or by both.

Duties of Lady's Maid: . . . well-mannered, respectable looking young woman . . . a tolerable good dress-
maker and a good hairdresser.

Her first morning duty is to dress her mistress.
About this it is impossible to give directions . . .

. . . It is the maid's duty to undress her mistress
and remain in attendance until she is dismissed.

A respectful manner is necessary in a lady's maid.
She is not to keep her seat when her mistress is speaking to her . . .

A good deal of sitting up at night is sometimes required from a lady's maid.

Duties of Valet: . . . attends to the lighting of the fire
and warming his master's bedroom. He then cleans his
boots and shoes . . . prepares his master's bath, and
is sometimes expected to shave his master.

It was published in New York and London by Macmillan
and Mrs. Melville had got copies for herself and Alice. "It's
such a sensible, down-to-earth book," she told her
daughter-in-law. "I don't see how it can ever be out-
dated."

Apart from occasionally helping Mrs. Grimble by shell-
ing peas or stirring a sauce when she was a small girl, Alice
had had no experience in the kitchen. Once, when she was
eleven or twelve, she had asked her mother if she could

learn to cook and her mother had replied, "Life is short enough without wasting time learning things that will never be of any practical use to you. I am the first to admit that fine cooking is an art but it is not one with which a young lady in your position need concern herself beyond cultivating a discriminating palate. Concentrate on your ballet and French."

Nonetheless she read the recipes in Mrs. Seely's book with fascination.

> *"Lobster à la Portland"* Take off the tails and big claws of three medium-sized female lobsters. Remove the string which runs through the center of each tail and cut crosswise in five or six pieces. Crack the claws and place them on a plate. Boil the bodies . . .
>
> *"Brains with Mushrooms"* Prepare the brain of an ox by washing and skimming it . . .
>
> *"Calf's Head"* The butcher should first prepare the head for use. Wash it thoroughly and remove the brains which may be kept for frying, as mock oysters, or may be added later. Cover with cold water, take off the scum as the head begins to heat . . .

They sat in one of the interviewing rooms of Mrs. Scott's Agency for the Placement of High Quality Domestic Servants. Mrs. Melville had made the preliminary arrangements and they had already engaged a young man by the name of Arnold Crump as Arthur's valet and a general Useful Man. A cook called Mrs. Walding had also been selected. Now they were in the process of completing the domestic staff with the choosing of Alice's maid, who would also be expected to help Arnold Crump with general cleaning and serving duties. They had narrowed the field to two and were sitting alone in the little room debating which would be the more suitable. Mrs. Melville favored the recently arrived English girl, Eileen Courtney—plain, stolid, willing, not too bright, easily ordered about. Alice held out for Maureen Juba whose mother had come from Ireland and father from the Ukraine. She was a small, red-headed, perky girl born in Brooklyn.

"She's the impertinent sort," Mrs. Melville said. "I know her type."

"But she's the one I'm going to have," Alice said. "It's my maid we're engaging."

Mrs. Melville looked at her daughter-in-law. She was not accustomed to being spoken to in that way. After a moment's hesitation she said, "I suppose it's only right to let you make your own mistakes. Have it your way."

Alice smiled inwardly but she gave no outward sign of satisfaction at having won her first argument with her mother-in-law. There would be more.

Though she felt some slight sympathy for Arthur, trapped, as he seemed to consider himself to be, between his wife and his mother, Alice had no intention of providing an easy solution to his problem by subordinating herself to Mrs. Melville's will. She was Arthur's wife and as such, it must be plainly understood by all concerned, was more important than his mother.

One advantage—the only one she could think of—of sharing this vast house with the Melvilles Senior was that she was spared from having to establish her own "At Home" day and time. Mrs. Melville's day was Tuesday and she told Alice that she expected her to be present.

Alice didn't fight it. Her own mother had always attached great importance to the custom which, she had said repeatedly, "is the most satisfactory and civilized manner of keeping up to date socially."

It was at the very first "At Home" of the new season, towards the end of September, which precipitated Alice and her mother-in-law into their first real trial of strength.

It was a better attended affair than usual, partly because there was so much news to catch up on after the long summer and partly because people were curious to see how the young bride and her mother-in-law were shaking down together under the same roof. Alice was talking to a Mrs. Selbourne, a large-boned, large-featured woman with a deceptively mild manner and a highly developed capacity for creating mischief. Alice remembered her mother saying, "That woman is a direct descendant of the serpent that caused all the trouble in the Garden of Eden."

"It must be so nice for you and your husband to be living here rather than in a place of your own," Mrs. Selbourne said. "I mean, so many young people these days want to be independent. It's refreshing to find a young cou-

ple who are willing to do what you're doing. Of course
Arthur and his mother have always been so close."

Out of the corner of her eye Alice could see Mrs. Melville watching them from across the room.

"Oh, we're quite independent," Alice answered. "Arthur
and I lead our own lives."

"Of course you do. Of course. But you don't have the
worrisome responsibilities of most newly married couples
and of course Arthur could never really be happy away
from his mother, do you think? It seems a perfect arrangement to me. You and your mother-in-law can share him."

Alice was well aware of what was happening. She saw
the web spread and the spider waiting for her to blunder
into it. Caution told her to get up and move away but Alice
was not by nature a cautious person. She knew other people were listening. She saw Mrs. Melville get up casually
and seat herself again within earshot.

"We don't *share* Arthur," she said crisply. "He's my husband. We are living here temporarily while we find a house
of our own."

"Oh really! Does your mother-in-law realize that?"

"Of course she does. That has been the understanding all
along."

"Oh, I was quite mistaken then. So you're busy looking
at houses. Have you seen any properties that appeal to you
yet?"

"No, not yet."

"But you are looking? What real estate firm are you
dealing with?"

"We haven't decided."

"So you're *not* looking at the moment. I must ask my
husband to get in touch with Arthur. He has some very
good connections with people in the property business."

"That won't be necessary. When the time comes my husband is quite capable of making the necessary arrangements himself."

"Oh, please don't be offended. I was just trying to be
helpful. You say 'when the time comes.' Of course the time
may never come. You may decide you like the protected
life here so much more than being on your own. I'm sure
Arthur and his mother would prefer it that way."

"I expect we shall move soon after Christmas."

That, at last, was too much for Mrs. Melville. "Oh, I

don't think so, dear," she said icily. "I'm sorry to butt in but I couldn't help overhearing your conversation. I don't think Arthur has it in mind to move as soon as that." Then, turning to Mrs. Selbourne, "They are entirely on their own. You are of course thinking of what the situation might be in a small house like yours but in a house this size we can go our own ways without interfering with each other at all."

"So you'll be staying here after all," said Mrs. Selbourne, turning to Alice.

"I expect so," Mrs. Melville said ominously without giving Alice a chance to reply.

"We'll be staying until we find a suitable place of our own," Alice said evenly. "As I said we shall probably move after Christmas."

"I don't think so, my dear," repeated Mrs. Melville. "Arthur and I have discussed the matter."

"Arthur and I have discussed it as well," Alice replied.

"It seems to have been very thoroughly discussed," Mrs. Selbourne said happily.

Mrs. Melville stood up. "And this is neither the time nor the place to discuss it further."

"I agree," said Alice, meeting her mother-in-law's glare with a steadfast stare of her own.

The winner was Mrs. Selbourne, Alice decided. Between the two Mrs. Melvilles it had been a draw.

Alice steeled herself for what would happen after the ladies had departed.

Chapter 17

Alice had gone up to their apartment just before the tea party came to an end. She half expected Mrs. Melville to follow her there in due course but now it was after five and there was no sign of her. Arthur, who had left after lunch to spend the afternoon at the New York Public Library, was due anytime now. She would explain everything to him. It was absolutely imperative that he see this situation from her point of view. This had to be his great moment of decision.

Mrs. Melville obviously thought of her as a nineteen-year-old girl who should show proper deference and do as she was told. She was a nineteen-year-old *wife* and therein lay all the difference. Mrs. Melville must be forced to recognize that difference and Arthur must help in forcing such recognition on her. It would not be easy.

When she wanted reassurance it had always been Alice's custom to go and survey herself in the mirror. She did so now and what she saw banished any possible wisps of doubt as to her ability to dominate the situation. She stood erect with her head tilted slightly back so that her chin had an aristocratic look about it. Her blue eyes stared at their reflection unblinkingly. "I am a Barrington," she said aloud, "the daughter of Amy Barrington, and I am more than a match for Agnes Melville." She thought of *The Boy Prince of Rajasthan* and the marvelous illustration of him with his sword raised above his head. "What a pair we would have made!" she said in a whisper. Then she smiled, because that was a childish thought and she had put away childish things.

She had asked Mrs. Walding, her newly acquired cook, to make fricasseed veal for dinner. It was a dish which, served with lots of little mushroom buttons and thick cream, had always been a favorite of hers even as a child and she thought it would help prove to Arthur that she was quite capable of maintaining a first-class establishment without any help from his mother. She was determined to convert him to the best dishes—the ones, that is, that she liked best and were more suitably sophisticated than those he professed to prefer.

There would be consommé first with sherry in it, stuffed tomatoes and potato croquettes to go with the fricassee, Chocolate Bavaroise to end with. All the recipes were taken from Mrs. Seely's cookbook so that if Mrs. Melville expressed any criticism when she inquired later what they had had, Alice would be ready with an answer which could not be quarrelled with.

This was to be her first attempt at something like a "special" dinner. Up to now they had been giving Mrs. Walding a chance to get "settled in" and, even though they now had servants of their own, they had had frequent dinners with the Melvilles Senior. The ones they had had on their own had been chicken and chops and such relatively plain fare.

Mrs. Walding, a pleasant, fair-haired widow of forty-two, whose husband, a New England fisherman, had been drowned, leaving her with three small children, had said, "I'm better with lobster but this will be no problem." Mrs. Walding's children were, Alice discovered, being looked after by paternal grandparents in Lynn, Massachusetts until their mother made enough money in the big city of New York to return and look after them herself.

Maureen had set the table with a low floral arrangement in the center, candles, and three wine glasses—sherry, claret, and port. Alice inspected it and approved. She herself had readied the ingredients for the martini cocktail which they would enjoy in the drawing room after they had changed and before going in for dinner—Boker's bitters, maraschino, Old Tom gin, vermouth, sliced lemons, and a silver bowl which would have lumps of ice in it. Maureen would carry the tray in when the time came and Arthur would do the mixing.

All was ready. It was nearly six. But there was no sign of Arthur. "He's talking to his mother downstairs," Alice thought. "On the floor below the battle has already begun."

At six ten Alice decided to change into the long, ice-blue silk dress with silver trimmings which her mother had ordered from Paris for her in time for her eighteenth birthday. Her mother had not been afraid of Agnes Melville and would have been ashamed of her if she had shown any timidity. No. Tonight she would prove herself. If Mrs. Melville wanted a confrontation she should have one. Alice would make it quite clear that she was a Barrington. She inspected herself in the full-length mirror and went back to the drawing room just as an agitated Arthur came hurrying in.

"What on earth have you been up to?" he demanded. "Mother is very angry. You must go down and apologize right away."

"I shall do nothing of the sort," Alice answered coolly. "If your mother wishes to apologize to me I am quite willing to forget the whole nonsense. As soon as you have changed, the martini cocktails will be ready for you to mix."

"Martini cocktails? I don't know what you're talking about. Mother is very upset."

"I expect she'll get over it. We might wander down and say good night to them before they go to bed."

"You don't seem to understand."

"Oh yes. I understand very well indeed. Either you are your mother's son or you are my husband. You're both, of course, but you've got to decide which has top priority."

"You won't go down and apologize to Mother?"

"I certainly will not."

"We're living under their roof."

"That wasn't my idea."

"Alice dear, do be reasonable. Mother may turn us both out."

"Really? You couldn't have said anything more encouraging."

"Do keep your voice down. The servants will hear."

"I'm sure they will. I'm sure they've heard a good deal of what your mother was saying about me downstairs."

"You know better than that. Mother would never criticize you in front of the servants."

"But she doesn't hesitate to do so behind my back. And you presumably agreed with her?"

"I didn't agree or disagree. I . . ."

"How very brave and decisive of you! I should have thought most husbands would have stood up for their wives."

"But Mother said you were extremely rude and humiliated her before all her friends."

"I was not rude at all. I merely said that we hoped to move into a place of our own after Christmas."

"That's the first I've heard of it and it certainly took Mother by surprise. After all the trouble and expense they've been to to create this lovely apartment, you suddenly announce we're going to move out. No wonder Mother was shocked. What kind of gratitude is that?"

"Your mother designed this apartment as a trap. She couldn't bear the idea of her one and only child, her darling boy, growing up and leaving home. She wanted him married, because all nice little boys grow up and get married, but she didn't want to lose control over him. So she would lure him into her trap—a magnificently furnished apartment—and burden him with an obligation of gratitude. Well, I don't feel obligated. I want us to lead our own lives and if you were half the man I thought you were when we married you would feel the same way."

Arthur paled. He opened his mouth to say something and closed it again. Then, finally, he asked, "Do you realize what you are saying?"

"Of course I do," Alice replied briskly. "Now shall I ask Maureen to bring in the tray so you can mix us a cocktail? I think we both need one after that little conversation."

He looked at her in amazement. "How can you possibly suggest such a thing? I certainly can't sit up here sipping a martini knowing that Mother is waiting downstairs. She is very upset."

"So you mentioned earlier. Then I shall have to drink alone. If I get Maureen to bring in the tray, perhaps you would be good enough to mix me a cocktail before you join your mother."

"You can't sit here and drink alone. You're only a nineteen-year-old girl."

"I guessed that might be the phrase your mother would use. I am not just a nineteen-year-old girl; I am the wife of Arthur Melville and I would like to be proud of that title. I'd like to feel my husband was a man."

There was a long pause.

"Of course I'm a man," Arthur said quietly at length. "You seem to have been having doubts about that ever since we got married."

"Only when you fail to act like one."

"Alice, please be reasonable. I'm only trying to keep peace. You know how Mother is."

"Sometimes the price of peace can be too high. If we

give in to your mother now it will be all the more difficult to stand up to her the next time. Can't you see that? You're in danger, Arthur, of never growing up—of remaining always the good little boy who would never do anything without asking Mummy first."

"It's easy for you to talk. Your mother's dead."

"Yes, my mother is dead and I miss her very much, but I'm not lost without her the way you will be when your mother dies. You'll be quite incapable by then of making up your own mind and there won't be anyone around to make it up for you."

"Tell Maureen to bring in the tray. We'll have a cocktail and then we must go down. Mother will wonder what's happened to me. I won't bother to change."

"And what did you do at the Library?" Alice asked brightly as they sipped their drinks.

"I read," Arthur answered miserably.

Before they had quite finished their cocktails Maureen appeared again and said, "Dinner is served, ma'am."

Arthur looked nervously at his watch. "I really should go down and see Mother. She won't know . . ."

"It's a very special dinner. You wouldn't want me to eat alone. After dinner we'll go down together. You would prefer we go down together, wouldn't you?"

"I don't think I'm very hungry."

"It isn't a big dinner. It won't take us long to eat. Your mother and father are probably at their dinner anyway and we couldn't, as you say, discuss things in front of the servants."

Arthur started out tentatively but the cocktail was beginning to work on him and, after a glass of sherry with the consommé, he tasted the fricassee of veal and apparently decided he might as well relax and enjoy life—for the moment, at any rate. He had two glasses of claret as well and, when the creamy chocolate dessert arrived, he smiled with pleasure. It was Alice who suggested, "Let's leave our coffee and port until we come back up after seeing your parents."

He agreed, Alice thought, with a trace of reluctance. He wanted to go downstairs now even less than she did. He couldn't conceal his nervousness.

Mrs. Melville was seated alone in the large, opulently furnished drawing room where the disastrous "At Home" had taken place earlier. She had changed, Alice noticed, and was wearing a long black dress with a purple sash and gold collar and cuffs. Mr. Melville had been banished or had banished himself to the library or, more likely, his gallery where he could sit in peace and silently contemplate his paintings. He did so quite often of an evening. "I'm sorry Edwin's not here," Mrs. Melville would say at such times, "but he needs his periods of solitude."

She glanced up as they appeared at the arched doorway. "How very gracious of you to appear," she said. "I trust you didn't let the fact that you were both being extremely rude to me in any way interfere with your appetites. You both look well wined and dined, I am glad to see."

"Very well indeed," Alice replied coolly. "We had fricassee of veal out of Mrs. Seely's cookbook."

"Mother, I would have come down sooner but . . ."

"Oh please don't apologize, Arthur," Mrs. Melville cut in. "You're a married man now and if your young bride wishes you to be cold and inconsiderate to your mother then I suppose that is the way it must be."

"You are not being at all fair, Mrs. Melville," Alice said. "If anyone is being cold and inconsiderate it is you."

"How dare you say such a thing? After all we have done for you?"

Arthur looked at his wife, appalled, but she pretended not to notice. "I've got her now," she thought. "She's lost her temper. If I can make her angrier still she'll lose more than that. Calmly does it."

"How dare you?" Mrs. Melville said again.

Alice sat down and managed a smile. "Do you want an honest answer?"

"Of course! What other kind of answer did you suppose I'd want?"

"Perhaps the kind of answer you get from people who are afraid of you, including Arthur at times."

"What nonsense! Are you afraid of me, Arthur?"

He didn't answer. He went and sat down too and in doing so, Alice realized, formed the apex of the little triangle—Mrs. Melville on the sofa, Alice on the low, armless chair, upholstered in red velvet, and Arthur now sitting crouched and uneasy on a green footstool which was too small for him.

"Well?" asked Mrs. Melville, turning to Alice. "Are we to have your answer?"

"Your question was: 'How dare I say that you are being cold and inconsiderate?' "

"That was my question."

"I don't say things like that easily," Alice replied, leaning slightly forward in her chair, "and I didn't say it in a fit of temper. I said it because whether you realize it or not, that is what you are being. You would sooner spoil our marriage than admit to yourself that Arthur is a grown man now and no longer needs you as he did when he was a child."

"That is a stupid, wicked thing to say. I have merely tried to do what is best for you."

"Isn't it time we ourselves decided what's best for us?"

"You are an insolent young woman. I should have thought your mother would have done a better job of bringing you up but, of course, she was dying during your most important years and lost control, I expect."

"If she thinks she's going to make me cry," Alice thought to herself, "she's wrong. Never, never, never would I give her that satisfaction."

"I have only been trying to do what your mother would undoubtedly have tried to do herself had she been stronger. I was singularly blessed in my own parents' guidance of me."

"My mother was frail physically during the last part of her life but her mind and her will were strong. She was strong enough to face the fact that her children were grown up. She would never have interfered." Alice was not certain, as she said this, that it was strictly true. She could imagine her mother at least trying to interfere, but not to this extent.

"I'm sure your mother did her best, considering her background. She was a governess or something like that when she met your father, was she not?"

"She was an assistant governess, the daughter of a minister. She worked very hard. Did you ever do anything useful, Mrs. Melville? Did you ever work hard?"

"I will not tolerate this impertinence one minute longer. I refuse to be insulted in my own house."

"Is it an insult to ask you if you ever worked hard?" Alice asked.

Mrs. Melville stood up. "Arthur," she asked dramatically, "are you going to allow your wife to speak to your own mother this way?"

Arthur had been sitting staring at the crumbling coals in the fireplace. Alice had glanced this way once or twice very quickly but she had not wanted to remove her eyes for more than a fleeting second from the stern face of her adversary. Now, however, she turned to look at him and, raising his head, he looked at her and their eyes met and locked for a moment. Then he looked up at his mother, who was almost towering above him.

Slowly he got to his feet and, turning to Alice, who was also standing now, made the speech of his lifetime. "Shall we go back up to our apartment?" he asked. "Our coffee and port are waiting."

"Arthur!" Mrs. Melville's voice was filled with pain and disbelief. "Arthur you can't . . ."

"Good night, Mother," he said. He bent and kissed her on the forehead.

Then he took his wife's arm and they walked out of the room.

Chapter 18

She felt no sense of triumph—no, not even a faint desire to parade her victory. There was no need. The evening was only referred to once again when, years later, she was sitting by the bedside of the dying Mrs. Melville and looking with admiration at the crumpled old face which retained still a vestige of its former pride and arrogance. "I love you very much," she said.

"You didn't always," the tired voice answered.

"I was very young."

"Was I horrid to you?"

"No, not really. I realized after that evening when we quarreled that you were an acquired taste—like olives."

The old face smiled. "You say the nicest things, my dear." She was holding Alice's hand in hers and she squeezed it.

Her twentieth birthday. She could have gone to the doctor a week before or a week later but she deliberately chose November seventeenth because she thought it would be fun to give Arthur a sort of birthday present in reverse and also, in years to come, she would say to her son, "I first knew that I was going to have you on my twentieth birthday." She decided that on the way home she would stop and get two bottles of champagne. They would have Arthur's parents up to announce to them that they were to be grandparents. It would be a happy, happy evening.

She knew when it had happened. Switzerland, after a long hike and a splendid dinner of spring lamb with local wine and wild strawberries with gollops of whipped cream. And then bed, with Arthur. They had had many good nights in Switzerland, but that was a very special one. That was when. They would call him Arthur, of course, but there should be a middle name, a Swiss name, perhaps Thun, to be a sort of secret family joke. No, not a joke—just a remembrance . . . a remembrance of that special night. There had been other special nights since, of course, but that was the one that mattered most. That was a night she would always remember—always.

When she got back Arthur wasn't yet home. She simply couldn't keep the news to herself. She thought of going down to tell Mrs. Melville, but that would spoil the surprise that evening. No one knew there was any possibility at all; no one knew she had been to the doctor. But she had to tell somebody or she'd burst, so she went into the kitchen and told Mrs. Walding. "I've just found out I'm going to have a baby," she blurted out. "You're the first to know."

Mrs. Walding was boiling bones to make stock and was just taking a sip when Alice burst in. She sipped more than she meant to and the burning liquid went down the wrong way. She coughed; her eyes watered but, putting the spoon down on the counter she turned and, to Alice's surprise and pleasure, embraced her and planted a brothy kiss on her cheek. "I thought as much," she said. "I saw it in your eyes two weeks ago."

Neither her mother nor Mrs. Melville would have approved of her being hugged and kissed by the cook, Alice thought, and that, for the moment, made it all the better. She kissed her back and said, "Not a word to the others." But, at that moment Maureen came in and so, of course, she had to be told too and Alice, giddy with the joy of it, said, "Let's all have a glass of sherry."

"I'll go and get Arnie," Maureen said and, before Alice could stop her, she was off to fetch Arnold Crump.

Mrs. Walding got the glasses, Arnold got the sherry from the sideboard in the dining room and filled them; and it was at that moment that she heard Arthur calling her. Instant consternation. Arnold Crump grabbed the decanter, apparently intending to rush it back to the dining room; Mrs. Walding turned towards the sink to empty her glass down the drain; Maureen stood stock still with the color mounting in her pretty cheeks. Alice smiled and, motioning them all to calm themselves, she went out through the pantry into the dining room and called, "Come into the kitchen, darling. You're just in time."

She held the door open for him. "What on earth is all this about?" He was quite obviously annoyed but puzzlement and shyness were the feelings that showed most plainly on his dark, handsome face. Alice didn't give him a chance to say anything. "I couldn't wait!" she told him. "I couldn't wait! I had to tell someone. You're going to be a father. You're going to be the father of a son and his name will be Arthur."

He looked at her first with something like incredulity on his face, and then that expression dissolved into astonishment and he smiled and took her in his arms right there in the kitchen in front of the servants. "Well," he said, releasing her, "isn't anybody going to give *me* a glass of sherry?"

After dinner, as they were sitting by the fire waiting for Arthur's parents to arrive so that they could bring out the champagne and announce the news to them, Arthur said, "I think perhaps we won't mention our little kitchen party to them. They might not understand."

"I think you're right," Alice told him. "It was fun though, wasn't it?"

He smiled—a grave smile, half for her and half for himself. "Yes, it was. I've never had sherry in the kitchen with the servants before. They're very decent people and I'm sure they won't take advantage of it."

When Mr. and Mrs. Melville arrived and were told the glad tidings, Mrs. Melville embraced her daughter-in-law almost as warmly as Mrs. Walding had done earlier. Mr. Melville gave her a somewhat sedate little peck on her left cheek. It didn't imply lack of affection. He was by nature shy and undemonstrative.

It was a happy evening. They finished both bottles of champagne but, as the parents stood by the door about to depart, Mr. Melville said a strange thing. "I hope your son will enjoy his life. It is not an easy thing to do."

When they were gone Alice asked, "What did your father mean by that?"

"I'm not sure. I've heard him say such things before. He's not really a very happy man, I'm afraid."

Alice was too happy herself to think anything more about it then, but later she remembered.

Mrs. Melville of course took a keen and at times almost obsessive interest in Alice's pregnancy. There was no further talk of them moving out. Alice, having won her battle, realized that she didn't really care all that much after all. They certainly couldn't move until after little Arthur was born anyway. It would be too cruel to deprive Mrs. Melville of the pleasure of having Arthur the Second born in her own house.

And Arthur himself was wonderful. How could she ever have doubted, even for a moment, that they would make a go of it together? He took to bringing her tea before breakfast. Despite the minor breakthrough of the kitchen sherry party she knew how hard it must be for him to go into the kitchen each morning in pajamas and dressing gown to collect the tray from Mrs. Walding. Then he would get back into bed beside her and they would plan little Arthur's upbringing and education. Sometimes the tea made her feel a little sick but she always greeted its arrival with pretended delight.

"I've never asked you why you were called Arthur," she said one morning.

"And I've never asked you why you were called Alice."

"Not after the Wonderland girl." She took a final gulp of her tea. It was finished at last. She put the cup and saucer on the tray beside her bed.

"More?" Arthur inquired eagerly.

"No, thank you. It was delicious. I was named after an aunt, an older sister of my mother. I never saw her but I had a miniature which was done just before she got married. When Prudence and Dorothea were so busy closing up the house and selling everything after Father's death they managed to lose it, which annoys me. She was a beautiful woman. So was Mother, of course."

"And so are you."

"I led up to that well, didn't I? Tell me about Arthur."

"Must you know?"

"Of course. Why not?"

"You might not guess it, but Mother is an incurable romantic and of course she always had absurd expectations for me."

"Why absurd?"

"I am named after King Arthur."

Alice's first inclination was to laugh but Arthur looked so miserable that she checked herself. "That makes me Guinevere."

"I suppose so," he said vaguely. He was obviously thinking of something and Alice didn't interrupt his thoughts. Finally he was ready to speak again. "One mistake we must never make, Alice, is to give little Arthur the idea that we expect too much of him. That's terribly unfair."

"What if it isn't a boy after all? What if little Arthur is a girl?"

"I won't be disappointed. Will you?"

"Of course not. I think we want an assortment."

He smiled gravely. There was more on his mind. She waited. "I don't quite know how to put this," he said, "but I think I should tell you that I appreciate what you have done for me."

"I haven't . . ."

"No, don't interruupt. You've given me something . . . oh, I don't know . . . a sort of freedom I've never had before. You were right to be critical of me even though I didn't react very well. You were right to stand up to Mother."

"I was probably horrid."

"No, you weren't. You were honest. You're the most honest person I've ever known."

"Oh, for heaven's sake, Arthur. Let's not get solemn."

"I feel solemn this morning."

"We won't be too solemn with little Arthur, will we?"

"No. No, we won't. I want him to be a happy boy. I had to sort of learn wit and charm. I want it to be natural with him."

"Why don't you ever have tea before breakfast with me?"

"I don't like it."

Alice opened her mouth to say something and then closed it again. Her morning cup of tea was a small sacrifice if it pleased Arthur.

She did everything the doctor told her. She drank lots of milk, went for walks in Central Park, ate sensibly, and didn't stay up late. Sometimes Arthur came with her on her walks. It was a mild winter with less overcast and more watery sunshine than usual. There was little snow until January.

Sometimes they talked politics. Arthur was critical of the big mergers that were taking place in some industries and "particularly of the United States Steel Corporation which is combining the already swollen corporations of Gates, Rockefeller, Carnegie, and others in a trust capitalized at

$1,400,000,000." The way Arthur said it, the figure seemed even larger.

"I don't like it," he said. "It's not right. And the insurance companies paying $100,000 to executives who do no work instead of reducing the rates." He didn't object, however, to the cheap labor imported from southern Europe in order to keep wages down. "The working classes must be disciplined," he told Alice. "They must be kept under control."

He picked up all this talk, Alice was well aware, at his club where he frequently took lunch but he passed it on to her as if it were the distillation of his own thinking. She didn't mind.

"In dealing with the big corporations we call trusts," Roosevelt said, "we most resolutely propose to proceed by evolution and not by revolution." Arthur approved of that.

"He's growing into the job," Arthur told her. "He's maturing."

Alice agreed. She would agree with almost anything Arthur said these days. He was so good and so kind. Marriage was a marvelous invention and childbearing was the most wonderful offshoot of it. Never in all her life had she been happier. Not even during that blissful summer when she was in love with Randy Maybank. This was the real thing. It was for this that she had been born.

At night, before she climbed into bed, she looked at herself in the mirror and gently stroked her swelling tummy. Little Arthur was in there waiting for his moment.

He was born almost exactly on schedule—May fifth. He lived for less than three hours.

Chapter 19

Alice felt occasionally that she spent a disproportionate amount of her leisure time—and it was almost all leisure time now—reflecting on the past. But what else was there to do? Approaching her mid-nineties there wasn't much point in speculating on what the future might hold. The present was a virtually featureless plane with regular signposts along the path she followed across it which read: "Get up," "Breakfast," "Lunch," "Afternoon snooze," "Tea," "Gin and tonic," "Supper," "Go to bed." Where she lived now the Pacific spread itself out mile after mile after mile to the west to the end of the world where the sun went down. But behind her was the wide land and, while her eyes looked out over the Ocean, her mind traveled back over the mountains and the forests, across the flat lands and more forests and hills and rivers to the Atlantic seaboard—to the City of New York which had been and always would be her home town.

She had never thought of it as an enchanted city and now, even in her most nostalgic moods, never did her remembrances of her girlhood and early married days bathe either the City or the time in a flood of golden light. Places and times might well be better now than they were then. She wouldn't have argued that. But New York had been her place and that time had been her time.

Mrs. Seely's band of followers had lived secure in their ignorance and a vast number of others lived now insecurely in theirs . . .

"Don't be foolish in regard to wearing a cap. It is a great improvement to one's appearance and is worn by all first class servants. Be sure to keep the hair tidy."—Mrs. Seely, *Don'ts for Servants.*

"I only work fourteen hours a day. My parents say I'm lucky."—Girl of eleven, factory employee, New York 1883.

"Hell, I'm rich. It's time I had some fun."—Diamond Jim Brady.

"I have been reading the morning paper. I do it every

morning, well knowing that I shall find in it the usual de-pravities and baseness and hypocrisies and cruelties that make up civilization."—Mark Twain.

"Farewell, Age of Iron: all hail, King Steel!"—Andrew Carnegie.

"In small households the cook has ever other Sunday afternoon and evening, one evening in the week after din-ner is served, and occasionally an afternoon, say from three to ten thirty. If no kitchen maid is kept, the cook prepares the dinner and the laundress cooks it."—Mrs. Seely, *The Servants' Hall*.

"They told me if I joined the union we could make them pay us enough to buy proper food for the kids. I know now I was wrong."—Pittsburgh miner at hearing, 1897.

"As soon as a guest is seated and has taken his napkin and bread from his plate, the butler puts down on it an-other on which are oysters, clams or melons, according to the season, neatly arranged on a small doily."—Mrs. Seely, *Dinners and Dinner-Giving*.

Such statements and a thousand more like them had jux-taposed themselves on Alice's consciousness for many years. Some of the cruel contrasts between the life she knew and the life of the poor disturbed her. A widowed mother from eastern Europe had killed her four children and herself leaving a note to say that she hadn't been able to find work and couldn't bear watching the children starv-ing to death.

"She must have been quite unbalanced," Mrs. Melville declared airily. "Why didn't she put her children in an in-stitution? I do wish the papers wouldn't print this kind of sensational nonsense."

A ball given by Mrs. Astor was reported, a good deal more prominently, in the same edition. The guests, all of them from the exclusive Four Hundred, had dined, "shortly after midnight, on smoked salmon, quail, suckling pig and other delicacies."

Such stories disturbed Alice more than they disturbed most of those around her. But they didn't keep her awake at night. There was nothing she could do about the way the world was. She was, after all, only a woman.

She also allowed herself to be comforted, if not entirely convinced, by Arthur and the others who assured her that the conditions in Europe from which "these people" had escaped were so appalling that their new lives in America were like heaven.

"This land is full of opportunities simply waiting to be seized by anyone with energy and ambition." Arthur told her. "At twenty-one John Rockefeller was merely a book-keeper from Cleveland and twelve years later he owned ninety percent of all American refineries. Andrew Carnegie at twelve worked in a factory and has just now made a deal to sell out his steel interests for $250,000,000. Do you suppose people like that expected people like you to go around feeling sorry for them?"

Alice supposed not.

That spring of the baby's death Alice had little inclination to concern herself with the pitiful lot of European immigrants. She had troubles enough much closer to home to occupy her mind.

Though Alice herself had naturally been deeply depressed by the event, Arthur had been almost devastated by it. The Reverend Barnstable hadn't helped matters.

Like most of their friends neither Alice's family nor the Melvilles had ever regarded religion as a vital necessity in their day to day lives. They felt, however, morally and socially obliged to identify themselves with a church and be seen to attend it fairly regularly. They felt much the same towards the Metropolitan Opera, which many of them had helped establish less than twenty years before. Both the Church and the Opera were important features of the urbane way of life which was, they realized, now that they had discovered it, the only sort of life worth living.

The Barringtons and the Melvilles and their friends had needed, however, a particular kind of church. It had to be Anglican, of course—or Episcopalian as they now preferred to call it—but not just a run-of-the-mill Episcopalian church. It had to be a church which not only understood their particular way of life but could also, to some extent, share it. Such a church must be presided over by a particularly sensitive minister. They found the church in St. Aiden's and the minister in the Reverend Austin Barnstable.

He was a large, comfortable man with thick brown hair, a florid complexion, and a splendidly deep, mellifluent voice which could endow the most commonplace utterance, such as a comment on the state of the weather, with deep spiritual significance. His popularity as a preacher was well deserved. Instead of leaving the church after the Sunday service feeling, at least for a fleeting moment, that they were indeed "miserable sinners," the faithful at St. Aiden's came away confirmed in their belief that they were exemplary champions of the Christian way of life.

Barnstable was particularly good at funerals. He always conveyed the unmistakable impression that the dear departed had been summoned because God needed his or her help in managing Heaven. When he said, "Let not your heart be troubled: ye believe in God, believe also in me," most members of the congregation truly felt that a belief in Barnstable and a belief in God were synonymous. When he went on to say, "In my Father's house are many mansions," these same people took it as reassurance that living conditions up above would prove as satisfactory as those they presently enjoyed in New York City.

At the age of twelve or thirteen Alice had been confirmed at St. Aiden's. She remembered her white dress; she remembered feeling very pure and quite worthy of the Boy Prince of Rajasthan when she renounced "the pomps and vanity of this wicked world and all the sinful lusts of the flesh"; she remembered that for lunch afterwards they had had boxed broiled chicken with mushroom sauce followed by chocolate mousse—two of her favorites. Beyond these memories the event had made no deep impact. She did recall, however, thinking Barnstable a pompous bore and feeling faintly guilty for doing so.

Very soon after Alice had been told of the death of her little boy, the Reverend Austin Barnstable appeared at her bedside. Arthur was sitting beside her, holding her hand in silence. Mrs. Melville ushered the reverend gentleman in and remained standing at the door of the room, like one of those strange gloomy women on the barge which bore King Arthur away across the mere.

Arthur stood up and Barnstable gave both him and Alice his smile of compassion and courage in adversity. "Blessed are they that mourn, for they shall be comforted," he murmured, modulating his voice beautifully to the size of the room. He took the bedside chair Arthur had vacated and, taking Alice's limp hand in both of his, said softly, "Like as a father pitieth his own children, even so is the Lord merciful unto them that fear him."

"I think, if you don't mind, I'll try to go to sleep now," Alice said.

"Of course," he answered sympathetically. "I won't stay. I take it you would like me to arrange for a quick and private interment."

Alice had closed her eyes, but she opened them again now. "I . . . I haven't even thought about that. There shouldn't be a big funeral, if that's what you mean."

"No, no of course not. That is precisely what I meant. We can't have a funeral at all in the proper sense. That's why I . . ."

Weary and sad as she was, Alice was still quite capable of reacting to a cryptic remark like that. "Why not a *proper* funeral?" she demanded angrily.

"My dear," Barnstable articulated, "I didn't mean to distress you. I assumed you realized."

"Realized what?"

"That the child could not possibly be buried in hallowed ground. He was unbaptized. The scripture makes clear that while there is no condemnation for them that believe and *are* baptized, for those who are not . . ."

"You mean he's going to hell?" Her voice, though weak, was saturated with anger and contempt.

"It is not an edict of my making. The prayer book states clearly that *after* baptism we may fall into sin and, by the grace of God, arise again and be forgiven. It does not, I fear, extend the same clemency to those who die *before* baptism."

He had got up from the chair as he said this, though still holding her hand. He had his benign face on.

"You can put his little body in the ground wherever you wish," Alice said in a quiet, even tone. "I don't visit graves."

"Of course," said Barnstable, relinquishing her hand.

"But I'll tell you this," she went on, raising her head as he turned to the door. "Christ said, 'Suffer little children to come unto me and forbid them not.' My little son is closer to Christ right now than you'll ever be."

Chapter 20

Arthur was very tender and gentle in his manner towards her—so much so, in fact, that after a few days Alice felt inclined to suggest to him that perhaps it was time to put the past behind them where it belonged and start looking to the future. She didn't do so for fear of hurting his feelings by seeming to be unappreciative of his solicitude.

Mrs. Melville didn't help the situation by dressing entirely in black and adopting an air of regal mourning. Mr. Melville too seemed to be deeply afflicted by the baby's death. Withdrawn and shy by nature he now enveloped himself in a sort of shroud of gloom. Alice began to feel, almost guiltily, that she, the mother of the boy, was affected less by his death than any of the others.

One evening, sitting before their fire, Alice knitting a scarf and Arthur pretending to read, he suddenly slammed the book shut, put it down on the table, and turned to her.

"You said I wasn't a man," he told her bitterly, "and now you've proved it."

Alice was startled. Everything had been so peaceful. "I never said such a thing," she stammered. "The baby's death had nothing to do with you."

"Of course it had," he answered angrily. "The mother houses the child until it is ready to be delivered but the father creates it and I created a sickly child. It was my sperm that was dilute and feeble."

"That's nonsense! Arthur, don't be absurd. We'll have another baby."

"Another?" He sounded frightened.

"Yes, of course."

"We'll . . . we'll have to think about it."

"I already have."

It took time but slowly the rhythm of the household routine reasserted itself and, though Arthur remained more solitary and subdued than Alice could have wished, he got back to work and life returned to normal.

In due course he submitted his first manuscript, *Under-*

standing French and English Painting, to a number of publishers, all of whom rejected it. He was not unduly cast down by this and, in fact, told Alice, "I know it's good. I may arrange to get it privately printed and distributed. The trouble is that the publishers don't know anything about painting themselves and they ask the advice of critics who are jealous of me and don't want any competition. I'll show them, though, and, when I'm better known than any of them, I'll be more generous to younger talent than they are."

He had read a good part of the manuscript aloud to her in the evenings as she sat knitting booties and such things by the fire in the last weeks of her pregnancy. She appreciated his companionship, even though she didn't really understand the book at all.

Alice was delighted at his resiliency in facing up to the publishers' lack of enthusiasm for his first literary effort. It did occur to her that if he couldn't make her understand and appreciate what he was trying to say about great paintings—she being most eager to do so—it was improbable that his book would have great appeal for the general public. She dismissed such doubts as unworthy and even perhaps disloyal. He would learn his craft. She must have no doubts that he would indeed make a reputation for himself.

So the summer dragged its weary, hot, humid length along. Alice would dearly have loved to escape from New York and go for a month or even a couple of weeks to some place in Maine or perhaps Atlantic City, but Arthur showed no interest in such a project. He had withdrawn into himself again, having apparently decided she was now recovered. He was much too busy, he told her, "collecting and collating" material. It was a dull and depressing time for Alice, with Arthur either away all day in libraries and art galleries or busy in his study covering page after page with his small, neat writing, but she was relieved to see him busy and apparently happy, and so was prepared to make the best of it. The Melvilles Senior went off to spend six weeks in Massachusetts with friends. So Alice was left for a good part of the time alone.

She took to going for long walks in Central Park. She was twenty and she longed for something more energetic, laughing friends, tennis, exploring rocky Atlantic coves, climbing hills. Anything but this sedate middle-aged promenading along the well-known paths. But what could she do? Everyone was out of town and Arthur was too preoccupied with his new book to spare time for her. If only little Arthur had lived. She wouldn't mind walking day after day in the Park if she had a baby carriage containing her son to push ahead of her.

"Arthur doesn't really love me," she told herself. He thought a wife was a pleasant and at times useful person to have around when he wanted her. But he didn't *need* her. She wasn't an essential and vital part of his life. For a little time it had been different and she had believed that all their troubles were behind them, that from here on life would be full of love and fun and sunshine and gaiety and the deep pleasures of making their lives together and together bringing up the children.

One day a young man spoke to her in the Park. He was a man of about her own age and only a little taller, with curly fair hair, clear blue eyes, and a humorous mouth.

"You seem to do a lot of walking," he said and smiled. "May I walk along with you?"

"If you would like."

"Are you married?" he asked her.

"Yes, I am."

"That's too bad. I've watched you the last three days, and I've thought to myself, 'One day I'll marry that girl.' Now my dreams are shattered. I shall probably go and jump over a cliff."

"There aren't many cliffs around."

"And I haven't got a pistol. Oh well, I expect I'll recover in time. Does your husband ever come walking with you?"

"He's busy."

"At what?"

Alice knew she should be cold and austere and show this brash young man that she was a respectable married woman and didn't make a habit of discussing her family affairs with the likes of him. He wasn't even wearing a tie. But he seemed so innocent and bright and she was so lonely, she couldn't do it. What would her mother have thought?

"He's an art critic," she said. "He writes books."

"Really! That's what I'm going to do. I mean I'm going to write books, not be an art critic. I'm going to write novels. I've already written a couple. Of course they're just in exercise books in my room now. I haven't sent them to a publisher yet."

"What are they about?"

"The best one is about a young bank teller who meets a very rich lady in Central Park and she makes it possible for him to leave the bank and they travel around the world. In the end he becomes very famous and very rich in his own right."

"You're the bank teller?"

"Yes, of course. And you're the rich lady."

They both laughed.

"I'm sorry things didn't work out the way you planned them."

"Oh, that's all right. As a matter of fact I come to the Park to watch birds."

"And keep an eye out for rich ladies."

"Not really. I noticed you because you're so beautiful."

"Thank you. You're on your holidays?"

"Yes. But only two days left." He sighed.

"Don't you like your job?"

"Oh yes, I like it well enough but I always feel that I'm a wasted genius. The trouble is that I'm the only one who realizes I'm a genius."

She looked at him again and saw how his eyes sparkled and the corners of his mouth twisted up happily in a mischievous grin. Here was a happy man. He would, she thought, be a wonderful husband for the right girl.

"You need a wife," she said. "All nice wives think their husbands are unrecognized geniuses."

"I'm looking for a wife, as a matter of fact, and I've got several possibilities in mind, but always, when I'm about to pop the question, I ask myself, 'Is she worthy of me?' And so far the answer has been, 'No. You'd better hold off for a bit. Something better may come along.' When I become famous I want a wife who can cope with the publicity and the receptions and all. I don't want a girl who is going to giggle and simper when we're invited to the White House for dinner."

"Yes, I see your point."

"On the other hand I can't wait much longer because I'm already twenty."

So they walked and talked and laughed together and,

when the time came for Alice to be getting back, he asked, "Will you come again tomorrow?"

"I expect so."

"Shall we have another walk together?"

"If you like."

It was absurd, of course. She should have snubbed him when he first approached her. He was just a cheeky little pipsqueak of a bank teller. He had no business talking to her the way he did. Yet there was something attractive about him. Alice didn't know of anyone in their circle of friends who was quite like him. She shouldn't, of course, go back. But she did. And, as she approached their meeting place of the day before, her heart beat a little faster and her step was lighter than it had been for a long time.

His name, it turned out, was Mark Wells. His father was a mechanic in Brooklyn and originally it had been intended that Mark should become a mechanic, too. "I worked for my father a couple of summers and one day he said to me, 'You'll do less damage in the world if you take an unskilled job like working in a bank.'"

They walked longer and talked longer than the day before. He told her how, ever since he was a small boy, he loved stories above everything else. He had composed his first story at the age of four and his mother had copied it down from his dictation and still had it.

"It's about a man who can turn himself into a fish and one day, he gets caught by a little boy; but once he is in the boat he turns back into a man and it all works out."

"I'm glad. I was hoping he wouldn't be fried in batter and served up with chips."

When the time came for good-byes he said, "I'm afraid I won't be able to come tomorrow. I always spend Sundays helping around the house and in the garden. You see, I live in a hostel during the week, even during the holidays because I'm paying for it anyway. Sundays I go back to Brooklyn. Then Monday I go back to work. Thank you for being so nice to me."

"I enjoyed it. I hope one day you really will be famous."

"I hope so, too."

For just a moment he looked as though he might kiss her and Alice wouldn't have repulsed him, but the moment passed. They shook hands.

It was nothing, but it certainly wasn't the sort of nothing

she could ever tell anyone about. How pleasant it had been. If she had met him first . . . ? No, she never would have met him. Sons of Brooklyn mechanics didn't go to the same parties she did. Even if they had she would never have been allowed to marry him. Yet, a little house in Brooklyn? Doing her own cooking and washing up and laundry and housecleaning and working in the garden?

In due course Mr. and Mrs. Melville returned from their New England travels and the dreary summer drew to an end. Mrs. Melville had enjoyed herself, but her husband was even less communicative than normal and Alice gathered he had not been well a good deal of the time.

As summer gave way to autumn and autumn to winter, Arthur became less obsessed with his work and had more time for his wife. They went to some parties and they gave some. Arthur had had a number of acquaintances but no friends before they were married. He didn't seem to care. Now, with Alice's encouragement, they began to find themselves members of a group of other young married couples with whom they spent pleasant evenings—sometimes at each other's houses, sometimes going to plays, concerts, or lectures, sometimes trying out new restaurants. They were the Sydney Carlyles, the Carlsons, the Ambroses, the Masseys, and others. Sometimes Arthur was silent and sometimes Alice could see that he was boring people, but often he was the same charming, witty man she had known before she was married. She was proud of him then.

Chapter 21

For Christmas Arthur gave her a diamond brooch from Tiffany's and she gave him the complete works of Shakespeare, bound in red morocco. He seldom read Shakespeare but the volumes, lettered in gold, were a most handsome addition to their bookshelves. They gave the Melvilles Senior a polar bear rug to put in front of their fireplace and the Melvilles Senior gave them a Turkish carpet.

There were some parties and some gaiety but, from Alice's point of view, it all seemed somewhat muted. She wasn't happy. She wasn't unhappy. She was bored and suspected that her boredom was her own fault. What could she or should she do to alleviate the tedium? She didn't know.

Then came the invitation and it, for a time at least, brightened the existence of all of them. The invitation, large and most handsomely engraved, was a request for the pleasure of the company of both the Senior and Junior Melvilles to attend the housewarming party for the new Whitney mansion at 871 Fifth Avenue on the corner of Sixty-seventh Street "on the occasion of the debut of Miss Helen Tracy Barney." Alice and her mother-in-law made no secret of their delight at this signal honor and, though Mr. Melville and Arthur pretended to be somewhat bored by the thought of the ball, there was little doubt that they were flattered.

As well they might be. Mr. Whitney was perhaps the most exciting and almost certainly the most discussed member of the Fifty Million Dollar Club or, as some preferred, the Barefoot Millionaires.

"I suspect," Arthur told Alice, "that he wants my father and me to view the Gobelin, Boucher, and Bockel tapestries, his Raphael and Van Dyck paintings. He may have more money than we have but I suspect he's unsure of his taste."

William Collins Whitney . . . Alice had of course heard of him—everyone had. He owned the New York Transit

System and all sorts of race horses and had been expected by his Yale classmates to be President of the United States or at least Justice of the Supreme Court. Alice asked her father-in-law about him one evening shortly before the ball when she and Arthur had gone down to play whist.

"I've met him only twice," Mr. Melville said, putting his fingertips together and resting his elbows on the card table. "He's a tall, handsome man of great charm. Some of those who know him much better than I say that he has squandered his undoubted talents in the pursuit of wealth. I am not qualified to pass judgment on that. He was, I think, a most satisfactory Secretary of the Navy." Mr. Melville paused and looked at his daughter-in-law. He smiled his sad, grave smile. "Even though he is a Democrat."

"He's a Harvard man," Arthur put in, as though that fact explained nearly everything. He did not add that Whitney had spent only one year at Harvard, as a student of law.

"I knew his second wife slightly," Mrs. Melville added, not to be outdone by her husband and son. "She was Mrs. Edith S. Randolph of Baltimore, a British army officer's widow and a charming person. His children disapproved of the marriage and didn't attend the wedding. It was all rather sad, really, because only two years later she was hit by a bridge and died about a year later."

"Hit by a bridge?" Alice asked.

"It was a low bridge," Mrs. Melville explained, as though that were more likely to prove fatal that being hit by a high bridge.

"I still don't understand."

"She was riding under it on a horse," Mrs. Melville said with a trace of impatience, "and she forgot to duck. The mansion was to have been for her. I'm surprised he had the heart to go on and finish it after her death."

"He still had his race horses," Arthur said.

"That," Mrs. Melville remarked coldly, "is a cheap remark." She picked up her cards. Arthur flushed. The game resumed.

The great night arrived. They proceeded through the impressive gates of bronze and wrought iron which had once graced the Palazzo Doria in Rome. Descending from their carriage, they continued on, through the onyx vestibule with its vast chandeliers, the entrance of white marble with

dark green columns and mosaic floor, up the grand staircase, where Mr. Melville paused to admire the Diana tapestries on the wall and Alice gasped at the huge banks of
poinsettias.

At the head of the staircase stood Mr. Whitney himself,
flanked by his sister, Mrs. Charles Barney, and his favorite
niece, Miss Helen Tracy Barney, in whose honor the ball
was ostensibly being given. Mrs. Astor, in a Marie-
Antoinette dress of purple velvet, a glittering tiara, a collar
of pearls and diamonds, and a diamond-studded stomacher,
preceded them slowly up the wide stairs, the center of all
eyes.

"This," Alice thought to herself in awe, "is what the Pal-
ace of the Boy Prince of Rajasthan must have been like."
She had always considered the Barrington and Melville
houses and others of their friends splendid but the magnif-
icence which confronted her now quite took her breath
away. She understood more clearly than ever before why
her father had never forgotten the ball at the Vanderbilt
mansion.

"And this," she heard a voice saying, "is my daughter-in-
law, Mrs. Arthur Melville." She looked around quickly and
up into the dark, unbelievably handsome face of Mr. Whitney. Instinctively she gave her hand and bent her knee.

Not being very good at curtsying, she almost lost her
balance but Mr. Whitney, holding her hand with gentle
firmness, helped her up.

"I know something about you," he said, smiling at her.
His voice was gentle, as was his manner, and yet there was
a hardness to them both. He had a suavity about him
which Alice found exciting and frightening at the same
time.

"About me?" she asked. "How could you know anything
about me, sir?"

"I have my spies. Does the name Mark Wells mean anything to you?"

It was so entirely unexpected that Alice caught her
breath. Mark Wells, the bank clerk from Brooklyn! What
on earth could he have to do with this?

"Why . . . yes . . . yes, I met him in Central Park.
We walked together."

Mr. Whitney laughed. "I didn't mean to alarm or embarrass you," he said. "The young man was sent as a messen-

ger from the bank a month or so ago and I came upon him gazing at Reynolds' *Portrait of a Lady* in the ballroom. He had taken the liberty of doing some exploring on his own while he was here. When he saw me I think he thought he was going to be arrested or shot or something. I asked if he knew anything about paintings and he told me he didn't but that he had met a lady in Central Park whose husband was an expert. He remembered your name and, knowing something of your father-in-law, I put two and two together. Brilliant, don't you think?"

Alice had recovered herself sufficiently to return his smile and answer, "Yes, indeed. Almost as clever as that detective invented by Mr. Conan Doyle. Have you read him?"

"Sherlock Holmes? I've read reviews. When life gets back to what I laughingly call normal I intend to delve deeper. Delighted to meet you. I hope I may have the pleasure of a dance later on."

So on into the immense ballroom from the castle of Baron de Foix, a field marshall under Louis XIV, panelled in oak and gilt with an inlaid oak floor, with magnificent red and gold tapestries and a two-hundred-year-old painted ceiling.

"And what on earth was all that about?" Arthur demanded, as he took her in his arms for their first dance.

"About a young man I chanced to meet on one of my walks in the Park while you were working. One of those silly coincidences."

"You never mentioned it to me. Now I'm the laughing stock."

"You're nothing of the kind. Don't be absurd."

"Mr. Whitney barely shook hands with me but he was all eyes for you."

"Arthur, stop worrying. Let's enjoy ourselves. He was just being gallant."

"Like the young man in Central Park with whom you had secret assignations? I suppose he was just being gallant, too."

"I do believe you're jealous," she laughed. "You're jealous of a bank clerk from Brooklyn."

Arthur said nothing more for the moment but Alice knew that the evening was dust and ashes in his mouth. The fact that Mr. Whitney did indeed seek her out at around midnight for a dance before the twelve-thirty supper didn't help matters, and when they returned to the ballroom afterwards to watch the fancy dress quadrilles, Arthur said, "Your name will be blazoned on every society page in the City tomorrow. Is that what you want?"

Alice didn't bother to reply.

When her name was not in fact mentioned at all in the paper the following day, Arthur seemed slightly disappointed.

Some two or three years later when William Collins Whitney perished after a severe attack of appendicitis, Arthur had reached the point where he could say, "Your old flame is no more," without sounding bitter.

Alice herself was a little sad at the news but she didn't admit to being so to Arthur.

It was a month or so after the ball—a raw, sleety evening. They were sitting, as they so often did of a winter evening, in front of the fire. Arthur, with a book lying open on his knee, was staring moodily into the flames and Alice, in her long pink dressing gown, was brushing her hair, which fell luxuriantly over her shoulders. Suddenly, Arthur seemed to have made up his mind about something. He closed the book, put it down on the floor beside his chair, got up and left the room.

"Where are you going?" Alice asked as he was going out. He made no reply.

A few moments later he was back with a great wad of manuscript and notes in his hand. He strode to the fire and, before Alice could intervene, he tore the brass-framed fire screen roughly aside and tumbled the papers onto the blaze.

"Arthur!" Alice exclaimed in alarm. "Arthur, what are you doing?"

He didn't answer at first but simply stood there watching with evident satisfaction as the flames hungrily devoured his hours of work.

She got to her feet and went to him but he thrust her aside. "I'm facing facts," he said, "That's what I'm doing. I can't father a baby; I can't write a book; I can't do a damn thing. I'm useless! Why go on pretending?"

"Arthur! What's wrong! Let's not go through all that

again. Little Arthur's death had nothing to do with you. You mustn't . . ."

"Don't tell me what I must or must not do. I've had that all my life. Don't tell me that the boy's death was no concern of mine. I was his father, wasn't I?"

"Of course you were but . . ."

"Of course I was. Then don't tell me that his death is not my affair."

"Arthur, don't shout. The servants will hear."

"Let them hear! Let everyone hear! They've all been smirking behind my back anyway all this time. They've known and you've known all the time. Now I know. So let's shout it out. Let's admit it to the world. Arthur Melville is no bloody good to anybody." He gave a wild laugh and then, collapsing into his chair, he covered his face with his hands and started to cry. Alice knelt at his feet.

That was the beginning of the troubles.

That first evening, though Alice was upset, she assumed that Arthur was merely overwrought and perhaps had had a little more wine than usual at dinner. It never occurred to her that this might be the first indication of something seriously wrong—an emotional and mental problem that would plague him for the rest of his life. He calmed down after a time and indicated, by manner rather than words, that he felt apologetic for his behavior. When they went to bed that night he appeared to have more or less recovered, though he was detached and frowning as though he were trying to puzzle something out. Alice was concerned and sympathetic, but not alarmed.

It was three weeks later, when she returned one afternoon from a meeting of the Orphan Children's Guild and found Arthur sitting silent in his chair with tears trickling down his cheeks, that she became really worried.

"What's wrong, darling?" she asked.

He made no reply.

She repeated her question, bending down and kissing him.

Still he didn't answer. He didn't seem to hear, gazing forlornly into space.

"Arthur!" she exclaimed, shaking his shoulder gently. "Arthur! What *is* the matter?"

"Leave me alone. What do you care?"

"I care very much. Are you still thinking about the baby? Your book?"

"I'm just thinking I want to be left alone."

"Can't I help?"

"No!" he said angrily. "No, you can't help."

This time his depression lasted for almost a week. He had little appetite and spent hours sitting with a book lying open on his knee, staring at nothing. Alice consulted her mother-in-law, who was no longer being quite as sepulchral as she had been immediately after the baby's death. To Alice's surprise, Mrs. Melville was not at all worried.

"He inherits this moodiness from his father," she told Alice. "I thought he had outgrown it. It's five or six years since we had this nonsense. When he was a child I would send him to his room without food until he pulled himself together. That worked very well. When he was fourteen, fifteen, sixteen and too old for me to spank I used to suggest that his father should whip him but his father didn't think that was the right treatment. I would just ignore him, my dear. He'll soon be his usual self."

Then, quite suddenly, he was more or less his normal self again and Alice decided that Mrs. Melville was right. Arthur, she told herself, was peculiarly sensitive and endowed with an artistic temperament. This, coupled with the baby's death and the rejection of his first manuscript, had cast him down unduly and she had probably not helped by being overly sympathetic.

Well, their troubles were over now. Arthur had started work with a great show of enthusiasm on a new manuscript tentatively entitled *Great Landscape Artists*. "This one," he assured her, "will establish my reputation. They won't be able to ignore it."

He was so intense in his confidence and enthusiasm and Alice was so pleased to see the end of his moodiness that she herself believed that this time all would be well. He had started to make love to her again and this gave her added confidence that the cloudy weather was over and the future bright.

Chapter 22

On the evening of February ninth, 1904 Alice and Arthur had dinner with the Melvilles Senior, as they did at least once a week. Alice, who was seated, as usual, on Mr. Melville's right, noticed that he scarcely touched his food and was even more silent than usual.

Though she had never really gotten to know him, Alice liked her father-in-law and she thought that he liked her. He always treated her with a grave courtesy and on three or four occasions had shown her special attention. Once, just before she married Arthur, he found her alone in the garden—Arthur had been called away somewhere—and they sat and talked and he told her stories of growing up as a boy in California and asked her questions about her own childhood. He was a good talker when he chose to be, but he seemed to prefer listening. The time Alice had felt she came closest to getting to know him was shortly after their return from Europe, when he had taken her on a personally conducted viewing of his various art treasures, particularly the paintings, in the gallery and around the house.

When Arthur talked to her about paintings his comments consisted largely of technical jargon which she found incomprehensible and boring, but with his father it was quite different. Without ever using a word she didn't understand and without a trace of condenscension in his tone he brought the paintings alive for her and, in doing so, showed her quite unconsciously more of himself than she had seen before. He was gentle and modest but with, Alice sensed, a strong and intensely private individuality.

But that evening he was, as he was so often, withdrawn, moody and monosyllabic when Alice attempted to start a conversation. Alice was not surprised when, after they had returned to the drawing room after dinner, he said to his wife, "I think if you and Alice will forgive me, my dear, I'll go and turn in. I'm not feeling quite myself."

"I'm sorry," Mrs. Melville said without emotion. "I had thought we might have a game of whist but, if you are in one of your moods, I don't suppose it would be much fun anyway."

"I don't suppose so," he answered. He spoke mildly but Alice was startled by the look he gave his wife, which was in sharp contrast to the softness of his tone. Mrs. Melville had turned away and didn't see it. It was not a look of anger, though there was something like anger in it. It was more a look which said, "You'll never understand, will you?"

He turned and left. From where she sat Alice could see him going slowly up the wide, carpeted stairs.

"What about pelmanism then?" Mrs. Melville asked.

Alice would have preferred to continue work on the sweater she was knitting for Arthur, but she knew Mrs. Melville, who had little general conversation, loved a game of some sort in the evening—particularly when she won— and Arthur liked to please his mother, so she said, "That sounds like fun," and presently they were seated around the table and Mrs. Melville was saying, "I know there's another seven here some place" as her jeweled fingers hovered over the face-down cards.

More by luck than by concentration Alice won the first game. So of course they had to play again. To Mrs. Melville's ill-concealed surprise and annoyance Arthur won the second. Alice didn't mind one game or even two but she really didn't want to play a third. However, there was no way out. "We can't stop now," Mrs. Melville said, speaking like a field officer rallying his troops for one final attack. "You must give me my chance. Three people. Three games." So the cards were spread out again.

Alice was amused but she was also vaguely annoyed, and besides she was tired and wanted to go to bed, read for half an hour, put out the light, and sleep. One voice inside her said, "Let the silly old thing win and have her childish pleasure." But another, stronger voice said, "She's inflicted this third game on you but she's going to be sorry. You're going to rob her of victory. You're going to win, my girl."

The second voice won and Alice pulled herself together, sat up straight, and concentrated on the play. Halfway through it was quite apparent to all three that the game had assumed an absurd tension. Arthur didn't much care one way or the other but he was acutely aware of the fact that his mother and Alice cared very much indeed. At that point Mrs. Melville had six pairs; Alice had four; Arthur had three. Mrs. Melville smiled grimly but in no way relaxed her concentration.

In the twenty minutes it took to finish the game Arthur won three more for a score of twelve; Alice won eight more for a score of twenty-four; Mrs. Melville won only two for a score of sixteen. Mrs. Melville gave a tight little smile. "Well, that's that for tonight," she said. "It's too bad we couldn't have played whist."

"Thank you for a delicious dinner and a very pleasant evening," Alice said.

"It was a good dinner," Mrs. Melville answered.

She allowed her son and daughter-in-law to kiss her and then all three started up the stairs. When they reached the second floor, where Mrs. Melville turned right and Alice and Arthur left, she said, "I think I'll just look in on Edwin and make sure he's all right. He's probably sound asleep."

"That's a good idea," Arthur told her.

They walked along the wide corridor in silence together. Alice knew Arthur was wishing that she hadn't been so determined to beat his mother in that silly game and wondered if he would say anything about it. They reached the end and were just turning right to go into their own quarters when from some distance there came a woman's scream. It was an anguished cry.

"That's Mother!" Arthur exclaimed in alarm. "Come on!" They turned and ran back down the hall. Servants were converging on the scene. Mrs. Melville was standing, framed in the doorway of her husband's bedroom. Her face, quite colorless except for the light touches of makeup on cheeks and lips, looked like a mask of wax. Her eyes, wide with terror, were fixed in an unseeing stare. Suddenly she took her hands from the sides of the doorway and covered her face with them. At the same moment she began to fall forward. Arthur caught her in his arms. "Someone get a chair," he said, "and someone else call Dr. Adler. Quick!"

A chair was found and Mrs. Melville, now semiconscious and sobbing soundlessly, was placed in it. Arthur knelt down at her feet and, looking up into her face, asked, "What is it?"

The unworthy suspicion entered Alice's head that he didn't want to go into his father's room to find out for himself what the trouble was. He was afraid. In an emergency he turned to his mother. Now he instinctively stayed with her even though her own maid, Valerie Nelson, who had been with her for years, was there by her side and there was nothing Arthur could do at the moment.

Alice was standing in the doorway herself now and turning to Benton, the butler, who was standing near her, she said, "I expect we'd better investigate."

"Yes, ma'am."

They went in and Benton closed the door behind them as a firm indication to the three or four other servants clustered curiously around the doorway that they were not invited. The large double bed, out of sight of the entrance to the left, had not been slept in.

"Mr. Melville?" Alice called softly.

On the floor near the bed a note had been dropped. Alice picked it up and glanced at it. It began "Dear Agnes." She didn't read on. She folded it.

She looked at Benton, and Benton at her. "Should we try the bathroom?" she asked.

"I suppose so, ma'am," Benton answered, without enthusiasm.

The bathroom door was closed and, even though it was virtually certain there was either a dead man on the other side of it or no man at all, the butler knocked deferentially and paused for a reply. None came. He opened the door and they went in.

Mr. Melville was slumped down in the bathtub, which was almost full of water. His head, turned toward them, was submerged. His right hip was thrust up and his right arm rested on it. They could see the slash in the wrist. Apparently for the sake of decency, not knowing who might find him, he had left his underwear pants on, but the rest of his clothing lay in a heap on the floor. The bath water was pink.

They gazed at him for a few seconds in silent horror and then went out. It never even occurred to them to try to haul him from the tub and revive him. It was obviously much too late for that.

She was in charge.

That fact didn't give her a feeling of exhilaration exactly but, even as she thought to herself that Arthur was not measuring up to his responsibilities in this crisis, she derived a strengthening satisfaction from the knowledge that she was coping for him. Mrs. Melville had now been taken to her bed and Arthur, for the time being at least, seemed to feel that his place was at her side.

Dr. Adler arrived. He was a thin, pale-faced man in his mid-fifties with a narrow, domed head fringed with unbelievably black hair, large and slightly protruding ears, opaque gray eyes, and the slowest and most deliberate manner imaginable. He was conducted to the bathroom by Alice and the faithful Benton.

After gazing at the grisly sight for several moments he turned to Benton and said, "I think—uh—it might—uh—be a good thing—to drain out—uh—the water." With obvious lack of enthusiasm, Benton removed his black coat (he never changed into informal clothes or pajamas until he was certain the family had retired for the night), hung it carefully on the door handle, slowly rolled back the shirtsleeve on his right arm, and, bending down, reached into the bloody water and removed the plug.

"Thank you," said Dr. Adler. He took his stethoscope out and, when the water had lowered sufficiently, he stooped and held it perfunctorily against the wet chest for a moment or two. Then he motioned Alice and Benton to leave and he followed them out.

"As a—uh—necessary formality—uh—you must summon—uh—the police," he told Benton.

The butler murmured, "Yes, sir." He had rolled down his sleeve and was in the process of putting his coat on again. He departed and Alice conducted Dr. Adler down to the drawing room where presently Arthur joined them. He was obviously and profoundly upset. "I left word with one of the servants to tell me when you arrived," he said. "Have you . . . have you seen my father?"

"I have," Dr. Adler answered in a sepulchral voice, slowly shaking his head.

"And?"

Adler looked gloomier than ever.

"I have felt it necessary to—uh—summon outside authorities."

"You mean the police are sent for?"

"A formality but—uh—a regrettably necessary one."

"I see," said Arthur. "My mother says he . . . he killed himself."

"That would—uh—appear to be the case."

"Why?" he asked in a voice brimming with misery.

Dr. Adler shook his head in silence, with an expression on his face intended to indicate that this was one of the few questions which even medical men, the wisest of the wise, could not answer.

"Perhaps you would come and see my mother?" Arthur asked.

It was not until she found herself alone with no further immediate responsibilities that the full horror of the situation struck Alice. She had stood up as the two men were about to leave. She had thought perhaps Arthur would like her to go up with them to see his mother, but he gave no indication of such a wish.

Now she sat down and suddenly the picture of the dead man's face under the water with its half-closed eyes and sagging mouth, pale, meaningless, and inexpressibly horrible, confronted her. "No!" she whispered. "No, I mustn't think of it." Kind, gentle Mr. Melville was dead, and dead not as her mother and father had died or even poor, miserable Laura Cosgrove. He was dead because he had chosen to be so. He had preferred death to life. It was horrible—too horrible to contemplate and yet she couldn't help herself. She glanced down and saw the note in her hand. She had forgotten it.

Her first instinct was to open it and read it but, even as she began to unfold it, she caught herself as she had done in the bedroom when she had first picked it up. Here was the secret, but it wasn't a secret for her eyes—not now or perhaps ever. Here was the most private of private letters—a dead husband's last letter to his wife. It would be the grossest kind of betrayal for her to read it. She refolded it and getting up, crossed the room and placed it in the ornate little brass box on the table with the green lamp. She was still shivering.

Then the front doorbell rang. It must be the police. She waited for Benton to answer it, sitting there hoping she looked calm and in control of herself. She forced herself to remain so until Benton appeared in the arched doorway. "The police are here, ma'am."

"Thank you, Benton. I'll come."

She followed the butler into the hall and found two young constables standing there looking cold, wet, and ill at ease. "Thank you for coming," she said.

"Shall I fetch Mr. Melville Junior or Dr. Adler, ma'am?" asked Benton.

"I think perhaps I'd better do that. If you wouldn't mind waiting here with the policemen."

"Very good, ma'am."

She went up the stairs. "Mr. Melville Junior," she thought to herself. "Not any longer. He's Mr. Melville Senior now . . . No, not until his father is buried. Until that time comes he is still Junior. Anyway, Senior or Junior have no meaning now. Arthur is the only male Melville left." She knocked gently on Mrs. Melville's door. It was opened by Arthur.

"The police are here," Alice said. "I think you or Dr. Adler should see them."

"Yes, I suppose so," Arthur answered vaguely, continuing to stand there. He looked like a man who was recovering from a long and wasting illness. He seemed only half aware.

"Well?" asked Alice.

"I'll . . . I'll tell Dr. Adler," Arthur said, and he turned back into the room.

Alice accompanied them up the stairs but didn't go into the bathroom a third time. She stood there looking at the unslept-in bed and listening to the men's voices without even trying to hear what they were saying. When they came out one of the constables said to Alice, "Dr. Adler says as far as he knows there was no suicide note. Would you know of any, ma'am?"

"No," replied Alice firmly, "no, I wouldn't." She had anticipated the question and decided on her answer.

"Well, sir," said the policeman, turning to Dr. Adler, "I expect the findings will be 'took his own life while temporarily of unsound mind.'"

"I—uh—don't think there will—uh—be any 'findings' at all," Dr. Adler replied. "I shall—uh—have the remains removed this evening and will have a word with—uh—the proper authorities tomorrow. I don't think an—uh—inquest will be—uh—necessary. Mr. Melville would not have wanted an inquest."

The final sentence, spoken without hesitation, indicated to the young constables that their rôle in this unhappy affair was peripheral. This was no ordinary suicide they were dealing with.

"We'll have to file a report," the other constable said apologetically.

"Of course," Dr. Adler answered, "you must follow your—uh—routine. I think—uh—a very quiet and confidential report, referring all—uh—questions to me."

"Yes, sir."

"And we don't—uh—answer any vulgar questions from the press?"

"No, sir. Of course not, sir."

"Very good. I shall mention that you were—uh—very cooperative. You may go now."

"Thank you, sir."

For a quiet, deliberate, and seemingly modest man it occurred to Alice that Dr. Adler had considerable authority. His patients were the rich and the very rich and he knew how they wanted things done and was able to do things their way. For all she knew he might be a good medical man as well.

Chapter 23

Alice went in to see her mother-in-law the next morning at about nine o'clock, when Mrs. Melville's maid reported that she was awake. Arthur, having spent the better part of the night with his mother, was now getting some sleep. Alice found Mrs. Melville propped up in bed and looking, despite her pale face, surprisingly well and in obvious command of herself. Alice bent to kiss her and felt Mrs. Melville grasp her upper arm and give it a firm squeeze of affection. She sat down beside the bed.

"It's going to be a difficult time," Mrs. Melville said firmly, "and I shall need your help. Arthur means well but he isn't a great deal of use in emergencies. I was upset last night, as you know, but even so I was well aware that you were facing up to the situation and that Arthur was using me as an excuse for not confronting his responsibilities."

"I don't know that you're being entirely fair," Alice replied quietly. "He is very devoted to you."

Mrs. Melville looked Alice square in the eye and smiled faintly. "You are a dutiful wife," she said. "I'm not sure Arthur deserves you but I am glad he has you just the same." She paused, looking steadily into Alice's face. "Now, we must set the wheels in motion. Would you ring for Benton, please? No, you'd better send a maid for him and tell her to ask him to bring a pad and pencil with him."

Benton arrived, looking, as he always did, impeccable and alert, with exactly the right blend of deference and authority.

He was a well-built man of medium height with thoughtful gray eyes, a firm chin, iron gray hair, and a quiet, respectful, but never servile manner. Even when Mrs. Melville was at her most autocratic, ordering Benton to take care of this, make sure of that, and not to forget something else, she never diminished Benton's essential manliness. He had begun his working life at the age of fourteen as a pageboy at The Plaza and had come to the Melvilles as a seventeen-year-old footman at a time when balls for three hundred people were annual affairs and dinners for twenty or thirty monthly occurrences. There were also, of course, the weekly "At Homes," frequent house guests, and numerous small affairs. Those were in the days of Mr. Melville's father and mother but they carried on into the days of the next generation for a time before—apart from the "At Homes"—they began slowly to taper off.

He stood now, just inside the door, awaiting his orders.

"First of all, Benton," Mrs. Melville began, "I wish you to instruct the servants that there is to be no gossip outside the house concerning the nature of Mr. Melville's death. The fact that he chose to take his own life is of concern only to the household and to no one else. I shall dismiss without reference anyone I suspect of idle gossip."

"I have already made that clear to the servants, ma'am."

"I thought you probably would have done so. The undertaker?"

"The remains were removed late last night on Dr. Adler's orders. Would you wish them returned here before the funeral?"

"No. They should go direct to St. Aiden's Church when the time comes. You and Mrs. Melville Junior will arrange suitable notices for the papers. Flowers, wine, and other refreshments . . . pall bearers . . ."

"Why don't you leave it up to me and Benton . . . and, of course, Arthur?" Alice asked. "We can arrange it all and confirm our arrangements with you."

Mrs. Melville looked at her sternly and Alice, for a moment, thought she had made a great mistake. Then the look softened. "You and Benton and, of course, Arthur are in completely charge," she said quietly. "There must be lots of sherry, Benton, because everyone drinks sherry before and after funerals. And flowers . . . a wreath with three dozen red roses and cedar sprays for the coffin and at least another ten dozen roses for the house . . . small sandwiches . . . nice things . . . You'll arrange it all. Edwin loved red roses . . . and boughs of cedar." She slumped back in the bed. Alice and Benton hesitated at the door. "And black-edged notepaper and cards," she added softly. "Order lots of black-edged notepaper and cards."

Four days had gone by since the funeral and the three of them were sitting one evening in Arthur's and Alice's drawing room after dinner. Since they had started again to have dinner at a regular time they had eaten together—either she with them or they with her.

They had been talking in a desultory fashion when, apropos of nothing that had been mentioned, Mrs. Melville said, "This is much too big a house for three people and especially for three people maintaining two separate establishments. I was wondering in bed last night how the two of you would feel about organizing things as one family. We really are, aren't we?" She glanced hastily at Alice. "I don't mean we would be on top of each other all the time," she added hurriedly. "You would still have your own privacy, of course."

For a moment nothing was said. Arthur turned to look at Alice as well. "Have you ever considered the possibility of selling the house and taking something smaller?" Alice asked. "We could make a separate apartment for you, where you could have your own personal things, and we would be much closer than we are now without actually sharing."

Even before she finished her little speech Alice realized that she might just as well propose that they find a down-at-the-heel frame house in Brooklyn painted up to make it look respectable, with a room for her in the basement.

"My dear Alice," she said, "you are not serious." She was, of course, still dressing in black and would continue to do so for many weeks yet. Weariness and grief had made her skin paler than usual and there she sat, bolt upright as usual, her face almost white above her high black collar, and looked at her daughter-in-law with something like horror. "This was Edwin's house," she said, "and as long as I am alive it will remain Edwin's house. It would be desecration to sell it, to auction off his priceless works of art, to dispose of the furnishings he assembled with so much care and pride and, in the end, see the place battered into rubble. It would profane his memory."

"I'm sorry," said Alice, awed by the depth of feeling in Mrs. Melville's voice. "I didn't mean . . ."

"The time may come," Mrs. Melville continued, ignoring Alice's protestation, "after I too am in the ground, when you and Arthur may decide to knock the place down and laugh as the walls tumble, but you will not do so during my lifetime."

"I was *not* proposing any such thing," Alice said heatedly. "I was only . . ."

"Not directly, perhaps, but the thin end of the wedge."

"Not even that. You said yourself it's much too big a house for three people."

"What do you want to do then? Do you suggest we turn it into some sort of hotel or cheap rooming house, and have Italians and Irishmen and all sorts of strange people coming and going and spitting on the rugs? Is that what you want?"

"You aren't being fair."

"Is it so unfair to wish to preserve my late husband's memory?"

Alice made no reply. What was the sense? Inwardly she seethed. She had thought that this battle had been won and that Arthur was on her side. Now she was not at all sure. He had sat silent and miserable during the exchange.

There was an uneasy silence, and then Mrs. Melville, speaking as though the argument had not taken place at all, said in a soft and slightly puzzled voice, "The night Edwin died I went to his room and there was a note on the bed. I only read the first sentence and then I ran to the bathroom because that was the only place he could be and . . ." She stopped, bit her lip and was silent, her eyes tight shut, her face rigid. Presently she opened her eyes and went on. "I was thinking about it last night. I expect the police have it. I'd like it back. Last night it suddenly occurred to me that one of the servants might have picked it up. I can't bear the thought. Could you get in touch with the police tomorrow, Arthur, and find out."

"Yes, Mother, of course."

"That won't be necessary," Alice said. "I know where it is."

"You do?" said Mrs. Melville. "Why did you not give it to me before this? You have read it, I presume."

"No, I have *not* read it. I intended to give it to you when you asked for it or when you were a little stronger, perhaps."

"A little stronger? Is it your business to decide when I am strong enough to be given my late husband's last letter to me? I've never heard of such arrogance. Did you know she had it, Arthur?"

Arthur shook his head in a desolate sort of way.

"I'm sorry," said Alice evenly. "It probably wasn't a good decision but it was not an arrogant one. I thought . . ."

"I'm not interested in what you thought. You didn't even tell your own husband. You're a very secretive . . ."

"I'm not a very secretive anything. Apart from hurried meals and a few moments first thing in the morning and last thing at night I have scarcely seen Arthur since Mr. Melville's death. He has spent virtually all his time with you."

The two looked into each other's eyes as they had done before—the young bride and the old widow. Then Mrs. Melville said, "You are right. I have appreciated Arthur's kindness and I appreciate as much your willingness to let him spend so much time away from you." Her voice was firm but there was kindness in it, perhaps even a hint of apology. "We mustn't quarrel," she said. "In the name of all we hold most precious we must never quarrel again."

"I'll get the letter now," said Alice. "It's in the brass box on the table in your drawing room. I didn't want the police to get hold of it."

When she returned she held it out to her but Mrs. Melville said, "I haven't got my right glasses. Give it to Arthur to read."

Arthur accepted it reluctantly and slowly unfolded it. "Shall I read it aloud?" he asked.

"Of course. We have no secrets."

"Dear Agnes,
    When you read this I shall be dead. I am sorry for the inconvenience and distress which my death will cause you and others but it will not, I hope, be of long duration. I have pondered this course of action for some time and decided this morning that it is the right one.
    For some years, as you know, my periodic headaches and moods of depression have been increasing in intensity and have been a burden to you and a source of some anxiety to me. During them I have at times suffered hallucinations and dark, irrational thoughts which have led me to fear that I may be losing my mind.
    I have done a certain amount of reading on the subject during the past year and have found considerable

evidence to support this fear. I have therefore decided that it is in the best interests of all concerned that I should act while I am still capable of doing so.

You have sometimes thought my moody spells were merely a selfish device for avoiding responsibilities and I preferred you to believe this rather than be concerned that they had a more serious origin. You have also said on occasion that you believe Arthur has inherited his periodic moodiness from me. I pray to God you are wrong about this and that I have not bequeathed my mental illness to him.

God bless you all and please tell Alice how devoted I am to her, even though it has been my misfortune to have known her for such a brief time. I am proud to think she is now a Melville.

Good night,
Edwin."

Silence.

Watching Arthur's pale, drawn face as he read the letter in a low monotone, Alice realized what an effort it had been for him to struggle through to the end without breaking down. He had managed to do so by a supreme effort of will and she admired him for it.

Mrs. Melville sat there immobile, unblinking, grim and solitary. It would have been an insult at that moment to have risen and kissed those thin lips or those pale, taut cheeks. Arthur refolded the letter and she held out her hand to receive it. Then she stood up to leave the room. Arthur rose to follow her but she said to him coldly, "I don't want you. Your place is here with your wife."

She went slowly but purposefully out the door, looking straight ahead of her, and Arthur and Alice watched her go. One never learned. Always, in the grip of an emotional crisis, one tended to say, "This is it! Never again can life possibly be as it has been. This has changed everything." Yet, even after the most shattering experience, the pieces had a tendency to fit themselves back together again and get glued in, not perhaps quite as securely as they had been before nor necessarily in precisely the same design, but near enough.

They did in the end consolidate housekeeping arrangements and Alice found a new position for Mrs. Walding, who needed, she said, "only one more job for a year before I've saved enough to go back to Lynn, Massachusetts, and the children. I'll never come to New York again but I'll always remember you, Mrs. Melville, and the kitchen sherry party." Alice's maid, Maureen, remained and Arthur retained Arnold Crump, his valet. Many rooms were, of course, shut up and there was no longer even a pretense that they would ever be used again. The house was greatly overstaffed, but the servants were a good lot and didn't take advantage of the fact to be unduly lazy. They understood that Mrs. Melville Sr. must always appear to be in command but that Mrs. Melville Jr. was actually in charge.

Under Benton's able leadership there was nothing they wouldn't do to help "Mrs. A.," as they called her among themselves, to cope with the unfamiliar job that had been thrust upon her. They liked and admired her. Benton almost revered her. "I'm the bachelor type," he confided in some of them one day, "but if I'd been the marrying sort and had had the money I'd of sought out a lady like Mrs. A."

Even the "At Homes" were reestablished and, as all the guests remarked, not always with approval, they were much more lively affairs. Alice persuaded some of her contemporaries to "come and ginger things up." They did so. Mrs. Selbourne, the born troublemaker, remarked to Mrs. Melville, "The old order changeth. It's not as it used to be."

Mrs. Melville skewered her with a glance. "No," she answered, "it's not. It's so much better. I'm glad you agree." Mrs. Selbourne nodded and drifted away.

Arthur went back to work on his new book and at times recaptured his old absorption in his work for some days on end. Then he would wake up one morning plunged in gloom and spend the day moping moodily in front of the fire. Nothing that Alice could do or say would shake him out of it.

They went out to dinner and they had people in, but Alice sensed that their friends understood the situation. Guests tended to leave early and their hosts tended not to be surprised when they did the same. "Arthur tires easily," Alice would say, and they would nod knowingly. But Alice herself didn't tire easily and she spent many evenings curled up in front of the fire reading and wishing that they could be dancing the night away at someone's lavish ball instead.

The approaching election captured Arthur's interest. He hoped and expected that The Party would nominate Mark Hanna in place of Roosevelt but, when Mark Hanna died, Arthur announced one evening, "I have decided to support Theodore Roosevelt. He is growing into the job. Though I must say the Democrats have for once a most attractive alternative in Judge Alton Parker. It will be a close thing." When Roosevelt swept the country with a majority of more than two and a half million votes Arthur said, "The Democrats are a lost cause. I doubt they will ever see power again."

Alice was quite sure that Arthur would not have remembered on his own that November seventeenth was her birthday. His mother must have reminded him. The fact having been drawn to his attention, however, he behaved in exemplary fashion. They went to the Ritz for dinner with two other couples—the Maitlands and the Harvey Gillans—and then they went on to see Geoffrey Hamilton star in *As You Like It*. Alice had seen him before, of course, and thought he was the most marvelous actor ever. When, at the end, Rosalind said to him, "To you I give myself, for I am yours" and Orlando answered, "If there be truth in sight, you are my Rosalind," Alice's eyes filled with tears.

When it was all over and they were back home again sipping a weak drink in front of the almost dead fire before going to bed, Arthur said, "I was watching you. You got quite carried away."

"I think he's wonderful, don't you?"

"You sound like a girl of thirteen who has developed a passion for some simpering Italian dancing master. He's only an actor, after all."

"But don't you think acting is as great an art as painting?"

"Of course not. It's only make-believe and it lives only as long as the actor does. A great painting lives forever."

"But there is a sort of . . . a sort of magic about it, don't you think? I mean a great actor really does make you forget for a moment who you are or where you are. He casts a sort of spell."

"He certainly seems to have cast a spell on you, anyway."

"It's not just that he's so handsome. It's not just his voice or his eyes. It's more than that." Her eyes were full of dreaming.

"He has a superficial talent, I suppose. I think he's been made too much of for too long. They say he's drinking and that he's on his way out."

"Oh, I hope not," Alice exclaimed. "I think that must be cruel gossip. I mean he didn't look to me as if . . ."

Arthur laughed dryly. "Are you in love with him?"

"Don't be absurd, Arthur. I admire his talent. I'm no more in love with him than you are with the Rubens nudes."

They were silent for a time and then Arthur said, "I expect you were contrasting Orlando and Rosalind with the two of us."

"Oh, Arthur, don't be so silly. It was only a play. Ours is a real marriage, not a make-believe one. I'll take you in preference to Orlando anytime." She got up and kissed him on the forehead.

He looked up and smiled. "I'm sorry. I don't mean to spoil your birthday. I . . . I want to deserve your love."

"You do."

He got up and embraced her, pulling her tightly against him. "Don't give up on me," he said. "Don't give up on me, Alice. I'm so afraid."

Chapter 24

"I don't suppose any of your old New York friends are still alive," Patricia remarked one Wednesday at tea.

"If they are, they're keeping very quiet about it," Alice answered. "I expect there are a number of Negroes, Puerto Ricans, and Mexicans who have a dim recollection of the strange lady who used to visit them at the Help-The-Children hostels but, if they don't recall me any more clearly than I do them, they can scarcely be classified as old friends. Jenny was the last. Of course there was Minerva Sparks. She wasn't really an old friend either, but when I saw her death announced in the *Times* on the way to San Francisco when I was coming here it gave me quite a jolt."

"Minerva Sparks? I don't remember you mentioning her. Who was she?"

"Have I never told you about Minerva Sparks?"

"Not that I remember." Patricia glanced at her watch. "My goodness! I hadn't realized it was so late. I must be going. Will Minerva keep to another time?"

"Minerva will keep," Alice said. She kissed her daughter good-bye and, after her departure, asked Mrs. Owens to bring in her gin and tonic.

So here she was, sitting at the window once again and remembering. She could have forseen that Patricia wouldn't be interested. Patricia hadn't the imagination to be interested in anything much beyond her husband and children, the Hospital Guild, the Vancouver Symphony, whether she should widen the perennial bed, and other such things of here and now. No, she wouldn't be interested in Minerva Sparks. In fact she might disapprove of Minerva almost as much as Mrs. Melville and Arthur had done.

It had all started when Alice and Arthur received an invitation to dinner "at the residence of Mr. and Mrs. James E. Sparks," which was situated on Seventy-third— not quite on Fifth Avenue, but not far off it.

"Never heard of them," Arthur said.

"Neither have I," said Mrs. Melville. "They are certainly not a Knickerbocker family. They must belong to the Suddenly Rich. I'm sure they are not our sort. I wonder how they made their money." They were at dinner. Mrs. Melville took a sip of claret.

"Initially in bathtubs and chamber pots and later in steel," Alice answered unexpectedly.

Both Mrs. Melville and Arthur turned on her in surprise. "How do you know about them?" Mrs. Melville demanded. "Did you say chamber pots?"

Alice was delighted with the stir she had created. "I did indeed," she answered. "I met her at an Afternoon at the Charles Schwabs' on Riverside Drive. She grew up in Cedar Rapids, Iowa and she's not afraid to admit it. Her older sister had known Mrs. Schwab or something like that and I think her husband was connected with Mr. Schwab in Bethlehem Steel."

"I see," said Mrs. Melville. Then, to herself, she muttered, "chamber pots and bathtubs."

"Minerva Sparks told me," Alice continued brightly, "that, when their house was finished, they had invited all sorts of people for dinner and bought expensive favors from Tiffany's to put under the napkins and, out of ninety-eight people invited, only thirty-two came."

"I'm surprised that she was so successful," said Mrs. Melville. "I can't understand these people who think that they can actually *buy* their way into society. It's disgusting. She probably even sent an invitation to Mrs. Astor."

"Yes, as a matter of fact, she did." Alice sounded defiant.

"Who, in heaven's name, does she think she is?"

"I can tell you exactly who she thinks she is, if you want to know," Alice answered.

Mrs. Melville regarded her daughter-in-law with a mixture of annoyance and curiosity in her face. Arthur remained silent, looking from one to the other. The curiosity won and Mrs. Melville said, "Well? Who is she then?"

Alice waited for the maid to remove the dishes from the table, bring in the fruit, and retire to the pantry. "She is— or at least believes herself to be—an illegitimate daughter of Commodore Cornelius Vanderbilt."

Mrs. Melville was in the process of swallowing a grape. It went down the wrong way and stuck momentarily. She coughed. Her eyes bulged. She turned red in the face and looked angrily at Alice. Arthur, looking very agitated, half rose from his chair but his mother motioned him back. "Vanderbilt," she gasped, as soon as she partially recovered the power of speech. "I might have guessed. A disgusting man. He spat tobacco juice onto Persian carpets and pinched the bottoms of the parlor maids. He was living proof, if any were needed, that manners, not money, maketh the man who is acceptable in society."

"What about a man of manners without any money?" Arthur asked. Alice was uncertain as to whether he was serious or not. It was unlike him to tease his mother.

Mrs. Melville herself seemed a little puzzled by the question and looked sharply at her son. Then she answered, "I never knew a man of true manners who did *not* have money. Money and manners generally go hand in hand except for some very unfortunate exceptions in both directions."

"That may be very true," said Alice, "but my mother and father were at a fancy dress ball at the William Kissam Vanderbilt mansion. They used to tell me about it when I was a girl and I've grown up feeling a sort of kinship with the Vanderbilts."

"A feeling," Mrs. Melville replied, "which, like the summer grippe, will, I trust, pass away in time."

"But Cornelius Vanderbilt was a Commodore, wasn't he?" Arthur asked.

"An ironic tribute," said Mrs. Melville. "He ran a ferry boat at one time."

Despite Mrs. Melville's obvious disapproval and Arthur's grave doubts, Alice accepted the invitation. As they were driving to the affair Arthur asked a question which had obviously been on his mind for some time. "Did she actually tell you she believed herself to be an illegitimate daughter of Cornelius Vanderbilt?"

"Oh yes," Alice answered airily. "She said that every time she passes his statue in Grand Central Station she waves a little greeting to it."

"That's obscene," said Arthur.

"I don't see why," Alice answered, adjusting her fur on her shoulder and just touching her pendant pearl earrings to make sure they were still there. "I think it shows a kind and forgiving spirit. She couldn't choose her own father, after all, and it's not her fault that Mr. Vanderbilt was a nasty old man."

"She needn't go around boasting about it."

"She didn't. I asked her if she had been born in Cedar Rapids and she said no, that she had been actually born in New York, but her mother had taken her to Cedar Rapids when she was very small and it was there she had met her husband who was to do so well in chamber pots and bathtubs."

"But how did Vanderbilt's name come up?"

"I was coming to that. I asked her who her father was and she answered, 'My mother thinks he must have been Cornelius Vanderbilt but she can't be absolutely certain.' Now, Arthur, you can't say that that is boasting about one's parentage."

"No," Arthur replied in a faraway voice, "no, I can't say that."

The house was large but by no means as imposing as the Melvilles' and almost lower middle-class compared to the Whitney mansion. They were greeted when they went in by Mr. Sparks, who was a short, balding, jolly man, and by Minerva, who was tall with red hair, sparkling here and there with jewels, large green eyes, unbelievably crimson lips, high cheekbones, and a firm chin. Her voice was strong and warm.

"Oh, Mr. Melville," she said, "how very kind of you to come. My husband Denny and I are very anxious to start gathering a modest but really *good* collection of paintings and, from all we've heard, you are the very best man in New York to advise us." She flashed a smile at him in which welcome and gaiety were blended with an almost intense admiration.

Watching the expression on Arthur's face dissolve from cold and almost hostile formality into a sort of wondering delight, Alice thought to herself, "She'll make it! Cedar Rapids to Fifth Avenue."

"We sure are glad you folks could come," said Denny.

It was not a large or ostentatious party. There were, Alice estimated, not more than thirty people. The menu was suitably simple. They had oysters, a choice of consommé or cream of chicken soup, smelts, mousse of ham, fillet of beef, potatoes, stuffed tomatoes, paté de foie gras in aspic, wild duck, celery salad, ice cream with cakes, cheese soufflé, and fruit.

When the gentlemen rejoined the ladies after dinner, Alice was delighted to see Arthur and Minerva Sparks in animated conversation about paintings. She herself was saddled with a Mr. Grantham, who had had too much to drink, and was trying to explain at great length that, if things had been different, he would be where Andrew Carnegie was now.

Driving home, Alice asked, "It wasn't too bad, was it?"

"It wasn't bad at all," Arthur replied. "It was quite delightful. We must see more of them. She is highly intelligent and eager to learn."

As they were going to bed Alice decided that he was in such high spirits that this was the time to break the news. She waited until he got both his legs out of his trousers.

"I've got good tidings for you," she told him.

"What's that?" he asked.

"We're going to have another baby."

He froze for a moment, sitting on the little pink chair in the act of removing his socks.

"Oh my God!" he exclaimed. "Are you sure?"

"Yes, I'm sure," she laughed, "and this time all will be well."

Patricia had been born in 1907. Alice recalled only fragmentary, disconnected moments of the ordeal. She recalled thinking that if the pain got any worse she could not bear it. There was a voice that said, "If she survives, it will be a miracle." She opened her mouth to tell them she was going to survive, but no sound came and it occurred to her she might be dead already. Everything was very dark but there were sudden flashes of brilliant light. At one point Arthur was kneeling by her bed. She thought he was crying and she wanted to tell him not to, but again she couldn't make a sound. She had wakened up and heard Mrs. Melville saying, "You're going to be all right, my dear. Just rest and take life easy. It's a darling little girl."

Almost from infancy Patricia was more Arthur's child than hers. She was, as Mrs. Melville said, "an apple dumpling with dark hair"—a pudgy, placid baby who was quite content to sit endlessly on her father's lap gazing benevolently at the world, burping occasionally and drooling continuously. There had been some thought at first of naming her Alice or Agnes but the name Patricia was decided on eventually for the very good reason, according to Arthur, that there was no Patricia in either family "and so she won't have to try to live up to false expectations."

Sitting by the window, her empty glass in her hand, Alice thought to herself, as she had done so often before, how strange it was. Patricia was now sixty-eight years old and troubled with arthritis. She and her husband Michael had three middle-aged "children," Michael, Patricia and Arthur, and they had produced seven children of their own. On the table beside her was a picture of Patricia, on the steps of the Melvilles', wearing a birthday dress and a ribbon in her hair. The dress was pink, Alice remembered, with frilly white trimmings. That was her tenth birthday. 1917. The year the United States came into the Great War.

When war broke out in 1914 Arthur had been exceedingly annoyed. "Apart from anything else," he told Alice, "it is going to play absolute havoc with all my art transactions in Europe and particularly in France." He was completely convinced that the whole thing was grossly exaggerated. His old distrust of Theodore Roosevelt flared up again as the former President clamored for America's entry into battle. He had always detested Wilson and was quite convinced that he had in some way deliberately arranged the sinking of the Lusitania in order to stir up American public opinion against Germany.

"When people find out what he's been up to," he assured Alice, "they will never vote Democrat again. I'm sure of that this time. He's destroying his party. I just hope he doesn't destroy America in the process."

When, however, the United States went into the war Arthur said, "Germany will now discover that there's a limit to our patience."

His one absorbing interest in life was his small daughter and Patricia soon learned that she could win from her father almost any concession by even the slightest show of displeasure. All the disciplining fell to Alice which, of course, strengthened the ties between father and daughter. Patricia was always on her very best behavior when she was with her grandmother, and so Mrs. Melville was no help one way or the other.

It was a difficult time. Arthur, despite his joy in his

daughter, was still subject to periods of deep despondency, ravaged by thoughts of his own inadequacy.

Alice lived now in an almost constant state of concern. When Arthur was having one of his spells—silent, morose, easily angered by the most innocent remark she might make, irritated even by little Patricia, avoiding his mother and given to morbid speculation as to what was to become of them all—her normal concern was intensified to the point that she could scarcely sleep at night. If she tried to stay with him he accused her of spying. When she forced herself to leave him alone he blamed her for being cold and indifferent to him in his hour of need.

So the war and President Wilson were good things if they distracted Arthur's attention from himself. Beyond that she didn't give them much thought. They didn't affect her life, and it was generally accepted among her friends that these were matters which men enjoyed discussing because it bolstered their sense of self-importance and general superiority. Years later when Patricia and Patricia's children, particularly young Arthur, who was the only one with whom she felt a real kinship, asked her, "What was it like?" she wished she could tell them more. She was ashamed that she had taken so little interest.

1923. She did remember that year. She was forty-two; Arthur was forty-six; Patricia was sixteen.

Women had gotten the vote by this time. Arthur didn't object, though he said, "It's just political posturing. One might as well pass a law allowing dogs to ride bicycles. Women will never exercise their franchise."

"Why not?" Alice demanded. "Why shouldn't I vote?"

"No reason at all. I'll be glad to explain, when the time comes, how you should vote and why."

"Couldn't I decide that on my own?"

"Men don't interfere in the running of the house and it would be better if women didn't interfere in the running of the country."

"You mean President Harding is doing such a splendid job? The oil scandals? The land scandals? Liquor? Narcotics? It's a whole orgy of corruption. You can't blame women for that."

"You've been reading the newspaper," Arthur said almost accusingly.

"Of course I have. You said yourself I should be better informed."

"Well, mistakes have been made. I admit that. Harding is from Ohio. That explains a good deal. I've never met a man from Ohio I could really trust. I don't know what there is about that state. I'm sure that Coolidge will be the next President, and he'll set things right."

But it wasn't the scandals which engulfed Warren Harding that made 1923 a memorable year for Alice; it was their own miniature scandal so much closer to home. Often she had felt tempted, during one of their little Wednesday afternoon parties, to mention it to Patricia, but she had refrained from doing so. Patricia wasn't very good at laughing at herself and quite incapable of laughing at anything her father had ever done. She would either be hurt by the fact that her mother had remembered the affair all these years, or be unduly solemn about it.

Chapter 25

After a year or two of home instruction Patricia had attended Ashcroft. Miss Conner was now Headmistress and had given the daughter of one of her favorite ex-pupils a warm welcome, but somehow or other Patricia didn't get as much enjoyment out of Ashcroft as her mother had done. There was too much of Arthur in her, Alice told herself privately. She had friends, but they weren't the gay and abandoned types like Jenny Robertson, the architect's daughter who had seen her brother naked, or Carla Sandhurst, who had gone with her to Coney Island. They were "nice" girls—well dressed, well mannered, and very dull, without even a pinch of pepper in them so far as Alice could make out. She showed no interest in boys.

"I always measure the boys I meet against Father," she told Alice once, "and so far I haven't met a single one who can compare."

"That's silly," Alice said. "How can you compare a boy of fifteen to a man your father's age?"

"I try to imagine what they'll be like when they *are* Father's age and none of them seem to be worthy."

Alice had never quite understood Patricia's deep devotion to Arthur. She didn't in any way resent it, but it puzzled her. Eventually she concluded that Arthur, finding in his daughter an audience who gave his utterances full and unquestioning concentration, treated her with the flattering respect that such a respectful and intelligent listener deserved. Patricia and her father shared, in their somewhat one-sided discussions, something of the companionship Alice had shared with her mother on their walks in Central Park.

Then one day Patricia had arrived home and announced that for her sixteenth birthday party she would like to have a dance. They were at dinner and midway through a creamed chicken dish. Alice paused with her fork in midair and gazed disbelievingly at her dark-haired daughter. "A dance?" she asked in disbelief.

Mrs. Melville, who had relinquished the head of the table to Alice and now sat opposite Patricia, said, "Why *not* a dance?"

Arthur echoed his mother's question. "Why not?"

"No reason at all," Alice replied, recovering herself. "I was a little surprised, that's all. I didn't think Patricia was all that interested in boys."

"I wasn't," said Patricia, "until I met David Spears."

"Who is David Spears?" Arthur asked.

"He's the nicest boy I've ever met. He knows almost everything. And he draws and paints too, Father, and can hardly wait to meet you. I told him you were a world authority."

"I think that's going a bit far," Arthur replied, smiling his tight little smile of pleasure. "I didn't ask for a catalogue of his virtues, however, Patricia; I asked you who he was. Do you know any Spears?" he asked, turning to his mother.

"There were the Wandsworth Spears," Mrs. Melville said vaguely, "but they went back to England years ago. He couldn't possibly be one of them."

"David never had any parents," Patricia said.

"How very unusual," said Alice.

"I mean they died when he was very small. He lives with an aunt in an apartment on Fifth Avenue. He's quite rich, I think, so I'm sure he's all right."

Patricia's birthday was the twenty-third of June. She drew up a list of the girls she wanted to ask but, apart from David Spears, she didn't know what to do about boys. "Couldn't each girl just bring the boy she wants?" she asked one evening at dinner.

"Certainly not!" Arthur replied before Alice had a chance to respond. "We wouldn't know who they were."

"I'll ask some of the girls' mothers for advice," Alice said.

So in the end, Alice wrote to the mothers of fourteen girls and the mothers of fourteen boys and the dance plans began to take shape. She didn't write to David Spears' aunt; she considered that unnecessary since Patricia assured her that the aunt had already been consulted and given her approval. Alice had first thought of a tea dance but Patricia had pleaded for an evening affair beginning at eight and ending at eleven and she had her way. Alice, of course, invited a number of the parents to join them "to watch the young enjoy themselves." So all was well.

The ballroom, which hadn't been used for years, was obviously much too large for such a party, so the library was cleared of its tables and the servants waxed the floor, brought up furniture from down below, arranged vases of flowers on tables, and generally made the room suitable for such a splendid occasion. At nine thirty a supper would be served in the gallery, after which they would dance again until the home waltz was played sharp at eleven o'clock. A five-piece orchestra was engaged through a booking agency which, fighting a losing battle against the wild goings on of the "flappers" and their crowd, advertised, "Catering for Refined Parties Since 1890."

Alice, with still vivid memories of that dreadful family dinner and dance at the Maybanks', was determined that Patricia and her friends would have fun. She thought a receiving line was quite unnecessary but she was outvoted by Arthur and his mother. So there was a receiving line and it was in that receiving line that Alice and Arthur first met David Spears. "This is David," Patricia said breathlessly, as though she were unveiling the Koh-i-noor diamond.

He was of medium height with olive complexion, contemplative eyes behind steel-rimmed glasses, a thin nose, the faintest suggestion of a moustache above a sensitive mouth, and a definite but delicate chin. His black hair was parted immaculately down the exact center of his scalp. "How do you do," he said, extending a thin, long-fingered hand. "I am very pleased to meet you." It was spoken as though he didn't want them to be over-awed by him and was doing his best to put them at their ease.

Alice accepted his hand and said, "We're very pleased to meet you too, David." She didn't know for sure what her face showed but, glancing sideways at Arthur, she could read his without any trouble. He did manage to shake hands very quickly and with obvious disinclination, as a timid missionary might have shaken hands with a lean and hungry cannibal.

The evening, which he seemed to have been looking forward to almost as much as Patricia herself and with similar trepidation, was irrevocably ruined for him now. Alice realized that. His dutiful greetings of the remaining guests was perfunctory at the best. Alice, to make up for her husband's sudden declination in spirits, more than compensated, she realized even at the time, by being unnaturally effusive.

"How *very* nice of you to come!" she kept saying. "We're delighted to see you." When she thought back on it later she felt vaguely embarrassed. That wasn't really her style.

Once the receiving line was over and the dancing had been started in a sedate and self-conscious way, the guest parents had to be taken care of and furnished with suitable refreshments, so it was some little time before Arthur could draw her away. Finally he managed to get her out into the hall. He was tense and distraught.

"What are we to do?" he asked urgently.

"Do?" asked Alice. "Do about what?"

"That boy's a Jew."

"There's nothing I can do about that. Blame his ancestors, not me."

"But Patricia is dancing with him."

"I don't think it's catching."

"But what will the other parents think?"

"I don't suppose they'll think anything one way or the other. You don't know that he's a Jew, and what if he is?"

"What if he is?"

"That's what I said."

"Patricia in love with a Jew boy?"

"Arthur, you're being absurd. What do you propose to do? Do you want me to go and make an announcement that we have just discovered that we think David Spears is a Jew and unless he can prove otherwise, the dance is over?"

"Of course not. You don't seem to be upset at all."

"I'm not."

"Why didn't you find out beforehand?"

"Oh, Arthur, for heaven's sake stop being so silly. I'm going back."

Arthur restrained himself from actively intervening with considerable effort and at great cost to his nervous system for the balance of the evening. Guests who tried to engage him in light conversation, however, found the experience unnerving; if he looked at them at all, it was only for the merest fraction of a second. Otherwise, his eyes were constantly on Patricia. Sometimes, when she was dancing, this required him to bob and weave about like a boxer. Sometimes he had to draw himself up to his full height; sometimes he was obliged to stoop. Occasionally whoever was trying to talk to him found himself automatically bobbing and weaving along with Arthur.

When the last guest had departed shortly after eleven o'clock and Patricia, her face radiant with pleasure, was about to tell her parents what a glorious birthday party it had been, Arthur turned on her and, flinging wide the doors of his anger, said, "That was a terrible evening. You will never have a birthday party again. How dare you bring a Jew into this house?"

"I don't know what you mean," Patricia replied, aghast.

"You know very well what I mean, young lady. You deliberately concealed the fact until it was too late for us to do anything about it. What will people think of you? It will be all over New York. Everyone will be saying that Patricia Melville has taken up with a slimy little Jew boy. Have you no pride? And, even if you have no pride, have you no consideration for our feelings, for our reputation?"

Patricia was instantly reduced to tears. Alice had been taken so off guard that for a moment she had been silenced. Now, however, she plunged into the battle. "Arthur!" she exclaimed. "How can you speak that way? David Spears was a guest in our house and a very polite and gentlemanly one. I had no idea you felt this way about Jews. I didn't realize how prejudiced you were."

"I am *not* prejudiced but I don't want my daughter to marry a Jew or a nigger or a Chinaman or one of those filthy anarchist Italians. That's not being prejudiced. I will not have that swarmy young man in the house again and Patricia might as well know it now."

"I had no idea . . ." Alice repeated in amazement.

"Well, you have now. I've been learning a lot I didn't know about Jews at the club. They're involved in a conspiracy to take over New York. They're squeezing honest Christians out of business everywhere."

Patricia had more or less recovered herself and was trying to interrupt, but Arthur brushed her aside. "Do you think for one moment Patricia would have been invited into a Jewish home? Of course not. But we invite them into ours. We invite them into our businesses. We trust them.

And then they cheat us out of all we own. I will not be a party to such . . ."

"I think Patricia has something to say."

"Well?" Arthur demanded impatiently.

"I don't know if what you say about Jews is true or not," Patricia said. "But David Spears isn't a Jew. He's Welsh. He was telling me all about it tonight. His grandfather was the Duke of something. He still has relatives in Wales and is spending this summer at Caernarvon with them. They're his uncle and aunt or cousins or something like that."

Arthur's mouth opened and closed like a goldfish which has just been returned to his bowl after a period out of water. "He wasn't Jewish at all then?" he muttered faintly.

"No," said Patricia. "I don't think Westside Academy takes Jews."

"Why didn't you say so?" he asked in a futile attempt to regain some semblance of justification for his outburst. But Alice had no intention of letting him get away with it.

"Do you expect Patricia to go around constantly explaining what her friends are not? I liked David Spears and I don't like him any more or any less because he turns out to be a Welshman and not a Jew."

The little moralistic speech was not entirely true, as Alice herself realized. She, too, was relieved to discover that young David was of more than respectable British forebears, but it was a good and right thing to say in front of Patricia.

"Spears doesn't sound Welsh," Arthur murmured.

"It's on his mother's side," Patricia answered. "His father was English."

"I'm going to bed," said Arthur.

Patricia flung her arms around her father's neck. Nothing he could do or say, Alice thought watching them embrace, would ever stand between them for long. Their relationship was a very, very special one. There was no jealousy in the reflection, but there was a tinge of sadness. It would have been nice to have had a child with whom she might have had . . . The thought trailed off into nothingness.

They were all down for breakfast the next morning, which was unusual.

"I liked your young man," Mrs. Melville told Patricia. "I thought his manners were charming."

"Yes," said Patricia blushing slightly, "he's a very nice boy."

"Weren't you proud of your daughter's choice?" she asked, looking at Arthur.

"Of course," Arthur answered. "I'm always proud of Patricia." Father and daughter exchanged smiles of mutual admiration.

Chapter 26

Mrs. Melville was sixty-seven—strange to reflect that she was younger than Patricia was now—and supposedly suffering from a heart condition, but this in no way inhibited her from taking a lively and frequently critical interest in Arthur's, Alice's, and Patricia's affairs. She particularly deplored the lack of social activity. It was no use for Alice to explain that it was senseless to plan for parties only to find when the time came that Arthur was plunged into the depths of gloom and could scarcely be persuaded to be civil with his wife and daughter, let alone be a gay and charming host to visitors.

"He needs to be taken out of himself. You must *force* him into situations. I should have done so more often with Edwin. I know that now."

It was incredible to Alice that her mother-in-law could have emerged from the frightful ordeal of her husband's death persuaded only, as she had been before the terrible event took place, that a little more firmness all round could have prevented it.

Yet over the years, in her loneliness, boredom, and frequent worry, Alice herself had sometimes been tempted to feel the same. Sometimes she had thought to herself, "If only Arthur would make an *effort*!" But the feeling quickly passed. She didn't understand his spells but she knew he was as powerless to prevent them as she was or, for that matter, as the doctor seemed to be. She was more or less reconciled to their placid, uneventful, and somewhat depressing way of life. It wasn't what she had once imagined, but now she had almost forgotten what that was. There was no point in dwelling on what might have been. The years had slipped by so quickly. She was unmistakably middle-aged. The mirror, which had once been her friend, now told her with cruel honesty that a routine of too much food, sherry before lunch, martinis before dinner, and almost no exercise was no way to preserve that body which she and others had once so admired. She thought of her mother at her age and of Mrs. Melville even now. Somtimes she

made vows to herself but she never kept them for more
than a day or two. Arthur didn't seem to care. It was easier
just to avoid looking in the mirror.

Yet, though their social efforts were few and far between,
they were not entirely ignored. Joseph Conrad was visiting
New York. It was known that he was in his middle or late
sixties, and in failing health. He would make no public ap-
pearances. He had arrived on the *Tuscania* and was to stay
for no more than six weeks. To read the papers one would
suppose that all Literary America was clamoring for a
glimpse of him. He had lunch with Colonel House and met
Paderewski, with whom he spoke of Poland. No lesser fig-
ures were likely to get within a mile of him.

But an invitation from Mrs. Curtis James arrived asking
them to meet the great man and hear him lecture and read
from his works. Arthur was excited. He had never read
Conrad before but he at once procured copies of *The Nigger of the Narcissus* and *Lord Jim*. He devoured them in
four days, even staying home for lunch. Unfortunately,
when the great evening arrived, Conrad read excerpts from
Victory, but that did little to diminish Arthur's great pleasure in the occasion.

There were a hundred and fifty people there, but in the
immense drawing room they seemed a comparatively small,
select group.

"I looked around and only the best people were there,"
Arthur told Alice on their way home.

"And we among them," Alice said.

"Yes," Arthur echoed, "we among them." Alice looked
at him and was pleased to see him so happy.

The next morning they sat for a time—just the two of
them—over their breakfast coffee. Patricia had gone off to
play tennis and Mrs. Melville had not yet come down.

"I was thinking after I got to bed last night," Arthur
said, "that I might try my hand at a novel."

"Why not?" Alice answered encouragingly.

"After all, Conrad was only a Polish sailor. He had to
learn the language and he still speaks with a very foreign
accent. I start out with the advantage of being able to write
pretty well, I think."

"What would it be about?"

"I thought that out. Shall I tell you?"

"Please do."

"You won't think I'm being foolish?"

"Of course not."

"The great thing is to write about the things and the people you know and understand. Conrad writes about the sea and ships and sailors. I would write about the world of Art. I really do know something about it, you know."

"Of course you do."

"Sometimes when I . . . when I get a bit depressed, I wonder if you really believe in me." He held up his hand to silence her as she was about to interrupt. "I can't say I'd blame you if you didn't. I haven't forgotten all the boasts I made when we were first married. I haven't forgotten how self-important I was then. And now? Now I'm well on in middle age and I've nothing to show for all my hours of work. I've nothing to point to."

"Of course you have. You and your father together have a collection that, for its size, equals anything in . . ."

"Oh, don't simply repeat my own words back to me to make me feel better," he interrupted impatiently. "I'm talking about doing something on my own. I want you to be proud of me, Alice. You have no reason to yet. But you will. I promise you. I will make a name for myself."

"Of course you will."

He searched her eyes with his. Was she just saying that to humor him, as one might say to a mentally retarded child, "That's splendid. You'll be catching up to all the others in no time"?

"Your novel," she prompted. "You were going to outline the story for me. Let's move into the sun-room. We'll be more comfortable there."

They were no sooner settled in the sun-room, however, before Mrs. Melville came in. "And how was your literary evening? she asked. "Tell me who all was there. I'm not interrupting a private discussion, am I?"

"I'll leave Alice to tell you about last night," Arthur said. "I have some work to do."

Arthur went as usual to the club for lunch and Alice, after doing her best to satisfy her mother-in-law's curiosity about the previous evening, spent the remainder of the morning doing housekeeping accounts. She then had sherry and when Mrs. Melville, who spent most mornings writing letters, rejoined her, they had lunch together. Then Alice had a nap and after that went out to have tea with Prudence and Dorothea at Prudence's house. The three sisters met about once a month. None of them enjoyed the meetings but Prudence always said, "It's so important to keep in touch."

She saw Arthur again when they were dressing before dinner. "You didn't say anything to Mother about the novel, did you?" Arthur asked.

"No, of course not. I thought you would want to tell her."

"I don't want anyone but you to know for the time being."

"When will you tell me the story?"

He didn't answer at first. And then he said, "You'll know it in due course."

Why had he changed his mind? Had he foreseen, when he said that, exactly how she would come to learn the story in the end? Of course not. How could he have? Yet, absurd as the idea was, it still nagged at the back of her mind . . .

It was that same spring of 1923 that they took Patricia to see Geoffrey Hamilton as Brutus in *Julius Caesar*. It was billed as a "Return Engagement" for the actor who had not been seen on Broadway for some years. The official story was that he had been on an extended tour of Europe but the cynics had a less charitable explanation of his absence. Whatever the truth of the matter, Alice had to admit reluctantly to herself that he no longer compelled her fascination as he had once done. The voice has lost its cutting edge; the eyes didn't flash with excitement as once they had done; he had put on weight. The theatre was little more than half-full and the applause was never more than polite. Patricia tried her best to see what her mother had told her she would see but she couldn't quite conceal her boredom.

"Why should I be surprised?" Alice thought to herself as she lay awake that night in the dark. "It's happened to me, too. I'm not exciting any more. The people who remember me as I was—including Arthur—must say to themselves, 'There was a time when she was lively and slim and attractive and she would toss her head and flash her blue eyes and smile. Now look at her.'" She must do something about herself. She really must. But what was the point? Who cared any longer?

Arthur was busy that summer—busier than he had been

for a long time. He went to the club as usual but, whereas before he had always returned in the afternoon, now he stayed in town for dinner two or three days a week and didn't arrive home until ten o'clock or thereabouts. Alice asked him where he spent his time and what he was doing. "I'm spending most of my time in the library at the club," he told her, "doing research for my novel. There are a good many novels there I can get hints from and of course the club has a number of literary members I can talk to." He seemed more at peace with himself than he had been for some time and though, from the sound of his speech and the smell of his breath when he arrived home some nights, she suspected that the research had been more convivial than scholarly, she didn't pester him.

There was one night he didn't come home at all. Alice waited until just before midnight and then telephoned the club. No, he was not there. He had left an hour or two before.

"On his way home?"

"I couldn't tell you that, ma'am. He left in the company of some other gentleman."

She worried and didn't sleep but the next morning, when he arrived home about ten, he was so abject that she didn't ask for any explanation. He told her a lie but she didn't bother to tell him she knew he was lying.

"We got involved in a long discussion at the club and first thing I knew it was after one. I decided that rather than disturb you I would spend the night there. I hope you weren't worried."

"Of course I was worried, but I guessed it must be something like that."

He didn't go back to the club for lunch that day and he slept for most of the afternoon.

One day in late August he got a letter from his friend Monsieur Parent in Paris.

My Dear Mr. Melville:

A very dear friend of mine, M. Jerome Le Royer, will be arriving with his wife in New York at about the same time that you receive this letter. M. Le Royer is, like yourself, a connoisseur and a collector of fine paintings.

When he told me of his proposed voyage to New

York to tour the galleries and to inspect some private collections I said to him, "There is one man you must make the acquaintance of. He is a man of great sensibility, superior taste, and impressive scholarship." It was in these words I took the liberty of referring him to you.

He will without doubt be in communication with you as soon after his arrival as possible and I hope it will not prove too great an imposition to show him a little of that hospitality for which Americans like yourself are famous throughout the world.

Although we have continued to correspond and to conduct business with each other over the years it is not at all the same as meeting together in Paris. It is over twenty years since you were here. When do you plan to return? I am much older but, thanks to God, I am still very active in all ways.

Your devoted servant,
Emile Parent

The letter delighted Arthur. All his self-importance, which he had renounced a few weeks earlier as a delusion of his weak nature, came surging back. For some time Alice had been concerned that he was getting thin. His dark Arabic face seemed at times almost sunken and the high cheekbones unduly prominent. Now all at once, miraculously, almost within minutes of reading the letter, his face seemed to fill out. As he stood up to hand the letter to Alice, he stood taller, his shoulders thrown back, his head more erect, his eyes gleaming.

"How very nice," Alice said, handing the letter back.

"Nice? It's better than nice. It is international acknowledgment at last. It was bound to come. Next summer we must go to Paris. We'll take Patricia. I'll write Parent and ask him if he would like me to give some lectures. You must help me brush up on my French."

"We might both take lessons this winter. Mine could stand some brushing up, too."

"Good idea. We'll get a tutor. All three of us will go at it together. I think I'll take the letter to the club. There are some there who will be interested."

"Of course there are."

"I'll bring it back to show Patricia at dinner time. I must

show it to Mother before I go." He almost bounded up the stairs.

"Oh dear," Alice thought to herself, "how little it takes to please him." His susceptibility to flattery had annoyed her when they were first married but now she found it merely pathetic. Surely if some of his manuscripts or even some of the brief "scholarly" notes he had sent off to publishers and editors had been published and he had had some actual achievements to point to he wouldn't get so carried away by Monsieur Parent's blandishments. Perhaps . . . perhaps not. There was something childlike, something a little sad about the absurdity of it all, but it did no harm. It was far, far better that he should be rushing about like an excited schoolboy who has just won the high jump than sitting and moping in his study. Unlike the boy, he hadn't won anything, but he thought he had and that was what really mattered. Far, far better than despondency and suicide in a bathtub. Anything was better than that.

"I won't be late," he told her when he came down from seeing his mother. "Don't tell Patricia. I'd like her to read the letter herself."

"You'll be home for dinner?"

"No, probably not. I'll be home by nine or shortly after. If Monsieur Le Royer should call, you will find out where he is staying, won't you?"

"Of course."

"And tell him I'll be in touch tomorrow at whatever time suits him. We'll have him and his wife for dinner, of course. Perhaps you'd like to give that some thought."

"I'll do that."

He kissed her good-bye, which was not his usual custom. "You are glad for me, aren't you?"

It was an appeal for love, for understanding, for reassurance that he did matter. There was an eager, childlike note in his voice.

"Of course I am, darling," she said. "I'm proud of you—very proud."

"I hoped you were."

"You'd think he had just won a Nobel Prize," she thought sadly to herself as he went out.

Mrs. Melville joined Alice for pre-luncheon sherry. She had one glass to Alice's three but she made no comment beyond a certain tightening of the lips as Alice poured her third glass.

"And what do you think?" she asked.

Alice knew perfectly well what she had in mind but, just the same, she asked, "About what?"

"That silly letter. Arthur is a dear child but he can lay no claim to 'impressive scholarship.' What has he done? I seem to have spent my life trying to get my husband and my son to *do* something. My father, as you know, was a prominent surgeon."

"Yes," Alice replied, "you've mentioned that."

"I have. I think of him often."

"You told me a little about him before Arthur and I married."

"Oh yes. You and Arthur had had a stupid quarrel. I remember. I don't talk much about him because he wouldn't approve. He was a modest man, though he had no reason to be."

"He was a great believer in discipline."

"Of course. 'Discipline,' he used to say, 'is the cornerstone of civilization.'"

"What happened to your brothers?"

"We've lost touch. Ben became an engineer and went to Oregon. Daniel and Aubrey went to Australia. They had a falling out with Father and never wrote. I used to get Christmas cards from Ben but I haven't for the past few years. Father was very disappointed in his sons. He wanted at least one of them to become a surgeon and he wanted all of them to be leaders—strong, important men like himself. When they settled for obscurity he thought they had let him down. I was my father's favorite."

"Your mother?"

"She was a timid little person. I don't know how my father happened to marry her. She died in her thirties. My father was the great influence in our lives. I scarcely remember my mother."

"You said your father was modest."

"I mean he wasn't like Arthur. He wasn't forever boasting about what he was going to do; he just did things. I didn't intend to imply that he was self-effacing or wishy-washy. When he came into a room people knew someone had arrived."

"I think you're hard on Arthur."

"I wish I'd been a good deal harder. I thought once that I could make his father amount to something; he thought of being an architect, you know. When that didn't work out I wanted him to work *with* an architect as a designer. He had the talent but he couldn't be bothered. He gave up so easily. I kept after him enough, heaven knows, but it didn't work. Then he started to get his moods and I gave up on him and devoted myself to Arthur but he's turning out just like his father. I still feel sometimes I'd like to shake him and frighten him as I used to do when he was a small boy. That used to get results, but they were short-lived, I'm afraid."

"You think I could have done more for Arthur, don't you?"

Mrs. Melville gave Alice a quick, penetrating glance and then looked off for a moment into space before replying. When she did answer she did so almost hesitantly, choosing her words carefully. "I hoped perhaps that you might succeed where I had failed. You seemed . . . you seemed an ambitious young woman, as your mother was. You seemed a fighter and I liked and respected that even when you fought me but . . . but somehow, somewhere you've lost your fighting qualities. You've given in. Am I being unfair?"

"No," Alice answered thoughtfully, "no, I don't think you're being unfair. Not entirely. I wish you had let Arthur and me have a house of our own. I thought if Arthur could get away from you . . . I don't know. It might have made no difference. Arthur is what he is. I love him."

"But you're disappointed in him, aren't you? You thought your marriage would be more exciting, didn't you? You don't need to answer. You and I have more in common than you realize, my dear. Perhaps I tried to keep Arthur under my influence for too long. Perhaps things would have been different if you had had a place of your own. I don't know. Worrying over what might have been is such a waste of time. Shall we have lunch?"

Alice thought of the conversation as she lay on her bed after lunch. Had this strong imperious woman sacrificed her husband and her son on the altar of her abiding admiration for her father? No, that was an old-fashioned thought. To think such a thing was an insult to Mr. Melville and to Arthur. How much more could she herself

have done for Arthur? How much more might she do for
him even now? How much more might she do to make
herself a better person? It was all senseless speculation.
Looking ahead at age eighteen was very different from
looking back at age forty-two. It must be so for everyone.
The thoughts nagged her just the same and, when she realized she wasn't going to sleep, she got up and went for a
walk. She hadn't been doing enough walking.

The dinner was not an absolute disaster but no one capable
of distinguishing between boiled cod and Filets of Sole
Messalina could possibly have described it as a triumph.

> *Quiche aux Poireaux*
> *Suprêmes de Volaille Sautés Cintra*
> *Pommes de Terre Nouvelles à la Vapeur*
> *Soufflé de Topenambours*
> *Fenouil à la Vinaigrette*
> *Crème au Limon avec des Fraises*

Mrs. Cuthbert, who had cooked for the Melvilles for
years, had selected the menu from her "No Nonsense
French Cookery Book." When Alice asked about new potatoes and strawberries, neither of which were in season, she
said, "I cut the regular potatoes down small and we use
strawberry preserve. No one will notice."

Alice had had her doubts and, as things turned out, they
were well founded. She had suggested to Arthur and his
mother that they might bring in a French chef for the occasion, but this idea was received with a shocked silence. It
was as though she had advocated bringing in naked
Chinese dancing girls to prance around the table between
courses. "It would be an unheard of insult to Mrs. Cuthbert," Mrs. Melville said. "She had coped more than ade-
quately with far more elaborate dinners than this one."

It was a dinner for twenty including, as Arthur assured
Alice, "the acknowledged leaders of New York's Art
world." Alice knew two of the wives slightly but none of
the men and, as the guests assembled, it became obvious
that Arthur was on anything but intimate terms with them.
He talked to a Mr. Van Nostrand for ten minutes before
dinner as they sipped their pre-dinner sherry only to have
the gentleman say, at the end of the time, "Actually, Mr.

Melville, I'm David Courtney. Van Nostrand is the tall
man over there talking to your wife."

The leek quiche didn't puff properly, the chicken breasts
were tough and tasteless, the artichoke soufflé tasted like
yesterday's oatmeal porridge with unidentifiable additives,
and the strawberries were sweet red mush. Dr. Jankel, Arthur's eye doctor, had recently given him glasses which he
wasn't yet used to and, peering closely at the Crème au
Limon avec des Fraises and poking at it tentatively with his
spoon, he said meditatively, "It looks as though someone
had been sick." Then, looking up at the faces of his startled
guests, he explained, "I'm sorry. I was thinking aloud. I'm
sure it's perfectly edible."

The talk was of course devoted almost exclusively to
paintings and painters. It meant nothing to Alice and at
one point she turned to Monsieur Le Royer on her right
and said, "I'm the ignorant one in our family. My husband
is the expert."

Monsieur Le Royer, an unpleasant little man with a
large mouth, small moustache, flat nose, and a receding
forehead, looked, Alice thought, rather like a complacent
lizard. "Your husband an *expert*?" he asked in astonishment. "No, no, madame. Your husband is an *amateur*, a
dabbler you say in English. Monsieur Parent told me so
himself. Your husband has no artistic sense. Like many
rich Americans, he judges paintings by their cost. If it is
expensive, it is good."

Alice had made her remark to Monsieur Le Royer during a lull in the general conversation and Monsieur Le
Royer's response to it was made in a loud voice to a silent
table. Alice looked apprehensively at Arthur. He flushed
but made no comment.

The men remained only a short time in the dining room
before joining the ladies and then they all visited the gallery. The comments of the visitors were on the whole polite. Monsieur Le Royer, looking more lizardlike than ever,
put on his pince-nez and peered at the various canvases
angrily with his large mouth tight shut. Arthur said little.

They didn't stay long. It seemed apparent to all that the
evening had not been a success and the sooner it came to
an end, the better for all concerned.

It was a cold, blustery night with sudden squalls of rain.
The guests hurried to their cars after quick, perfunctory

thank-yous. Arthur stood outside on the botoom step watching them go. When the last guest had departed Alice held the door open, waiting for him to come in, but he didn't do so.

She called and there was no answer. Patricia, attending her first grown-up dinner party, and Mrs. Melville were behind her in the hall. "Shall I go and find him?" Patricia asked.

"No," said Alice decisively, "I will. She put on her raincoat and went out.

He wasn't on the driveway, so she went round to the garden at the back. The rain had increased and was sweeping in angry gusts across the wide lawn. He was standing there facing it, his hands by his side, his head up like a Christian martyr about to face the lions.

"Arthur, you must come in. You're soaked through."

"I'm a dabbler," he said. "I'm a dabbler. Everyone knows it now, even Patricia. You knew it before and so did my mother but Patricia thought I was something."

"You *are*, Arthur! You are! Please come in." The rain lashed their faces. She kissed him. "Please, please come in."

"They're right. Of course they're right."

"Please come in."

He didn't answer. He stood there with his eyes wide open and the rain beating against his face.

"I believe in you," she told him. "Doesn't that mean anything to you?" The face was immobile. "Arthur please! Please come in!"

"I'm a dabbler," he repeated tonelessly. "I'm a dabbler."

"Let's go in out of the rain," Alice said softly.

"All right," he answered at last. "Let's go back in."

Chapter 27

In the summer of 1925, Patricia joined fourteen other girls on a conducted tour of Europe. In the space of two and a half months, including Atlantic crossing time, they visited England, Scotland, Ireland, Wales, France, Germany, Holland, Switzerland, Austria, and Italy. She had been very doubtful about going; it was the first time she had left home for longer than a weekend. Arthur didn't help matters by telling her that "Europeans, particularly Frenchmen and Italians, are at their most dangerous when they pretend to be charming. You must be constantly on your guard. If you find yourself in a situation where you have to talk to them you should discuss the beauties of ancient architecture and the weather."

It was a lonely time for Alice. Arthur was far from well—nervous, petulant, and prone to long periods of morose brooding. For a time he even stopped going to the club for lunch but, even on those days, he preferred a sandwich in his study to lunching with her. Whether he went to the club or not he generally left home in the evening and seldom returned before it was time for bed. She suspected, of course, that he had a mistress, though that scarcely seemed Arthur's style, but she didn't ask him where he went or why. She wanted to know but she was afraid of what the answer might be. So she remained silent and worried instead.

She consulted Dr. Adler again and he prescribed "Horsford's Acid Phosphate." She read the leaflet that came with it so that she could extoll its virtues to Arthur. "Prepared according to the directions of Prof. E. N. Horsford of Cambridge. A preparation of the phosphates of lime, magnesia, potash and iron . . . for dyspepsia, mental and physical exhaustion, weakened energy, nervousness etc. . . . universally recommended and prescribed by physicians of all schools . . . best tonic known, furnishing sustenance to both brain and body."

Arthur looked at it gloomily when Alice presented him

with it. "It claims to do nothing that whiskey doesn't do," he said, "and I suspect whiskey does it better."

"You can have both," Alice told him. "It says that 'its action will harmonize with such stimulants as are necessary to take.' "

"Leave it in the bathroom. I'll think about it."

There it remained untouched for weeks until finally Alice threw it out.

Yet all was not doom and gloom. There were a few good evenings when the clouds seemed to blow away and the sun shone through. One one such occasion he took her out for dinner and then to Daly's Theatre to see *After Business Hours,* which made them both laugh.

"Why did we never go back to Europe?" Arthur asked as they were having a nightcap before going to bed.

"We still could," Alice said. "Why don't we plan a trip for next spring?"

"We'll go to Rome and Greece this time and I won't spend all my time in galleries. We'll explore together and drink wine at sidewalk cafés and watch the honeymoon couples and pretend we're young and foolish again." His eyes shone with pleasure at the prospect.

"Oh, Arthur, I'd love it! We'll go to Venice and ride in a gondola."

"And then on to Egypt to see the pyramids and ride camels. Oh, Alice, if you know how I've hated myself all this time for being such a drag on you. But I'll make it up. I really will."

"You haven't been on a drag, darling. Please don't say that. You just haven't . . . you haven't been well. That's all. And I'm afraid I've been dull. Let's both make more of an effort."

"I agree. I do really agree, Alice, and I'll try."

"How's the novel coming? When am I going to get a chance to see it?"

He was serious in an instant. "You may see it in due course," he said. "I'm working at it."

She wished she hadn't asked. Her question broke the spell. She tried to get the talk going on the trip again.

"I'd like to visit the Greek islands, too," she said. "I was reading about them just the other day."

"We'll think about it. I don't see how we can just pack up and leave Mother."

"She'll be well taken care of. We won't be gone that long. She would want us to go."

"We'll think about it."

They finished their drinks and went to bed. The next morning he was in low spirits once again. There was no further talk of the trip.

Despite her initial misgivings, Patricia enjoyed her trip enormously and arrived home brimming over with enthusiasm. "Now," she announced, "I know Europe."

It cheered Arthur to have his daughter back and Alice was delighted to watch and listen to the two of them in eager conversation about all Patricia's adventures. She herself was seldom included. Patricia was very much her father's daughter. Perhaps, if little Arthur had lived, he might have been very much her son. If she could only have had more children—half a dozen at least—how wonderful it would have been. If . . . if . . . if . . . It was stupid to think that way.

Patricia didn't stay put for long. A month after her return she received an invitation from a girl who had been on the tour with her to pay a visit to Boston.

"But you've just come back," Alice protested. "I really think you should settle down and get on with your French and music."

"Please," Patricia begged. "It's only for two weeks."

"I'll let your father decide."

That, of course, was the same as saying "yes." Arthur was quite incapable of refusing Patricia anything she had set her heart on.

But she knew he was hurt to see her go away again so soon after returning home, and the night after Patricia's departure was the worst since he had walked out into the rain. He had stayed home most evenings with Patricia but, on this particular evening, he went out again. He arrived home just after ten and Alice, who went to meet him in the hall, knew at once that they were in for trouble. There was a sort of vacancy in his face when he was in one of his moods.

"I'm leaving," he announced. "I can't stand it here any longer. I don't owe you anything and you don't owe me anything. We should never have got married."

"Why don't we go to bed?" Alice suggested. "We'll talk about it in the morning."

He looked at her bleakly, almost as though he was trying to work out who she was. "I'm not going to bed. I'm moving out as soon as I pack my things. You think I've had too much to drink, don't you? Well, I haven't. I've had just enough to give me the courage to tell you the way I feel. I should have told you a long time ago. You've always despised me. I know that. Well, tonight I'll tell you something. I've never loved you. The only good thing you've ever done for me was to give me Patricia. And she's *my* daughter. She's mine. You've always been too superior for me. It was my mother made me get married. Now I'm quitting. I'm getting out. I'm going to lead my own life. You can't keep me here any longer."

"No one's keeping you here, Arthur. Please come to bed. You don't know what you're saying."

"I know what I'm saying. I should have said it long ago. I know other things too. I know I'm a failure. You don't have to keep telling me that. I won't be around for you to tell it to. I'll be gone. But you and my mother made me that way."

"Arthur, I've never told you you were a failure. You mustn't say things like that."

He stood there, tall and gaunt. His eyes were bloodshot and his black hair, now flecked with white as though salt had been sprinkled on it, was tousled. His shoulders were stooped and his tie was loosened. There was stubble on his chin. Incongruously Alice remembered the beggars on the street she had seen when her father took her to the store. She felt a great surge of pity for him welling up inside her.

"Don't pity me," he said, reading the emotion in her eyes with uncanny accuracy. "You don't have to pity me. I'm going to be all right. As soon as I get away from here I'm going to be just fine. I don't want your pity. Save it for yourself."

Benton, aroused by the loudness of his voice, now hovered solicitously in the background. Alice was glad to see him there. Since the night of Mr. Melville's suicide she had come to regard him more as a trusty friend than as a servant.

"Why don't you let Benton help you up to bed?" she asked gently.

"I'm not going to bed. I'm leaving. I'm getting out. I told you that. You can't make me stay here. My mother can't make me stay here. I hate this place. I never liked it. Even when I was a boy I hated it. It's like living in a museum." His voice dropped suddenly to a conspiratorial whisper. "But I'll tell you what I'm going to do before I go."

"What?" Alice asked.

"I'm going to take a carving knife and slash up the paintings. I haven't been living in a real world. I've been living in a world of paintings. The only people that have been real to me are the people on canvas. I'm going to carve them up. They never took me seriously anyway. I'm going to kill them. They always thought I was just a dabbler. A dabbler! I'll show them who's a dabbler! I'll slash them to pieces. It's either them or you and my mother. Why not everybody? Why not slash everybody up? Why not? My father slashed his wrists. Why didn't he slash our throats? That's the answer."

He fell suddenly to his knees, mumbling and muttering incoherently, holding his hands over his face as though to blot out some terrible vision. On a nod from Alice, Benton moved in and, helping him gently to his feet, guided him up to bed.

Alice helped herself to a glass of brandy to steady her nerves and presently Benton reappeared in the doorway.

"He seems to be asleep now, ma'am," he said.

"Thank you, Benton. You have been a great help. I don't know what I'd do without you."

"These are difficult times for us all," he said quietly. "If you need me, Mrs. Melville, please don't hesitate to ring."

"I'm having a glass of brandy. Why don't you join me?"

He hesitated momentarily but all his instincts were against it. "We won't make a habit of drinking together late at night," Alice said. "Just this once."

"I think not, ma'am. I appreciate the offer."

So there she was alone in the great big house. Mrs. Melville was sound asleep in her great bed with her teeth soaking in a glass on the bedside table. Arthur would be snoring. Presently she would look in on him. She would go up and lie down beside him and lie awake looking at the darkness. Then, if he seemed settled, she would go to her own bed, but probably not to sleep.

Patricia arrived home and announced, "I have met the man I love and he's coming to stay with us next weekend to ask if he can marry me. I told him there wouldn't be any problem. He's a foreigner."

"A foreigner?" Arthur asked in alarm. "He's not Boston-Irish or Italian is he?"

"Of course not. He's a young doctor doing postgraduate work. He's a Canadian and lives in Vancouver, British Columbia."

"A Canadian. He speaks English then. Is he part Indian?"

"Of course not. You couldn't tell him from an American if you didn't know."

So Michael came. Alice thought him a rather solemn young man but he called Arthur "sir" and endured with seeming enthusiasm a lengthy tour of the art treasures, so Arthur thought him an ideal prospective son-in-law. The nightmarish incident in the front hall was never referred to again. Alice wondered if Arthur recalled it at all. Mostly likely he thought it a dream. At any rate, during Michael's stay he was quite himself again. He stayed home, didn't drink too much, and went out of his way to make the visit a success. Mrs. Melville too was charmed by the young man. "I didn't realize Canadians had such nice manners," she told him. "I thought you'd be rougher."

It was all arranged and six weeks later, Michael having completed his work in Boston, they were married, and the young couple set off for Vancouver. They would have a honeymoon in Carmel on their way.

It all seemed very much a whirlwind affair and Patricia "much too young." But the two were unquestionably deeply in love. Michael was eminently satisfactory. Also, Alice had the feeling, which she never expressed to a living soul, that, if Patricia didn't take this opportunity, another might be a long time in coming.

Summer 1936. Alice was fifty-four, Arthur was fifty-eight, and old Mrs. Melville, her mind and tongue as sharp as ever but her body shrunken with age, was seventy-nine.

The Depression years had not affected their lives appreciably, though they had intensified Arthur's abiding distrust of the working classes. He had an almost pathological hatred of Franklin Roosevelt. "He has not only betrayed his own class," Arthur was fond of saying, "but, worse than that, he has betrayed the nation." When one evening some rowdies hurled rocks through the dining-room window and were not apprehended because the police failed to arrive in time, Arthur held Roosevelt personally responsible. "It would never have happened under Hoover."

It was Hoover who had said, "You cannot extend the mastery of government over the daily life of a people without somewhere making it master of people's souls and thoughts." Arthur was fond of quoting this and Alice nodded and agreed it was a wise thing to say, though she couldn't quite see what it had to do with hoodlums throwing stones at their windows. Nor was it very apparent to her what comfort such eloquence might be to a man, with a wife and two or three children, who couldn't find work.

"I sometimes wonder," Arthur had told Alice in 1932, when Roosevelt had beaten Hoover by some seven million votes, "I really do sometimes wonder if, in times like these, it might not be better to suspend universal suffrage. The ordinary man on the street is so fickle. He doesn't really know what is best for him."

To Alice's great relief Arthur stopped drinking too much. He still went most days to the club for lunch and he still frequently didn't arrive home until almost bedtime, but they had some evenings together and, when he did stay home, he was gentle. Once or twice Alice asked him about the novel or whether he was working on something new, but such questions seemed to upset him and presently she stopped asking them.

Most of the rooms in the big old house were shut up now and most of the servants had gone. The faithful Benton remained and a curious young man by the name of Argus Clayton kept the lawns reasonably trim, the gardens reasonably free of weeds, and the walks cleared of snow in winter. Alice's maid Maureen had left long since to get married and Arnold Crump, Arthur's valet, had also gone. Mrs. Cuthbert with her "No Nonsense" cookery books remained in command of the kitchen with a girl to help with the washing up. A couple of cleaning women came in three times a week.

Patricia wrote long and happy letters from Vancouver and suggested they come for a visit but Arthur, though he longed to see his daughter, was opposed to making the lengthy journey. Alice though it would be fun to fly but Arthur said, "I certainly will not go up in one of those contraptions and the train journey is much too long. Besides, everything west of Chicago until you reach California is dry and dusty and transportation is exceedingly unreliable."

The first child was Michael after his father; the second was Patricia after her mother; the third was Arthur. "Three is our quota," Patricia wrote. Alice wondered, if there had been a fourth and the fourth had been a girl, if it would have been named after her. She would have liked to have a little girl carry her name into the future.

She spent a good part of her time with Mrs. Melville, often sitting reading by her bedside waiting for her to wake so they could talk for twenty minutes or half an hour before the old lady drifted off again. She was almost blind now and slept, Alice thought, as much out of boredom as from any physical necessity for rest.

When they did talk it was often about Arthur as a boy. "If I had it all to do again," she would say, "I'd send him to a good boarding school, perhaps a military academy, where he would have had men and other boys and discipline."

"He would have hated it," Alice said.

"Perhaps," she replied in her thin old voice, "perhaps. I'm not sure it is bad for the young to be made to do some things they hate. It builds character. My father made me do things I hated at the time. I don't think I ever lacked character."

"No," Alice assured her, "no one would ever accuse you of lacking character."

Mrs. Melville's smile was grim but not without humor. "No one would make that accusation of you either," she said. "When we had our differences they were differences of ladies of character." She seemed pleased with the thought. "We're birds of a feather," she said. She intended the remark as a compliment—perhaps the greatest compliment in her power to pay—and Alice accepted it as such.

Then, one morning when they were having coffee together and Mrs. Melville seemed perhaps a little more lively than usual, she stretched out her skeletal hand to Alice, who took it in hers. "I think I'm going now," she said. She put her cup down rather suddenly on her bed tray and lay back on the pillows. A slight gasp and that was it.

Alice sat on for a moment or two, the dead woman's hand still enfolded in her own, looking at the old face with its mouth slightly ajar, its eyes almost closed, not much paler in death than it had been latterly in life. Then she got up and laid the arm back on the sheet. She removed the tray to the floor and went out to find Benton and to call Dr. Adler.

When she called the club Arthur hadn't yet arrived but she left instructions for him to telephone. He did so a few minutes later.

"It's your mother," Alice told him. "You'd better come home right away."

"What's happened?"

"She's dead, Arthur."

There was a long pause. "I'll be there as soon as possible," he said.

Alice had feared that Arthur might be temporarily destroyed by his mother's death and suffer a recurrence of his black depression, but he took it surprisingly calmly. It was only after the funeral that he gave her more than a glimpse of the emotions that had been at work deep within him.

"I feel guilty that I didn't spend more time with her these past months. It was shame, I suppose. Did she speak of me?"

"Sometimes."

"She thought I was a failure, didn't she? She felt I'd let her down. When I did go and sit by her the reproach was in her eyes. I know that reproach; I've had it all my life. Both my father and I were disappointments to her. She wanted always to remake us in her own father's image."

"She loved you very much."

He half smiled in the grave way he had. "You don't have to say things like that. I don't need that kind of comfort. I don't think my mother was capable of love in the way most people use the word. I'm not certain you are either, if you want me to be honest. I suspect I was attracted to you because you have so many of my mother's qualities. I was still very much under her influence when I married you." He stopped suddenly. "Is that something I shouldn't have said?"

"No," she answered, making an effort to keep her tone

level, "no, there's nothing we can't say to each other. You're wrong. You didn't marry me; we married each other. I accepted your proposal because I loved you. I thought you asked me because you felt the same."

"I know I'm not easy to love," he went on, talking apparently as much to himself as to her. "I'm not very fond of myself. One day, however, I may prove my mother wrong. I may even surprise you."

"Arthur," she pleaded gently, "don't please torment yourself. Don't say things that will spoil our life together. The reproach you keep talking about is as much in yourself as . . ."

"I know that," he interrupted. "I know that perfectly well. It was bred into me. But I'm overcoming it now. I've had some help. I *am* overcoming it. I'll surprise you yet."

"Your success wouldn't surprise me. I don't underestimate your talents. Please don't speak as though I had always been nagging at you or looking down on you or something like that."

He raised his head and looked at her and there was kindness in his look—kindness and sadness both. Then he shrugged his shoulders and said, "Let's forget everything I said, shall we? I've been a lucky man really. You've been a good wife and Patricia is a good daughter. I know that."

Except on weekends Arthur continued to go to the club for lunch but he began to spend more evenings at home. Outwardly he seemed reasonably calm and contented but sometimes, as they sat reading and making occasional desultory remarks to each other, Alice knew his mind was neither on his book nor on her.

She had taken to having her own lunch on a tray in the sun-room where she would read the *Times* and sip three glasses of sherry before the salad or the soup and sandwich arrived. She had listened to Arthur talk politics and, when she was a girl, she had listened to her father, but beyond realizing that nice, well brought-up people who had the best interests of America truly at heart were Republicans and the shortsighted laborers, who were greedy for more money than they were worth, were Democrats—beyond that realization she had never given the matter much thought.

Now, all at once, she began to find herself more interested, and the more interested she found herself, the more she began to doubt that her father and Arthur and their various friends and acquaintances had all the truth on their side.

These United States were, she realized, in very deep trouble. Nearly one quarter of all the workers had no jobs. She looked at the photographs of long lineups outside soup kitchens and she heard Arthur tell her that everyone at the club believed that Roosevelt was determined to destroy the "American System." Mrs. Dowker, a relic of the old "At Home" days, telephoned to say that she and some of her friends had formed a telephoning committee to urge all their friends to turn out and vote for Landon. "That wicked man in the White House is determined to be a dictator," she said in her twangy nasal voice. "He is lavishing money on the shiftless and ignorant in order to get them under his control. I know that's true. I have inside information. You will vote, won't you?"

"Yes," Alice told her. "I intend to."

"Landon is the only man who can save us from revolution," Mrs. Dowker told her.

Alice thought of the crowds of laboring men and their families she had seen with Carla Sandhurst on their trip to Coney Island. She remembered Mark Wells, with whom she had walked in Central Park and who had explored the Whitney Mansion goggle-eyed. Those were "the people" everyone kept talking about. They didn't want to start a revolution. All they wanted to do was make a living. Even her ineffectual kidnapping friend only wanted enough money to get back to Wilmington.

Well, next week she would stage her own little revolution. Next week, while Arthur and all the other people like him were marking their ballots for Landon, she would vote for Franklin Roosevelt. She didn't know much about Roosevelt but she was convinced in her own mind that he was much more likely to help those happy throngs at Coney Island than was the folksy, ineffectual ex-governor of Kansas.

She never got to cast her ballot.

She had breakfast in bed but was up and dressed when Arthur came in. He stood uncertainly with one hand on the back of a chair. He looked at her as though he were squinting into a bright light. The blood seemed to have drained from his cheeks, leaving them yellowish in color.

"Arthur! What's wrong? You look ill."

"It . . . it was coming up the stairs. I . . . I don't think I'll go to the club." He spoke quietly and with obvious effort. "I think . . . I think I'll . . ."

His knees suddenly buckled under him and he tumbled to the floor.

Chapter 28

Dr. Adler came and went and came and went and came and went and huffed and said, "I'm afraid it's just a matter of time."

"I expect that diagnosis applies to all of us," Alice retorted. She telephoned Patricia, who was devastated by the news. "I'll catch the very next plane." Then, after a moment for reflection, she said, "You've taken me by surprise," in an accusatory tone, as though Alice should have planned Arthur's last illness with greater forethought. "I'll let you know."

Patricia called back sometime later to announce that she wouldn't arrive as soon as she had hoped because Michael Jr. had just broken out in a dreadful rash and Michael Sr. was at a medical convention in Victoria and she couldn't possibly leave just then but would arrive as soon as she could and please not to even think of meeting her at the airport.

Arthur lay on his back, staring up. Sometimes he was conscious of Alice being there; at other times he seemed quite unaware of anything. Sometime around midnight she left him with the nurse and went downstairs for a cup of coffee. She had forgotten all about the election but now she remembered and turned on the radio. Roosevelt had been reelected with a popular majority that looked as if it might reach ten million votes when all the returns were in. He seemed likely to carry every state but Maine and Vermont. It seemed somehow disloyal to Arthur to be glad about it at that moment. She switched off the radio, finished her coffee, and went back upstairs.

An hour or so later he said, "Cathy isn't here, is she?"

She had his hand in hers and she squeezed it and asked, "You mean Patricia? She'll be here as soon as she can."

"That will be nice," he whispered. "But I wanted Cathy, too."

"Who's Cathy?" she asked gently.

"It doesn't matter," he said.

There was silence for a time, broken only by his deep,

irregular breathing. Then he said something so softly that Alice didn't catch it. She stood up and leaned over him. "What was that, dear?"

Again he whispered in a throaty way and this time she got it. "The election?" He nodded almost imperceptibly. "It looks like a great victory for Landon."

He smiled very faintly. "I knew it," he said. And those were the last words he spoke.

It all came back so vividly and yet, in some ways, so like a dream—real and unreal the way things so often were. She had been sad that Arthur was dead and yet that sadness was more, perhaps, at the fact that he had found so little real pleasure in life.

Benton was there. Benton was always there when he was needed most. What would she have done without him? How could she have coped without his calm, strong, deferential manliness? The world didn't produce Bentons anymore and the world was the poorer for it.

The world was the poorer for a whole lot of things for which Benton served still in her mind as a sort of symbol—an order and sense of fitness in society, integrity, loyalty. People thought all those things were old-fashioned now.

Dorothea's husband had retired a year or two before Arthur had died and they had moved to Florida. The last time Alice had seen her was at Prudence's funeral. Not that that mattered. What mattered most was that somehow or other she had let her friends slip out of her life. Of course, with Arthur's moods so unpredictable, both entertaining and being entertained had proved difficult and so . . . No, that wasn't fair. She had only herself to blame. She was using Arthur as an excuse when, all the time, it was her fault. Of course it was. One had to work at friendship just as one had to work at music or needlepoint or . . . yes, or even retaining one's youthful figure.

But she had found most of the people that might have been her friends so boring. They played bridge and took Italian lessons and read books on philosophy and chitted and chatted about all sorts of things that didn't interest her at all and so she had sort of slumped back into her useless routine and done nothing much more than was absolutely essential.

She was alone and she had no one to blame but herself. But now she had to bestir herself. She couldn't possibly live on in this great museum of a house. What had happened to all her dreams? What indeed? If there had been children perhaps. Well, there hadn't been. Only one. Only one that lived. But even if there had been they would all be grown up now. What a puzzle life was. But, puzzle or not, the time was fast approaching when she was going to have to do something.

Patricia had arrived from Vancouver in time for the funeral and stayed on for a few days after it. Alice was pleased to see her but found her we-must-all-be-calm-in-the-midst-of-our-grief attitude pretty hard to take.

One evening, as they were sitting before the fire sipping a glass of after-dinner port, Alice said, "I expect you'll be wanting to get back to Michael and the children. I hope you aren't staying on because you think I need you."

Patricia looked solemnly at her mother—a female version of Arthur if ever there was one—and said, "Michael and I had a talk about you before I left and we quite agreed."

"Is that unusual?" Alice asked.

"We talked about what would be best for you and we . . ."

"I think if you don't mind," Alice interrupted, "I'll decide what is best for me. I appreciate your and Michael's concern but I am sound of wind and limb with a mind of my own. I'll make my own decisions for a time yet."

"We weren't trying to interfere," Patricia objected. "It was just that we thought you might like to come and live with us. It would mean, of course, a large remodeling job on the house so you could have your own private quarters. Michael and I think the older generation are entitled to their privacy."

"That is very broad-minded of Michael and you. You mean I wouldn't be expected to share a bedroom with the children?"

"Mother, please don't be difficult. I know how upset you must be about Father's sudden death but life must go on and we must . . ."

"Patricia, my dear, we must all do what we must. If I did move to Vancouver I would take an apartment of my own and I would see no more of you and Michael than suited you both and me. I am considering various possibilities of which that is one."

"The last thing that Michael and I have in mind is to

interfere in any way with your life. We wouldn't dream of it. Michael often says, 'Older people have got to live their own lives.' "

"That's very generous of him," Alice said coldly.

"Oh Mother, don't be like that. We're only trying to help."

"Of course you are, dear, and I'm trying to tell you not to bother. I don't want your help. If you must know I have spent most of my life fighting back an almost irrepressible desire to do wonderful, mad, feckless things that no one I knew would possibly approve of. On the whole I've been successful. There have been a few occasions in my life when the impulse became too strong to be resisted but, by and large, I've behaved myself. Now I'm free. Your father, to whom I owed my first loyalty, has no further need of me. You, my only child, are on your own with your own family to care for. You don't need me any more either. I shall sell the house, pay off the servants, and indulge myself. It's late in life but not too late, thank the good Lord. There's time for a last fling."

"Good for you," Patricia said vaguely. "What have you in mind?"

"I have various ideas, some of which you would not approve of."

"You make me sound like an awful stick-in-the-mud."

"Do I, darling? I don't mean to. I'm really paying you a compliment, in a way. You're much more sensible than I am. You have inherited that from your father."

"I . . . I really don't understand what's got into you, Mother. I've never known you like this."

"Of course you haven't. You didn't know me as a girl. By the time you came along, my dear, I was a staid married woman. But deep inside me there was still some of that naughtiness. I hadn't used it all up as a child. I'll use the rest of it up now."

Then, all at once, she saw to her horror that Patricia was making a valiant but not entirely successful effort to fight back tears. "Oh, my dear, please don't cry. What is the trouble? I know how close you were to your father."

"You . . . you said you'd spent most of your life fighting back a desire to do wonderful things but now at last you're free. You sound as though you were glad Father was dead. I don't understand. I don't understand you at all."

Alice moved over to sit beside her daughter and put her arm around her shoulder. "I'm not sure sometimes I understand myself," she said. "Don't cry, please. I loved Arthur. You *must* know that. I've been happy and I hope . . . I hope I gave him some happiness. I gave him you, after all, and you were his greatest happiness of all. When I said I had to fight back a longing to do exciting things I didn't mean it was a constant struggle. In many, many ways I've been lazy. I've decided to stop being lazy now. Now that Arthur is dead I've got to make a new life for myself, and, without him, that new life has to be a very different one. You can surely understand that."

Patricia didn't answer at first, but then she dried her eyes and said, "You were just trying to be brave in front of me. Was that it?"

"Yes," said Alice. "I expect that was it."

"You'll be thinking of closing up the old house and making plans for the future, I expect," Benton said to Alice one morning as he finished serving her breakfast. Patricia had returned home the day before.

Alice had invited him to sit down at the dining-room table with her for a cup of coffee. He did so more easily there than in the drawing room. Somehow it seemed more neutral territory.

"Yes," Alice answered, "yes, I'm going to make plans to do that. Quite apart from the expense I couldn't possibly continue to live on here all alone."

"I'd like to assure you, Mrs. Melville, that I'll stay as long as I'm needed and I'll leave as soon as I'm no further use."

"Thank you, Benton. I knew you would understand the situation. It must be sad for you just the same."

"No, not sad." He sipped his coffee, thinking of the right words. Alice didn't rush him. Eventually he said, "Butlers are almost extinct now. They live on mainly in murder stories and silly English comedies. I remember the day when my greatest ambition was to be a butler. I'm afraid a boy today would think such an ambition either comic or pathetic. Times change. It's not sad."

"Have you any plans?"

"Oh yes. My brother has a grocery store in Yonkers. I'm going to go and work for him. He thinks an ex-butler behind the counter will be quite a drawing card." He smiled his quiet smile.

"But, with what the family left you, you could retire, couldn't you?"

"I could but I don't think retirement would suit me." He finished his coffee and put down the cup. "I think, if you'll excuse me," he said, standing up, "I'd better get busy. I'm making an inventory of all the household furnishings and linen and silver so you'll know what we have and can decide what you wish to keep and what you wish to dispose of."

"That's a good idea," Alice answered vaguely. She was trying to imagine Benton as a grocery clerk in Yonkers.

Apart from the paragraph near the end, Arthur's will was entirely predictable. There were some bequests to charities, some paintings to the club, generous rewards to Benton, Mrs. Cuthbert, the "No Nonsense" cook, and to Valerie Nelson, now retired, who had been Mrs. Melville's maid. Patricia was left one hundred thousand dollars and the remainder went to Alice.

Yes. Except for that paragraph all was clear and straightforward. It, however, made all the difference.

"To Miss Catherine Maine, 46A, The Dorchester Court Apartments, 2715 Fifth Avenue, New York, N.Y., the sum of One Hundred Thousand Dollars with heartfelt gratitude for her kindness and comfort to me."

This must be the Cathy he had spoken of when he was dying. Who was she? Was she his mistress? If that were so why couldn't he have paid her off in cash? Why put her in his will in such a mysterious way? He would know that it would trouble her to find the name of another woman there. Had that been his purpose? Was it a carefully devised plan to humiliate her? No, surely not. Why then? Yet Arthur wasn't the type to have a mistress. Or was he? Once it was apparent that she could never bear him another child their sex life had ceased to exist. Alice had always assumed that that was by mutual agreement. Now she wondered. Perhaps he had missed it more than she realized. He had not found comfort in his wife and had had to look elsewhere. That must be it.

After the will was read Patricia had asked who Miss Maine was and Alice had replied that she was a nurse, now retired, who had been very good to both Mrs. Melville and later to Arthur. That seemed to satisfy her, though she had said, "He must have been very grateful indeed to have left her such a large sum."

Alice had to know. She *had* to. But how? Could she simply telephone her and ask, "Were you my husband's mistress?" And supposing the bold hussy answered, "Yes, I was." What then? She couldn't reply, "Thank you. I just wanted to know." Or the woman might say, "No, I wasn't." What then? Should she then ask, "What were you?" It would be an impossible kind of conversation. Yet she *must* know.

She looked the name up in the directory and sure enough, there it was. All she had to do was dial the number and she would hear the voice at the other end. Yet she didn't do it. She was afraid.

Then, a few days later, Benton answered the phone and said, "It's for you, Mrs. Melville."

"Mrs. Melville?"

"Yes."

"It's Catherine Maine speaking. I thought I might hear from you but when I didn't I thought I'd give you a call. I expect you'd like to know who I am."

"Yes . . . yes, Miss Maine, I would like to meet you."

Chapter 29

She wondered how she should dress. Perhaps the gray suit would be safest. Yet the last time she wore it, she had thought it made her look stouter than she was. She certainly didn't want to dress in such a way as to imply that she attached undue importance to the meeting, but she didn't want to look dowdy so that it would be quite apparent to Catherine Maine why Arthur felt obliged to seek comfort and companionship elsewhere. She could wear black but that would suggest mourning and that seemed an obsolete custom to persist in black after the funeral. In the end she settled for a very plain, dark green silk dress. It looked, she hoped, dignified but also stylish.

She had invited the woman to lunch with her at twelve thirty at the Chez Laurent. Like her dress she thought of it as being fashionable but in no way flashy. She would, of course, arrive ten minutes late as a further indication that she attached no particular importance to the occasion. If, as she hoped, Catherine Maine found herself somewhat ill at ease in the muted elegance of Chez Laurent, the ten-minute wait would further undermine any brash self-confidence she might feel at the encounter.

"Thank heaven," Alice thought to herself, "that I wasn't the one to make the call." After her somewhat fumbling response at the beginning of the telephone conversation she had recovered herself and struck, she thought, exactly the right note. She had been courteous but aloof. When Catherine Maine had said that Wednesday would suit her Alice had hesitated and then said, "No, I'm sorry, Wednesday is quite impossible for me. I've got appointments all day." That should show her that she was in no particular hurry and that what little curiosity she might have was well under control.

Now it was Thursday and she was on her way. When cars had begun to replace carriages Mr. and Mrs. Melville had discussed the possibility of buying one but, at that time, Mr. Melville considered them "nothing more than a passing craze." When he was forced to retreat from that position he fell back on the fact that they were "noisy and unreliable." Later, when they disposed of their carriage, they made use of a limousine service which supplied black, shiny Packards driven by polite uniformed chauffeurs. "This way," Mr. Melville had said, taking his final stand, "we have all the convenience of owning a car without any of the worries." Arthur had accepted this idea. It had, he knew, been his mother's antipathy to cars that had dictated his father's objections.

So it was from an Apex Limousine Service vehicle that Alice descended at the door of Chez Laurent. The cars were unmarked so no one could tell whether they were privately owned or not. Alice waited for the liveried chauffeur to open the door for her and said, "I'll call when I want you. I may do some shopping and take a taxi home." She was nervous but she hoped it didn't show.

The entrance hall with its deep-piled tawny carpet, old gold furniture, and low marble-topped tables was, as always, dimly lit and seemed particularly so on such a raw, overcast winter day. Alice paused for a moment just inside the door. Then she removed her coat and gave it to the checking girl. She turned to find herself face to face with a woman about her own height who asked, "Are you Mrs. Arthur Melville?"

She had not intended to be caught unawares in this way. "Yes," she answered and then added, "yes, I am," as though this other woman had indicated some skepticism.

"I thought you must be. Your husband had told me what you looked like."

"I'm sorry I'm a bit late. I've been so busy."

"Oh, don't worry about that. I just got here myself a couple of minutes ago. I was afraid I might keep you waiting. We're only supposed to have an hour for lunch but a couple of the girls said they'd fill in for me if I made it up to them next week. Of course I had to bring a good dress to work so I could change. That took time."

"You're a librarian or an art gallery person?"

She laughed. "Oh no. Sorry to disappoint you. I'm a waitress."

"A waitress?" She blurted it out without meaning to and then made matters worse by saying, "I'm sorry . . . I . . . You don't look like a waitress."

"I'm not wearing my cap and apron, if that's what you mean."

She was a woman in her late forties or early fifties with gray hair, blue eyes, a somewhat pointed nose, and pale lips. It was a pleasant enough face, but one which looked as though it had been washed in bleach so that most of the color had faded out of it. Her manner was modest but not self-effacing. If she found the sophistication of Chez Laurent in any way daunting, she did not show it as the head waiter led them to their table and as she accepted a glass of sherry—Alice had already had one before she left—and ordered cream of chicken soup and an omelet. Alice ordered consommé and calves' liver with bacon.

"I hope you didn't mind me calling you," Catherine began. "Your husband was such a fine person and so very good to me that I thought I ought to meet you, so I could thank you for sharing him with me."

"I hadn't realized, until I read his will, that I had shared him with anyone other than his parents and our daughter."

"Do you mind? I mean, now that you do know, are you resentful?"

"I don't know that resentful is the right word. I'm surprised."

"Of course. I can understand that."

"How very broad-minded of you." When she had planned the conversation in advance Alice pictured herself as remaining cool and collected no matter what the provocation, but the conversation was not following the pattern she had intended. This plain, faded woman in her blue woolen dress showed neither shame nor defiance. Furthermore, she spoke to Alice as an equal, almost as if they could be friends.

"You must wonder how we happened to meet," Catherine went on, ignoring Alice's sarcasm.

"Oh yes, I'm vaguely curious. Arthur knew all sorts of people."

"I'm a waitress at the club. Have been for years. Before that I was with Dumont Catering. It paid well but it wasn't steady. So, anyway, I'm a waitress at the club and I got to know Mr. Melville in a sort of way because he was there a lot of the time. Quite often he ate alone and even when he had lunch or dinner with other gentlemen I noticed that he never said very much. He seemed lonely somehow."

"He was quiet and reserved. That was his way."

"He talked to me. Maybe I'm the sympathetic type. I don't know why it was but he never seemed to have trouble talking to me." She paused and took a spoonful of soup and a thoughtful nibble at her cracker.

"One night he was by himself. He had been having some drinks with other gentlemen before but, when they left, he stayed on. I tried to persuade him not to have any more to drink. I just wanted him to have something to eat. I thought that was what he needed, but you know how men are in that mood. He insisted. Then, all at once, he'd had too much. He knew it, too. I suggested he spend the night at the club but he wouldn't do that. He said he would get in a taxi and drive round and round until he felt well enough to go home."

"Couldn't you have got one of the male servants to cope with him?" Alice asked.

"I didn't want to embarrass him. He was a nice man and never told vulgar jokes in a loud voice and he seemed so lonely."

"He had moods when he appeared lonely. Drink sometimes had that effect on him." Alice curbed her anger as best she could. Was this woman—this club waitress—presuming to tell her what her husband was like?

"It was a Monday," the woman went on. "Monday was always a slack night. Most men stay home Monday nights. The only man I could have got hold of easily was old Landers Webster, who was on duty in the front hall. He wouldn't have been much help and anyway I didn't need him. Mr. Melville and I were alone in the Oak Room. The dining room was just about closing down. I got him a cup of coffee and a sandwich and made him take them. He talked to me and asked me where I lived and things like that."

"What do you mean by 'and things like that'?"

"Nothing much. If I was married. If I had many friends. I told him I lived with my mother in a rooming house she ran. My mother was a widow; she's dead now. He asked if he could have a room there for the night and I said he could. We went there by taxi when I got off duty. That was the start. Then, after my mother died, he fixed me up in the apartment I'm in now. He gave me money for rent and some extra for clothes and things. He was very kind."

"And he called on you in the apartment."

"Yes. He came quite often in the evenings. I'm not on duty much in the evenings any more. Sometimes he spent the afternoons there working at his novel. He let me read parts of it. Have you seen it?"

Alice considered lying but decided that was too dangerous. She compromised. "He discussed it with me, of course, but I haven't seen the manuscript."

"I think it really belongs to you now. It's really about you, isn't it? I mean the heroine, if you can call her that, Esther Lansbury, is sort of based on you, isn't she?"

Oh my God! What could she say? She took a small forkful of her calves' liver and chewed it meditatively. She hoped that she appeared to be considering the literary validity of Catherine Maine's question. "I suppose every writer of fiction, knowingly or unknowingly, endows his imaginary characters with traits he has observed in people around him."

"I suppose," the woman answered vaguely. "I thought Esther Lansbury's character was deeper than that."

"Deeper? Deeper in what way?" It came out more sharply than she had intended and startled Catherine.

"I'm not educated like Mr. Melville and you. I'm not sure I can explain exactly. I've read a lot though. My mother started us off reading early and, even before that, my father read aloud to us. He read poetry and Charles Dickens. He used to say, 'Books are the only real education.' My oldest brother is a teacher in Kansas."

"Esther Lansbury?"

"What I meant by deeper was that it seemed to me that he thought of you and her as sort of the same person. I think he respected her the way he respected you and thought maybe he wasn't . . . oh, I don't know . . . maybe wasn't worthy of her. I mean the man in the book who is something like Mr. Melville . . . I mean *he* didn't think he was worthy of her. I've probably got it all wrong. You'll have to read it yourself."

"You always refer to my husband as Mr. Melville. Didn't he ask you to call him Arthur?"

"Yes, he did, but I could never do that—only a few times in special circumstances. I was so lucky to be able to help him a little bit. I would never have taken advantage. If I'd ever called him by his Christian name as a regular thing, it would have seemed to me I was trying to take your place and I never thought of that. I could never have been like a wife to him."

"Why not? If you had met him first, why couldn't you have been his wife?"

"Because that's not the way things are," Catherine Maine answered without hesitation. "Men like your husband don't marry women like me and, if they do, they're sorry afterwards."

"Why?"

"I don't know why. It's the way God made the world."

"God never made rules like that. Perhaps Arthur would have been happier with you."

"Oh please don't say that, Mrs. Melville. Please don't even think that. I was nothing to him compared to you. I would never ever have called you if I'd thought you'd get ideas like that. I was *nothing* to him compared to you. He always told me how fortunate he was to have you as his wife. I was a part-time companion. I was satisfied with that." Her voice trailed off.

"You were good to him."

"I tried."

They finished their meal in silence.

Disturbed as she was, Alice knew even then that she had no reason to be angry with this pale, friendly woman across from her. This was no contriving, conspiring rival. The woman had had no reason to get in touch with her other than a desire to clear up what might have been a mystery. There was no guile. Alice could have fought that, but there was nothing here to fight.

"Would you like dessert?" she asked.

"A cup of coffee would suit me fine."

There was another long silence while the waiter cleared away and brought the coffee.

"Shall I send you the novel?"

"If you don't want it."

"I'll put it in the mail. It should really be yours. Your husband meant you to have it in the end. I'm quite sure of it. That's why he put my name in his will. I expect, too, he wanted us to meet so that, if you ever found out that he'd had—you know—another woman, you'd know I was never a real rival."

"Perhaps," Alice said.

They stood up to go. There was an awkwardness. Alice felt out of breath. She had come prepared to fight but it had turned out that there was no opponent; there was just Catherine Maine, a waitress who had been kind to Arthur. Was that really all? Had the woman hoodwinked her?

They collected their coats and allowed themselves to be helped into them by the attentive flunky. "Thank you," Catherine said. "That was a nice lunch."

"I'm glad you could come."

"Well, I guess I'd better be getting back."

"I'll wait for my car."

They shook hands and looked briefly into each other's faces. "He was a nice man. I'm sorry he's dead."

"So am I," Alice answered.

"I only hope Paul will turn out as well."

"Paul?" inquired Alice. "Who's Paul?"

The blood rushed into the cheeks of Catherine Maine. She was suddenly no longer the composed, tranquil woman of a moment ago. "He told me you knew," she said huskily. "He said you didn't mind because . . . because . . ." The tone was anguished, and then her voice trailed off into silence and she bit her lip.

"Well?" Alice demanded. Her voice was hard to hide her own fear.

"He said you didn't mind me bearing him a son because you couldn't. He said you knew. He really did. I wouldn't have said anything except that . . ." Despite her utmost effort to hold them back the tears forced themselves out of her eyes. "How dreadful for you to find out suddenly this way. It's not fair. If I'd only . . ."

Hurt and angry as she was Alice realized that her hurt was not inflicted at this woman's hand and her anger must not be directed at her. A compassion compounded of many emotions she could never untangle so overwhelmed her that she put her arm around Catherine Maine's shoulders and said, "Don't cry. Please don't cry. I'm glad for you."

"That's why he left me so much money."

"Of course," said Alice. "I understand."

Catherine Maine gently disengaged Alice's arm and, dabbing her eyes, she composed herself.

"Would you like to meet him?" she asked in a quiet voice.

"Perhaps one day. How old is he?"

"He's just turned twelve."

"What have you told him?"

Other diners were coming out into the entrance hall. The two of them moved to a corner of the room away from the door. "I . . . I've told him his father was a sea captain who died saving one of his men from drowning. I thought a memory like that might make him brave. Should I tell him the truth?" Her eyes were wide and searching.

Alice smiled and the smile was a mixture of sadness and amusement and other feelings. "No," she said, "let him believe that his father was a sea captain. I hope he will be very brave indeed. I would like to meet him one day, but not just now."

"Should I call you sometime?"

"Yes . . . yes, do call me sometime."

Catherine Maine turned away, hesitated, turned back and murmured, "Thank you." Then she walked quickly away and went out.

Alice waited until she was sure that she must be well away, and was just about to go out herself when a loud voice said, "Mrs. Melville! How nice to see you. I've been meaning to telephone you."

Alice turned to confront Minerva Sparks.

Chapter 30

"I'm so very happy to see you. We've been meaning for simply ages to have you and your *marvelous* husband over for a quiet family dinner. We *so* wanted his advice about our paintings and now of course it's too late, isn't it? I saw in the paper that he'd gone and I said to myself, 'That's what you get, Minerva, for procrastinating.' I'm terribly *terribly* sorry. You must have been quite heartbroken. Who was that lady I saw you with just now? I'm sure I met her at the Cuddikys' but her name quite escapes me."

"No," said Alice numbly, "I don't think you met her at the Cuddikys'. She's an . . . an acquaintance from out of town."

"Really! I could have sworn I'd met her before. She seemed very upset. That's why I waited. I thought perhaps she was your husband's sister or something."

It occurred to Alice to reply, "No, she's the mother of my husband's son." She rejected the notion. "I really must be going," she said. "I have an appointment and I'm late already."

"Is your car waiting?"

"My car?" Alice asked faintly. All she wanted was to be left alone. Pray God let this woman go away! She had once defended her to Arthur and his mother. It didn't matter that she might or might not be the bastard daughter of Cornelius Vanderbilt. What did matter was that Arthur had a bastard son by a club waitress. She had to be alone. She had to sort things out. Her head throbbed.

"Are you all right? You look pale. Would you like to sit down for a few minutes?"

"That might be a good idea," Alice said. Then, as they were moving towards a pair of golden chairs, she reconsidered. She didn't need the help and solicitude of Minerva Sparks. What, in the name of heaven, was she thinking of? "No!" she said suddenly, "no, I really must be going." She could feel the color flooding back into her cheeks. "I'm walking to my appointment. I always walk whenever possible, as my father did. So nice to have seen you again."

"Are you going out?" asked Minerva, relinquishing Alice's elbow.

"Out! Of course I'm going out. Why do you mean?"

"I mean, are you accepting invitations?"

"I don't know. I haven't had any." Alice realized she was sounding unduly aggressive but she didn't care. She had to escape. She had to get away from this frightful woman. She had to walk.

"We're giving a reception for Geoffrey Hamilton," the woman said. "Denny and I are spearheading a group to raise money for a return performance. Would you come? It's Friday at seven thirty."

Alice looked at her. Geoffrey Hamilton! She had once longed to meet him face to face to find out if he could possibly be, in real life, as magic as he was on the stage. It was a long time since she had heard or thought of Geoffrey Hamilton. A long time.

"I'll have to check my engagements," she told Minerva Sparks crisply. "Could you give me a call?"

"Yes," Minerva answered. "I'll do that. You're quite sure I can't give you a ride?"

"Absolutely positive!"

There had been no real snow yet—just flurries that melted as soon as they hit the pavement. This afternoon was another afternoon like the many they had had, but the wind seemed sharper and the sleet stung her cheeks. She was glad she had on her tweed coat. It was as warm or warmer than the mink and one couldn't really walk in a fur coat. And she wanted to walk.

No, she didn't just want to. She felt a compulsion to walk. It was a long time since she had walked farther than around the block—and then only if it was warm and sunny. Mostly her outdoor walking was confined to going from the front door to a car and from a car to the front door. Many times she had made vows to herself that she would begin a regular and vigorous walking routine. She would eat more sensibly, drink less, and walk for at least an hour a day. Usually she had dedicated herself to such a regime when she was cosily snuggled in her bed at night with sleep only minutes away. It was comforting to make such resolutions at such a time. But when the new day dawned there always seemed to be some reason for not implementing them that day. "I'll start on Monday for sure," she would tell herself.

She welcomed the rawness of the sleet, the overcast sky, the wet sidewalks, the sucking sound of tires on the street, the smell of exhaust fumes, the anonymous throng of people, hurrying silently along, each of them grimly intent on some individual mission. She plunged on, her head bent slightly down. The wind between the gray cliffs of buildings fought against her and she fought back like an ocean tug.

This was what she wanted. There might be some who preferred the sunlit uplands but she wanted the grime and the soot and the hard gray, impersonal cruelty of the big city. She didn't even want Central Park at the moment.

There was no reason to hate the woman. No reason at all. Catherine Maine had not been smug. She had not suggested the meeting in order to embarrass her. Not at all. She had simply thought that she ought to make herself known. It had been an act of courtesy, of gratitude.

And all the time she had assumed she knew. Because Arthur had told her she knew and didn't mind. Why should she mind?

In the end Arthur had found happiness with a middle-aged waitress. Why? That wasn't too difficult a question to answer. Because he had not found happiness with his wife. Nothing complicated about it. No point in feeling sorry for herself. No point at all. Yet she had tried. Surely she had done her best. No, of course she hadn't. She had let things slide. She had never made any real effort. Now it was too late. It was too late. She had let her own happiness and Arthur's go by default. She should feel grateful to Catherine Maine for having given him perhaps the only real happiness he had experienced . . . for giving him a son. She should feel grateful.

But she didn't!

The boy Paul. What about him? His father was a sea captain and he was going to grow up to be brave and manly and . . . and . . . Oh my God! A sea captain! Sir Francis Drake? Nelson? Columbus? How pathetic. His father was Arthur Melville, who had lived all his life in fear of his own mother. In fear of himself. No, Catherine Maine couldn't tell the boy that. She probably didn't even know it. Cathy, as Arthur had called her on his death bed, must certainly have known a different Arthur from the one she

knew. Perhaps, to her, he appeared as a frustrated mariner.
If Catherine Maine did call, what would she do? Should
she agree to meet the boy? How could such a meeting be
explained to him? What would they talk about? Yet the
notion of his father being a sea captain was perhaps no
more fanciful than her dreams of the Boy Prince of Rajasthan.

Occasionally she bumped against people. Occasionally
they bumped against her. She continued on regardless. She
didn't really notice. She had to keep walking. There was no
doubt about that. It was important that she keep putting
one foot after the other. She didn't know where she was
going or why or how far. That didn't matter. All that mattered was that she should keep going.

What dreams she had once had. They were gone now.
No more dreams. Nothing. She had had her chance. She
could have made something . . . a great deal of her marriage to Arthur but she had given up. She had never made
a real effort. She had made excuses to herself, using Arthur's moodiness, but that was nonsense. It was her laziness
really. Nothing but laziness. That and lack of imagination.
If she had only tried a little harder.

She paid no more attention to the other walkers, flowing
with and against her, then they did to her. Everyone was
hurrying to some place to do something. No one had time
for anyone else. It was too cold and miserable for that.
Everyone was late and had to walk fast to make up for lost
time.

There was no way she could make up for lost time now
no matter how fast she walked. Arthur was dead. She
might have helped him but she hadn't done so. He had
come back from the grave to reproach her through that
poor washed-out woman who had obviously meant more to
him than she ever had. There was no point in feeling sorry
for herself. She had only herself to blame and she would go
on blaming herself for the rest of her life. There would be
no second chance.

She was at an intersection. She had turned this way and
that without heed. She had paid no attention to where she
was going. The sign said Broadway.

"You look as if you could use a drink." The voice was
deep and warm. She heard it without a first realizing it was
intended for her. "Would you join me?"

She turned and there he was, standing just behind her. He was tall, unshaven, dressed in a worn blue coat. He smiled down at her and it was a kind, sympathetic, interested smile, and yet there was amusement in it too.

Before she could answer him he seized her elbow. "Quick," he said, "the light's turned green." Before she knew it he was propelling her across the street.

"Who are you?" Alice demanded once they had reached the farther shore in safety.

He looked down at her and smiled again in his mischievous, ironic way. "I've almost forgotten who I am, if I ever knew, but if you'd care to join me in a cheer-up little noggin I'd be glad to tell you what I know of myself, which isn't much. The place I have in mind is just down a block and around the corner."

"I don't even know you," Alice said.

"Nor me you but there's no place that's better to begin than at the beginning. We'll never meet again. There's no complications. Alpha and Omega someone once said. Let's chance it."

She was cold, tired, wet, angry, despondent. She looked up into the face of this strange man and it radiated warmth and friendliness and, perhaps, even understanding of her sorry confusion, though of course he couldn't possibly know anything about that.

"Let's chance it," she said in what she thought was a wicked tone.

They didn't talk on the way. He conveyed her down the street and turned right. They went in a door, down a few steps, and presently were sitting at a round table before an open fire with steaming mugs of Irish Coffee before them. It was a dream. It was a very pleasant dream. She took a sip from her mug and felt the warmth and comfort of it penetrating and permeating and seeping into the nooks and crannies of her being.

"Who am I?" he said softly, gazing across at her. "You asked me that, didn't you? You wanted to know whether it was quite respectable to come for a drink with the likes of me. Am I right? Am I wrong?"

"You're right and wrong. I'm not sure. I'm not sure about anything very much."

"Good for you. You speak precisely the way I feel. To make the matter clear I'm a sort of descendant of James

Francis McDonnell who was the son of Peter McDonnell of Drumlish, County Longford. My own name is Peter McDonnell as well." He laughed and his teeth were white as white. "I'm a disgrace to the family. I make my living in sundry ways. I've never set foot in Ireland and I don't suppose I ever will. Who am I? I'm New York."

Alice was enthralled by the man. She would never see him again. It was a moment caught by accident in a butterfly net. She would make the most of it.

"What is New York?" she asked.

"It's a city of enchantmant. It's a garbage dump. It's whatever you think it is." He sipped from his mug.

"And what do *you* think it is?

"I'm one of its bastard sons. I'm prejudiced in its favor." He had reddish hair, bushy eyebrows, big ears, ruddy complexion, and dimples.

"He's an absolute scalawag," Alice thought to herself, and the thought did nothing to diminish her enjoyment.

"Why do you say you are the sort of son of New York you said you were?" she asked daringly. She couldn't bring herself to use the word he had used, the word she had applied in her mind to Arthur's son Paul.

He grinned. "I'm the product of a love affair between Ireland and America, between Drumlish with its two hundred simple, honest folk and New York with its brawling masses of unwashed and unkempt living in gutters and mansions and clawing for dollars like starving cats at a creel of fat trout. I'm not one nor the other. I'm not simple and honest like the people of Drumlish and I'm not a lean and ravenous cat. I'm a mixture of the two—kind of a half-breed. Now isn't that a fine bit of philosophy? Let's have another mug of this nourishing coffee and then we'll part forever."

"No," Alice said, "no, I've had quite enough."

"Nonsense! You can never have 'quite enough' if another one would make you feel even better. It is a far, far better thing to be merry than to be sad and if Irish Coffee makes a noble contribution to that end, then who are we to thrust it aside? It would seem to me a churlish act. If it would make you more receptive to the idea, I shall graciously allow you to pay for the second round."

She was enchanted by him. He was, at this particular moment, exactly what she needed. The Irish Coffee was a wonderful soother. He was right. One had to take one's pleasures where and when they could be found.

"All right," she said. "Since you put it that way." Her voice didn't sound quite normal to her.

"It's no never mind which way I put it," he answered, beckoning a waitress over and handling her the empty mugs. "The resultant happiness for all concerned is the same precisely as it would be either way round. So long as establishments of the likes of this one continue to dispense their comfort to the likes of you and me in our hours of need I'll continue to believe that, next to Drumlish, New York is the finest city in the whole wide world. I've never known another so I'm well qualified to pass judgment on the subject. Did you ever know what Mr. Rockefeller said?"

"What did he say?"

"He said a fine thing. He said a thing that every school child should be made to commit to memory. The words are branded on my mind like the brand on the backside of a cow. 'I believe the power to make money is a gift of God and, having been endowed with the gift I possess, I believe it is my duty to make more and still more money.' Did you ever hear such a lovely thought? I wish I was as friendly with God as Mr. Rockefeller."

Alice laughed rather more loudly than she intended—so loudly, in fact, that she was aware of people at the next table turning to look at her. She didn't care. Never in all her life had she met such a thoroughly delightful man. Never in all her life had she tasted such a thoroughly delightful drink. She needed it. She deserved it. She took a good gulp and was surprised to find that her mug was almost empty. They were very small mugs. She would buy him one more and then she must be getting home. It seemed a shame not to prolong this happy time for a few moments more.

"We might have one more," she said, and once again there was something not quite right about her voice. Perhaps she was getting a cold.

He looked at her and smiled. What a charming man he was! It did her good just to look at him.

"Are you sure?" he asked in his delightful way.

"Of course I'm sure," she answered. "They really are very small mugs. Are these the same ones we had before?

They seem so much smaller. We'll have one more and then . . . Excuse me, I don't think I'm feeling quite well. It's suddenly turned very hot in here."

"What's your address?" a voice asked.

"My address?" There was a roaring sound in her head and her eyes refused to focus properly.

"Where do you live?"

"Live?"

"Your house?"

"I'm Mrs. Arthur Melville," she announced loudly.

Chapter 31

She revived in the taxi with the cold wind from the open window blowing in her face. He was sitting beside her.

"Feeling better?" he asked.

"Yes. I don't know what came over me."

"I can't imagine myself, unless it might be that coffee doesn't agree with you."

When they reached home he declined her somewhat half-hearted invitation to come in, but he did allow her to pay the return taxi fare.

"A shining moment I shall treasure for the rest of my born days," he told her.

"I'm glad you think so," Alice replied. "As for myself, I regard it as a sordid little episode and I shall try to put it out of my mind as quickly as possible. Are you in the habit of picking up middle-aged women and plying them with drinks?"

She realized, even as she spoke the words, that she wasn't really being fair. She was taking her anger at herself out on him. The taxi driver was taking it all in and smiling happily.

"Yes," Peter McDonnell answered, "it's my favorite hobby." He grinned broadly.

Alice could think of no suitably scathing reply and so she turned away abruptly and made her way, somewhat unsteadily, up the front walk. She hadn't had *that* much to drink, she told herself defensively. It was a combination of things. What an offensive man!

In preparation for the selling of the house she was down to two full-time servants—Mrs. Cuthberg and Gladys. Benton, his inventory completed, had departed a few days before to begin his career as a grocer.

Gladys Humber was an old-timer, though she had never figured prominently in the household hierarchy. She had been taken on as a kitchen helper by Mrs. Melville years ago and had occupied that humble position ever since. Mrs. Cuthbert had made several attempts to teach her the rudiments of cookery but without success. "I don't read good enough to follow them fancy directions," Gladys would always say. "I specialize in boiling potatoes. If ever I marry, my man had better like boiled potatoes. I do cabbage pretty good, too."

Marriage was an unlikely possibility because Gladys knew no men. On her afternoons off she went to the movies and sucked gumdrops. The rest of her waking hours she spent scrubbing the kitchen floor, washing dishes, pots, and pans, preparing vegetables, and, her favorite activity, boiling potatoes. She had begun her career as a girl fresh out of school and now, in middle age, there was still a girlish freshness about her. Her cheeks were plump and pink, her eyes were round and blue, and she moved with a bouncing motion.

When Alice had asked Mrs. Cutherbert to nominate one servant to remain with her until the final closing up, Mrs. Cuthbert had said without hesitation, "I'll keep Gladys. She works hard; she does what she's told and she doesn't get to thinking. The ones I can't stand are the ones who get to thinking."

So Mrs. Cuthbert and Gladys were the only ones remaining of the once considerable establishment which had maintained the Melville mansion. She had found it a surprising and welcome relief not to have a large staff of servants for whose efficiency and welfare she felt responsible. She wasn't certain in her own mind, however, that such a feeling of relief was not, in actual fact, a kind of laziness.

Gladys had for some time been "taking on poundage," as she herself put it. Alice thought it made her sound like a merchant ship, but she was fond of her and knew the feeling was reciprocated.

As soon as she was in the front hall there was Gladys to greet her. Alice had paused briefly before opening the front door to pull herself together. Perhaps she had had more sherry before leaving for lunch than she realized and then more sherry and the shock and the long walk and the Irish Coffee. Well, there must be no weakness in front of the servants. She stood very erect.

"We been terrible worried about you, Mrs. Cuthbert and me," Gladys blurted out. "We couldn't think what could of happened to you since you just went out for lunch. You look all funny like. Was you sick?"

"I had some business which detained me longer than I expected and then I had a cup of coffee and I think the cream must have been sour. It made me feel quite ill."

"But you don't take cream in your coffee," Gladys said.

"Not normally. I think perhaps I'll go to bed for a time."

"What about supper? It's all ready—nice mutton stew with little fatty bits floating around in the gravy. Just what you need on a cold night like this. And mashed potatoes and cabbage. It would do you a world of good."

"Perhaps later," she said firmly. Gladys had taken her coat and Alice started to mount the stairs—carefully, with a hand on the banister.

"What will I tell Mrs. Cuthbert?"

"Whatever you think best."

She was aware that Gladys was gazing up at her with her mouth open. She didn't care. The only thing that mattered was to get to the bathroom before she was sick on the stairs and then to prostrate herself on the bed.

When she woke she had vague, uncomfortable memories of having proclaimed to the world, "I am Mrs. Arthur Melville." She blushed at the thought. What had come over her? She couldn't possibly have had too much to drink. Two little mugs of Irish Coffee? Nonsense! Surely the sherry had worn off before that. It was fatigue and shock. What had Gladys thought? What would Gladys have said to Mrs. Cuthbert? She must go down and reestablish herself. Perhaps a bowl of soup would be nice.

Swinging her feet off the bed she glanced at her watch and saw to her astonishment that it was nearly ten o'clock. She had slept for hours! A faint knocking at the door.

"Come in."

"It's just me," said Gladys, peeping around. "Me and Mrs. Cuthbert's taken turns to come up to see you was all right."

"I'm quite all right, thank you," Alice answered in a firm, cool tone. "I was cold and very tired, that's all."

"Should I bring you some soup or something?"

"If it wouldn't be too much trouble, I think that would be nice, Gladys."

She was undressed and properly in bed by the time Gladys came puffing in with a tray—chicken broth and toast.

"Don't bother to come back for the tray," Alice told her. "You can take it down in the morning."

"I sure hope you're feeling better in the morning," Gladys said. "Me and Mrs. Cuthbert was real worried."

"There was no need to be," Alice said primly. Then, because Gladys looked hurt, she added, "But it was kind of you both just the same."

"Good night, Mrs. Melville."

"Good night, Gladys."

When she finished her soup she turned off her bedside lamp and lay down, but her mind was full of many things and sleep was a long time coming.

The promised call from Minerva Sparks came two days later.

"I do hope you're feeling quite yourself again. Denny and I are so hoping you'll feel up to joining us. I should probably explain that Ben Wiseman, the theatrical producer, is going to be there along with Geoffrey Hamilton. He thinks it's terribly important that Geoffrey Hamilton should return to the stage in a big Shakespearean role. He's quite all right now, you know—I mean Geoffrey Hamilton, not Ben Wiseman—and he's hardly drinking at all. He's been back to England in some wonderful play I forget the name of and the reviews were absolutely *marvelous*. Mr. Wiseman wants to form a committee of some of the best people who are willing to give their moral, social, and financial backing. As soon as he mentioned the idea to us you were one of the very first names that came to mind. I can assure you that we're not inviting just *anybody* to join us. We are, in fact, being *very* selective. Friday at seven thirty."

She paused for breath.

Before she could get started again Alice made a quick decision. "Friday at seven thirty. I'd be delighted to come."

"That's absolutely marvelous. We'll so look forward to seeing you. It's nothing elaborate. Just champagne and odds and ends to eat."

"Thank you for thinking of me," Alice said and hurriedly replaced the receiver.

She was in the sun-room where she had been taking her usual pre-lunch sherry, but she had scarcely taken another sip when Gladys appeared at the door in a great state of agitation.

"There's a messenger boy at the servants' entrance with a parcel for you, Mrs. Melville, and he won't let me have it. He says he has orders to give it to you yourself. What should I do?"

"A parcel. What sort of a parcel?"

"A brown paper one about the size of a square frying pan."

"I can't think of anyone who'd be sending me a square frying pan," Alice said. "You'd better send him around to the front door and I'll take it from him there."

Still Gladys hesitated. "He's a nigger boy," she said doubtfully.

"Don't be absurd," Alice said crisply. "Send him around at once." She had suddenly realized she was being stupid. She knew what the parcel was. It must of course be Arthur's novel, and Catherine Maine had taken precautions to make sure it fell into nobody's hands but hers.

Alice went to the front door to meet the boy and by the time the boy arrived, Gladys was back in the hall, hovering protectively in the background. Alice, having received and signed for the parcel, turned to her. "Gladys, what is the trouble?"

"You can't trust them," she said. "They attack people. I heard where a lady opened her door to a nigger and next thing she was tied up hand and foot and he had made off with all the silver, the rugs, her jewels, and a painting of Europe."

"He must have been very strong," Alice said.

"You laugh if you like, Mrs. Melville, but I think the sooner we send all the niggers back to Africa, the safer we'll all be." She hurried away in something of a huff.

Carrying the parcel back into the sun-room, where her interrupted sherry was waiting, Alice recalled her father's explanation of the Negro problem. It was one evening when she had been allowed to stay up and have dinner with her parents. For some reason, long forgotten, she had asked where all the black people came from.

"A long time ago," her father told her, "the families who grew cotton in the South couldn't get enough help picking it so they paid the passage of a lot of Negroes from Africa to come across and help them. These Negroes were very ignorant because they hadn't been to school and the men who brought them over said to them, 'We can't afford to pay you proper wages but we'll give you little houses to live in and we'll give you food and clothes and we'll take care of you when you're sick, if you'll help us pick our cotton.'"

"Some of the Negroes were very good but others, after a while, began to cause trouble. By this time they had had far too many children and they didn't take care of them properly. A lot of the Negroes started to make mischief then and said they didn't want to work for no wages anymore. They said they wanted to be free. So we had the Civil War and Abraham Lincoln, who was very wise, said that when the North won the war they could be free. And that's what happened.

"A lot of them came up north then and we discovered that the people in the South had been right all along. The Negro is not someone you can trust.

"So nice people don't like having them around except as servants. That's why I won't let any of them into the store."

"Besides," her mother had added, "they don't take regular baths or dress cleanly and neatly."

"Some do," Alice had protested, "I saw a black family with a little girl about my age and . . ."

"You've asked your question and you've had your answer. That will be quite enough. There are other more pleasant things to talk about."

She sat with the parcel on her knee. She wouldn't—she couldn't—open it now. There was no doubt what it was. Catherine Maine's name and address were on the label.

She would open it later. There was time enough. Time enough for what? She couldn't go on and on thrusting everything before her into the future and saying to herself, "I'll cope with that in due course." That was no way of facing up to life. She must plan and act. But what was she planning for? Musing, with the unopened manuscript on her knee, she wondered what it said of her. Was Arthur's son in it—the son that should have been hers as well?

Well, one thing was certain. She had to get out of this house as soon as she possibly could. So long as she went on living here, she would be too encumbered with the past to make sensible plans for the future.

She picked up the telephone beside her and dialed her

lawyer's number. She didn't have to look it up. One of the few things she still prided herself on was her ability to remember telephone numbers.

"I want to speak to Mr. Durant. It's Mrs. Melville . . . I'm sure he *is* busy but, in spite of that fact, I wish to speak to him *now*. . . . I'm not concerned about the other client. I have been a client of Mr. Durant's for many years. Would you please tell him that Mrs. Alice Melville wishes to speak with him? . . . Mr. Durant? . . . Alice Melville. That stupid girl of yours wouldn't put me through. I won't keep you. I would like you please to arrange to have this house sold with all its furnishings and paintings and so on and also to get me a nice apartment with two bedrooms overlooking Central Park. If you could arrange that within the next two weeks or perhaps even a month I would be most grateful."

She hung up, looked for a moment into space, and then refilled her sherry glass.

Chapter 32

Patricia had taken to authorship. She had embarked on a book which was tentatively entitled *Tales for Tots*. She had also taken to artistry and was illustrating the book with her own colored-pencil drawings.

Alice had done her best to sound suitably congratulatory when her daughter had brought the first samples of her work to show her, but she had found the cute little moralistic stories almost unbelievably banal and the illustrations grotesque. Her words of praise were obviously too faint for Patricia's creative nature and she had said, with something of a rebuke in her voice, "How very interested Father would have been to know that he bequeathed me something of his talent."

"Indeed," Alice answered. She thought more but refrained from saying it.

So, when Patricia arrived for the regular Wednesday get-together and announced, "I've brought along something that I thought would amuse you," Alice had an instant misgiving that the "something" must be a further installment of *Tales for Tots*.

"What is it?" she asked, trying to sound bright and curious. There was a fearful undertone which she herself could detect.

"It's an article from the magazine section of *The Sun* called 'Stage Idols of the Past' and it has several paragraphs about Geoffrey Hamilton. Do you remember taking me to see him as Brutus in *Julius Caesar*?"

"Yes," Alice answered, "in 1923."

"He wasn't very good, as I remember," Patricia went on, "and then he dropped out for a time I gather. But he did make a comeback."

"Yes, he did. He played Prospero in *The Tempest*. Later he returned to England and became *Sir* Geoffrey Hamilton."

"You met him once, didn't you? I seem to remember something in one of your letters."

"Yes," Alice answered, "I met him."

"Was he wonderful?"

"It was a long time ago." She took a sip of her tea.

"According to the article he was quite a man for the women."

"Was he? Have another cup of tea, my dear, and tell me how *Tales for Tots* is coming on."

The Pacific was calm as calm could be. It looked as if one could row a boat across it all the way to Japan. It would take a long time, though. It would take a very long time. She had rowed a boat only once in her life, when one afternoon in Switzerland she and Arthur had gone out on Lake Thun, one of Interlaken's lakes. Or was it the evening after hiking all day? Or, perhaps, in the morning before setting off on a walk? She couldn't remember for sure. It didn't matter.

She would sip her gin and tonic very slowly and make it last the whole hour before dinner. There was much to think about . . .

The Sparks reception had been large and noisy and, she realized almost as soon as she arrived, not at all the sort of party she should be present at so soon after Arthur's death or, for that matter, while he was still alive. These people were definitely not her kind. They were obviously the Suddenly Rich. *Very* obviously. The only reason she had been asked was to lend tone to the affair, and that she would not make any effort to do.

Everyone was clustered around the great Geoffrey Hamilton. She certainly wasn't going to be a part of that chattering mob. She sipped champagne, nibbled on a caviar sandwich, and carried on an exceedingly dull conversation with a Dr. Ainsworth and his wife who obviously wondered, as much as Alice did, why they were there.

Then she felt a tap on her shoulder and, turning, found herself face to face with Peter McDonnell, her Irish Coffee companion.

"Mrs. Melville," he said in a loud, clear, mellow voice, "what a wonderful delight and pleasure it is to greet you again. When we parted the other day I thought sorrowfully that I should nevermore set eyes on your lovely countenance, but Fate has decreed otherwise. Blessings on Fate!" Turning to Dr. and Mrs. Ainsworth he said, "Mrs. Melville and I are drinking companions."

Mrs. Ainsworth, a tall, gaunt woman with incongruous patches of rouge on her pale cheeks, twitched her thin lips faintly to indicate amusement. Her husband, fat with a toothbrush moustache and pink eyes, said uncertainly, "We've never been at a theatrical party before and don't quite know how to take remarks like that, I'm afraid."

"Aren't you the one who removed a boil from Minerva's bottom?" Peter McDonnell asked.

Dr. Ainsworth turned scarlet. He opened and closed his mouth like a fish but no sound came.

"She loves you dearly," McDonnell went on. "She told me so herself."

Alice was outraged. "I knew," she said—and icicles hung from every word—"that the Sparks might be hard pressed to find enough socially acceptable guests to attend this gathering, but I had not realized that they would find themselves obliged to recruit simply anyone available for a free drink."

Peter McDonnell laughed heartily. "You have it all wrong. I've never met the Sparks until this evening. I was invited by the guest of honor. I'm sort of an actor myself and Geoffrey and I have been friends for ages. He brought me along to give him moral support. You have met him, haven't you?"

"No," Alice answered, "I have not and the discovery that he is a friend of yours quite effaces any desire I might have had to do so. I must be going." Dr. and Mrs. Ainsworth indicated with mumblings and anxious sidelong glances that they, too, were already late for another appointment.

"You're not being fair," Peter McDonnell told them and Alice, caught off guard by the hardness of his voice, looked up at him and saw that he was serious and perhaps even angry.

"In what way?" she demanded.

The Ainsworths, sensing a confrontation they wanted no part of, drifted off.

"In what way?" Alice repeated.

"You really want to know?" There was no doubt of his utmost seriousness now. "Shall I tell you?"

"If you wish."

There was a sort of wildness in his ruddy face and expressive eyes and yet it was a wildness, she thought, of temperament rather than of quick anger.

"The trouble with the likes of you," he began, leading her into a reasonably secluded corner to avoid a clucking group that seemed to be descending on them, "is that you don't want to look at the world the way the world is. You think Franklin Roosevelt is a demon determined to destroy your way of living and you don't realize that your way of living became extinct long ago. You can cling to it for a while, like a drowning man might cling to a wood chip in the water, but it won't keep you afloat."

"I admire Roosevelt and would have voted for him, if the election hadn't been on the day my husband died."

"Did you ever see Sean O'Casey's *Juno and the Paycock*? It came out about ten years back."

"No, I didn't. I've heard of it."

"You've heard of it, indeed. I'm glad of that at least. I played Jerry Devine, a socialist. He was in love with Mary and she recalled the verses he'd once read at the Socialist Rooms."

"I'm sorry I didn't see it," Alice said.

> *"An' we felt the power that fashion'd*
> *All the lovely things we saw,*
> *That created all the murmur*
> *Of an everlasting law,*
> *Was a hand of force an' beauty,*
> *With an eagle's tearin' claw."*

He stood there silent and Alice saw that his eyes were shiny, but, whether with joy or sadness she didn't know.

"So what are you trying to show me?" she asked at length.

"I'm trying to tell you that with all the misery that's going about, it's more important than ever it was for us not to get too terrible solemn. If we get a chance to drink champagne once in a long while—or even Irish Coffee a little more often—we ought to take it. If we don't work to keep gaiety alive no one else is going to, and can you imagine a world without jollity and laughter? I believe the good Lord Jesus laughed from time to time and I think he'd want us to do the same."

"I believe you're right," Alice said almost repentantly. "I really believe you are. Where does it all end? I mean, what's going to happen?"

"Oh, I know that," he answered with careless confidence. "I know that as sure as I know my name. We can be like that doctor friend of yours and go sniffling and mumbling away because he doesn't want to admit that women have bottoms. We can be like you who look around at the people assembled here and think you're too good by half to mingle and mangle with them. Nothing of that will prevent what's coming from coming."

"And what *is* coming?"

"There's misery and there's hunger and there's a plethora of troubles this side of the ocean and the other. Whenever too many of the poor begin to starve and fidget and cause trouble, someone says, 'Let's have a war. That's what we need.' They get together and decide what the war will be about and then they have it."

"But even if you're right," Alice protested, "and I don't really believe you are, how could your theory apply to our country?"

He smiled at her and she saw in his face, dimples, and bushy eyebrows a deeper understanding than she had conceived possible. She felt a sort of shame for having underestimated him.

"I'm not waiting to find out," he said quietly. "I'm an adventurer and I might as well be in it from the start. I'm leaving for Spain tomorrow."

"For Spain?" Alice asked in bewilderment.

"Yes. Haven't you heard? The troubles heve started there already. Now, come and meet Geoffrey Hamilton. You'll be enchanted by him. He's a grand man."

She took very small sips. It must last her until Mrs. Owens came to announce that dinner was ready. Dinner indeed! A small filet of sole, perhaps, a small overboiled potato, some heated up frozen beans, and then red or yellow Jell-o with a dab of whipped cream on top. Dinner! She should have been underground long ago. It was idiotic to have dragged on for such a time—a long time—too long a time.

Geoffrey Hamilton had come back to the house after the party. Peter McDonnell had brought him, but Peter left early because he was sailing for Europe the next morning.

He smiled and, with the firelight on his face, there was still a theatrical magic in the twist of the lips and in the gray eyes which excited Alice as she had not been excited for a long time. Time had marked his face, but there was little hint of dissipation in it. There were lines around his eyes and at the corners of his mouth but the wonderful eyes were clear and the skin had a healthy tone to it. The chin was as firm as ever.

They were silent for a time after Peter McDonnell left and then Geoffrey said, "In case you're worried, I'm not planning to spend the night. Peter wanted to spend this last night with his girl and I have a mortal horror of leaving a drink unfinished. About five more sips and I'll go."

"Go where?" Alice asked. "I'm not the least bit worried."

"You're very kind. I feel as though I'd known you for a long time."

"I have known you for a long time. You didn't say where you were going."

"I have a room in a building not far off Broadway with a communal bathroom down the hall. I call it my apartment."

"You're not acting at the moment."

"I am 'at liberty,' as we say in the trade, and amusing myself by acting as night watchman at the Phoenix. Sometimes, in the stillness of the small hours, I stand on the empty stage and declaim to an audience of shadows. Tonight is my night off. The shadows will miss me."

"Will you go back?"

He didn't answer at first but sat looking steadfastly at the fire through his empty glass, which he held in his fingertips. "Did you know," he asked at length, "that Lawrence Markheim is opening next month at the Crown in *Henry the Fifth*? I could outact him nine ways from Sunday. He's even more of a fraud than I was once." He paused and then, very quietly,

> *Let me speak proudly: tell the constable*
> *We are but warriors for the working-day;*
> *Our gayness and our gilt are all besmirch'd*
> *With rainy marching in the painful field:*
> *There's not a piece of feather . . .*"

He stopped. "I really must be going," he said.

"Why? Why don't we have one more drink and then you can go to bed here. We have lots of room."

"Your maid gave us such a suspicious look as we came in, I'm surprised she hasn't been up to check on you."

"Don't worry about Gladys," Alice laughed. "The only man she's ever known was her father."

"All right," he said, "why not? Shall I pour them?"

"Did Wiseman speak to you at the party?" he asked when they were once more seated before the dwindling fire.

"Yes, just as I was leaving. He's coming to see me on Tuesday."

"You know what he wants, of course?"

"Backing for your triumphant return to Broadway. That's it, isn't it?"

"Something like that," he replied musingly.

"I thought that was the whole purpose of the Sparks' party. Wasn't it?"

"Yes, I suppose you're right." He sounded tired. "The Sparks and Wiseman want to use me for their own purposes and I must decide whether or not I'm prepared to be used."

"Use you? I don't understand."

A long silence.

"Peter will be killed," he said softly.

"How do you know?"

"He wants to die for a noble cause and I suspect I'm willing to live for an ignoble one. We're both actors. We're both playing make-believe games."

"You're tired," Alice said. She felt a sense of pity and yet, in a strange way, a sense of exultation. This was Geoffrey Hamilton. He was sitting here before her fireside. No, it wasn't pity; it was something much stronger than that. She must not show it. It was absurd! But from somewhere deep within her there welled up a frightening surge of emotion that she was almost incapable of subduing.

He was speaking and his voice, though nothing more than a whisper, seemed to fill the room.

"You do look, my son, in a mov'd sort,
As if you were dismayed; be cheerful, sir.
Our revels now are ended. These our actors,
Are melted into air, into thin air;

> *And, like the baseless fabric of this vision,*
> *The cloud capp'd towers . . ."*

His voice drifted off into silence. He wasn't asleep but he was thinking of where or why or how and he was wondering about when and if. Alice sat watching his fine face for some long time before she eventually said, "Isn't it time you went to bed? You look very tired."

He rubbed his forehead with the fingers of his left hand. "I suppose perhaps it is," he said.

She showed him up to the bedroom that had once been Mrs. Melville's. As some sort of domestic memorial to her the room had been maintained in pristine fashion since she had died and the bed linen changed every week.

What Mrs. Cuthbert and Gladys would think when they knew a man had slept in that bed—an actor, indeed—Alice could imagine, but she preferred not to imagine it that night.

At the doorway he took her in his arms and kissed her. It was as if they had known each other for a hundred years. As she went to her own bedroom she was perplexed and even half ashamed at the fact that she was weeping like a schoolgirl.

Chapter 33

It was easy enough, looking back on events later, to see that, right from the start, he was simply amusing himself. The possibility had occurred to her at the time, but she dismissed it from her mind. Even now, she liked to believe that perhaps now and then, there had been something more to it than acting. Surely there had been moments when he felt something genuine and warm in their relationship. It hadn't all been her imagination.

There had been the evening, for instance, just after the financing of the play had been arranged, and he had quit his job as night watchman to devote all his time to preparations for the great come-back.

He wasn't actually living with her, though sometimes alone, sometimes with friends, he spent many evenings at the house and stayed occasional nights. He wanted her money, of course. She suspected that but didn't resent it. She had more of it than she knew what to do with and it was natural enough for him to enjoy spending money on luxuries again after being unable to do so for so long. Despite her lawyer's advice she had put two hundred thousand dollars into the production itself and another ten thousand into a fund from which Geoffrey could draw to tide him over until *The Tempest* opened.

There were just the two of them that evening. Mrs. Cuthbert and Gladys had been told that Geoffrey was a cousin from England and they accepted the story. He was very charming with them, treating them with a sort of mock gallantry that quite won their hearts.

"If all Englishmen was like him," Gladys confided in Alice one day, "I'd up and marry one."

He had come for dinner and Mrs. Cuthbert, anxious to please him with a good old English dish, had made beefsteak and kidney pudding with boiled potatoes and brussel sprouts, which she followed with trifle. Geoffrey had delighted her by going out to the kitchen afterwards and telling her that the dinner had brought back happy memories of his London boyhood.

Now they were sitting in front of the fire, he sipping brandy and Alice with a glass of port.

"One of the things that's wrong with the world," Geoffrey was saying, "is that not enough people love poetry. Children have a natural, inborn love of poetry but somehow or other, it's cut out of them—out of boys anyway—because it's considered soft and bad, like a rotten spot in an apple. I was lucky. I had a wonderful English master in my early school days. He made us understand that poetry was a terribly important thing."

"Tell me about him."

"Some day, perhaps."

"Why not now?"

> "*Had we but world enough, and time,*
> *This coyness, Lady, were no crime.*
> *We could sit down and think which way*
> *To walk and pass our long lives' day,*
> *Thou by the Indian Ganges' side*
> *Shoulds't rubies find . . .*"

"Go on," she said when he stopped.

He laughed. "I've forgotten the rest. It was written over three hundred years ago by Andrew Marvell. How strange he would think it that we remember. My father had no use for poetry."

"You've never really talked about your family."

"There's nothing much to talk about."

"Tell me."

"I was born in England, the youngest of three boys. My father was clerk to Sir Aubrey Wilkins, who was a distinguished and fashionable London barrister. My father was very keen that one of his sons should become a barrister and, when my older brothers departed for Australia, he concentrated his hopes on me.

"I was quite enthusiastic for a time. I used to attend trials during school holidays and I rather fancied myself conducting a brilliant cross-examination in gown and wig. But I had all sorts of other dreams as well—explorer, member of Parliament, Admiral of the Fleet. I was always the hero in my dreams." He paused and touched his chin with the tips of his long fingers—a characteristic gesture.

"Then," he went on, with a slightly rueful smile, "one

day I realized I didn't want actually to *be* anything in particular; I just wanted to pretend to be all sorts of things. I'd been in school plays, of course, and greatly enjoyed them, but the idea of actually making my living acting never occurred to me until I was sixteen. When it did I could think of nothing else.

"My father was appalled at the idea and my mother, who was the gentlest person I have ever known and hated any disagreement in the family, tried to agree with us both. I blackmailed my father in the end by threatening to run away from home unless he would send me to the Royal Academy of Dramatic Arts. He did it for my mother's sake. He knew it would break her heart if I ran away. I did well at RADA and at eighteen I decided to come to New York. My mother bought me a return ticket out of her meager savings and gave me fifty pounds spending money. It was a magnificent gesture and I repaid it by cashing in the return half of the ticket as soon as I arrived.

"On the ship I had met a New York agent. I pretended to have had all sorts of experience. I convinced him I was a boy genius and he was lucky to have met me. I don't suppose I really impressed him that much actually, but he decided to give me a chance to show what I could do. His name was Abe Kuchner.

"I saw my parents once again when I went back to England as something of a star. My father thought it would have been better if I'd become a barrister but my mother was delighted. They came to see me as Prospero. My father's only comment was, 'You memorized your lines very well.'"

"Your older brothers?" Alice asked.

He shrugged his shoulders. "I have no idea whether they are still alive or, if they are, what they are doing or where they are doing it. We never knew each other very well."

"I know what you mean. It was much the same with my older sisters."

"Yes indeed," he murmured, "what curious twists and turns there are in life."

They were silent for a time and then Alice asked, "When you were a boy, did you ever come upon a book called *The Boy Prince of Rajasthan*?"

"Indeed I did. What do you know about it?"

She told him. She told him many things about her own

childhood, about her Paris kidnapping, about her long lone-liness, about . . . She couldn't remember all she told him. She did remember that they ended up together in the dark room on the big sofa with his strong arms enfolding her in a warm embrace.

It should seem obscene now. But it didn't. Surely, that night, surely he had meant it. He must have been at least a little bit in love with her.

The day to close the house and move to the apartment came only three weeks before the opening night of *The Tempest*. Geoffrey was of course very busy indeed. She saw him fleetingly from time to time. One night he had come in just before ten. He had said he might be in for dinner but had not arrived.

"I'm sorry I'm late," he said. "We had a production meeting before, during, and after dinner. I thought it would never end." He inclined his head and kissed her on the forehead. "I brought these as a peace offering," he said, handing her a long box of flowers he had been carrying under his arm. She opened them by the sink—a dozen long-stemmed red roses.

"Oh Geoffrey," she said, "they're beautiful." She turned, held out her hands, and he took her in his arms and em-braced her, putting his stubbled cheek against her smooth one. The only flaw in the ecstasy of that moment was that she smelt whiskey on his breath. Well, what of it? She'd had a drink herself.

"Can you reach down the tall white vase in that cup-board?" she asked.

He did so and she watched him. He made even a simple action like that a thing of grace and beauty. His legs, his arms, his neck, his head, his whole body excited her. His eyes, his mouth, and the sound of his voice thrilled her in a way she had never been thrilled before. She found herself flushed and short of breath and took longer to fill the vase and arrange the roses than she need have done, telling her-self all the time to calm down and not to be absurd.

"What would you like?" she asked. "The coffee can be ready in five minutes."

"I thought we might have a small drink to celebrate the new home. I've given up booze, as you know, but I thought

I might make an exception tonight in honor of the occasion. I've almost forgotten what the stuff tastes like."

It startled her that he could lie so suavely and she found it in her head to say, "You must have a very short memory. That wasn't mouthwash I smelled when you kissed me." The words were in her head but not in her heart and so instead she said, "You'll find the bottles in the right-hand cupboard of the sideboard. I'll get the glasses."

And, of course, it was all wonderful. He had only two drinks and showed no signs of having had too much. Perhaps she had merely imagined the smell on his breath because she was nervous about him and wanted so much that he should be a triumphant success. And he would be! He must be!

With his long legs stretched out before him and sitting well back in his chair, his glass held by his finger tips, he talked about rehearsals and particularly about Gertrude Keiller who had been imported from England to play Ariel.

"She's quite marvelous," he told her, gazing beyond his glass into the far distance, "and unlike so many in this idiotic world of make-believe which people call the theatre, she carries her charm and wit with her all the time. There is something magic about her. I mean about the girl herself. It's not something she puts on with her costume and makeup."

"And the others," Alice asked, trying not to sound tense. "You're happy with the whole cast?"

"Perfect. Dennis Parker is the best Caliban ever. I do wish you could come to a rehearsal, but they're being very strict. No one not officially involved. A few photographers have been allowed to take some publicity shots. That's all. The first night, as I told you, really will be a first night."

"Not long now."

"No," he said thoughtfully, "not long now. The rebirth of Geoffrey Hamilton." He gazed thoughtfully into his glass.

Life magazine, which was still very young and very much in demand, gave him a two-page spread with pictures from triumphs of long ago and a shot of the cast in rehearsal. It quoted Jon Doyle, the director, as saying, "I believe that Geoffrey Hamilton will bring the greatness back to the American stage that seemed to disappear when he left it.

He has had hard times since and so has the classical theatre, but now we are in for a great reawakening."

The *Herald Tribune* had an interview. The *New Yorker*
did a profile in "The Talk of the Town." *Time* magazine
said: "Sated by superlatives we may be, but Geoffrey Hamilton's return to the Broadway stage has to be described as,
potentially, one of the greatest events in American theatrical history. A new generation, many of whom had never
heard of him or thought him long since dead, are about to
experience for themselves the excitement of truly great acting. They won't have to take their parents' word for it any
longer."

He brought these and other such things home to show
her, but he was far from being overly elated by them. "It's
all puffery," he said. "Of course I'm pleased with the recognition. Who wouldn't be? But the play's the thing. If it flops
I could disappear from view again as quickly as I emerged.
This time it would be for good."

"Please! Please!" she told him. "You mustn't say or even
think such things. You are going to be absolutely marvelous. I know that and so does everyone else."

He kissed her and then, with his strong hands on her
shoulders, he looked searchingly down into her face and
said, "You've done so much for me. I hope I can repay
you."

"But you have repaid me. You've more than repaid me.
I would have been so lonely in these weeks and months
without you. I wish . . ." She stopped suddenly. She had
been in danger of making a pathetic spectacle of herself
again. She had caught herself just in time.

"You wish?"

"I wish you everything you wish yourself—fame, fortune, and lasting happiness."

He looked at her quizzically. "That's not what you were
going to say." His fine lips curved up in a half smile; his
eyebrows were slightly raised and he seemed to see right
into her mind.

"Not exactly. Perhaps what I was going to say comes to
the same thing in the end."

He continued to look at her for a long moment, and then
he said softly, "Perhaps it does."

Of one thing, however, she was certain, and that was
that she was no match sexually for Gertrude Keiller. She

had never met her, but she had seen some photographs and Geoffrey talked of her.

"Why not invite her over for dinner some night?" Alice suggested. "She must be lonely."

"Gertrude lonely?" He laughed. "No, she has all the dinner engagements she can handle. She's not the lonely kind."

So how could she possibly measure up? He might or might not need youth and beauty, but almost certainly he needed the sort of effervescent excitement with which people like Gertrude filled every waking hour of every day, and there was no sense in her trying to rival that. Once perhaps, a long time ago, she had something of that quality, but not now. Time and circumstances had sapped it. She was past middle age and she was now so dull compared to Gertrude Keiller.

Yes, but he was old enough to be Gertrude Keiller's father. She mustn't forget that!

Chapter 34

The day for leaving the great house came at last. Alice had been steeling herself for weeks. People now didn't feel about houses as they once had done. They bought them and sold them with careless abandon, like any other commodity. They might be big or small, handsome or ugly, well or poorly constructed, but they were essentially merely places to live. How could she ever explain to Patricia, or anyone else for that matter, how she felt that morning? They wouldn't understand.

"What's the sense of bringing in a lot of cleaners?" Mrs. Cuthbert had demanded a few weeks earlier. "A month after we're gone the place will be rubble and dust anyhow. Why they want to tear it down and put up one of them big ugly apartment buildings surpasses my comprehension." She had obviously been pleased with the oratorical flourish of that phrase. "I'm only glad that Mrs. Melville is gone. She wouldn't of stood for it."

"People don't want big houses like this anymore," Alice had explained for the umpteenth time. "I can't stay on here all alone."

"Well," Mrs. Cuthbert sniffed, "I hope you know what you're doing. Next thing you know they'll be tearing down the Statue of Liberty and there won't be nothing left of New York."

Alice didn't argue. She knew that all the confusions of the last months and now the news that the old place was to disappear forever had been almost more than the poor old soul could bear. She had been there before Alice arrived as a new bride. It had been her life for all these years, and it would all soon be gone and she would find herself with a room in a boarding house in some unattractive neighborhood. She would hate all the other lodgers. She would read her "No Nonsense" cookbooks and remember. No, Alice could not find it in her heart to rebuke her. In a few days they would both be gone their separate ways. The acid reply would hurt without serving any useful purpose. There was no point in trying to keep Mrs. Cuthbert in her place any more.

When the day came she gave Mrs. Cuthbert and Gladys a check for two months' wages plus five thousand dollars. Gladys burst into a torrent of tears and asked chokingly, "What's to become of us all? Who will look after you with us not around?"

"I shall try and look after myself," Alice replied crisply.

"Look after yourself? I always thought you was going to a kind of hotel."

"Don't be hysterical!" exclaimed Mrs. Cuthbert crossly in a brave attempt to conceal her own emotion.

"But will you make your own bed?" Gladys continued.

"Of course she will!" said Mrs. Cuthbert. "It's her *food* I'm worried about."

"I'll miss you both," Alice told them and she spoke from the bottom of her heart.

Then the car Alice had arranged to take them where they were going arrived. They both embraced her, Mrs. Cuthbert overcoming, on this occasion, her natural aversion to such an act, and they were gone. The furniture, other furnishings, and art collection had been transported to their various new owners during the past few weeks and, earlier that morning, a van had arrived to take her five trunks and nine suitcases to her new home. A few special belongings had already gone to the apartment. A few bits and pieces which remained would be called for later by the Salvation Army.

A Mrs. Gorman from Macy's had undertaken the "fitting out," as she called it, of the apartment. "When you move in," she assured Alice, "it will be like stepping from one room to another in your own home." Alice doubted it would be that easy, but at least she would have some familiar things around her and she would have her own bed again. She had scarcely slept a wink last night on what had once been a servant's bed, moved into her room for the final night.

Never could she remember having felt so alone as she did at that moment, standing in the cavernous, marble-floored entrance hall and gazing up the wide stairs. She remembered climbing them as a new bride with her new husband—followed by Benton and a footman, the last of the footmen, carrying their bags—just back from their European honeymoon which now, in retrospect, seemed like a far-off, blissful dream. She remembered climbing them after that first dreadful "At Home" when that frightful woman—what was her name? Oh yes, Mrs. Selbourne—had so provoked her about moving out and had precipitated her quarrel that evening with Mrs. Melville. She remembered watching Mr. Melville climbing the stairs one at a time, purposefully, going to his death.

As she went up the stairs now for the last time she was glad that, despite Mrs. Cuthbert's advice, she had had the whole place cleaned. Mrs. Cuthbert had logic on her side, but logic was not everything. It would have been shoddy and disrespectful to the old house to have let it go to its end uncared for and unkempt and, despite the best efforts of Gladys and the cleaning women, there were many rooms which had received no attention in years. It had taken a cleaning gang nearly two weeks to do the job and it had cost her nearly a thousand dollars, but it had been worth it. "Besides," she had told Mrs. Cuthbert and Gladys, "it provides work at a time when jobs are scarce."

She turned right at the top of the stairs and, opening the door, looked in at Mr. Melville's room, which had never been occupied since his death. She didn't go in. Then she walked slowly back along the hall and, as she entered the wing that she and Arthur had occupied, she passed the door of Arthur's study where he had worked so long and fruitlessly at his Art research. The door was slightly open and, from inside the room, came a faint scratching sound. She went in to look around. The window was open and there, in one corner of the bare room, was a robin, fluttering up against the panelled wall seeking vainly for a foothold.

She moved cautiously towards it and, stooping down, reached her hand out for it but, just as it was almost within her grasp, it eluded her and fled to the corner on her right. She tried again with the same lack of success. A third time. A fourth. Now she was determined. She closed the door so that it could not escape into the hall and pursued the bird round and round and round the room until at last, emotionally and physically exhausted, it huddled on the floor in the center of the room, its beak slightly open, its eyes bright with fear, awaiting its fate.

Picking it up and holding it couched in her two hands,

she felt its heart palpitating under its soft feathers. She put it carefully on the window sill and stood back watching it as it sat there for a long, long moment. Then, just as she was wondering if she should perhaps take it downstairs and put it on the lawn in the sunshine, with a swoop it was gone.

She closed the window behind it and, after standing looking out for a moment, she went back down to the front hall to await her taxi.

"As part of our service," Mrs. Gorman of Macy's had told her, "I've arranged for a girl to be at the apartment when you arrive to help you get settled. She'll make up the beds, unpack what you want, and fetch and carry for you."

She had almost declined the offer because of Mrs. Gorman's annoying assumption that she would find life quite impossible to cope with without servants. "You mean you are not even going to have a general maid?" she had asked at one point and, when Alice had confirmed this decision, she said, "You're a very original person, Mrs. Melville." By "original" she obviously meant eccentric.

However, when Alice had let herself into the apartment and was confronted by her assembled luggage, ranged through the hall and into the living room, she was glad that she had not spurned Mrs. Gorman's offer, and a moment or two later a pretty and efficient looking girl of about twenty arrived and announced that her name was Sheila Harmer and she had come to help.

She was capable, willing, strong, and cheerful. She was engaged to an electrical engineer who had just finished his training, she told Alice, and they were to be married as soon as he found a job. She had curly brown hair, intelligent brown eyes, a snub nose, a determined but humorous mouth, and a firm chin. "She'll make a good wife," Alice thought to herself as she watched the deft way she piled sheets, pillow slips, and towels on the shelves of the linen cupboard. And, following that thought, she could not resist the secret wish that Patricia might have been a little more like this one. It was absurd, of course. She scarcely knew the girl.

"Are you an only child?" she asked as they were making up the bed in one of the spare rooms, which she hoped would be Geoffrey's bedroom for a long time to come.

Sheila laughed. "Not by a long shot," she said. "There are seven of us. I have a twin sister, three younger brothers and two older. Dad owns a grocery store and always says he's his own best customer, but we kids eat up all the profits."

They stopped for lunch. When Alice, who, with much advice from Mrs. Cuthbert and cooperation from Mrs. Gorman, had had her refrigerator and cupboards stocked with enough food to enable a family of seven to withstand a week's siege, said she would get them something, Sheila replied that she had made an extra ham sandwich and a big thermos of coffee for them and "wouldn't that be simpler?"

So they sat together at the kitchen table munching their thick sandwiches, drinking their coffee, and chatting away, as Alice thought later, "like two schoolgirls."

By five o'clock they were finished, or as finished as they could be for the time being, and Sheila said, "Well, I guess that's about as much as I can help you with, Mrs. Melville. The building superintendent said he'd send men up to take the trunks to the storeroom in half an hour. I hope the curtains really are all right now, and I'll certainly tell Mrs. Gorman what a sloppy job they did hanging them in the first place. We've done the dusting and vacuuming and the books are on the shelves but in no special order. That leaves you with the pictures, the ornaments, and the final sorting out of the kitchen. I think it's sorted out enough to be getting on with." She smiled, breathless, happy, and bright-eyed. "Does that sum it up?"

"That sums it up beautifully. I'm so grateful to you, Sheila, for all your help."

"It's been a real pleasure, Mrs. Melville. I'd like to think we might meet again someday, but I guess that's not very likely."

"Why not?"

Sheila smiled and didn't even attempt an answer to the question. "Stan's taking me out dancing tonight," she said. "I've got to get home, have supper, and make myself look pretty before eight o'clock. He gets mad if I keep him waiting."

"Just a second," Alice said hurriedly. "I just remembered something." Hurrying into her bedroom she took her handbag out of her top drawer, opened it, and extracted from its mysterious depths a five-dollar bill. She looked at it doubtfully for a moment and then, impulsively, plunged her hand in again, rummaged around holding her bag tilted toward the window and peering into it until she found another five dollars. Then she hurried back to Sheila.

"I'm sorry to have kept you waiting," she said, "but I wanted to give you this as a sort of pre-wedding present. I hope you and your young man will be very happy and that you'll have lots of children."

Chapter 35

She had thought at first of having a dress made especially for the evening but, in the end, she decided on the long, shimmering gray-blue silk. Now that she had lost weight it fitted her beautifully again and it really had, she always thought, a "timeless elegance." Mrs. Melville had ordered it from Paris as a Christmas present years ago. She would wear her sable wrap and long platinum and pearl earrings. She had a hair appointment with Antoine for the morning of the opening.

Geoffrey had offered to get her two tickets so she could take a friend but she had said no, she would go by herself. She knew perfectly well that those few acquaintances she had left had been having a marvelous time gossiping about her. She could almost hear them.

"Can you imagine Alice Melville taking up with that actor, and her husband scarcely cold in his grave? I think it's disgraceful. What on earth would old Mrs. Melville have thought?"

"Do you think he trapped her or did she trap him? I always thought she had a sense of refinement. The whole thing is grotesque. Of course there always was something wayward in her nature. I remember Mrs. Melville telling my mother so."

"Yes, I know, and we all felt sorry for her, saddled with poor, dear Arthur—such a dull stick, but one would have thought she had a greater sense of decency. Do you suppose she's become slightly unhinged mentally? I'd like to help her but I really don't see what I can do. I certainly can't go and call on her. That would seem to be condoning the relationship."

"I don't think there's anything any of us can do except keep an eye on the situation and, when it all blows up as it's bound to do, be ready to help her pick up the pieces and settle down to a normal life. It's so sad." She could hear it all in her imagination so clearly.

No. She would go alone. He got her an aisle seat in the tenth row.

Geoffrey had been very busy in the days leading up to the big day. He was busy many evenings and, when he did come to see her, he was frequently withdrawn and uncommunicative. That was only natural, she thought. No wonder he was tense and, at times, brusque. His whole future hung in the balance. It would have been surprising and even alarming if he was overly calm and relaxed as the testing time approached.

He did occasionally stay the night and sleep in the bed she had made up for him and, on those nights, though nothing exciting happened, she allowed herself to imagine the possibility of them working out some permanent arrangement when the time came. What that arrangement might be she tried hard and unsuccessfully not to speculate on.

Of one thing she was quite sure: there was nothing in any way sordid about their relationship. Let the gossips cluck away to their hearts' content, she had nothing whatever to be ashamed of.

The evening before the opening, he came for dinner and announced he would stay the night.

After dinner they sat and talked over their coffee and he asked her to tell him again about her girlhood. He'd heard it all before but he said he'd like to hear it again. So she told him about going to the shop with her father, to Central Park with her mother, and to Coney Island with Carla. She told him about Randy Maybank and the lovely tennis summer. She left out bits and pieces, like the nasty man who wanted them to take off their dresses and the death of poor Laura Cosgrove. She improved the stories a bit. She even brought the Boy Prince of Rajasthan back to life. "I still have it in the little bookshelf beside my bed," she told him.

He told her more about his boyhood in England and how, at the age of fourteen, he had fallen madly in love with a girl called Cynthia Broadbottom. "Poor girl," he said, shaking his head slowly at the memory, gazing into the distance and smiling, Alice thought, as only he could smile, "I do hope she got married and was able to change her name. Actually she had rather a small bottom. I remember it well."

They had both deliberately avoided mention of the opening night, but it was bound to come up and it did so, just before bedtime. "What say we have a tot of brandy and drink to tomorrow's success?" he asked.

"Are you sure you should?"

"Of course not. I'm not sure of anything at the moment. It's an uncertain world. It seems like a good idea."

"If it's a good idea for you, then it's a good idea for me."

For no obvious reason she felt suddenly on the verge of tears. How would it all end? He was a wonderful, wonderful man. After tomorrow . . . ? After tomorrow would he disappear in a cloud of glory? Well, even if he did, she still had tonight.

"That's more than a tot," she said as he handed her her glass.

"It's a tot and a half."

Then, for a time there was a silence. She could feel him looking at her.

"After the show we're going to Sardi's to wait for the reviews. Would you like to come?"

She hesitated, toying with the idea, and then she said, "No. I don't think I fit in, somehow. I'll wait for you here."

"I'll be very late."

"That doesn't matter."

"There's something I may want to tell you when I get home."

"I'll be waiting."

He was up by seven thirty. She heard him bumbling about the kitchen and got up to see what all the confusion was about. "Where the hell's the thing you make coffee in?" he asked irritably.

"It's right here on the counter. You sit down. I'll make it." He sat at the kitchen table and watched her. He was wearing his dark blue pajamas and his red silk dressing gown. There was gray stubble on his cheeks and chin, and sleep was still in his eyes. She thought to herself, "If only he were really and truly mine. There's nothing I wouldn't or couldn't do for him." Yet she didn't really know him. It was a silly, middle-aged schoolgirl crush. They had seldom talked with any real intimacy and his affection for her had been mostly a cool, detached, half-humorous one. What had he meant when he'd said, "There's something I may want to tell you when I get home?" If he had said "something I want to *ask* you," she would have understood.

She got the coffee and collected the newspaper from the hall. For some time they sipped and read in silence. At last she said, "I expect we'd better have some breakfast."

"It says the Governor and the Mayor are going to be there," he said.

"All the more reason for us to have breakfast and build up our strength. Would ham and eggs suit you?"

"I suppose so. I'm not really hungry."

"You're an absolute delight to cook for. I've never known anyone so appreciative."

He looked at her, smiled, and then laughed, not very convincingly. "I'm sorry. My mind isn't really on food. Ham and eggs would be wonderful."

After breakfast he left the kitchen and went back into the bathroom. She made the beds, washed the dishes, got dressed, prepared the salad for lunch, and began to wonder if he was ever going to emerge. He came out finally and went into his own bedroom. It was her turn at last. It was idiotic, she thought, to have only one bathroom in an apartment this big.

"I think I'll go for a walk," he said. It was just after eleven. "Would you like to come with me?"

It was a gray, gusty day with autumn leaves swirling across the street. They walked along without saying anything for two long blocks. Then, suddenly, he stopped and, looking at her intently, he said, "If I make a mess of it tonight, what then? That will be the final and absolute end, won't it?"

"Don't be absurd. You're going to be a triumph. You know that and so do I." The wind blew against their faces. She felt cold and nervous. "Oh my God," she said suddenly. "I forgot my hair appointment. I'll look a perfect fright."

"No, you won't. I like your hair just the way it is." He put his hands on her shoulders and kissed her right there on Fifth Avenue.

When they got home she said, "I've given up before-lunch sherry but I'm going to break my rule. Will you join me?"

"I promised myself I wouldn't have anything to drink today, but promises are made to be broken, aren't they?"

"On days like today they are indeed."

"On days like today?" They were in the dining room. He

sat at the table and watched her filling their glasses from the long-necked, cut-glass decanter. "On days like today," he repeated. "Pray God there will never be any more days like today." He accepted his glass and drained it in a gulp. "I'll have one more," he said. "This time I'll sip it."

He had another glass of sherry after that one and then she persuaded him to have some salad and a hot roll. He had a cup of coffee and stretched out on the sofa. She watched him for a time, finishing off her own coffee, and then, just as she had thought he was asleep, he began to speak.

> "There be some sports are painful, and their labor
> Delight in them sets off: some kinds of baseness
> Are nobly undergone, and most poor matters
> Point to rich ends."

"Prospero?" she asked.

"No, Ferdinand, the son of the King of Naples. It's not one of my speeches."

"I'm not sure I understand it."

"I'm not sure I understand it myself."

He lay for a time staring up at the ceiling, and then his eyes closed. She continued to watch him and wonder. Then, after a time, she got up quietly and went out to the kitchen to make him a chicken sandwich which he could eat before he left or, if he preferred, take with him to the theatre. As she buttered the bread she thought, "This is idiotic. I'm more nervous than he is."

She surveyed herself in the mirror and was satisfied with what she saw. It didn't really matter that she had missed her appointment with Antoine. Her hair was silvery and sleek. It was not as long as it had been in her youth but it curled pleasantly at the nape of her neck. She held her shoulders back and her head erect. The dress hung beautifully. She would show them that Alice Melville was still a woman to be reckoned with.

The lobby was crowded with everybody who was anybody. Looking around, Alice recognized Mrs. Sydney Carlyle, Mr. and Mrs. Stephen Ambrose, Mr. and Mrs. Anthony Carlson, and others. Mrs. Durrell came up to her and said, "My dear Alice, how *are* you? I've been thinking of you *so* much. *So* sad about poor dear Arthur but you *mustn't* creep into a shell and stay there. I'm so *glad* to see you here this evening. If I'd only *thought*, Charles and I would have asked you to join our party. We'll get together for lunch next week and make some plans. *Lovely* to see you and you're looking simply *gorgeous*. You've always been one of my *very* favorite people." Then, as Alice was opening her mouth to say, "What a shame it is that the feeling isn't mutual," she was gone. Probably just as well. Silly old bat.

She was well aware of the fact that people were looking at her and pointing her out to other people. She didn't care. This was Geoffrey's night of triumph but, in a sense, it was also hers. They could say what they liked and they could think what they liked, but she was secure in her knowledge that, if it hadn't been for her, they would never be here to witness the triumphant return of Geoffrey Hamilton. Yet there was a nagging worry. When she had been in the bathroom just before he left for the theatre she had heard him go into the kitchen and later, after she had kissed him good-bye and wished him good luck, she had found a glass with the dregs of a drink in it.

Chapter 36

She was glad she had decided against Sardi's. She would remain in the background. It was better that way. She would wait for him at home. Wait for what? There was no way of telling. She wouldn't think about it.

Two rows ahead and to the right she spotted Ben Wiseman looking debonair with a dark-haired woman in a silvery dress. Wife? Mistress? Girl friend? Somewhere behind that curtain Geoffrey was sitting in his costume and makeup. He was waiting back there and she was waiting out here. Was he thinking of her at all? No, he had too much else to think of.

The theatre was filling up. Behind her she heard the murmuring of voices and rustling of dresses. She glanced over her shoulder. It was what the papers would describe as a glittering audience. The men were all in evening clothes and the ladies were bejeweled and befurred. And they were all here because she had rescued Geoffrey Hamilton from oblivion.

The lights dimmed. The murmuring subsided. The footlights came on. Silence. Then a great crash of thunder, a howling of wind, the thundering of waves on the shore, and the curtain came up with a rush to reveal a ship that was indeed about to founder on the rocks. It was magnificent.

How they achieved it she couldn't imagine, but presently the wrecked ship seemed almost to dissolve before her eyes and there was the wonderful lush island with Prospero and Miranda standing before his cell, the palm trees stirring in the breeze and the calm blue sea in the background. He looked magnificent—every inch the rightful Duke of Milan with his long, flowing hair falling over his shoulders, his fine beard, his full, rich robe, and, best of all, his fierce resonant voice filled the theatre. "Be collected. No more argument. Tell your piteous heart there's no harm done."

Someone, somewhere started to clap and suddenly everyone was on his feet, clapping and cheering. They were welcoming Geoffrey Hamilton back after a long, long absence. He was just as great as they remembered him being or as their parents had told them he was. There had been some snide suggestions that he never had been worthy of the reputation he had acquired. One reporter even went so far as to suggest that he might turn up drunk for the first night. He had given the lie to them. He looked out over the audience with an aristocratic haughtiness as a true Duke would. He never dropped out of character for a moment. The play had scarcely started and already it was a brilliant success. The audience sat down and the play went on.

There was only one intermission and Alice did not go out for it. She preferred to remain in her seat absorbed in her happiness for him and for herself. Nothing in her whole life could ever measure up to this evening. There would be more. Many more similar evenings she could look forward to. But this one, this triumphant return from oblivion, would always remain in her memory as the greatest.

After the intermission, the play seemed to rush to an end. She wept to hear him say:

> ". . . These our actors,
> As I foretold you, were all spirits and
> Are melted into air, into thin air
>
> . . . We are such stuff
> As dreams are made on . . ."

Then, only a moment later it seemed, he was speaking the epilogue.

> "Now my charms are all o'erthrown
> And what strength I have's mine own,
> Which is most faint . . ."

They were on their feet again cheering as he made his farewell bow. The ovation went on and on and on. Never, Alice thought to herself with the tears streaming down her cheeks, would she ever witness anything to compare to this.

She pulled herself together and hurried down the aisle to grab a taxi before they were all taken. She would have her ultimate moment of glory a few hours from now.

When she got home she hung up her sable coat, poured herself a glass of brandy, and sat down to collect her thoughts. "Now, you must be sensible," she said aloud. "It is very important that you be sensible."

The brandy was very comforting indeed and she had a second glass. When that was finished she looked at her watch and decided that it would be at least four hours before he was home. She would set the alarm for three thirty and lie down for a bit so she would be all fresh to welcome him on his return. She hung up her dress very carefully and got out her Chinese red kimono with the golden dragons on it and hung it on the door. Her father had given it to her years and years ago and her mother had disapproved, but she had found it when she was moving out of the house and brought it with her. It was a little creased but that wouldn't matter. Tonight was certainly the night for it.

She didn't think she would sleep but she did and woke up with a start when the alarm jangled. He would probably have had lots of lovely things to eat at Sardi's but, in case he felt like onion soup, she had got two very expensive cans of it from Campano's. She opened them now and put the saucepan at the back of the stove to heat very slowly. She arranged the crackers and cheese on a wooden platter and put them ready, covered with wax paper. He could open the champagne when the time came. Then, with all things ready, she donned her kimono, poured herself one more glass of brandy, and sat down to wait. It was just after four.

At five she went back out to the kitchen and turned off the soup, which was bubbling in a sulky fashion. He would be here anytime now and they would have champagne first, so there would be ample time to heat it up. She tried to read but she was much too excited.

Then, finally, just before six, there was the sound of his key in the lock and she leapt up. "Anybody home?" he called.

"Of course I'm home," she called back and rushed out into the little entrance hall to greet him.

There he was, only very slightly drunk and with bits and pieces of his makeup still clinging to his face.

With him, looking radiantly beautiful with big blue eyes glittering with pleasure, was Gertrude Keiller, the young girl who had played Ariel with such sparkling charm and lightness.

"Come in. Do come in," Alice heard herself saying. "I've got champagne in the refrigerator and onion soup on the stove. Which would you like first?"

Geoffrey looked at Gertrude and asked, "What do you think?"

She laughed charmingly, sparklingly, airily, as she had done in the play. "I think I've had enough," she said, "and you certainly have, but tonight is a night to remember. I vote for champagne first."

"The reviews?" Alice asked. "How were the reviews?"

"Marvelous!" Gertrude answered. "Absolutely marvelous. I'm going to the bathroom while you two get the champagne."

"It's the first door on your right along the hall," Alice said. She must not cry. She would not cry. It had been her idiocy, not his.

He followed her out to the kitchen and there, before she could open the refrigerator, he put his hands on her shoulders, turned her round to face him, and kissed her on the lips.

They stayed less than half an hour—just time for two glasses of champagne. The chatter was bright and merry but Alice didn't understand most of it. She precipitated their departure by saying, "What about the onion soup?"

"Oh my God!" Geoffrey exclaimed, leaping to his feet. "I'd almost forgotten that the taxi was sitting down there ticking away like a time bomb. We must be on our way. Wonderful of you to wait up for us, darling," he said, kissing Alice on the forehead.

"You won't . . ." Alice faltered.

"I'm at the Waldorf tonight. Last port of call. I'll telephone around noon and we'll arrange something."

"It was simply *marvelous* to meet you," Gertrude Keiller said. "I've heard *so* much about you, and now I understand how important you are to Geoffrey and why."

Then they were gone.

Alice went back out to the kitchen, poured the onion soup into a bowl to cool, wrapped up the cheese in wax paper and put it in the refrigerator, turned off the coffee but left it on the stove. She would have a cup or two of it for breakfast before throwing the rest of it out.

They hadn't even commented on her Chinese red kimono with the dragons on it. Whatever it was that he had said he might tell her had apparently slipped his mind or else, more likely, he had decided against doing so.

Sitting at the kitchen table after a few sleepless hours in bed and sipping the warmed-over coffee, Alice decided to be sensible. It was idiotic to be upset over last night. It was good of him to have come at all. And to bring along the leading lady as well! She should be flattered. He was the toast of the town and he had come to see her when hostesses all over New York must have been clamoring to have him. He had said he would call at noon. She must not, on any account, sound hurt.

Perhaps he would just turn up. That was a possibility. It was after eleven already. She got dressed, made her bed, washed the dishes, and did a quick dusting. When the telephone rang, almost on the dot of noon, she was all set. She let it ring twice before she answered. There was no point in letting him think that she had been sitting, waiting to pounce.

"Alice? . . . It's Jenny McDougall—Jenny Robertson that was."

"Jenny?" She had expected his voice. It took her a moment to readjust.

"Ashcroft. My father designed your . . ."

"Of course! I was expecting a call from someone else. How nice to hear your voice. I thought you'd moved to Boston or San Francisco or someplace . . . Me? Oh, I've been busy. As you've probably heard I seem to have become deeply involved in theatrical affairs . . . No, of course we're not engaged!" She laughed. "Oh yes, of course, very exciting. I've always been very keen on the theatre. Monday? Yes, I'd love to. It sounds delightful . . . Oh, you're not very far from me then. . . . Yes, of course I know. Thank you so much. I'll look forward to it. . . . Monday at six. . . . Good." She hung up.

A female cocktail party at Jenny Robertson's! At any place for that matter. She had been invited out of curiosity; she was sure of that. "I dare you to invite Alice Melville," someone had said to Jenny. And Jenny would take the dare. The tongues would go clackety-clack. There would be sly insinuating questions.

Well, let there be. She could stand up for herself. Who were they to criticize, anyway? There wasn't one among them who hadn't had her little flutter at some time. What about Irene Carpenter and that Italian sculptor? And Gloria Sanderson and that incredible Hungarian Count? Her relationship with Geoffrey was no mere flutter. They would know that in time.

Geoffrey's call came an hour later.

"I've been frightfully busy," he said. "It's the price one pays, I suppose."

"I understand, of course," Alice said.

"I thought I'd bring some friends around on Monday evening and then, after they've left, we'll have a time together. Would that suit?"

"Yes . . . yes indeed! I've accepted an invitation to a silly party early in the evening but I could . . ."

"I'm thinking of around ten or perhaps even eleven."

"That would be splendid. I'll be back long before then but, in case you arrive early, you have your key and I'll leave things out ready."

She wished now that she hadn't accepted Jenny's invitation, but perhaps it wouldn't do Geoffrey any harm to realize that she didn't just languish at home waiting for him to appear.

Monday. She did remember her hair appointment this time and she chose a dress she hadn't worn for years— black silk with a hat to match. She wore a pearl necklace that had belonged to her mother. Standing erect before the mirror and surveying herself, she was satisfied. She adjusted her mink stole over her shoulders and tossed her head in the old way. If they supposed for one minute that Alice Barrington Melville had lost her looks or her defiance, they were in for a rude shock.

"I'm so glad you arrived early," Jenny said. "I nearly called you back because I do hope you'll stay on for a bite to eat after the others have gone. It will be just soup and leftovers. We've got so much catching up to do, and I want you to meet Colin." She laughed and her laughter trilled and ended in the same delightful gurgle as it had long ago. Alice was suddenly back forty years. Why had they lost touch?

"I'd love to stay for supper," she said. "We must see more of each other. I can't think why we haven't."

"Oh, neither can I. We get so busy with one thing and another. The children are on their own now except for our young one, and he's seventeen and off to Europe this summer, so we will get together. You have children, Alice?"

"One—a grown-up daughter."

"Lucky you. I had five."

"Your parents?"

"Mother died last year. My father's in a nursing home. He's still busy designing wonderful houses that he knows will never be built. Speaking of the old days, you'll never guess who's coming this evening."

"Who?"

"Miss Conner."

"Good heavens. I haven't thought of her for years. If I had I would have assumed she had died years ago."

"I think that's one of the hazards of being a school teacher. Ex-pupils always think of their teachers as being on the verge of senility a year or two after they themselves have left school." She laughed again and Alice laughed with her. Like the old days.

It was a good evening. There were all sorts of people Alice hadn't seen for years and they weren't gossipy and unkind as she had thought they might be. They seemed genuinely happy to see her.

"You've been hibernating," someone said.

"Hibernating? Sleeping in a cave and waiting for spring? I've been prowling about looking for game." They all laughed and Alice laughed with them.

"What's he like? Is he as glamorous offstage as on?"

"Not when you see him at the kitchen table at breakfast time."

"Do you go out much together? We'd love to have you over for dinner."

"We go our own ways. Geoffrey works very hard. When he has time off he usually catches up on his sleep."

"What happened to your plan to have ten children?" Miss Conner asked. "You were going to travel over the world, too, I remember."

"I changed my mind. We settled for one child and stayed at home."

"You look lovely," someone told her. "How do you manage to stay so slim?"

"I run in Central Park."

Yes, it really was a delightful evening. She had braced herself for an ordeal and found, to her happy surprise, that it was nothing of the sort. She hadn't had so much fun for a long, long time.

The guests trickled gradually away and, when the last had departed, Jenny called out, "It's safe now, Colin. You can emerge." Colin McDougall appeared, a big, burly Scot. He was an engineer, Alice thought from something someone had said.

They had soup—rich creamy mushroom—and toasted cheese sandwiches. They talked easily and Jenny laughed that wonderful laugh of hers.

At last Alice said, "I really must be going. May I call a taxi?"

"Of course not," Colin said. "We'll have a small nightcap and then I'll drive you home." His voice was rich and deep and his manner warm and friendly. "You mustn't rush away. I'm so pleased to have met you at last. Jenny's spoken of you often. You drew trees together."

"Yes, do stay," Jenny said. "It's such fun to see you."

"I've stayed too long already. It has been wonderful. Yes, I'd love a drink and then I really must go. A very weak bourbon."

When Collin had gone out to get the drinks, Jenny said, "Isn't Miss Conner wonderful? She was delighted to see you again."

"She is indeed. I'm ashamed of myself for thinking she was dead. She hasn't really aged much and she knew me right away."

"Of course. You were always one of her favorites. She's spoken of you several times."

"You've kept regularly in touch then?"

"In a vague way. She comes to tea now and again. I've sort of dragged my girlhood along with me as I've grown older. I've tried to keep the best from the past and add other things. Colin is wonderful. We're very happy."

"You've done better than I have," Alice said quietly.

"Oh no. I didn't mean that."

"I know you didn't. It's true just the same." Alice suddenly felt the tears pressing hard behind her eyes. She shook her head.

"I didn't mean that at all," Jenny said. "I wasn't making comparisons."

Colin came back with the drinks. Alice didn't have to answer.

She stayed much much too late, allowing herself to be talked into another drink and sitting chatting about this and that. Reliving the past. Alice's mind wandered. Would Geoffrey be there by now? She was torn. No! It would be good for Geoffrey to realize that she didn't think she had to rush back.

Colin told them about a man who wanted to convert the first two stories of an aged apartment building he owned in Yonkers into an elaborate health spa and beauty salon. Colin did a feasibility study for him which involved a consulting architect and various other engineers and craftsmen. In due course he reported back that the proposition was not really viable. "In fact," he told his client, "I think the building should be condemned."

The man had received the news in a placid fashion and said, "I expected you would say that. Your verdict is symptomatic of what is wrong with America today. I hoped you might regard this as a challenge but you allow yourself to be defeated by mundane matters like strength of materials. I've already sold the building so, if you have the nerve to submit a bill for such a negative report, you can send it to the new owners."

"But if you were going to sell the building, why did you engage me?"

"I was curious."

Colin laughed and his laughter was as warm and friendly as the man himself. "I got my money in the end but I had to go to court about it. In a way I was sorry when I won. He was a nice old geezer. We got to be quite good friends before it was all over. There aren't enough eccentrics left. He congratulated me when the thing was finished and said, 'If I ever get involved in such a business again I'll ask your advice.'"

It was after eleven. She really had stayed much too late. Jenny would say to her husband, "Well, we certainly won't have Alice again for a while. She is a stayer, isn't she?" and Colin would agree. It had been fun though—great fun. She had needed it. She would phone Jenny in the morning. Colin drove her home.

Gales of laughter greeted her as she opened the door of the apartment. Geoffrey was reading aloud and his voice rose above the background hilarity.

" 'I shall do what I must. It may be that God had des-

tined me for an early death but, be that as it may, my duty
to God and the Queen must come first.' " More laughter.

She took off her coat and hung it up. No one seemed to
have heard her arrive. Geoffrey's voice went on. " 'He
raised his sword above his head and the richly jeweled hilt
glittered and sparkled as did the eyes of the Boy Prince
who wielded it. "I know not the meaning of fear," he cried
aloud. "I put my life into the hands of Fate." The cheers
rang out loudly across the wide, sun-drenched plain.' "
More laughter, some clapping and ironic cheers.

Alice went to the archway into the living room. Geoffrey
sat in the large chair in the corner. Sprawled on the floor at
his feet were Gertrude Keiller, two other young women—
one with fluffy yellow hair and the other with pink hair
and very red lips—and two languid young men in sweaters
and baggy trousers. Geoffrey, enjoying himself hugely, was
reading *The Boy Prince of Rajasthan* to them and, as he
finished each page, tearing it out and letting it fall to the
floor.

For a moment none of them noticed her standing motionless at the door and the mocking voice continued. Precisely what happened in the next few seconds Alice recon-
structed in a general way later but, at the time, she acted
without any conscious thought whatsoever.

It was as though she was seized by a giant, invisible
hand and propelled into the room with a force over which
she had no control. A great wave of outrage and fury
surged up within her. She had snatched up the tall cut-glass
vase, which stood on the table in the hall and, as she
rushed at him, he leaped to his feet. She struck at his head
and then, as he took a step towards her and stretched out
his hand in an apparent attempt to seize the weapon from
her or to ward off another blow, she struck again. He fell
sideways half across a small, thin-legged table which gave
way under his weight. There was screaming and confusion.
Then there was silence and she was kneeling beside him on
the rug and weeping.

They got him onto the sofa and Alice bandaged his head
while the others stood around in nervous uncertainty, looking at each other. While she was doing the bandaging and
gently sponging the blood from his colorless cheeks, Alice

told Gertrude Keiller to call the doctor. "His name is Sayers and he has an apartment in this building."

Geoffrey lay on his back with his head on a cushion breathing deeply. Alice got a blanket from his bedroom and covered him. No one said anything. The girl with the yellow hair was crying softly on the shoulder of one of the young men.

Dr. Sayers, like Dr. Adler of long ago, was a discreet man. He was accustomed to dealing with the rich and the famous and it was said of him, by envious competitors for the lucrative fashionable market, that his charm and discretion concealed his lack of professional skill so well that dying patients apologized to him for not responding to his treatment. In his mid-fifties, he was tall, urbane, and almost too good-looking. His female patients were known to invent imaginary ailments in order to experience his healing touch.

"Well," he said softly, carefully removing the bandage and looking at Geoffrey's wound, "we've had a little accident, have we?"

Geoffrey heard the words and, managing to half open his eyes, whispered, "It was an accident."

"I think we'll take you into the hospital where we can have a better look at it. Could I use your telephone to call an ambulance Mrs. . . . Mrs. . . ."

"Melville," Alice said.

"Yes, of course."

When he returned from calling the hospital and the ambulance he said to the others, "I think perhaps it would be best if you all went home now before the ambulance arrives. I know you will agree with me that for the sake of Mr. Hamilton and any others concerned, the less said the better. It is obvious that Mr. Hamilton tripped and hit his head on the table as he fell. I shall so inform the press." As he spoke he picked up the tall vase and placed it on another table. "You agree, I'm sure," he said.

There were murmurs of assent and they dispersed. "Now," he said to Alice, when the three of them were alone, "I'll leave you and get to the hospital so as to be there when he arrives. The ambulance should be here in about ten minutes. He'll be all right. You have nothing to worry about." He touched her gently and reassuringly on the shoulder and then he was gone.

Alice stood in the center of the room. It had all been like a terrible nightmare, but there lay Geoffrey on the sofa with his eyes closed and the ugly wound on his forehead caked with congealed blood. No, it was real. It had happened. She felt numb.

She was still standing there when the ambulance men arrived. They lifted him expertly onto the stretcher and tucked some blankets around him. While they were doing this he opened his eyes and looked at her, but neither of them spoke.

When they were gone she stood for a few moments more gazing bleakly about her and then, dropping to her knees, she began to pick up the pages of *The Boy Prince of Rajasthan.*

Chapter 37

Wednesday afternoon.

Mrs. Owens had left the tea things ready and gone off to visit an elderly cousin. Alice sat looking out the window at the ocean twinkling and sparkling in the distance.

The telephone rang. It was Patricia to say that Michael was not at all well and she wouldn't be in. So she was alone. She hadn't been feeling very well herself, and so she wasn't sorry not to have to make conversation.

What she needed, she thought, smiling to herself, was a good dose of Dr. Buckland's Scotch Oats Essence. As a child she had repeatedly asked her mother why it wasn't in their medicine cabinet. Although it was "in no sense a Patent Medicine" it cured "sleeplessness, paralysis, opium habit, drunkenness, neuralgia, sick headache, sciatica, nervous dyspepsia, locomotor ataxia, headache, ovarian neuralgia, nervous exhaustion, epilepsy, St. Vitus dance and many other things." She remembered asking her mother if she developed the opium habit or locomotor ataxia if then she would get a bottle. It only cost a dollar. Her mother just laughed.

There was another magic restorative, too, the advertisement for which she had read with interest. She could still see the illustration clearly—an attentive, bonneted lady leaning solicitously over the back of a couch on which her sick friend reclined against a pillow. In the foreground a little girl was administering a restorative to a sick doll. At the time she had first seen it, the picture had seemed to her positively saturated with human drama. There was a verse under it:

> Don't give up, my poor, sick friend
> While there's life there's hope, 'tis said;
> Sicker persons often mend;
> Time to give up when you're dead.

The advertisement proclaimed the virtues of Dr. Pierce's Golden Medical Discovery. "Try it and obtain a new lease of life."

No, it was too late for either Dr. Buckland or Dr. Pierce to help her now. A dose of medicine might banish her slight cold, if that's what it was, but no one had invented a cure for extreme old age.

She seldom thought of the later years. When her mind wandered back it didn't dwell on them. They seemed like a pressed flower discovered in an old book. By contrast, the earlier years were still as bright and real as could be.

It had been just after that frightful final evening with Geoffrey that she had dug out Arthur's novel. She remembered feeling that, now that the Boy Prince of Rajasthan was gone forever, she might just as well face up to final truth with Arthur as well.

She had thought of throwing it out unopened when she moved to the apartment, but had decided that would be a cowardly act. Now she cut the string, removed the thick manuscript, letting the wrapping paper fall to the floor at her feet. "Esther Lansbury," she read, "was the sort of woman all men admire but no man can ever really know. Her romantic dreams and aspirations were too great ever to be satisfied by an ordinary marriage."

She never read any further. Getting up from her chair and clutching the pages to her with both arms, she went out to the little janitor room off the kitchen where the trash can was and dumped them in. It was at that moment she knew she didn't ever want to set eyes on Arthur's son, Paul, and that, if Catherine Maine called, she would tell her so. But the call never came.

What would Patricia think if she knew that she had a half brother who believed his dead father had been a sea captain? Alice smiled faintly at the thought.

It was time for tea.

She got up slowly, went out, plugged in the kettle and then decided she didn't really want tea after all and un-plugged it. It was too early for a drink and she wasn't in the mood for reading or watching television. She hovered uncertainly in the archway between the kitchen and the dining room. She felt shivery.

Who said it was too early for a drink? If you couldn't do what you wanted to do when you wanted to do it at the age of ninety-five, then there was something wrong with the way the world was organized. She would have a glass of whiskey. That would warm and comfort her. She hadn't had a glass for ages. She kept it only for Michael and the grandchildren on their rare visits.

She used to like it with ice, but now she thought she'd prefer it with slightly warm water. Returning to her chair she sat and looked out the window, clasping the glass firmly in her knobby, arthritic fingers. "I knew Mr. William Kissam Vanderbilt," she heard her father say. And then her mother: "You're eight years old and so it's time you began thinking like a young lady."

Arthur looking at her dish of frogs' legs . . . Mrs. Melville's "At Homes" . . . Mr. Melville going up the stairs . . .

And so many loose ends. Had her Paris kidnapper made it back to Wilmington? Had Mark Wells, her friend in Central Park, met a beautiful girl and become a successful novelist or a poet? Benton would have retired from the grocery business long ago now. He was probably dead. Of course he would be. Arthur in the rain after that dreadful dinner party. Randy Maybank and the Snow Ball. The sherry party in the kitchen. What a jumble.

Once she dreamed of conquering New York and now here she was in a foreign country on the other side of the continent. Yet, in a way, she had known what it felt like to be a conqueror of that great city. Walking along the paths of Central Park with her mother, with the nursemaids and other, lesser, children eyeing them with respectful awe, she had known more surely than she ever had since that she was indeed a "superior person."

Since those days she seemed to have spent her life looking for something but, if she had ever known what it was, she had long since forgotten. All she knew was that she hadn't found it.

Gladys had cried when she was leaving the great house and had asked, "Are you going to make your own bed?"

The young evangelist she had watched last Sunday on television because she was too lazy to turn him off thought he knew all the answers, but he had no more idea of what it was all about than she did. Life asked far more questions than it answered. Poor Roger, the Barringtons' coachman, had wondered about life, too. She remembered their talks when he drove her to Ashcroft. She smiled.

Geoffrey Hamilton . . . no . . . no, she didn't want to

think about Geoffrey. She still heard his voice sometimes and remembered, despite herself, the night when he had held her in his arms.

No more . . . enough memories for one day.

The whiskey was as warm and comforting as she had thought it would be. Just a tiny splash more before Mrs. Owens came back.

The pangs in her chest began as she bent down by the sideboard cupboard. She guessed what they meant. By an effort of will she was able to straighten up, put her glass in the kitchen sink, and return to her chair.

And that was where Mrs. Owens found her on her return. Her hands were folded on her lap; her lips were slightly parted; her eyes were staring sightlessly out across the wide ocean.

*The irresistible love story
with a happy ending.*

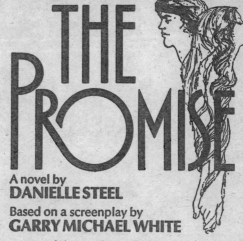

THE PROMISE

A novel by
DANIELLE STEEL

Based on a screenplay by
GARRY MICHAEL WHITE

After an automobile accident which left Nancy McAllister's
beautiful face a tragic ruin, she accepted the money for plastic
surgery from her lover's mother on one condition: that she never
contact Michael again. She didn't know Michael would be told
that she was dead.

Four years later, Michael met a lovely woman whose face he
didn't recognize, and wondered why she hated him with such
intensity

A Dell Book $1.95

Dell Bestsellers

- ☐ BEGGARMAN, THIEF by Irwin Shaw $2.75 (10701-6)
- ☐ THE BLACK SWAN by Day Taylor $2.25 (10611-7)
- ☐ PUNISH THE SINNERS by John Saul $1.95 (17084-2)
- ☐ SCARLET SHADOWS by Emma Drummond..$2.25 (17812-6)
- ☐ THE PROMISE by Danielle Steel based on a screenplay by Garry Michael White $1.95 (17079-6)
- ☐ FLAMES OF DESIRE by Vanessa Royall $1.95 (15077-9)
- ☐ THE REDBOOK REPORT ON FEMALE SEXUALITY by Carol Tavris and Susan Sadd $1.95 (17342-6)
- ☐ THE HOUSE OF CHRISTINA by Ben Haas $2.25 (13793-4)
- ☐ THE MESMERIST by Felice Picano $1.95 (15213-5)
- ☐ CONVOY by B.W.L. Norton $1.95 (11298-2)
- ☐ F.I.S.T. by Joe Eszterhas $2.25 (12650-9)
- ☐ HIDDEN FIRES by Janette Radcliffe $1.95 (10657-5)
- ☐ CLOSE ENCOUNTERS OF THE THIRD KIND by Steven Spielberg $1.95 (11433-0)
- ☐ PARIS ONE by James Brady $1.95 (16803-1)
- ☐ NO RIVER SO WIDE by Pierre Danton $1.95 (10215-4)
- ☐ CLOSING TIME by Lacey Fosburgh $1.95 (11302-4)
- ☐ A PLACE TO COME TO by Robert Penn Warren $2.25 (15999-7)
- ☐ ROOTS by Alex Haley $2.75 (17464-3)
- ☐ THE CHOIRBOYS by Joseph Wambaugh $2.25 (11188-9)

At your local bookstore or use this handy coupon for ordering:

DELL BOOKS
P.O. BOX 1000, PINEBROOK, N.J. 07058

Please send me the books I have checked above. I am enclosing $_____
(please add 35¢ per copy to cover postage and handling). Send check or money order—no cash or C.O.D.'s. Please allow up to 8 weeks for shipment.

Mr/Mrs/Miss_____

Address_____

City_____State/Zip_____